What readers say about *Phoenix/Maine...*

"With her legislative experience and deep feelings for Maine, Nancy Payne captures the essence of Maine's political scene with a marvelous tale. Phoenix/Maine *is a stimulating yet leisurely read sure to please; it combines the home-town feel of Mitford [the fictional town in Jan Karon's novels] with the realities of Maine sensibilities."*

—U.S. Senator Olympia Snowe

"Nancy Payne's collection of vignettes gripped me from the first line to the last page. Her writing style rings with her essential genuineness. One senses Nancy's integrity as the story weaves through the pages. I will always cherish this book as I cherish its author."

—Rabbi Harry Z. Sky, cofounder, Osher Lifelong Learning Institute, Portland

"This book is unique nowadays: it tells its story straight from the start to the satisfying finish—all without any introspective detours. The characters are likeable and wholesome without a single neurosis in the bunch. The author is clearly a happy person who shares with us her lifetime insights and goodwill. Enjoy her accomplishment."

—Judge Robert Donovan (retired)

"An exciting love story set in the wilds of Maine, with an intriguing solution to the state's negative political climate, its 'two Maines' philosophy and both adult and juvenile civility, all with a surprise ending. A must-read for Mainers."

—Hon. Mary H. MacBride, former Maine state representative for Presque Isle

"A delightful and authentic novel about Maine life and politics at its best, reflecting the author's own experiences. Its accurate portrayal of both rural and urban life in Maine reflects the state's strengths and weaknesses. A must read for all who love Maine."

—Merton G. Henry, Esq., Chairman,
Margaret Chase Smith Library

"Nancy Payne, with wisdom, fertile imagination, and deep feeling for Maine, addresses society's lack of satisfaction, direction ,and pride. Her Phoenix/Maine, *through intriguing characters and poetic descriptions, proposes to restore mutual respect, integrity, and civility through an 'As Maine Goes' campaign.""*

—General Wallace Nutting (retired)

"Like my parents and grandparents, I grew up Roman Catholic, Irish, working-class, and a lifelong Democrat. Yet I loved this novel written by a former Republican legislator and National Committee-woman. Why? Because it is about what good politics should be—honest, wholesome, collaborative, respectful, and directed toward improving the lives of people."

—E. Michael Brady, Ph. D., Dept. of
Human Resource Development, USM

"Nancy Payne uses her warmth and humor, plus an impressive command of the nuts and bolts of campaigning, to spin an entertaining and inspiring tale of how one small state could transform its politics to reflect the highest ideals of our democracy."

—David T. Flanagan, former CEO of Central Maine
Power Co. and Independent candidate for governor

Phoenix/Maine

Nancy Payne

To good neighbors —
Nancy

Rathaldron Publications
Falmouth, Maine

Dedication

To my children, who will now have to find a new project to keep the "old girl" out of trouble, Bill, Lewis and Tony Payne, and Nancy Alexander.

Acknowledgements

While writers, artists or composers all like to think their creations are 100% their own product, in the deepest area of our consciences a bell tinkles stubbornly and with honesty "Thank you, thank you".

My bell thus rings for all those who suggested, supported, informed, and encouraged me, particularly Julie Zimmerman, Jean Blanchard, Patsy Wiggin, Merton Henry, Doris Russell, Nancy Connolly, Denis and Nancy Firth, Judge Robert Donovan, and Rep. Gerald Davis. The most profound gratitude is expressed to the "surgeon" of great skill who removed the nonessential, the fat, and left no scars, Kate O'Halloran.

Published by Rathaldron Publications
P.O.Box 66792
Falmouth, Maine 04105

ISBN 0-9727217-03

Contents

Chapter 1: Winter 1987

He wiggled his toes luxuriously in the comfortable old hunting boots and shifted his behind in the plane seat, hoping to find a more comfortable position. Peering out the window he could still see, in the failing light, the dark green of the woods and the black of the occasional lakes beneath. The plane was over the largely uninhabited great woods of northern Maine.

Returning from a business trip to Cairo via Zurich, Webb Lewis was glad to be taking this route. Even just flying over Maine meant a great deal to him. The happiest summers of his life had been spent somewhere in that woodland below him.

An only child whose father had been killed in Korea, Webb had been brought up by his mother and grandmother, who could give him love and guidance but few extras. An unmarried uncle, sensing the child's need for space, competition, and the self-confidence that comes with them, had sent him to a Maine boys' wilderness camp for several seasons. There he had been initiated into the male world, protected still, but male.

The flight was now about fifteen minutes from Bangor, where the plane would refuel and passengers could clear customs before they continued to their final destinations. Webb rose, slid past the empty seat on his right and, opening the storage bin over his head, removed the warm jacket stuffed in there. His overcoat, his tailor-made suits, custom-made shirts, and shoes, were riding in the hold. Traveling was made more bearable if he wore comfortable clothes rather than the clothes he thought of as his business uniform.

Clad in jeans, flannel shirt, and the old L.L. Bean parka, he would meet his wife at O'Hare. She would be annoyed; almost everything he did seemed to have that effect in the unhappy game of their marriage. This outfit expressed his reluctance to return home. A small enough rebellion, considering. Phyllis would drive in from their home outside the city expecting to be taken to the Harvard Club for dinner. She would be dressed impeccably, with style and elegance. There would be no enthusiasm in her greeting. Her conversation, if any, would concern only the business. She would ask nothing of what he might have learned or accomplished. He would not have been missed.

Now, as he slipped into the parka and felt its light warmth, it seemed as if he was putting on a different skin, another persona. No longer the travel-weary president of a large industrial chemical company, he was a vigorous mid-thirtyish man about to fill his lungs with clean air that hopefully would recharge his attitudes and sense of purpose.

Winking at the little boy across the aisle, he picked up and returned to him an obviously loved stuffed dinosaur. Glancing out his window he saw nothing but white. The plane was going through a cloud or a sudden snowstorm. As he started to sit down again the plane bucked and shuddered. Before he could even get buckled up, the intercom came on.

"This is the captain. There is some turbulence ahead in a good old-fashioned Maine blizzard, so I ask you to fasten your seat belts and . . . . " His voice ceased on a high note. The huge plane bucked again, gave a sickening plunge, and the sound of its descent became a wild whine rising even as the plane dropped.

Webb was attacked by flying seats, luggage, bodies and jagged metal; the air filled with screams. There was a final crumbling thump and a brief settling, then stillness. Only the winter wind made any sound.

Later, in a silent, cold, almost black world, Webb realized that he had been thrown into deep snow outside the plane. Lying on his stomach he carefully moved each part of his body. No major bones seemed broken, though every muscle screamed. He took a deep breath, gathered courage, and forced himself to open his eyes. Blood stained the whiteness just in front of him. His?

The snow was swirling heavily down, blurring what little he could see. What was left of the plane lay like a beached and dismembered whale some forty or fifty feet to his right. Nearer to him, sticking out of the snow, was a squarish black object that must be the emergency door he'd been catapulted through. It was covered with heavy ice.

Other black shapes—metal, flesh, or plastic—lay scattered about. Most appalling of all, he realized, was the utter lack of light or voices. Not a cry, not a whimper, not even the ominous crackle of flames. Nothing. Just Webb Lewis in an erasing whiteness, and this absence of sound, broken only by the occasional mourning keen of the blizzard wind through snow-laden branches. So many lives, so vibrant, human, and eager to land so short a time before, had been simply snuffed out.

Using what strength he had he called out, listening listened intensely for even the faintest answer. None. Though all strength seemed to have ebbed out of him, he knew he could not lie there without making sure that there was no one who could use what little help he could give. He lifted his head higher, raising himself up on one elbow to assess his position. It was almost impossible to believe he really was the sole survivor of the several hundred he had flown with from Zurich, but it seemed, very simply, so.

The nearest bundle didn't seem too far and he crawled toward it. Something was covered by a blanket. He pulled at a corner, and discovered a headless body! Sheared right off! His cry seemed obscene in that silence, the sound of his retching was worse. Instinctively, though even weaker, he searched for the head, to somehow make things right and tidy, but it could be anywhere, or already buried. The corpse was that of a man, dressed in a business suit, neat and normal—just without a head.

Shakily he crawled on, nearer the main mass of the plane, inspecting—even shaking—more bodies, some grotesquely twisted and some lying as if they just slept. Then he was stopped by the branches and trees that had brought the flight to a halt, a dense and spiky thicket.

Resting, he took stock of his situation. He was lost and alone in the deep woods of Maine, God knows where, in a blizzard, with no food, only snow to melt for liquid, no shelter, and no idea of how soon the plane would be missed—or blow up. Was the plane's last location known? How long would it take searchers to find it on the ground?

Plunging his stiffening hands in his pockets he was surprised to find ski mittens and matches. This jacket was so ancient that he'd had it while he was still smoking. Well, that young Maine camper of many years ago could now try to build a fire. And he had at least one blanket, as the poor devil who was wrapped in it certainly didn't need it any more. Maybe there were other things on that body that it could spare. He stopped crawling and rested again on his elbows, exhausted, but thinking hard.

"Hey, Webby. Your immediate future, till just a little while ago, was not alluring. Landing in Bangor, stretching your legs, getting through customs and flying on to Chicago to meet Phyllis and then take up your basically unsatisfactory life again, that was the only game plan.

"You're in your mid-thirties, financially comfortable, probably mildly respected as a businessman, fairly decent citizen and an average golfer, so what's turning you off? You're no longer in love with your wife but you don't hate her. You're married to an insecure woman you once loved dearly, who has to feel superior to you to keep her own fragile sanity intact. Phyllis is not a bitch, not a tramp, not even dishonest or extravagant. She is simply sucking the lifeblood of self worth from you and probably doesn't even know it. You will not divorce her and thus destroy her minuscule self-esteem, and you can't even give her grounds for divorce as that would have the same effect.

"You no longer have burning ambitions or lofty goals, no kids to watch grow up and to guide. As a pair, with really hard work, you and your wife have built a fairly successful business, taking over a small one from her father. By pooling her chemistry talents with your business skills you've done OK . But, very importantly, you're getting uneasy with the world of chemical products, a feeling underlined by what you've learned in Cairo. It is the year 1987. January. Otherwise no big problems ahead except trying to remember how it feels to be happy."

A strange idea was forming in his head as he lay there in the snow. He tried to push it back, to erase it, to make the snow bury it. But it kept coming back, more logical, possible, clever, and actually more reasonable every second.

Several years ago Webb's closest friend and college roommate had visited them for a few days and, late one evening as the two men had a final Scotch, Joel had said, "There's a helluva lot of tension under this roof, isn't there? None of my business but I sure would like to see you two happier in this life."

Joel knew of how Webb and Phyllis had met at Harvard grad school, Webb on a grant seeking an MBA and Phyllis, graduate of Wellesley, going for a Masters in chemical engineering. She was pretty, bright, and very goal-oriented. Webb had not been able to party his way through his undergraduate Harvard years as Joel and other friends had, busy with their club life, dances, and ski weekends. Webb was on scholarship and had outside work, waiting tables, cutting lawns, doing anything he could to make ends meet; he had no time for even halfway serious relationships with girls.

Brought up in a fatherless home, Webb had little understanding of wedlock. He hadn't given it much thought. This shy, attractive young woman with no real financial need to seek a career intrigued him. She had few outside interests or concerns and no close friends. Respect for the other's mind, recognition of similar reactions to many things, and a strong physical attraction satisfied them both. And weddings seemed to be popular; they were almost expected after grad school.

Her "Mummy" had been enthusiastic about the match as she had quickly recognized that Webb seemed much like "Daddy." Manageable. His Harvard background was nice to drop into bridge-table chats when the engagement was announced. Phyllis had finally done something right.

They were married the summer after receiving their graduate degrees. Docile, submissive "Daddy" found places for them both in his plant, which at that time specialized in chemical fertilizers, and all seemed rosy. A pleasantly correct but hardly impassioned existence; they had expected little more.

Three years later Phyllis became pregnant and it was then that Webb first became really aware of her paralyzing fears and lack of self-esteem. To her father she wasn't the son he wanted, and it had never entered his chauvinistic head that a girl might be capable of following in his footsteps. Her lack of interest in her mother's social values had caused real problems between them. "Mummy's" need to manage and control was stifling; Phyllis had felt for years she could do nothing that really pleased either of her parents. Having Webb choose her had been seemed a miracle. Though still ridden with anxieties, she had felt better about herself. Pregnancy magnified her stress.

Tragedy struck during the seventh month. Phyllis miscarried a hopelessly deformed fetus and was told she could not bear another child. All the degrees in the world, all the money, and she could not do "what any stupid little fourteen-year-old female savage could." She defensively built in her head an unshakably strong denial that the baby's problems had been in any way connected to her. Therefore, it must have been Webb's genes that were flawed. To save herself, she began—almost subconsciously—to punish him at every opportunity, putting him down, rejecting his support, freezing their relationship.

So Webb lost not only his chance at fatherhood but also, in many ways, his wife. He was so sorry for her that he couldn't and wouldn't fight back. He knew that to suggest counseling would have been the last straw for her His support was therefore immense patience; he had never demanded that she think of him. Tension, yes, Joel, lots of tension.

Now in a frozen hell so unreal that logical, reasonable thought was impossible, he remembered sitting that night in his warm den, nursing his drink and answering Joel's query about happiness. He had simply said, without bitterness or drama, "Maybe this is all there is for me."

And Joel, unwilling to let it go at that, replied "Buddy, we go this way but once."

Webb hadn't argued. He seldom did, and avoided confrontations almost entirely, often earning more of Phyllis' disdain because of it. He really didn't know how to handle unpleasantness, even yet. The strong women in his life had discouraged argument. Even his mother had a held-over Victorianism that found sweeping problems under the rug preferable to taking stands. Bad manners.

So what were his options right now? He could dig a hole in the snow, line it with broken branches, and hope to be found. Knowing something of these woods and mountains, it might be a matter of just a few hours after daylight, or a matter of several days, before rescuers came, depending on the strength and length of the storm and the natural obstacles to the site.

Then it would be back to civilization, a lot of television and press hoopla, phony tears of joy from Phyllis and a return to his regular routine and frustrations. A future almost as bleak as the frightening world he had been discussing in Cairo.

Or—and what a huge "or!" —do we really go this way but once? How about a try at twice?

He was now aware of the smell of gasoline. There were no flames, and possibly the cold had cooled the engines enough so that the gas would not be ignited from heat. In his woozy head he recalled the Vikings' funerals he'd seen in countless Saturday afternoon movies as a kid, and particularly the splendid cremation of Gary Cooper in *Beau Geste* at Fort Zinderneuf, in the shimmering heat of the Sahara. Heat, a lovely word. But he knew there might be too much, quite soon. Move!

Struggling through snow well over his knees to where he believed the gas tanks would be, he was rewarded by the sight of the tinted snow where the fuel was starting to form a pool.

Passing a particularly large branch he tossed his wallet into it, with the exception of a few small bills and change. Good-bye credit cards, good-bye ID's, passport, birth certificate, driver's license, insurance cards, library card, club membership cards. Incontrovertible evidence he was among the victims. He was tempted to whistle "Taps" or some other appropriate number, and finally did give the "late Webb H. Lewis" a salute.

He staggered as rapidly as he could to where he'd left the blanket, picked it up, and kept moving, the dry snow so cold it squeaked with every step. Looking back he saw wind-whipped flames already jumping, dancing, advancing on the plane.

He had no idea how great an area might be affected by the explosion and certainly didn't want to get hit by falling and possibly burning materials. A bit ahead was a large snow-covered rock. He was just able to stagger that far and get behind it; he didn't have long to wait.

With no warning the whole area became bright as day, the air was almost sucked out of his lungs, and the bang that followed was beyond anything he had ever heard. He shook, uncontrollably, for a long time.

Webb H. Lewis was kaput, gone, over. His "widow" Phyllis was now in charge of the business and plant that seemed her only pleasure. She had a lovely home, plenty of money, and a new life of her own to live. Maybe she too would find his "death" a release and take the opportunity to find a modus vivendi that was truly satisfying. Maybe he was giving her a second chance, too. Good luck, once-dear Phyllis!

He had a few fairly close friends where they lived, golf buddies mostly. His social lifewas slight as Phyllis was shy and could not enter into the talk about children that other wives enjoyed. His mother and his kindly uncle were long gone. Though he was active in United Way campaigns, served on a few boards of nonprofit agencies, spoke up occasionally at town meetings, he did not consider that his loss would matter much. Camp and college friends were scattered and he had only kept in really close touch with Joel. There was Tommy, a kid he'd met at the Boys' Club and who had become sort of a protégé. Now, hopefully, someone else would take him on, a boy of promise.

With the decision made and action taken came a miraculous spurt of energy, though he hurt like hell. The main thing nowwas to move along so that no searchers would find him. He must create a shelter of sorts, eliminate any tracks that the wind-driven snow wasn't filling, and try to remember everything he'd ever read about amnesia. Pulling the hood of the parka further down over his head, he fought his way against the wind and deepening snow to get a real distance from the fire, aleady thanking the mechanic who had not properly checked the locking of the emergency door, thus allowing the miracle of his own deliverance.

Exhaustion finally overcame him. It took real determination to scoop out an adequate hole, piling the snow in a wall around it. Lining it with a few boughs, he curled up on them, wrapped in the blanket. Prayers were no longer a habit, but tonight was different. "Now I lay me down to sleep" seemed ridiculously childish. As he settled in and started to make himself breathe deeply and slowly, there came into his head, and then flooded over him, from many Sunday school years back, a hymn of faith and hope: "Abide with me; fast falls the eventide; the darkness deepens; Lord with me abide. When other helpers fail, and comforts flee, Help of the helpless, O abide with me."

The late Webb Lewis, exhausted, woozy, and cold, fell asleep, in peace.

* * * * *

Every muscle, every bone, every nerve ending, and parts of his body he hadn't known he had, ached and screamed in rebellion, proclaiming their misery. The area around his nose was sore and very tender. He was pretty sure it was broken. There was caked blood from what was probably a deep cut on one cheek, near his eye.

Curled up in the small snow and bough-lined cave for what may have been hours, Webb was cramped, stiff, hungry, and very, very cold; his nostrils were still frozen shut and there was ice on his chin where his breath had hit the cold air. He unfolded gradually, pushed off the blanket which itself was blanketed with snow, and finally had a space cleared through which he could inspect the new day.

As so often happens after a northeast storm, there was an almost contrived innocence in the bright blue sky, benign sunlight, and frisky little breeze. "Sorry if I inconvenienced you a bit, it's all over now. Grab your shovels, snowshoes, or whatever, for this is the day that the Lord hath made," so saith the weather sprite.

This sparkling wilderness greeted him, with no hints or reminders of last night's nightmare. The wind no longer even whispered through the pine boughs and the only sound was an occasional, almost imperceptible, plop of soft snow chunks falling from branches onto equally soft snow below. It was easy to dream, in such a wintry Eden, that he would soon smell coffee perking, bacon sizzling, or at the very least, the welcoming odor of wood smoke from a friendly chimney. Even in his condition, he absorbed energy from such a day.

God, he was hungry! In books, stranded heroes always found stale chocolate bars in their pockets; he wondered if those novelists had ever really starved. Did they all carry emergency chocolate bars themselves? He couldn't imagine not finishing one, much less pessimistically storing a remnant. Eat the damn thing and enjoy!

Eventually he achieved a standing position and stretched, slowly and painfully. Everything worked, but not without protest. Then, as he was about to climb out of his refuge and check his surroundings, he heard sounds certainly not forest-made. Looking up, he spotted the helicopter immediately and ducked back into his shelter.

In performing that simple, reflexive act he realized that he was really making a commitment to this disappearance drama he had orchestrated; he wasn't going to run out into a clearing waving his arms and sobbing with the relief of the rescued. He was now, from this moment, a major character in a new game, a refugee, escapee, Jean Valjean, a man on the lam. Yet, appallingly, he felt alive, not dead as the news would have him but truly, pulsatingly alive for the first time in years. He was honest enough to admit that if the going got too rough, or if he felt it was a cruel mistake, he could always stage a resurrection, a miracle, and be right back where he started.

After a while there was a new sound added to the continuing noise of the circling helicopter, abrasive, demanding, irritating, and also thoroughly foreign to the woods he knew, or had known. Snowmobiles! Sounded like a goddam army of them, whining and churning through the snow, like chain saws. He again sank back into his shelter.

Approaching from several directions, three machines came closer. To his horror, they stopped for an apparent rendezvous so near that he could actually hear the drivers' conversation once they throttled down.

"No signs yet, are there? Can you receive from the choppers?" one asked. Answered in the affirmative, the other drivers chose to take a break. The smell of tobacco drifted into Webb's lair. Not a smoker for six years, he would have given almost anything for a cigarette now. As his nostrils quivered and a long-ignored area of his interior cried out for nicotine relief, he heard yet another sound, a beeping and static that could only be air-to-ground communication.

"They've found it! Thank God, we mighta had to search for weeks. Ya, ya, got it! Over to Muskrat Pond, just a little way in from the south shore? Prob'ly not more'n a mile from here? OK, I got it!" The speaker reported to his friends, "We're wanted ASAP. Good thing we were all together for the news. Damn, though, I was kinda hoping to warm up in that camp on the east shore of Kidney. T'ain't far from here, coupla miles due north. It's stocked pretty good, woodstove 'n all. Oh, hell, let's go."

Motors were started up. Roaring, throwing a fine snow spray, they disappeared to the east. Webb waited a while, then stood again and looked around. It was hard to believe he had struggled so far last night before he felt safe enough to stop. Almost a mile!

He could hear the 'copter in the distance, the snowmobile crew wouldn't be back and, by the grace of God, he now had a clue to where he might find refuge and warmth, at least long enough to sort things out in his head. Erasing all the personal landmarks of thirty-five years and concocting new signposts was going to be harder than erasing the signs of last night's lodgings; he needed time, not to mention a worthwhile plan of action.

Studying the sun's position and the length of shadows he could pretty well determine true north. Certainly the chance of finding even a crude camp in this wilderness was worth taking; he had nothing to lose. Removing all traces of his stay, he headed carefully through the underbrush.

The traveling was hardly speedy. The snow was deep, and each footstep made him aware of his bruises and fatigue, but he had an optimistic bent that kept him going. Finally, about midafternoon, he emerged from the woods onto the shore of a frozen lake, much of it already in shadow. The sun had most surely been sinking a bit on his left, so he followed the shoreline to his right, venturing out on the ice, which made for easier walking.

Webb was so exhausted that he almost missed it, but all at once the angular lines of a cabin stood out against the irregular, curving lines of tree boughs; a crude porch provided horizontals in contrast to the vertical tree trunks, and he knew he had a chance. He almost fell against the crude front door, half hidden by a drift of snow. He rattled the doorknob with no results, and then common sense told him to search for a key. Camp owners in remote sections knew that determined interlopers could get in anyway, but they didn't want to make it too easy. Where to look? Shutters, behind the shutters. On his third try, he found it, on a rawhide loop, hanging from a nail.

Kicking away the snow, he entered the cabin. It would have seemed like pretty unattractive accommodations a week ago, but now he felt as if welcoming arms had reached out to hold and comfort him. Ridiculous. He was breaking and entering, wasn't he? But in that one room, smelling of mouse droppings, decaying wood, long burned out stove fires and slightly moldy blankets, he felt at home and, more importantly, safe.

Crude camps such as this were found throughout the Maine woods, often owned for generations by working-class families from the cities. Here the men could come once or twice a year to hunt and fish with chosen companions, spending the days outdoors and the nights playing cards, drinking, and outlying each other with straight faces. In Maine all rustic retreats didn't belong to millionaires or paper companies.

Just enough light glowing from the west helped Webb to locate a lantern, blessedly filled with kerosene. An old coffee tin housed matches and, once he'd illuminated his surroundings, he took inventory: four bunks with blankets, a table, chairs, some logs piled by the stove—he knew there'd be more stacked outside. A pile of old newspapers, mostly the Maine Sunday Telegram, made starting a fire in the stove easy. Some cans of beans, of tuna, and one of coffee were on the shelves, frozen, of course, but they could be heated. The snow would provide water. What more could one ask?

Sooner than he had expected, the stove gave off blessed heat and his hands tingled as they warmed up. Running the chance of discovery because of smoke from the chimney was worth this ecstasy of expanding comfort. He rummaged through a drawer in the table near the stove and found a can opener.

Which would it be? Beans or tuna? Tuna would bring back a lot of school lunches and summer picnics, but beans were stick-to-the-ribs food, with a sweetness and richness that was superbly satisfying. Heating the opened can on the stove he didn't even look for a plate, but ate the beans, swimming in their special sauce, right out of the can.

Webb banked the old stove, set the drafts so it would burn slowly all night, cupped his hand over the top of the lamp chimney and blew out the light. As he lay down on a bunk, covered with several blankets, warm and full, he knew he was going to make it. He was almost content.

There was a lot of serious thinking to do, a new identity to create, and most important, some purpose to follow. Not many people get a second chance at life, and the thought was exciting. He'd have to be careful that Webb Lewis never emerged again, though he was tempted to contact Joel. Should he fabricate a new name and background or would he, at least temporarily, be an amnesia victim, playing it by ear? Before he even finished his list of questions, he was dead to the world.

As the cabin filled with soft dawn light, Webb looked at his watch, actually for the first time since the accident. A little after six and he knew, regretfully, he had to move on. Only a few miles separated him from the rescue parties and he would surely be discovered. He filled his pockets with some stale crackers he'd found in a tin, another can of beans, and the opener. Making a roll of the plane's blanket, he slung it on his shoulder and opened the door.

But something nailed to the inside of the door caught his eye, something he had missed in the dark of last night. Beside a yellowed pinup of a scantily clad girl was tacked a faded and discolored map. Studying it carefully he soon found a penciled X. Was that to show where he was at the moment? Sure enough, he could just read the words "Kidney P." The map probably covered a twenty-five mile area showing in detail streams, elevations, swampland, and lakes.

Certainly he didn't expect to locate a sizeable town, but there might be a small village. The print was so small and faint he had to trace each lake and pond shore with a finger to be sure he missed nothing. Finally, success! At the foot of a considerable lake, Mistoki, there were the words "Harding's Corner." Now he studied the map in earnest, plotting the best route from X. A rough estimate would be about six miles, with luck.

He placed the last of his money on the table and tore the map from the door. He knew that if circumstances forced him to alter his chosen route he would be hopelessly lost without it, and he already felt like a thief anyway. He would like to someday thank, in person, the owner of this mansion. Closing and locking the door, and hanging up the key, he took off for the suddenly enormously important "metropolis" of Harding's Corner, Maine, U.S.A.

By midafternoon he knew he was close. He could almost taste the hot coffee that he would order, sitting up at the counter of a warm little convenience store, while being looked over by the few regulars. Let 'em look; he would have made it! He would make the momentous decision of choosing a plain donut or a sugarcoated one, displayed on a glass-covered plate. He conjured up in his mind the warmth of the mug in both hands.

The last half mile seemed endless, but finally the woods thinned out. Finding himself on a recently plowed narrow road, he blessed that ancient map with true affection. Civilization, such as it was! The road curved off to the left, and he knew he'd find his goal just beyond. He felt like running, like shouting, but his feet just didn't get the message. He was staggering.

And there it was. Harding's Corner, a tiny crossroads in an empty land of snow. One very small building, roof partially fallen in, tilted drunkenly toward one rusted gas pump. An old tin Coca-Cola sign swung in the slight wind, hanging on to the building by one nail. The door was open, sagging.

The building was stripped, totally stripped of whatever merchandise or comforts it had once provided. Linoleum curled up at the edges of the one room, stopped from rolling further by a counter that was actually weatherbeaten. His luck had run out; his future was as empty and bleak as that little store.

Webb sank onto the high end of a collapsing step, put his head in his hands, and almost expected tears to come. Even that system was evidently too tired, too discouraged to function. Being saved, God knows why, from death, overhearing the conversation that had led him to the cabin, finding food, warmth and the map had been miracles certainly. Now he'd used up his share, he was licked. Being on a road didn't help when he couldn't take another step; it was getting dark and the temperature was dropping again.

He unfolded the map to search for some other place name, some new goal, though he doubted that his strength would get him far, certainly not tonight. The light had faded too much for him to read the map at all. Common sense told him to go inside the building for what little shelter it might provide against the night cold. He stood up , swayed, and fell onto the snowy ground by the pump, unconscious.

* * * * *

Just before the plane had actually crashed Webb had been bumped around, in the dark, no idea of what was happening. Now almost the same feeling came over him as his body tried to maintain balance in a vehicle that also threw him around. Had the woods episode just been a dream? The crash an imagined reprieve? How crazy was he? Eyes slowly opened and he looked out on a winter road illuminated by the headlights of whatever he was riding in.

He turned his head to the left and saw the profile of a man who concentrated on maneuvering what seemed to be a very old truck down a very crude logging road.

Webb must have made some sound louder than the motor, as his chauffeur turned, looked at him and grinned, "Good evening, son. Your quarters back at lovely downtown Harding's Corner didn't seem quite adequate. How about sharing mine with my wife and me for awhile? Not elegant, but warm, good food, and a hot tub?"

Webb felt quite definitely that he had died and gone to heaven. And it was the first time he could ever remember a man calling him "son."

They finally lurched into the dooryard of what seemed in the dark to be a moderately large farmhouse, with attached barn and sheds. What was probably the back door opened, allowing light to reach the truck and, at the same time, to silhouette a figure peering out at them.

For the first time Webb could clearly see the profile of his rescuer. The outstanding feature was a splendid nose; below that, interrupted by a clipped moustache, was a neatly trimmed beard, covering what was probably a very strong chin. The man seemed to be in his late sixties, judging from the almost white hair and the lines etched deeply around the eyes and mouth. Formidably bushy eyebrows were in harmony with the other features. A "man's man," thought Webb, "a stern face when in repose."

"Need any help in getting to the house?" he was asked, so he answered by kicking open the truck door and climbing out, stiffly but on his own two feet. Bumpy as his ride had been, some strength had returned to him.

The figure in the light was that of a woman, now hurrying out to meet them. Clad in jeans and a flannel shirt under a heavy jacket, with her hair pulled back in a long pigtail, she immediately struck Webb as gentle, probably wise, a nurturer. Her face was one that he would wish to find on the head nurse in an operating room if he was about to be anaesthetized for major surgery, a no-nonsense, caring, straightforward lady. He was amazed that he would, or could, make such a quick appraisal. Webb felt safe, even though she had a smudge of paint on her nose, green paint.

At the same time a big dog, mostly, if not all, black lab, circled the truck with enthusiasm, well-mannered enough not to jump on any of them, but exuding joy and hospitality.

"Well, my dear, I've brought us company. Let's get him in the house, warm up a bit and look him over. Why don't you take one arm, Susan, and I'll handle the other. Seems he's had quite a trip. And, Rousseau, mind your P's and Q's and let us go in first."

Walking between them into a warm, softly lit kitchen filled with homey odors was almost a religious experience for Webb, like unexpectedly hearing glorious music in just the right setting.

Jackets were taken off and hung on wooden pegs by the door. Boots followed, to be lined up neatly, and his blanket was folded and placed on a chair by the wall.

Webb was suddenly embarrassed by his condition, knew he stunk to high heaven, looked like a derelict, and had no idea yet of how to introduce himself.

"Now Susan is going to pour you some coffee, and while the tub is filling I'll I rustle up something for you to wear. Make a new man of you." Little did his host know how close to the truth that was.

"Incidentally I'm Stan, Stan Warner."

He was led down a hall into an old-fashioned downstairs bathroom, complete with an iron tub on clawed feet, narrow and deep, a tub for soaking. The man turned on the water, then left to return with towels, razor, and an armful of faded but serviceable clothes.

Webb saw himself in the little mirror over the sink, and didn't know whether to laugh or cry. His nose was swollen to immense proportions and listing to one side. A deep cut ran diagonally from a cheekbone up through an eyebrow, and he finally laughed, realizing that his present appearance was exactly what he had tried to achieve for long-ago Halloweens—mean, vicious, and perfect for scaring poor householders. He turned to his host. "Good God! Trick or Treat?"

Before he was left alone he suggested that if he did not appear within a reasonable time to please come and rescue him from drowning, as he had an idea that that tub was going to be pretty soporific.

Starting to shave it occurred to him that a beard might not be too bad an idea, and he certainly had the start of one. Between gulps of good hot coffee to keep him going, he achieved quite a neat appearance. He had avoided hirsute appendages during the hippy era; now he would experiment. Maybe that stuffy non-rebel had died in the crash too!

Swinging his leg over the side of the tub was agony, but worth it. He soaped, scrubbed luxuriously, and then sank back into the faintly scented soapy water till just his shampooed head was visible. He wondered dreamily if the human race would have survived as long as it had if hot water had not been available. Were the countries with natural hot springs early leaders in civilization? Choking, he realized that he'd dozed off in a philosophical reverie and that it was time to investigate the kitchen or drown.

While Webb had been soaking, Stan had filled his wife Susan in on all he knew of their guest. Then, as she prepared supper, he had picked up Webb's blanket to put it in a more suitable spot. As he shook it out to fold more neatly, a logo woven into it caught his eye. He recognized it as Centralia-Airlines, and thoughts tumbled around in his head.

He said quietly to Susan, "This guy has been through something big, I think. Let's hold any questions for a bit; let him tell us what he wants." She looked a bit worried, but trusted Stan's judgment. She always had, or almost always.

Webb, still looking weary, but obviously refreshed, joined them to enjoy a stew he was told was rabbit, with hot corn bread and, interestingly, a glass of goat's milk. Big molasses cookies served as dessert.

The old kitchen was illuminated by tall-chimneyed Aladdin kerosene lamps, which gave a steady bright light. Webb had noticed the sound of a motor running somewhere when they had arrived, but that was now silent. He reasoned, correctly, that their electricity was produced by a generator, and they used it as little as possible, as fuel was undoubtedly precious.

The meal, the warmth of the room and of his companions, and the occasional thump of Rousseau's tail were all doing what no massage or even tranquilizer could have possibly done. Now, to make it storybook perfect, he felt what must be a very large cat rubbing in and out around his legs, purring. He reached under the table to investigate and Susan chuckled. "I guess we'll let you stay. Grandma Moses has accepted you. Now, off to bed. Sleep tight," as if to a little child," and we'll see you in the morning.'?

Later, with her head on Stan's shoulder in their big bed, Susan waited for him to speak. She felt uncannily sure that their lives had taken a new turn, that this stranger was not just a pass-through.

Stan's hand stroked her now loosened gray hair.

"Y'know, I think this guy has done just what we did, for different reasons and in a different way. I'm sure he was on that plane that crashed, and I'm guessing he's taking advantage of that accident and easing out of a life he wasn't very happy in. I shouldn't have done it, but I went through his jacket before coming to bed. No wallet, no identification, just a can opener, and a faded old map. It had an X on Kidney Pond, which isn't too far from where they found the plane, but far enough to tell me he was moving away from it. Nice-looking guy, well-spoken, polite. OK with you if we give him a chance? He may even play amnesia games, but let's let him. He needs time to get things sorted out."

His answer was a contented sleepy grunt from Susan before she turned over and lay against him, so they were like spoons in a drawer. When he was sure she was asleep he carefully and gently cupped one big hand over her breast, and relaxed. Grandma Moses, on the comforter at the foot of the bed, stretched luxuriously, and all was still.

* * * * *

Chicago

Phyllis Lewis had been just about to leave for O'Hare to meet Webb when a call came from the airline. She was told that the plane from Zurich had simply disappeared just outside some Maine airport, in a blizzard, sending no clue as to location or problem! They would keep her informed.

She had actually continued on through the kitchen into the garage before it hit her that there was no need for the trip. Not yet at least. The caller had suggested she ask a friend to wait with her near the phone and TV. No close friends with whom to share such a vigil, barely any real friends at all, came to her mind. This was the first time she had even realized, much less thought about, what an isolated and almost antisocial life she led.

Webb was her only intimate, her destroyer, her one-time lover, her silly docile sheep, but always her knight in shining armor when it came to protection and support. She needed him right this minute to help her through this disaster, and then stopped—the disaster was that he wasn't here, and might never be here again!

Big, handsome Webb, whose spine she considered made of jelly, who never fought back under any circumstances and unfailingly gave her the same tender care that she had given his fragile gardenia corsages so many years ago. Both she and the gardenias had ended up in the refrigerator.

Starting to feel shaky, she hung up her coat and returned to the living room, to stand in front of what was left of the fire she'd lit earlier, the fire Webb had laid just before he left for Egypt. His hands had touched those logs which were also disappearing, forever.

Her eye lit on the TV. Maybe there would be some news. Her clicks of the remote brought talk shows, sitcoms, rock'n'roll bands, old movies, basketball, vulgarity, ads for mouthwash. None, for God's sake, interested in whether her husband was alive or dead? 10:45, there should be a news broadcast at 11:00. That was what Webb always felt he had to watch before he came up to bed, to his room.

But before five more minutes had passed the phone rang again. It was the airline. "Mrs. Lewis, I hope you have someone with you. No? Maybe you would rather hear this in the morning?"

Phyllis sank into Webb's chair. "No, no, tell me. Have they found him?" Not it, or them, just Webb.

"What we know so far is that a huge fiery explosion at ground level was seen in the area we believe they were flying over at the time of disappearance. There are no homes or roads near the spot, but a small private plane spotted flames and reported. We've waited to see if any more information came in before calling the families of passengers. That is all we know now. Mrs. Lewis. Mrs. Lewis, are you there? Are you all right?"

Her voice seemed very far away. It reminded her of her replies when she was little and Mummy would call from town or the country club to see if she'd come promptly home from school. Phyllis now replied mechanically, "Yes I'm here. I'm all right, and thank you. Yes, oh yes, please keep me posted. Goodnight."

She hung up, watched the last log crumple and fall into the red ashes, and whispered to the empty room, the empty house, the empty world, "I'm not really all right. I am terrified."

She believed that their business associates and rivals all thought she was the strong one who really ran the company, and that her few social acquaintances also saw her as the decision maker. But though she regularly found herself impatient with Webb's malleability and seeming lack of executive aggressiveness, she had always known that she depended heavily on his judgment. Webb not only gave support in business matters, but more importantly, he kept her glued together. His strong arms held her when the panics set in, he listened when she tried to explain the inexplicable horrors that lived inside her but for which she had refused professional help. No therapists had ever been allowed to treat this woman. They and their pills might take control of her, so no, no thanks.

In books and movies this was the moment when the heroine tottered to the bar and mixed a drink, Phyllis thought wryly. She had never touched alcohol for fear of it, fear of losing that same precious control. She just continued to shake, and could feel the old, familiar and dreaded panic symptoms building up. She turned on the TV; it was just 11:00.

Local news first, always, and it was always the same, a murder or two in the slum section of the city, a devastating car crash on the interstate, a mother tearfully saying her son was such a good boy he couldn't have raped a six-year-old, and yet another disaster in Bangladesh. Then came the weather: light snow, clearing in the afternoon.

Commercials, gorgeous human models draped over glistening late-model autos, carpets cleaned by cartoon busy bees, cereal your child would like more than ice-cream. Here it was, finally.

"This afternoon, over a snow-covered Maine wilderness, an overseas flight simply disappeared. The plane, carrying almost 400 people, was due to land in Bangor, Maine, just minutes after a recording of the captain's voice urged passengers to buckle up because of turbulence in unexpected blizzard conditions. Then came sounds of a crash and nothing. Search parties are out now, trying to cover hundreds of square miles in case there may be survivors."

All through this were shown airplane views of nothing but trees, snow-covered mountains, and flat areas she assumed were lakes. Not even a church spire, a suggestion of a road, or the black ribbon of an open river.

"There are believed to be well over 200 Americans aboard, but we have no passenger list at this time. This station will keep you posted with newsbreaks as they may develop."

She shut if off. What to do now?

Her phone rang. It was Daddy, and she was sure Mummy was on an extension, ready with directions but little understanding.

"Phyl, baby, is Webb home all right? No? He wasn't on that plane over Maine, was he? Phyl, Phyl, are you there? Oh my God. Phyl, we're on our way over."

Her mouth had gone dry, she was sweating now, and shaking more than ever. She felt like fainting but knew she wouldn't because she never had, no matter how badly off she was. Just her classic panic symptom.

Her parents were coming, just what she needed the least right now. They would take control as always, run her life through this situation by treating her as a child, calling it love but robbing her of all dignity, all feeling of maturity and intelligence. Damn, damn, damn, where was Webb? He would fend them off.

Phyllis went into the powder room under the broad stairway, put on fresh lipstick, smoothed her flawless blonde page-boy, patted the velvet ribbon in the back, and was ready to go into her "I'm the mistress of myself and this house" act. She was very good at it, and no one but Webb knew of the trembling, fragile moth of sanity that fought for existence inside her somewhere. Tires soon crunched outside on the frozen driveway. Her parents had arrived, and she opened the big front door for them.

Taking her mother's heavy mink coat, she laid it on a chest in the large entrance hall. After allowing herself to be pecked, she motioned to the living room. To stall at least for a second or two she opened the handsome wood-box and, folding back the fire-screen, carefully put another log on the embers, her back to her parents as she fought for control.

"Phyllis dear," purred Maude Jarrett, "we have decided that you must pack a few things and come home to us till this is decided one way or another."

The words seemed supportive but Phyllis heard loud and clear the unspoken "or else" that had characterized their conversations since her babyhood. Her mother straightened out lives as compulsively as she straightened pictures on the wall. Order, not empathy, was her strong suit.

"Home to where?" thought Phyllis. She been a married woman with her own home for almost ten years. Did they think she was just on an extended sleep-over?

Her mother continued. "I've thought it all out. The phone company can transfer all your calls to us, we will take care of our poor little girl and keep the press and all your friends from bothering you at this difficult time."

"Mother, mother, let go the reins, give me a chance." Wordlessly.

"And, dear, we do have to think ahead. Do you have a decent black dress? Just in case? We ought to go through your closet now before you get caught in a whirl of decisions. I want my little princess to look her very best for the ordeal." Her mother, typically, was only thinking of image, not of her daughter's needs or feelings.

Arthur Jarrett straightened in his chair and actually interrupted his wife. "That's nothing to discuss right now, Maude. Let's give Phyl a chance to speak up and tell us what she wants, what she really needs right now." He sent his daughter a gentle smile and a little wink of encouragement.

Phyllis faced her mother and hardly recognized her own voice as she replied. "Thank you, Daddy. You are both very kind but I have no intention of leaving here. This is my home, I have few friends so I won't be bothered, and the press has over 200 other American families to badger. Yes, Mummy, I do have several black dresses, none of which you probably like, but I am" her throat tightened but she kept right on "appalled that you are worrying about such a trivial thing when we don't know whether my husband is alive or dead."

She rose and, interrupting her mother's startled defense of herself, continued. "Needless to say, I am very tired. I appreciate your having come over, and now I think I'll say goodnight." She walked into the hall, lifted her mother's coat and held it for her, then gently patted her father's arm.

As the car went down the drive, Phyllis Jarrett Lewis locked the front door, turned off the lights in living room and hall and, with back ramrod straight, went up the broad stairs. In her bedroom she stood before her dressing table and looked at a picture of Webb taken when he assumed presidency of the company. She really studied the kindly, handsome face, always so open and warm. She whispered, "Maybe the little princess did some growing up tonight, in several ways. Help me in this, Webb. I think maybe you've already started."

* * * * *

Waking up she did not immediately remember the night before. She did not miss Webb in the bed, as they had had separate rooms for several years. Phyllis stretched luxuriously and then stopped, paralyzed, midway. The horror came rushing in and she wasn't sure whether it was one of her bad dreams, or reality. Then the phone rang. No one called this early as a rule.

"Yes, yes. Oh, Joel, it is good to hear your voice. So far, yes, I'm OK, I guess, but it's only just begun. No, there's no one here I want to trouble, no one except my parents, and you know how I feel about them. But I'll manage. What?"

From a snowy suburb of Boston, Joel McLean continued to talk and to offer his help, starting immediately. He would come out for at least the time it would take to get through the planning and occasion of a memorial service and the beginning of legal and business decisions.

"I've even looked up flights, as I'd made up my mind to come whether you wanted me or not. Can someone meet me at 12:45, United Flight 641? Now, turn over and go back to sleep, Uncle Joel's on the way."

Friends first at camp in Maine as boys, then later roommates at Harvard, Webb and Joel had never lost touch with one another. They had a rare relationship. From quite different social and economic backgrounds, they had somehow managed to share joys, sorrows, and values.

Phyllis said "I'll meet you myself. Bring Carol if you can." She was quite grateful that Joel was coming to help her, not even considering how much he needed to do this for his own sake as well as hers.

Between more calls, some from her office and a few business friends, she was able to dress, in pale gray slacks and a soft violet cashmere sweater, topped off with a filmy scarf. It was a sober costume but not strictly mourning.

Downstairs, Mrs. Johnson, who came in by the day, offered fresh orange juice, coffee, and Phyllis's favorite raisin toast, but not before getting up her courage to give her employer a truly motherly hug. Their relationship was quite businesslike generally, but not today. And Phyllis responded with a surprised feeling of warmth and a smile.

"I've told all callers at the front door to just give me their names and you may get in touch. Lotsa newspaper men and women, even TV. I may be suspicious, but I'll bet some are in the bushes outside right now. Wish we had a great big mean-looking dog, that'd fix 'em." As she puttered around the sunny kitchen and Phyllis sank into a chair by the window with her coffee, the doorbell pealed again. When Mrs. Johnson came back she announced in a more impressed voice, "It's the minister, Mrs. Lewis. You know, the new man at St. Peter's."

Webb and Phyllis were nominal members of St. Peter's Episcopal Church, though rarely attending together. Webb occasionally went to the 8:00 AM Sunday Communion, but Phyllis, unless sure of an aisle seat in the rear, had learned that panic attacks thrived in the hushed and proper atmosphere of church services, lectures, and other occasions requiring passive and unobtrusive behavior. Her piety was simply not up to that agony. She had not even met this new rector, and really didn't know whether Webb had or not.

"Might as well get it over with," she muttered to herself, and went to greet him.

The Rev. Arthur Morris was middle-aged, of middle height, unremarkable in features or coloring, but he had a pleasant smile, warm eyes behind his bifocals, and little of the phony good cheer or pious humility she had dreaded. And, instead of being all in black, he wore gray flannels and a heathery tweed sport coat over his black vest and clerical collar.

When they were seated before the living-room fire and the usual small talk and formal condolences were taken care of, he asked if she had given any thought to a memorial service for her husband.

"My mother was anxious about whether I had a decent black dress, but that's about as far as I've gotten. Isn't one of the beauties of the Episcopal Church the fact that we have a standard sort of service and don't have to be very creative?"

He smiled and recrossed his feet. "You might suggest some favorite hymns, or Bible readings, even loved poetry if applicable. Do you have any ideas about those? Of course, we don't have to decide anything now, but you might be thinking along those lines."

All she could think of along those lines were "Fair Harvard" which was not exactly what he had meant, or the campfire song from those long-ago summers at that camp she'd heard so much about. Endlessly, it seemed.

Mr. Morris said how sorry he was to not have had the opportunity of knowing her husband more than as a familiar face at the communion rail. Maybe she would find time to write down a few things about him that could be used in a little homily, to personalize the standard service?

"That would be nice," Phyllis murmured, wondering what on earth she would think of. "There will probably be just a few people there," she added. "We weren't very social, no country club life or that sort of thing, and for family there are only my parents and a few cousins who may not come anyway. My husband's parents are gone, and he had no one else."

She knew she was being negative and not at all helpful, so she clutched at a straw. "Webb did enjoy singing. Maybe later we could go over some hymns that we all could sing." He smiled again, talked a bit about the church custom of having flowers only on the altar under these circumstances and then, sensing she had nothing more to add, shook hands, gave her shoulder a careful little pat, and left.

Phyllis Lewis closed the door behind the departing clergyman and leaned against it. Eleven thirty already! Telling Mrs. Johnson that she was on her way to the airport she threw on a coat, grabbed her purse and ran for the car. As she drove along the expressway a new thought hit her. Not once, since that first dreadful news last night, had she thought of the office, the lab, the pile of problems on her desk. What had she been thinking about? Webb? Or Phyllis?

* * * * *

Augusta,Maine

In Augusta, Maine's capital, schools were closed because of the blizzard. The plows were noisily clearing the main avenues and streets, and news broadcasts announced that the Maine Legislature was going into session at noon rather than at the regular nine o'clock hour. Snow still fell, but lightly.

Rep. Patsy Hudson, R., from Portland, enjoying a leisurely second cup of coffee in the Senator Motel's dining room, turned to her companion. "You say you've hunted those woods often for deer. What access is there to where they think the plane is? Will there have to be just haphazard probing by helicopter and snowmobile or are there logging roads? No chance of open fields is there, much less a landing strip?"

Rep. Norman Jackson, R., a retired teacher from Caribou, laughed. "Little city lady, we're talking real Maine woods, not your Sebago Lake State Park. In this weather, with no visibility from above, with every lake, opening, and tree covered in white, it will take days to find that plane. The pilot's last signal, if you recall, was his telling the passengers to buckle up." He stirred his coffee. "Not a hint of the trouble and no location points at all-at-all." He drank, then reluctantly put down his cup.

"I'm going down to the State House and work at my desk. Want a lift?"

"Thanks, Norm, I'll be ready in a minute. Meet you at your car. I'll help dig out yours if you'll help find mine."

They were "roommates," as their motel units were next to each other. (One referred to legislators sitting next to one in either the House as "seatmates.")

She'd been recently widowed, her children were both living independently, and she had run for the House to help fill a suddenly very empty existence. A few days short of fifty-five when Bill died, she knew she must find an absorbing new life, not just busy work. She was too young to just vegetate and, though well educated, was untrained for any specific career. Bill had had strong feelings about where a woman's place was: in the home. Her life so far could be described as student, wife, mom, and community volunteer, period. Politics? Why not?

Though born, bred, and wed a Republican, she was not a dedicated ideologue; she had simply never considered any other affiliation. Her only political experience had been volunteering on various local campaigns, but this lack had been eclipsed by her energy and determination. To the surprise of many in strongly Democratic Portland, she'd won the seat, handily.

Would she find a new lifestyle, even a new Patsy? She'd worked awfully hard to create the present model.

Most legislators lived too far from Augusta to commute daily. Patsy, who lived only sixty miles away, had no reason to go home to an empty house. The Senator Motel was a Republican stronghold, while the Dems patronized a motel on the other side of the turnpike.

Living at the motel was just the education even a middle-aged freshman legislator needed, and in many subjects, not all political. Here, after their workday, tired lawmakers came back to their rooms, freshened up a bit, opened their inside corridor doors and, glasses in hand, visited back and forth. Sometimes, they jokingly claimed, their biggest decision of the day was where to eat dinner, and their biggest financial problem was whether to choose chicken or steak, not whether the State could afford new bridges or increased Medicaid programs. It was in these informal, friendly evenings that Patsy met people from all over the state, listened as they discussed their local problems and bills, and learned the inside workings of the House.

So immersed in this job had she become that the pain of her recent loss was mercifully dulled, and it was only on weekends, when she took up her former life in an empty house, that the suffering was still intense. How she would have loved to have Bill share it all. He had been the one interested in politics; her decision to run had been partly a memorial to him.

She and Norman climbed the snow-covered steps to a side entrance of the Capitol and she let him go ahead into the building. Turning, she gazed out over the almost empty and snow-covered parking lot and across the Kennebec River to distant hills, recalling standing there six weeks ago on Opening Day. She had silently mouthed a message then, looking up. "Bill, this is almost another good-bye, as I'm starting a new life without you, but this is exactly the adventure I know you would have chosen for me. Thanks for all you've taught me to care about, and for the support you've always given. I'll do my best for all that you and I believe in. Wish me luck, darling."

But already she was finding how ignorant she was on many issues, and how ambivalent she was about some she had thought were black and white. While Bill would have been delighted to find there were many members, mainly from the rural areas, as strongly conservative as he, Patsy was discovering that she was considerably more flexible (liberal?), listening to both sides carefully, though so far always voting with her party. Many bills appearing on her desk sounded like great ideas, while others seemed grossly unnecessary. However, when discussed in Committee or on the floor, perfectly sound reasons were given both for and against. If a problem had a simple solution there probably would have been no need for a bill in the first place.

So far she had few axes to grind or missions to accomplish, other than trying to make sure that Maine citizens got the biggest bang for their buck. Services should be efficiently delivered to where they were needed, at the least possible cost, a goal that sounded simple enough. She was finding in actuality that the Band-Aid upon Band-Aid approach of past legislatures had covered up but not cured many festering problems for too long, and for reasons she was just beginning to discover.

To the citizens of northern and eastern Maine, Portland and vicinity was likened to another state, a liberal Democratic aberration, and "Portland bills" were suspect, DOA and to be voted down, particularly the expensive welfare programs. Abused runaways, addicts, and the homeless converged on the state's largest city from their small towns. In the eyes of many they thus became Portland's problem and responsibility, so let Portland support them.

A Republican representative from Portland was almost an anomaly, but here she was. Though beginning to feel, with a certain amount of shame, strong symptoms of partisan paranoia—a contagious disease in Augusta—Patsy did enjoy feeling part of a team.

A Republican governor, a Democratic House, and a Republican Senate made a perfect breeding ground for party rivalry. The climate was perfect for a gridlock epidemic. In joint session the R's had a two-vote majority, if discipline held firm. Patsy could see that good decision making too often bowed to the satisfaction of frustrating the opposite side in the endless fight for power. Though often having to blindly follow the party's leadership votes because of ignorance, she also sincerely wished to be considered a loyal team player. This game-playing, however, was a surprise, and not what she had come to Augusta to do.

On opening day the freshmen had been handed, in addition to impressive license plates and locker keys, their notebooks, personalized stationery, books of Rules, notepads, maps of Augusta, etc. Patsy finally groaned "When do we get our gym suits? It's just like school?" The swearing-in ceremony was impressive. Senators came to the House and sat in front of the rostrum. Messengers from both Houses were chosen and sent to the governor's office to issue his invitation. In due time they returned, announcing that the message had been received, and soon His Excellency was escorted down the aisle. Elected members stood, repeated the vow he directed, and duly became the 113th Legislature of the State of Maine.

At lunch Patsy had asked where her office was, where she could keep all this equipment she'd been handed, take telephone calls, and receive constituents. When the laughter had ceased she was told that her desk was her office, except for one file drawer, if she was lucky, in the Committee Room to which she would be assigned.

Later, her party's leadership had reviewed for the freshmen the procedures governing every step of the legislative process. She had learned that bills originated from several sources: the governor's office, legislators, constituents, and special interests. The latter two chose sympathetic legislaors to write and present their concerns. Now, though still naive about the sophisticated manipulation of Robert's Rules, she felt pretty comfortable with the daily routine and some of the more obvious maneuverings. So far there had been little actual voting, as bills had to go through many steps, including committee hearings, before they reached the floor. This gave her time to catch her breath.

All Committees were made up of both Houses, and co-chaired by a Majority senator and a Majority representative. Because of her considerable experience with Board work for nonprofit agencies and charities in Portland, Patsy had been put on Health and Institutions, which pleased her, as those were subjects with which she felt comfortable.

But after the very first Committee hearing she admitted to herself how much she had to learn, particularly the social work vocabulary and use of acronyms that were so prevalent in the discussions. There was also constant reference to past legislation with which she was unfamiliar, and worst of all was the use of bureaucratese. This language had no rules, no grammar. Some day, some very fine day, she would feel confident enough to speak up and say how intimidating and arrogant such jargon was, essentially a foreign language. Gobbledygook!

She put her coat and boots in her locker and rode the elevator to the third floor. She had been surprised and impressed with the dignity of the House chamber when she first saw it, high-ceilinged, with large Palladian windows beautifully draped, and fine paneling wherever possible. Her large leather chair and mahogany desk, complete with voting buttons and microphone, were near the front in the middle of a row. She had a fairly good location, though she had had little choice. The parties were not separated by the aisle, but mixed together. Republicans being in the minority the Speaker, all-powerful, saw to it that freshman Republicans were given only a choice of the seats that would isolate them from their experienced fellows. His Democratic tyros sat together in large clusters, old hands instructing them on every bill, trick, and maneuver emanating from his rostrum. Typical power play.

Patsy's desk was covered today by copies of new bills, a freebie copy of the Maine Times and a message to contact her committee chairman.

Placing the new bills in her huge three-ring notebook, in numerical order, she glanced at their stated purposes. One caught her eye. LD 2310 addressed the problem of spraying the money-making blueberry barrens with chemical fertilizer from the air. Residents of that sparsely settled northeast area were concerned about what was getting into the aquifers from which their drinking water came. They wanted the practice to cease. A perfect example of both sides of a question having rights and interests.

She shut the notebook, placed it in the bin at the rear of her desk, and walked back across the rotunda and down the hall to the Senate Chamber. This was an even more beautiful chamber than the House. The senators' desks and chairs seemed massive, and they had more room in which to store their papers.

Sen. Bob Hawkins, R., a bit portly and balding, stood up as she approached his desk. He had been a friend of Bill's, also in the heating oil business, and so he'd been hospitable to Patsy from the start.

"Thanks for coming over. No one is using the president's office, so let's talk there." The president of the Senate was that body's equivalent of Speaker. Patsy followed Hawkins into a sumptuous room behind the Chamber, with sofa, several easy chairs, and a fireplace that crackled cheerfully this snowy day.

They sat down, and Bob got right to the point.

"Patsy, this isn't just malarkey. Ever since you've been here I've been impressed in committee with your ability to strip away the jargon and see what each person testifying is getting at, and why. Your questions have been extraordinarily perceptive and also refreshingly open, even in English all can understand."

Patsy was delighted with his enthusiasm, but tried hard not to show it. "Thanks, Bob. Some boards I've been sitting on recently seem to use a language so carefully nonabrasive that no one knows where anyone stands. Phrases like 'I think what I'm hearing' instead of 'you said', and 'at this point in time' instead of good, old-fashioned 'now' make me sick. And I'm almost embarrassed to admit that I had a reputation for telling it like it is. Saves a lot of time and keeps the air clear."

Relaxed now, she waited for him to get at whatever it was he wanted to talk about.

"We R's evaluate and analyze, in many different ways, the progress and contents of all the bills being heard. Each committee already has one person from each party who reports weekly to their leadership the current position of each bill assigned to it. Is it being worked on, or is it lying fallow and possibly headed for oblivion? Some of us want more than that. In just eighteen months we'll all be campaigning for reelection, and we need facts and figures to base our issues on. The D's do the same.

"As you know, one great difference between our parties is that we, the R's, believe in the least possible government, while the Dems just as sincerely believe that programs initiated by government and administered by same are the only way to go. Of course a lot of their programs are giveaways and they know that nobody shoots Santa." He just had to get that dig in.

"For example, someone is already keeping track of all the bills to be processed this session and next that could have a direct impact on the family. We often consider many of those bills intrusive, while the other party considers them examples of true compassion.

"I'm asking you to keep track of all bills that would affect business, particularly small business, in this state. Your husband talked a lot over with you, I know, so you've got some background for it. Many bills will very obviously fall into this category. It's those others affecting business by their ripple effect that are harder to spot and evaluate. Small businessmen are screaming about the regulations that pour out of here and Washington, generally concocted by legislators who have never had to meet a payroll, who have never had to hire more and more extra employees just to handle the required paperwork, or who have never had to redesign a whole plant because the bureaucrats can't see that there are other common-sense remedies for workplace safety or pollution.

"Consumers fault business for rises in prices, not realizing that that is inevitable when regulations, often demanded by Labor, make production so expensive. Whenever the liberal powers in Washington want to raise more money to give away, they raise taxes on business, yet business becomes the villain when workers have to be laid off or prices go up.

"None of us claim that Big Business is totally innocent. Some of its loopholes and excesses are almost obscene, such as CEO salaries that almost match a ballplayer's. But where the hell would most revenue come from, or new jobs, if business didn't have the courage to take risks and expand, using venture capital invested by stockholders?

"Sorry, I didn't mean to make a speech, but the state and the country just can't afford much more of this slow strangling of the goose that lays the golden revenue eggs and supplies jobs.

"If you'll take this assignment, several of us will stand ready to help. Do you want to think it over, or can you answer now? It won't affect your other Committee work at all."

Patsy didn't hesitate. She knew already, because of her freshman and GOP status, that her constituent work in Portland was not going to amount to much. She was a person who was happy only when meeting challenges and thereby earning recognition, a trait that had dominated much of her life. This assignment might even be a step up politically.

She stood and extended her hand, eyes glowing with pleasure. "You've made my day, Bob. Thanks, and when do I start?"

She hadn't felt as self-confident since the results came in on election night. On her way back to the House she stopped in the ladies room to inspect the new Patsy. Standing before the long mirror she took stock. About middle height, with a still trim figure and hair in short, natural waves that fell into place and softened her face, she knew that she looked younger than she was. What really gave Patsy the appearance of youth was the energy that radiated from her expressive face and the constant amusement in her eyes as if waiting, always optimistically, for something wonderful and probably funny to happen.

"Recognition has always been your greatest need and very best therapy, m'girl, and you now look and feel great. It's been a long time, hasn't it?" She glowed with enthusiasm. Maybe there really was a place for her here. If not, she might make one. Who knew? Today might be a new start. She pulled in her tummy a bit, put on fresh lipstick and right then the House bell sounded, warning legislators to take their seats.

More members had arrived but because of the storm, the chamber was far from full, barely a quorum. The Speaker and the Clerk were in their places. The Speaker pounded his gavel, declared the House in order, and asked Rep. Horace Perkins, D, a retired minister from Dover-Foxcroft, to come to the podium.

"The guest clergyman who was scheduled to open our session has not been able to even get out of his driveway, so would the Rev. Perkins lead us in prayer this day?"

Rep. Perkins bowed his head, the members stood, and his prayer was simple. "Dear Lord, who made it possible for us to be here together today, take into your loving arms those 387 souls whose plane crashed in your beautiful Maine woods yesterday afternoon. The wreck has been located in a wilderness area some 75 miles from my own home. Snowmobiles have reached the scene and there are, as you know, O Lord, no survivors. May you give comfort to those families involved, and to all of us who join them in mourning this tragic loss. We ask Thy blessing. Amen".

* * * * *

Chicago

Joel McLean closed the notebook on his lap. He was glad to be on his way to help plan with Phyllis and to do what he felt Webb would want done. But oh how empty he felt! Few knew how close he and Webb had been, exchanging not only letters but often long phone calls, keeping in touch and serving as backups to each other. Phyllis was the only subject that was off limits.

And Phyllis, on the phone, had sounded like such a robot! He'd never really felt he knew her, or that she trusted him. Quite the reverse, he felt she was jealous of his closeness to Webb. He wished he could work up more personal sympathy for her, but she was so appallingly self-centered, so uptight, so neurotic. She'd made no comment on what Webb might have gone through as the plane crashed, what pain or terror he might have felt. Those were questions uppermost in Joel's mind. He was grateful for the fire, the cremation. Final and clean.

He was on his way now to be damn sure that Webb, his best friend and alter ego, got a send-off worthy of the man in spite of any cockeyed, self-protective ideas Webb's widow might have. In his luggage were the 10th Anniversary Report of the Harvard Class of 1972, his personal phone list of friends from Camp Namakant, and some random thoughts he'd jotted down. More scribblings were in the notebook on his lap.

Chatting with Phyllis earlier, he had gathered that she didn't think the service was going to be a big deal, that it would be mostly family and precious little of that. It was pitifully obvious that she had little or no knowledge of or interest in Webb's life outside their shared involvement in the business. Though this was another subject that Webb had put off limits, Joel had gathered that since the loss of the baby their marriage was pretty well kaput. Carol, his own normal and wonderfully uncomplicated wife, had told him to be charitable, sensitive and to keep his antennae focused on how Phyllis was really feeling. He'd try.

Passengers were told that they were due to land in just a few minutes and Joel gathered up his coat, flight bag and notebook. He was not a person anyone would look at twice with much interest, just a pleasant-appearing, fit man, with sandy coloring, most of his hair, a flat belly, and clothes that spoke of Brooks Brothers, tailors, and Cole Haan. Ivy League clubman was written all over him, and he was comfortable with it. Known in the insurance world as well-connected, capable, and clean as a whistle, his business associates suspected that a few nice family trust funds saved him from having to be very competitive. He was quite predictable, and solid as a rock.

Approaching the reception area he spotted Phyllis, chic as ever. He waved and, reaching her, gave her a hug. She clung to him rather longer than he'd expected, but finally they were on their way to the baggage carousel, then the parking lot.

Having to travel a good deal, Joel had learned that sometimes conversations in automobiles between driver and passenger were very productive, as there could be little eye contact and few interruptions. A car was also almost neutral turf.

"How are things going, Phyl? Where do I fit in and how can I help?"

She seemed almost not to hear, but then pulled herself back from wherever her mind had taken her.

"In a formal way everything is all set, I guess. We've arranged a memorial service for the day after tomorrow at 2:00 PM, the minister is all set; he's asked to have some of the choir there in case there aren't enough people to sing a hymn or so decently. Webb's regular Saturday foursome, or what's left of it, will usher. Flowers have been ordered for the altar, and the Ladies Guild of the church will put on a sandwich, cookies and punch reception after the service."

Of course there would be no committal, so that was that.

Not surprised by her unemotional laundry list of details, showing no feeling, he congratulated her on the planning. They drove in silence for a while, getting away from strip shopping areas, secondhand car dealerships, and fast-food restaurants and into the suburbs. Soon they came to an area of good-sized estates with long driveways and careful plantings, now snow-covered.

"Phyl, I've known Webb since we were kids. As you know, a lot of services no longer just stick to the book of Common Prayer, and the clergy often permit input from the congregation, from close friends. People seem to like it. Would you mind if I said a few words about Webb?."

There was a pause, longer than he'd hoped for, but she finally agreed.

Did she want to get the service over with as fast as possible? He remembered her fears of being caught in crowds, of panicking and possibly making a spectacle of herself.

"How about the obituary for the papers? All taken care of?"

She answered almost sharply. "Oh yes, I asked Webb's secretary to do that for me. She knows far better what boards he was on and what organizations he belonged to. The newspaper probably has material too. It will be in tomorrow's paper."

Joel made a mental note to get in touch with that secretary ASAP. He wanted Webb's obit to be as rich and complete as it should be, not just a list of boards, clubs, and survivors.

They finally reached the Lewis driveway and, pulling up to the house, he reached over and patted her hand, limp in her lap. "Thanks for meeting me. And I think you're doing a great job. May I take this car to the hotel, settle myself in, and make a few calls? And then may I invite myself to dinner?"

She agreed, and after taking her to the door, he got back in and drove off.

* * * * *

At about 1:30 two days later a limousine left the Lewis home bearing Phyllis, her parents, and what few cousins she had to the church. In the main room of the Parish House, which adjoined the church, the Ladies Guild had placed refreshments for them. Joel was waiting, looking at ease, but with none of his usual twinkle. His wife, Carol, stood beside him and greeted Phyllis warmly.

The organ was playing, setting the mood for the mourners filtering into the church proper. It was a Norman-Gothic edifice, very Episcopalian. Wealthy parishioners had over the years provided splendid memorial stained-glass windows and charming, whimsical wood carvings on the ends of pews and on the choir stalls. Ladies of the parish had produced exquisite needlepoint coverings for kneelers in the pews and at the communion rail.

The Rev. Arthur Morris, robed for the service, approached Phyllis and Joel. "I just peeked into the church and there is quite a crowd. Many more than I was led to expect."

There was an almost happy satisfaction in his voice.

"I've asked the ushers to be ready to bring out the folding chairs." Too bad we don't pass the plate at funerals, he mused, and then was ashamed of himself.

At two sharp he led the family from the Parish Hall into the church through a door beside the organ. They took their seats in the front pews, and he continued to the chancel steps. The church was filled to capacity, with many people standing in the rear, even in the vestibule.

"I am the resurrection and the life, saith the Lord. He that believeth in me, though he were dead, yet shall he live...."

Following several other well-known prayers and passages, the rector asked the congregation to join him in the 121st and the 23rd psalms. Then everybody sang "O God our help in ages past." All so far was par for the course, no surprises, very dignified.

The Rev. Morris then announced that he'd been requested to give friends of the deceased an opportunity to speak of Webb, to remember special qualities, and to share their common grief. But he would first like to read a few lines from Webb Lewis's 10th Harvard Reunion Report, thoughts Webb had felt were important.

"We're still pretty damp behind the ears, and have a lot to learn," Webb had written, "but of one thing I am sure. Little can be permanently accomplished without genuine goodwill, or unless we truly try to empathize, treating each other with genuine respect and trust. I have been criticized, and justly, for my lack of participation in the anti-Vietnam demonstrations at Harvard during our years there, but I saw them as just leading to more ugliness, violence, and guilt. Good minds coming together with good intentions and trust are what I will always work for. I hope I am never put in a position in which reason and flexibility cannot prevail."

The Rev. Morris closed the report. "Now, Mr. McLean, if you would care to proceed."

Joel rose from the second row of pews, gave Phyllis an encouraging smile, and mounted the steps to the lectern.

"Good afternoon. I am Joel McLean, one of Webb's oldest friends, from camp days and later at Harvard." His friendly warmth reached everyone listening. "I know Webb has only been among you in this community for about ten years, so I'd like to tell you a little about his life before he arrived here."

Joel's manner was so relaxed and assured that the mourners settled back comfortably, even began to look forward to the remainder of the service. Though it was now definitely out of Phyllis's control, she found her heart beating more regularly and her throat loosening up.

"I believe that memorial services should not be sentimental, gloomy, or self-pitying. They should be a loving, even occasionally humorous, celebration of a life, with reminiscing possibly bringing out facts that may enrich all our memories, and possibly our lives. Sometimes we listen to the unexpected more carefully than to the traditional services.

"Webb was not yet an acknowledged leader in this town or city, yet this church is full. Why? What was he or what did he do to bring you all here? Of course many are friends of his wife and her family, here to support them in their loss, but I'll bet that many of you are here because in some way, somehow, Webb made a difference to you. Maybe he just made you feel better about yourself, maybe helped you to make a decision of which you are proud. Maybe," and he paused, "you're here just because he was an awfully good listener, the very best I've ever known.

"He made a real difference to me. We met twenty years ago at a boys' camp in Maine. He was a high-school kid from a small town in upper New York State while most of us were from the Boston area, school friends. Preppies, if you will. We learned that Webb was an only child, his father was dead, and he had been raised by his mother and grandmother, both lovely ladies but pretty old-fashioned.

"At fifteen he was a tall, skinny kid, a good ball player, but we thought he was sort of a wimp. Pleasant, but making few jokes, clean or otherwise, no imagined or real adventures with girls. He never fought back, never defended himself, never got in trouble. But it was almost impossible to get mad at him, as he had sort of a presence we couldn't ignore. Why so unflappable? Was he awfully naive or maybe, perish the thought, mature?" A chuckle rippled through the church.

"The camp was more or less like the Outward Bound camps. Each camper was pressed beyond the limit of his self-confidence but, bolstered up by his team, he generally accomplished what he thought he never could. We learned that to reach the goals the camp had set for us, and that our parents were paying to have us learn, we had to trust each other, and help the other guy with our own very best efforts, mental and physical, at all times. Heavy stuff for pubescent teenagers. Our lives often seemed to be one long commando course.

"One of the greatest challenges was jumping, or preferably diving, into the ice-cold waters of an old quarry, from an awesome height, really awesome."

Many of the congregation were smiling now in sympathy with those long-ago teenagers. Rites of passage into manhood could be pretty scary, whether in primitive rituals or elite summer camps.

"One night at campfire it was announced that Webb's tent was scheduled for that dive next morning. I dropped in on them on the way to my tent, and quite a discussion was in progress. One kid, who'd been trying to bluff his pseudo-macho way all summer, was obviously panicking. 'They have no damn right to make us do this. We might get killed. I'm going to call my dad and he'll straighten this camp out.'

"Another kid, a good athlete, groaned. 'You jerk. If they were in the habit of making kamikaze pilots out of us, do you think the camp would be in business? You were scared to death of the rope walk too, but you got your fat self across, didn't you?'

"Laughter made the griper even madder. 'If you had more brain and less muscle in your head you'd fight back too,' he yelled.

"More and saltier insults flew, personal and crude, and more kids joined in, seeking relief from their personal anxieties. Some pillows and then boots were thrown and I realized that the unity of the tent, built up slowly and carefully in the preceding weeks, was disintegrating very fast. It wasn't my tent and I felt I should stay out of this.

"Suddenly, over the ugly noise, there was a clang of metal on metal, as arresting as a pistol shot. Webb once again banged the end of a cot with his steel tennis racquet. The silence became complete. All eyes were on him. His other hand held a big bottle of Coke, which he waved over his head with energy..

"'Hey, we're all shook up, like this Coke. If I keep shaking it we might just have an explosion, lose all the Coke, have flying shattered glass all over the place, and possibly injuries.

"'However,' and he put down the racquet and took a knife from his pocket, 'I'm going to loosen the cap v-e-r-y slowly,' and he opened the knife, 'v-e-r-y slowly, and there'll be enough Coke to go around, for a toast to tomorrow.'

"Every eye watched as he gently pried the cap off the bottle with a minimum of fizz. A collective release of pent-up breath filled the tent as he tossed the cap on his cot and, after putting the bottle to his own lips, passed it to the nearest boy. 'And now,' he said, stretching,' if you gentlemen will let me, I'm going to get some sleep.'

"In a few minutes the bottle was empty, pillows and boots were retrieved, and the lamp was turned down. Just the sounds of eight boys settling on creaking springs could be heard as I left and went to my own tent, impressed. But a concern stayed with me.

"Only one boy had been silent, had stayed out of the whole thing from the first, little Harvey Perkins, a really nervous kid who looked terrified all the time anyway. I guessed he was about paralyzed that night so I made a mental note to keep my eye on him in the morning..

"But, not being in that tent, I had to learn secondhand what happened later." Joel had the undivided attention of the congregation.

"Something woke Webb up early, and he noticed that Harvey's cot was empty. He got up and looked for him in the wash-house, no success. Worried, he ran through the woods toward the quarry. Breaking out of the trees he saw Harvey standing at the quarry's edge, confused and pale, in the one place most of us knew we shouldn't make the dive because of submerged boulders.

"Harvey called to Webb that he was practicing, then jumped just as Webb cried out 'No, not from there!' Still hollering, but now for help, Webb ran along the edge and dove in at the same spot himself.

"Some campers and counselors heard his yells and came running. Webb's head broke the surface but, in spite of so many of us there to help, he went back down. And it was Webb and another boy who brought Harvey to the surface, bloody and awfully limp. They got him ashore, and thank God, he was revived

"When we looked around to fuss over Webb, he'd disappeared. He'd done what was right, he knew it, and that was all the approval he seemed to need. He never really did talk about it, just kept on doing the right thing and caring about people. No one ever thought of him as a wimp again. We just wondered what made him tick, and kinda envied him..

" For this instance, for the many other lessons you taught me," and Joel looked up into the soaring arch above him, "I say, thank you, Webb."

Phyllis gave him the glimmer of a smile as he returned to his seat, and it pleased him.

From the rear of the church came a big man, who walked with the assurance that comes with leadership.

"I'm not going to be up here long, but Joel suggested you might like to meet me. I'm Colonel George Schmidt, US Marine Corps. I'm also that fat, pain-in-the-neck kid who has never forgotten that night or morning. I learned the perils of not listening to orders, but far more importantly, a door I had never known existed opened up for me, showing a world where true compassion, true courage, and true cooperation proved more effective than threats, fists, or whining. I am a military professional, working for peace, and I like to think these traits are part of all my decisions.

"You might be interested to know, though it hurts to think of it, that Harvey was killed by a stray bullet while he was trying to help defuse the riots in Washington, DC, at the time of the King assassination. Another real hero. Thank you, Webb." Looking upward, he saluted.

At this point the minister rose and announced "We will now, at the request of many of you, sing the campfire song of that camp. The words were written by a camp director's wife many years ago, with apologies to William Blake. It is sung to the music Sir Hubert H. Parry wrote for Blake's "Jerusalem." You will find the words in the programs you were handed."

The congregation stood, the organ played opening bars, and then, from the area where Schmidt and other camp alumni sat, came the strong, sure voices of the many men who had come from all over the country for this service. Soon others joined in till song filled the church with conviction and emotion.

We are the sons of Namakant
Strong with the wisdom of his clan.
Learning to live to take our places
Around the campfires of Man.
We all have learned from each young brave
Our strength is built on trust and right.
Love and respect for all that's living,
Make us all instruments of might.
When giant waves toss our frail craft
When all about us thunder roars,
We'll call upon this inner power
And make it to the sheltering shores.
Around this campfire, brothers pledge
To always give a helping hand
So each may reach his mountain top
A strong united woodland band.

As the very moved congregation sat down, waiting for whatever came next, one of Webb's local golfing friends whispered to another, "You know, that may seem corny now, but it sure brought back Boy Scout camp and all the good stuff we talked about there."

His friend smiled and said, "I could practically smell the wood smoke and taste burnt marshmallows, and it really made me homesick for the kid I was then. It was good stuff, and still is. When and why did we lose it?"

A gentleman older than Webb's contemporaries rose next, assured and obviously at home with the local mourners.

"My name, for those of you who don't know me, is Steve Hamilton. Webb and I are, uh, were business acquaintances in the city. At least, that's how we started, but then he began to show up on some of the same nonprofit agency boards I've been on, so I got to know him better."

"At my age one starts, unfortunately, to attend quite a number of funeral or memorial services for contemporaries, but today we are experiencing something unusual. Webb Lewis was too young to die, we all agree to that. It may be the first service some of you have attended for one of your own. But the difference is more than that.

"He has not lived here long, he has made no headlines. Not a tycoon, or pop singer, or statesman, not even the best golfer at our club, though he tried awfully hard to often break par. He was not really a mover or shaker, he did not rock boats, was not in the limelight. Quite the contrary.

"This church, I think, is full, because he exemplified endangered if not almost extinct qualities, those he mentioned in the Class Report, civility and respect to all.

"As I look around I see the faces of a real cross section of this town, many people I had no idea even knew Webb. I see my barber, the secretary from the United Way office, a waitress from the diner, and many others who are the good people that really make this town tick, not just the company chairmen or bank CEOs. Some of you seem just as surprised to see each other, for the same reason.

"It makes us look at ourselves, doesn't it? Will we have the same comprehensive drawing power at our own services? Will this community feel the same sense of loss?

"What we're learning, as Mr. McLean said we'd learn, is that it doesn't take financial power, media-produced popularity, Cadillacs or private jets, to fill a church. I think Webb Lewis was one of the most decent men I've ever known, believing in himself and trying to be the best of that self, with no posturing, image making, or status seeking. Webb was probably the best listener I have ever known, and he really cared about what he heard. Humble almost to a fault, he was always willing to give of what little time he had to make this community better.

"He's done it again, in absentia, because by being here together today we all have a deeper sense of community; we have discovered an important common bond with neighbors who up to now we've considered strangers. I know I'm going out of here with the feeling that a cleansing breeze has blown a lot of foolish, unimportant, even cheap notions and stupid values out of this bald head this afternoon.

"So I too say, thank you, Webb Lewis." He paused, then looked to the rear of the church.

"Now, there's a young gentleman here that both Webb and I met at the Boys' Club. He's not the most experienced speaker in the room, but I think he might like to say a few words. If not we'll all understand. His name is Tommy Parker."

Heads swiveled around and finally, slowly and as if he was approaching a horror movie torture chamber, a string bean of a boy about fourteen came forward. Looking at the faces turned toward him, he felt he had friends. There were many smiles, kind smiles, even amused smiles. He was all slicked up for the occasion, combed and shiny as he faced them.

"My name is Tommy Parker, and I live over by the railroad station with my mom and two sisters. Dad ain't been home for a while. Mr. Lewis was my friend. I'm in 8th grade at the Roosevelt School and I'm playing hooky to be here, but my Mom knows."

With that admission the crowd was his, and any rustling ceased. All wished to catch every word of that scratchy voice, raspy with self-consciousness.

"After school every day I go to the Boys' Club for a while before I start my evening paper route, 'cause Mom says it's important that I mix with other men." A kindly ripple of laughter interrupted him briefly.

"I deliver the Sunday papers too, and have to collect my route money on Saturdays, so at first I didn't see much of Mr. Lewis when he visited the Club, which I guess he did a lot. Then one Sunday morning early, when I was just a kid, a real rainy Sunday, a big car stopped beside me on the route. Mom has always told us not to go nowhere with strangers, but I felt Mr. Lewis was really a friend, so when he asked me, I got in his car. And," his freckled face lit up, "he helped me deliver every one of them papers! In the rain! And then he drove me home. You should'a seen my neighbors' faces when I got outta that BMW."

Tommy was freewheeling now; he'd never had an audience before in his life and he liked it.

"Guess what? Mr. Lewis showed up almost every Sunday after that, unless he was outta town, and helped. I was only eight then, and Sunday papers was awful heavy. And guess what? He'd had a paper route himself!

"Well, he's been helping me on and off ever since, and we have talks between deliveries. It's been kinda like having a dad, I guess. He used to talk about trying to always do the right thing, and how we really like ourselves when we do. We've had some real neat times, too, like ball games. I learned a lot from him. Like school's important. If I work hard maybe I'll have a big car and nice clothes like he has. Would it be OK if I said 'Thank you, Mr. Lewis,' too?" With long steps he loped awkwardly back to his seat, head down, but beaming.

Joel knew that there were others who had planned to speak, but he also knew that anything would be an anticlimax after that. No wonder the minister didn't know Webb well; he too had been about the Lord's work Sunday mornings.

Joel indicated his decision to the minister, who rose to proceed with the service. But it was no longer his, and he cut it as short as possible. A vigorous Recessional hymn, "Rise up, oh men of God," the benediction, and it was over.

Many of the congregation went into the Parish Hall, greeted Phyllis and, toying with cookies and sandwiches, tried to express to one another their feelings about what they had just experienced. Failing, as they hadn't had time to sort it out, they found they just wanted to stay there anyway with these people, strangers and friends, who had shared with them a very moving event. And any who had been embarrassed by the emotional reminiscences or the possibly dated notion of human nobility had the good sense to keep their mouths shut, and possibly decide to do a little unaccustomed soul searching.

Phyllis was the most surprised of anyone by the range, depth, and effect of Webb's seemingly quiet and even dull life. Why hadn't she known? For one very simple reason: she had never bothered to ask. That night, as she lay waiting for sleep, she reviewed what she had learned. What might Webb have accomplished if he had been a fighter? Where might the business be today? While she respected him now for this unsuspected standing in the community, she could feel her old irritation at his perceived submissiveness just as strongly as ever. Business decisions would be hers now. Would, or could, she make a difference? She thought back to the service, the crowd, the spotlight on her. She hadn't panicked, had even been so engrossed in what was happening that she'd forgotten herself. Interesting.

And Joel, emotionally tired but too keyed up to sleep, paced around his hotel room. His thoughts kept going back to the words read from Webb's class report, so candid about a very sensitive subject. He had never questioned Webb's courage, but he wondered if there had been in his friend some psychological barrier that would have always kept him from deeming a cause worth fighting for. Would the "gentil, parfit knight" ever have unsheathed his sword? Or accepted a challenge in the lists? Flung down his glove? He looked out over the sleeping city, unhappy at even having raised the question to himself. Because it was too late. He would never know the answer now.

* * * * *

Harding's Corner

For the next few days life in the Warner house kept to its regular routine, but on tiptoe. Stan brought in wood for the stove, cared for the animals, and continued with the seemingly endless maintenance chores to be tackled in these winter months.

Fresh bread came out of the oven, sweetening the air with its simple and elemental odor. The old treadle sewing machine produced the last of new kitchen curtains, buckets for gathering maple sap were checked and cleaned, and Susan even found time to work on her latest painting. Grandma Moses lay happily in sunny spots on the rugs, and Rousseau supervised all. The mystery guest appeared for meals, chatted quietly, then retreated once more to his room. No questions asked or answered.

Susan's painting was of the big blue spruce that served as a sentry on the hilltop behind the house. She had painted it many times and each picture expressed a different feeling for it, or perhaps a different Susan. This one was another winter scene, but in the past few days warming sunlight hues had crept onto her palette. Looking at it, one could sense the cold losing its grip, a melting taking place under the crust of snow. The sky was an almost-spring blue. As the dark days and bitter cold continued and promised no such thing, this mood came obviously from her imagination and spirit.

Discovering this old farm during a camping trip early in their marriage, Susan and Stan had loved it for the classic though fast-deteriorating Federal-style house, the huge barn, and the matchless view of lakes, forests, and mighty Mt. Katahdin. But, above all, its isolation drew them. It was a place where one could be oneself. They had been able to locate the owners, heirs of long gone and discouraged settlers. The well had proved sound and pure, old apple trees and berries were plentiful, and they even discovered the boundaries of an earlier vegetable garden. The amount of work necessary to transform this "estate" into a comfortable, productive vacation home was staggering. Exactly what Stan craved, and he would do it with his own two hands, with pride. They bought it with hardly a second thought.

Stan knew that here, on vacations, he could satisfy his urge to get back to the all-but-forgotten lifestyle and values of his youth. He had had a happy, secure childhood with parents careful to teach him self-reliance and responsibility. It had been a well-ordered existence not far removed from Victorianism, one in which honor, courage, and courtesy were the attributes by which one was judged, tempered by a strong work ethic.

Since his return from WWII, Susan had found herself married to an increasingly angry man, a man trying to find the world he had dreamed of while overseas, one which certainly was not ruled by the new gray flannel suitism or status seeking, so brittle and materialistic, that he had found. Stan, unbidden, took his soapbox to every dinner party. Popularity was the goal of most, the key to success, both socially and economically, but he didn't give a damn. He felt that exchange of ideas was more important than that of plastic pleasantries, and he would state his in no uncertain terms, leaving little room for discussion. Stan's listening skills were limited. His capacity for anger was not.

His values, principles, and ideals were considered by many to be old-fashioned. His politics were based on pre-New Deal thinking, and his moral code was rigid. He felt he had returned from overseas to an increasingly permissive, wishy-washy society seeking endlessly for pleasure and comforts while breeding irresponsibility and destroying initiative. Man-made rules, created by the burgeoning bureaucracy or corporate policies, ate at his vitals constantly. Out-of-control toleration became intolerable.

On the other hand, the frustrations and disasters caused by nature disturbed him hardly at all; he was of it and could live with its vagaries. There were no bureaucrats in Nature, and no self-centered manipulation that could affect it. This farm, Susan had hoped, would be a safety valve, enabling him, between vacations, to continue to work in New York City with more enthusiasm and ambition. He might even stay in one position for a while and not quit in a rage, as he had done several times already.

Susan was actually an independent too, and sometimes impatient with the lives her neighbors found satisfying. She was not a garden-clubber or fashion show enthusiast and didn't give a hooray for the "Joneses" or the "latest" of whatever was "in." Years ago, when she was perhaps ten or eleven, her playmates decided to spend one winter afternoon making a snowman together. Not Susan. Off to one side she made her own snowman, smaller, not any better than theirs, but it was hers; she'd had to do it on her own.

She had wondered that day why she refused to be part of their fun. Years later she remembered that afternoon, and finally understood. Personal creativity was her passion, and hours could magically disappear as she worked on her projects, while other women were just as happy lunching or shopping together. She loved the challenge, the choices of design or materials, and didn't let inexperience or rules hold her back. The farm would be a perfect workshop, needing much that she could learn to make in those precious summer months. Her hands were her link with spirituality, her imagination almost unlimited.

The house became more and more livable each summer. The roof was repaired, rotting sills and panes of glass replaced, and gallons of paint stroked lovingly over peeled or bare surfaces indoors and out. Every year they became more proficient in the crafts and husbanding of independent rural living. They were seldom bothered with summer guests, as it was too primitive for their country-and-yacht-club-minded relatives and friends. One visit usually satisfied the curiosity of those who even ventured that far. Little Jerry was born, Stan was receiving promotions quite regularly, and Susan was almost content with her life as housewife and mom, after years of teaching.

Then one March day in the mid-fifties Stan had come home to their Connecticut house on an early train, with a bulging briefcase under his arm and fire in his eye. "We're moving to the farm." He hung up his London Fog very deliberately, gave Susan a kiss, went to the bar in the kitchen and poured a stiff bourbon, though it was just midafternoon.

"I've done it again, jumped out the window with no mattress under me. Quit." It was said honestly, with no apologies.

Susan's heart jumped into her throat. It had been OK when he did this while she was working, before Jerry was born, when they could afford to put principles before principal. Now not even a suggestion of finding another job. So we're going to the farm, just like that? She looked at him, a long look, then started to pick up the toys strewn around the living room, to at least bring order into some small segment of their life.

Had he thought ahead at all? Had he considered her needs or Jerry's future? Or was he so old-fashioned in his views that it never occurred to him she might have an opinion or even the right to one? Why should she expect this magnificent male chauvinist she had chosen to share life with to do otherwise? Men made the big decisions, women the day-to-day ones, and like biblical Ruth she was expected to go where he chose, live the life he felt best, and magically make both ends meet, keep up their living standard, and smile, smile, smile. And she would doubtless rise to the challenge again. His feeling of rightness convinced her every time. She loved him too much to let him down. But damn, damn, damn. Perhaps it was that day that the first tiny bricks of a wall of resentment were laid in place, a protective wall.

"I was called in to see Ralph Young this morning, and he looked unusually pleased with himself. We made a bit of small talk and then he, with such patronizing pleasure, announced that I was to be promoted, good raise, and I was now to be head of the marketing division." Susan had almost gasped; this was just what they'd dreamed of. What had gone wrong, so wrong?

"I expressed my gratitude and pleasure, we talked a bit about what he hoped I could put together and accomplish, and then came the crunchers.

"That damn fat-assed bastard said that of course he would expect me, us, to change our lifestyles to fit the job and its prestige. He started out on my appearance. No more tweed jackets and flannels, only well-tailored dark three-piece suits. No more Madras bow ties—too casual, from now on regimental stripes. No more pickup truck but a solid sedan, at least a Buick or Olds. He listed off some clubs both in the city and here that he wanted us to join. And here's the clincher, when I almost put his expensive capped teeth down his gullet: he wants us to spend our vacations on Cape Cod, Martha's Vineyard, Long Island, or in some Maine resort with a good yacht club and old families' 'cottages.' The whole damn thing sounded like a parody on the worst of IBM's rules and regulations.

"With my usual charm and tact, I told him I could sell just as well bare-naked as in his fancy three-piece suit, he was counting on my talent, not the horsepower of my car, and he could take the whole deal and shove it, and I knew where if he didn't. Then I simply walked out, packed up a bit of my desk stuff, kissed good old Mrs. Morrissey soundly with thanks for putting up with me as her boss for these past years, and walked out the door. I don't even know if there will be a check in the mail."

Jerry had announced at that point that he was awake from his nap, Susan went to get him up, and she had taken this opportunity to clench her jaws, bite her tongue, and come downstairs the perfect picture of supportive wife and loving mother, no matter what. But also an animal mother, ready to protect her young.

So they had sold the Connecticut house for a good bit more than it had cost, added up the modest incomes each received from family trust funds, sold almost all their furniture except for pieces that would fit into a Federal period farmhouse with undeniable rustic charm but few amenities, and moved, timing it perfectly so that they arrived when mud season was over and they could brave the dirt road, lately slough. The resident woodchucks were eradicated before a new litter joined their elders. The vegetable garden they soon planted would now be vital to their sustenance, no longer just a hobby or a cafeteria for critters.

Stan had complete faith in his abilities to learn the skills he would need in this new life. Susan had total faith in Stan. They bought a heavy-duty truck with a snowplow attachment, perfect for navigating back roads. A rugged old secondhand tractor came next. They dickered for, and acquired, a reliable work boat with which to bring in supplies from the little town at the far end of the lake when the roads were impassable. News of the world reached them via a battery-operated radio and the *Wall Street Journal* (picked up when convenient at the distant post office). An occasional all-day trip to Bangor was like Christmas as they brought home books, fabrics, and old 78 RPM and later LP records to play on their windup Victrola.

Their property was in Unorganized Territory, with no local government, schools, or services. Taxes were paid only to the state. One summer a man from the Maine Department of Education came calling, by boat, to inquire if they had school-age children. The state would educate them if the parents were willing to get them out of this wilderness and to a relative's or friend's home for at least the school week. Susan had explained that she was a certified teacher and would take care of Jerry's education at home, thank you.

By disciplining herself to mentally walk in Stan's moccasins, feel what he felt, reason as he reasoned, and thus respect and understand his needs,

Susan had adjusted pretty well. She had always accepted his differentness and loved him all the more for it, was actually proud of it. No puppet he, this big, handsome man of hers.

Each year improvements were made. A propane gas generator provided power when they wished to pump water from the well, or Stan needed it for his power tools. He even wired the house for electric lights, though they generally used Aladdin lamps which gave a fine white light without too much flicker. And eventually also running on propane were a refrigerator-freezer, and finally a stove, to aid Susan in the canning of quarts and quarts of vegetables every harvest. She had felt almost sissy when they acquired a washing machine, but it certainly gave her more time to paint.

Animals became members of the family, two milk goats, sheep, numerous hens, a yearly pig, and two or three fluffy lambs each spring to gambol and frolic and thrive with Jerry every summer, only to end up on the table in the winter.

There were as yet no near neighbors. Chores and infrequent trips to town for supplies and occasional mail did not lead to socializing. Fortunate in good health, they did not even have a doctor, and Jerry was spared the childhood diseases he would ordinarily have picked up at school. Because no one checked on them again, even the state was in ignorance about a child who was in none of its files.

But Susan yearned to leave a small, faint trail of her own moccasins, and she put all her energies and aspirations into raising their son, enriching his life at every chance. He would be her memorial, the splendid product and proof of her time on this earth, a child who, as an adult, would make a difference.

One day, when he was five, she was reading him a story about the woods, and a blue spruce was mentioned in the text. Jerry had interrupted with vehemence.

"But Mom, trees are green. The sky is blue, the water is blue, blueberries are blue but TREES ARE GREEN." She had chuckled, swept him up in her arms, and promised, "The next time we go to Bangor we will buy a blue tree and we will plant it and it will be your very own." And they had done just that, picking a spot from which the special tree would always have a special view and could grow as straight and tall and strong as Jerry would.

Then one fine summer's day, three years later, while Susan was in the kitchen making strawberry jam from their very bountiful crop, and Stan was hilling up the potatoes, eight-year-old Jerry went fishing out on the lake in the sturdy little boat Stan had built him. The sky had suddenly darkened, almost green-black, and a squall exploded across the water. Stan and Susan had run, stumbling, down the hill to the shore, but could see nothing in the downpour. They found Jerry's body the next day almost a mile down the lake, his life jacket ripped off and floating nearby.

Wordlessly they had clung to each other, then Stan had carried the dripping little body up to the house, to its room. Susan had sat with it all night, too paralyzed with grief to cry, or scream, or to find a way to vent anger at whatever fate had ordained this tragedy. Stan, in the shop off the barn, had made a small, tight coffin. Jerry was buried under his blue spruce.

Susan's mind could not accept this loss. After all the years of hopes she had poured into this child of her body, she totally denied that he was gone. His place was set at the table for every meal, and she would explain to Stan that Jerry was in his room reading, or visiting family in the Midwest, or even, finally, at boarding school. Stan, just as devastated, played this tragic game with her, hoping that his acquiescence was a comfort, as he had no notion of how to talk it out. Discussion of feelings had always made him uncomfortable, and there was no action he could think of to help.

On Jerry's birthday each year one of them would suggest, as if it was a bright new idea, that they pack a picnic supper and climb the hill to enjoy the view. And they would sit silently under the boughs of the growing tree, drinking in the beauty of the sunset while suffering agonies they couldn't talk about. And at Christmas time balls of suet, tied up in red yarn, would mysteriously appear on the tips of branches, swinging in the December winds, for the birds to share.

Little by little Susan's wounded spirit had healed, yet when she finally accepted the truth she couldn't or wouldn't let Stan know. She felt that his supposed acceptance of her delusion was his loving but clumsy way to amend for his pigheaded choices of lifestyle. So the charade continued. The wall had been built between them, and both were wrong, though it was built on love.

Susan found she could not give all of herself to him; some part of her had to be kept safe and inviolate. Stan, puzzled, decided this was due to Jerry's loss alone, unaware that what she increasingly craved now was full acceptance as an equal with personal dignity.

Now as Susan painted, twenty-nine years later, she felt unusually relaxed. Was this stranger, about whom they knew nothing, anything like what Jerry might have been? Was he going to have a real place in their lives? What was Stan thinking? How long before they learned something of this man, and he of them?

Chapter 2: Spring 1987

Harding's Corner

"How long does it take to get over an accident and trauma like this?" Webb asked himself as he woke up from his third nap of the day. Terror, cold, exhaustion, memories of horror, hunger, pain—all had taken their toll. Nightmares were common, often complete with dreams of huge bonfires, explosions, numbing cold. And then there was The Decision. To kill himself off and then give birth to a new persona was certainly a shock to his well-ordered mind. He had spent hours on this bed trying to concentrate on an acceptable reason for his behavior, and some plan for his future. But the sight of the long lake in the valley below, the clarity of almost monochromatic wintry scenes, and the sound of wind singing in the trees generally put him right back to sleep.

But he couldn't lie here forever. It wasn't fair to these good people who had taken him in.

At some time they had mentioned a son, and this was obviously his room, or had been, as it contained the treasures of an eight- to ten-year-old. Good reproductions hung on the walls, of paintings with subjects a boy could get into, make up stories about, imagine himself to be part of. Ranging from Greek warriors and athletes to N.C. Wyeth illustrations, they were more exciting than comic books, which were notable by their absence. There were no athletic posters, baseball gloves, or even a Cub Scout cap in evidence, but charts of songbirds, of animal tracks, and trees native to Maine. A good fly rod stood in the corner. It would have been fun to grow up in this house. Where was this young man? Did he ever come home?

Some of the many books were those of Webb's own childhood, some classics, some modern. When he had time he wanted to reread some, such as *Charlotte's Web*, Robin Hood, Tom Sawyer. He discovered a well-worn and obviously loved copy of *The World of Pooh*, an old friend. He flipped through it, happy to see Tigger, Eeyore, Kanga, and, of course, Pooh and Piglet.

At some point during his first summer at camp, his new friend Joel, feeling midmorning pangs of hunger, had casually remarked that he had an "eleven o'clockish feeling." Webb, responding to the cue, had added correctly "Time for a little something." Pure A. A. Milne, pure Pooh. Thus their mutual familiarity with Christopher Robin and his friends forged their first real bond. Joel, deliberate, reliable, and comfortable, became Pooh, to Webb's loyal and admiring Piglet. They still occasionally called each other by those names. Joel McLean and their long friendship were right now his greatest loss.

As he sat on the edge of the bed, pulling on his boots, Webb reviewed his new but temporary home. Though the kitchen was the center of activity there were also a parlor and a book-lined den, both with fireplaces. The walls of the spacious dining room were paneled, not with fake wallboard but with the real thing, finished to a soft golden glow. And he would swear that in the entire downstairs there was not one piece of department store furniture. Where had they found these original treasures? He'd have to ask.

Susan had said something about painting, but could these expert oils be hers? Had she ever shown? Maybe her work was well known. Many of the rugs were hand-hooked, designed with flowers so painstakingly done that they might have been brought in from the garden that day and tossed onto tan or cream wool mats. Were they made from wool from their own sheep? He had noted a spinning wheel in the living room, but was it more than decoration? And the stoneware mugs and dishes they used every meal could have been found at a fine craft show or.... .At that point he realized that he'd seen nothing made of plastic, nothing. Most of all, Webb felt that this was a home with a personal, lived-in feeling. The furnishings were certainly not on display, but created to be used. What a contrast to his own house, designed and decorated by professionals, reflecting no one's personality.

To create all this Susan must have a studio somewhere in this rambling structure, maybe on the second floor, which seemed to be otherwise unused. Always interested in good craftsmanship, he hoped to be invited to visit where she worked some day. From bits of conversation and the occasional sound of power tools, he guessed Stan's workshop was in a shed off the barn.

The relationship between Stan and Susan interested Webb also. They were obviously comfortable in their marriage, courteous and respectful to one another, living in a harmony that comes with years of practice. But he sensed a reserve, particularly in Susan, as if part of her led a very private life in addition to the one that was obvious. Though unfailingly pleasant, he felt she had boundaries of self, of protection that even Stan dared not cross. To a casual observer Stan seemed to rule the roost, but even after just a short time Webb believed Stan tiptoed in their relationship. While always pleasant, it was a house of little laughter or great joy.

The bedroom was darkening and all at once he craved companionship. Had he mended at all, or was he malingering to make this irresponsible recovery last as long as possible? Time to bite the bullet, Webb. Out you go, boy.

Tucking his shirt tails in and admiring the new beard as he combed his hair, he was glad to see that the bump and scab on his face were fast disappearing, though his nose would probably always have considerable list to it and his face would be twisted a bit by the scar. Perhaps this slightly different face would be useful in his new identity. When he had one.

Susan and Stan were both in the kitchen. Stan must have made one of his infrequent trips into the nearest town earlier, as he was settled in the rocking chair reading a paper. Susan was peeling potatoes at the soapstone sink. As Webb came out they abruptly stopped a conversation, exchanged looks, and greeted him. Webb walked over to the sink, gently took the knife from Susan, picked up a potato, and said "I'm working my way through college, ma'am." She laughed and turned to sprinkle crumbs over a frozen trout fillet headed for the oven.

"Any news in the big world?" Webb hoped there was none about the plane, but he had to know, and what else would you say to a guy reading a newspaper?

"That plane that went down so near Bangor is all the *Bangor Daily News* can think of writing about, even after almost a week. Might be something about all those cretins in Washington on the back page, if they're up to anything. Honest to God, I don't think most of them have both oars in the water. Middle East's heating up again in spite of that Cairo conference. Want the sports page?"

"Plane going down? Near here, or aren't we close to Bangor? Y'know, I haven't the foggiest where I am." Webb put down the knife, dropped the potato in a pan of cold water and turned around. They were both watching him with interest, more than just polite interest.

He lifted his head, looked Stan and then Susan right in the eye and asked "Do you two know anything about amnesia? If people really forget? or how much they forget, and is it just their identity that goes? Can they still read and write and do their times tables? Or state capitals? Can you answer any of those questions for me? I don't know who the hell I am today or who I'll be tomorrow, but 7 times 8 is still 56. It's damn scary."

His carefully thought-out speech was over; he had made his point and hadn't told one real lie. It was a beginning.

Susan spoke first, calm and upbeat. "Let's see if there's anything in the encyclopedia about it. I don't think my handy-dandy book of home remedies goes into that stuff." And she went into the den where reference tomes were kept.

Looking over his glasses, Stan tilted his big head a bit, though he kept his blue eyes bland and innocent. "You know anything about that plane wreck?"

Eyes just as innocent, he hoped, Webb replied, "Should I?" He had learned long ago to keep the ball in the other guy's court, answer a question with a tougher question.

"Dunno. You arrived in the middle of nowhere, with no visible means of transportation, kinda beat up, and now amnesia. If you were in my shoes, what would you think? Take your time answering. We've got all winter." He looked toward the den. "Here comes the font of all good knowledge."

Susan settled on a hassock, a fat volume in her lap, and pulled her glasses down from the top of her head.

"Disappointing, too little and I'm not sure I understand what there is. Quote: 'Loss of memory for long or short intervals. It may be caused by physical injury, shock, senility, or severe illness. In other cases, a painful experience and everything remindful of it, including the individual's identity, is unconsciously repressed. Possibly a defense mechanism to modify reality and make it more tolerable.' That gives answers to none of your questions except possibly 'why?'"

Again he tried the question technique. "Have I mumbled anything in my sleep, or when semiconscious, that would give us a clue? A name? You laundered my clothing, and thank you again. Were there any clues there? Other than I seem to be an L.L. Bean fan. No wallet, no ticket stubs, no I.D. of any kind? Was I beaten up and robbed and left by the side of the road? Where was I headed? in what? and where is that car?"

He drew closer to them, standing behind what had become his chair at the table, and putting his hands on the back.

"I know just a few things. One, that I will be eternally grateful to you two for taking me in for so long, no questions asked. Two, I think I may be fairly decent person, not a cold-blooded killer or a drug dealer. Playing mind games in the other room, I have thought up ethical dilemmas and tried to answer them honestly. The answers are straight Boy Scout, but maybe I'm kidding myself."

He turned to them helplessly, spreading his hands. "Maybe I'm married. No ring, but a lot of men don't wear 'em. Do I have kids? Am I divorced and my wife has custody? I don't think I'm a substance abuser or I'd have been screeching for a drink or a fix by now, wouldn't I? "

Stan unfolded his six-foot-three-inch frame from the chair and grinned. "Now that you mention it, a drink might be just what we all need. Your pleasure, sir?"

"Bourbon, if you have it, on the rocks with a bit of branch water, please."

"My drink too," and the bartender dug a bottle of Jim Beam out of a cabinet. "Susan, what'll yours be? "

"You know perfectly well, after all these years. A perfect chilled dry martini!" And she soon produced goat cheese and crisp homemade crackers.

His drink was passed to him in a short glass decorated with the Yale seal. He almost bit his tongue to stop an automatic Harvard "not a goddam Eli?" from popping out of his mouth. But he felt wonderfully at peace, though afraid the drinks and the discovery of a fellow Ivy Leaguer might loosen his tongue. But, oh God, that drink tasted good.

* * * * *

The days assumed a pattern of work, meals, and quiet evenings of reading, music, or Scrabble. Stan's offer to let him stay the winter gave Webb the confidence to emerge from the shelter of his room full time, to regularly do a day's work. Insisting on being given those jobs of which he was capable, he gradually felt less like a parasite and was pleased on the several occasions when Stan complimented him. Together they thoroughly cleaned out the barn, inventoried sprays and fertilizers, stacked wood, and gave the generator an overhauling. He became familiar with the routine care of the animals, and quite proud of his goat-milking proficiency.

The two men got to know each other better and better, each enjoying an exchange of ideas covering a diverse range of knowledge and interests. Webb grew accustomed to Stan's pronunciamentos and learned how to occasionally disagree without provoking an explosion. Sometimes, though not often, he felt he had moved Stan an inch or two from a fixed position.

Stan was impressed by the quiet way Webb made his points, never raising his voice, attacking, or closing off the conversation. Though they shared many of the same concerns they often had very different solutions to them, and Stan was struck by the respect with which Webb listened to his positions. Too often, he began to realize, he himself had irritated others into silence by his unsolicited and presumptuous pedagogy. He found himself inordinately pleased to have not only a new audience, but one who responded with intelligent theories of his own.

Webb's greatest joy was in soaking up all he heard and noted of the arts of country living, a completely new world to him. He was particularly impressed and humbled by the variety of projects involved, by the knowledge necessitated, and mostly by the love of it Stan radiated. Goats or goslings, beans or bacon, lambs or lettuce, all were important, intertwined on the food chain. Not to mention mechanics, chemistry, even meteorology.

A few people would consider this place and lifestyle heaven, but only for a while. Others would relish its quaintness, take pictures, and then talk amusingly about it at suburban cocktail parties. Many would find it appalling. But to the Warners, this home and life were the way things were intended to be, honoring self-reliance and respecting nature's rules and even whims. They were fully absorbed in doing what they felt they were put on earth to do. Free from the social commitments engendered by suburban living, they'd had the time to experiment, accept challenges, and revel in honest satisfaction.

Webb thought that it was certainly more natural to man's makeup than honking a horn in NY gridlock, or catching the 6:21 from Grand Central after drinks at the Oyster Bar. Amused, he wondered what Joel, the preppy traditionalist, would think of it.

Even their isolation didn't seem to bother Stan or Susan. Webb had remarked on that one evening and they had both laughed.

"We're nowhere near as isolated as we were at first. Over the years about twenty families have moved as close as a mile from us, not counting our lane, though most are farther than that. We just don't do much neighboring, and neither do they." Then Susan broke into giggles.

"A few years ago, in late spring, I was here at the sink when Stan came stomping in, all riled up, and Grandma Moses stomped right behind him, her tail at noon with outrage. Stan had his hat in his hands and bellowed 'Damn it, look at this!' That hat was full of brand-new kittens. 'What are you going to do about it?'

"I suggested that we find the father and a preacher and make an honest cat of Grandma, who at this point had shamelessly leapt onto the table and was preparing to remove her babies to a safer place. 'It's a little late to find a home for unmarried cats, don't you think?'"

Stan chuckled, not minding her kidding. "Let me have the last word," he suggested. "That woman knew exactly why I was so upset. If Grandma'd got pregnant it meant that there was something other than wild bobcats out there. We seemed to have neighbors who were too damn close, but I knew better than to suggest we move. I just left a kitten or two on the closest doorsteps. No more came of it, but every fall, when the leaves are off the trees, I'm afraid I'll see smoke coming from a new chimney. I need elbow room."

Susan had shown Webb her portfolio of paintings, her weaving room in what was once the summer kitchen, and the potter's wheel and kiln Stan had built for her. He slowly became aware that in all these crafts her current designs seemed bolder and brighter, as if she was emerging from a gray world she had inhabited for a long time. That pleased him, for her.

For his entertainment and hers, she occasionally asked him to serve as a model. These exercises gave her a chance to study his face and possibly his soul. Some of the sketches were as he had looked at first, stubble-faced, scarred, with swollen crooked nose. His eyes had struck her as being very tired, even as he recovered. Occasionally she attempted to paint or draw him as he must have looked before they knew him, clean-shaven, in white shirt and tie, unblemished. But the eyes were still those of an unhappy, tired man. Why?

* * * * *

Augusta

Patsy was beginning to feel truly charged up in Augusta. Committee work was absorbing. She had had no idea of the huge network of agencies and programs, all created by earlier legislatures, with which she must become at least on nodding terms. Every week she learned more of the devastating conditions in which many Maine people lived, often gallantly, and she wanted to help most of them.

She found herself less and less patient with welfare critics who claimed that most of those receiving help were shiftless, lazy cheats. Those comfortable, protected critics obviously had no understanding that years of malnutrition, lack of disciplined work ethic, and bureaucratic bungling sap any feelings of pride or self-sufficiency. Of course there were abuses, of course reform was needed, but that would take time. Bill would probably have been appalled at her thinking.

Working hard on her compilation of bills affecting business was a satisfying assignment, as her reports already surprised and concerned her party. But a nagging thought kept repeating itself. New legislators such as herself had run on the naive premise that by representing the people of their districts they would be the ones making the decisions that governed the state. Hah! What pitiful innocence. The Legislature sat for just six months the first session of each term, and only for three the next year, supposedly dealing then with just emergency bills or bills from the governor. But the bureaucrats, those hundreds if not thousands of state employees working for this commission and that bureau, were active twelve months of every year. They all were anxious to justify their existence by the administration, reports, and rules and regulations they fabricated for the legislation passed during the session. A very powerful bunch, unelected but almost untouchable.

Then there was the media. Maine had just two or three newspapers of considerable influence, one of which also had its own television station. There were a few other papers, like the statewide *Maine Times*, a self-professed gadfly, and, of course, the small local weeklies. Here and there independent reporters observed, taped, and interviewed, but one had to seek out what they had to say. On TV news what advertisers of what products were paying to have commentators say what? Like the bureaucrats, the media was not elected. Patsy, however, accepted their power and was, as subtly as possible, cultivating several reporters. Home recognition was important; she wanted her constituents to be reminded of her, often and positively.

She was also astounded by the sheer numbers of special interests, vital to the state's economy, a list like the catalog in an epic poem. All were dependent in many ways on legislative decisions and financial support, therefore invested heavily in lobbyists. No lobbyists had approached Patsy yet. She realized that freshmen weren't very important to them, and during this session, the Senate was key anyway, of the same party as the governor. However, as many lobbyists were former legislators, and therefore good resources, she had actually sought several out for information.

Discovering the political weight of the entitlement programs and environmental groups was another eye-opener. The Christian Civic League and the religious right also had powerful voices. Add to these demands on the state purse the day-in day-out expenses of maintaining the roads, providing health services, protecting the environment, and citizen safety. All were components of a healthy democracy, all were expensive, and all drew affected voters to the polls.

There were many voices in the capital, all trying to catch the legislators' ears, and it was their job to listen, to sift, and to weigh. No amateurs sat on the Appropriation Committee. Over the years government had become a far larger undertaking than she had ever imagined, an invisible plastic-wrap bubble encasing almost every activity, protective but often making growth and even existence difficult.

The legislature was a cross section of hard-working men and women, some better educated than others but possibly less experienced in realities, and so far she had sniffed out no sleaze, no payoffs. Her fellow House members might not be the big-shot leaders of their communities any more than she was; those people were at home, leading. Her co-workers were just what their title implied, representatives, and they were working long hours for little pay, giving up normal family life for the winter. Some self-interest was involved, of course, but precious little. It was a citizens' legislature, not a professional one, at least not yet.

She was often depressed to learn how unappreciative voters were. Sometimes she wondered if productive serving was all a childish fantasy, if legislators were really just little kids in a specially designed playpen, self-important, busy with their toys and games, and making not whit of difference. Then she would remind herself of the many committee hearings that had been crowded with citizens caring enough to come to Augusta in midwinter. Courteous and treated with matching courtesy and interest, they had their say as proponents or opponents of bills. True democracy at work.

Nightly, Patsy's mind raced, focusing particularly on the gridlock caused by partisanship. A huge glass case on the first floor contained two stuffed moose, great antlers locked while they engaged in deadly combat. Visiting schoolchildren were fascinated by the violent display. Wasn't what went on upstairs much the same? Just as the animals once fought to dominate, didn't those civilized men and women, using different weapons, enjoy their combat and struggle for power just as much? But hadn't they been elected to solve problems, not to make them? How many fellow legislators felt as she did? or did most accept the wasteful power duel?

Patsy was also discovering that being a legislator wasn't all committee hearings and floor debates. Legislators had an effect on many people's lives.

One Thursday night in late March heavy wet snow had once again carpeted the state, turning the roads to grease, keeping children home from school, and discouraging the few little crocuses that had dared make their appearance. People groaned; enough was enough. In the morning, Patsy dug her boots from the back of her closet, sloshed out to the car, and slipped and slid down Western Avenue and Capitol Street's hill to the State House. A cup of coffee tasted good, and she chatted a bit with a friend from Aroostook who would be making the long drive home tonight. Then they both became aware of an unusual number of women and children milling around the rotunda. The Sergeant at Arms was directing them to the stairs leading to the balcony.

These women were mostly in their thirties, many dressed in long, full skirts hem-heavy with melted snow. They wore sturdy boots, wool caps, and shawls. No makeup, many with pigtails or hair in simple buns, they seemed to be from another century or culture. The children, awed and silent, clung to their mothers' hands, often with the free thumb stuck comfortingly in their little mouths.

"Oh Lord, I thought we were through with hippies," groaned one legislator. "Wonder what they're up to?"

"I'll bet they're here from Washington County because of that blueberry spraying bill," said Patsy's friend. "Think of how early they had to get started to be here by nine! And with little children, on these roads today!"

That bill had already generated considerable interest as it affected the multi-million-dollar blueberry industry that employed many in the poorest section of the state. Most legislators felt the bill went too far and needed further study. The health hazards caused by spraying were not yet well documented. More work was needed.

The bell rang and the members not already in their seats drifted into the House. Before she sat, Patsy turned and looked up into the balcony. The women and children had taken seats in the front row, and there seemed to be something new happening up there. There were about forty of them, and Patsy saw glints of metal on the railing that ran the length of the front of the balcony. As she tried to puzzle that out, the Speaker called the House to order, so she had to turn away.

The daily routine of the House was followed, the gavel pounded as each piece of business was finished, and finally came the time for committee reports. The chairman of the Agriculture Committee rose. "Mr. Speaker, Ladies and Gentlemen of the House, the Agriculture Committee has voted unanimously that L.D.2310, a bill to forbid any spraying of blueberry barrens in Washington and Hancock counties, ought not to pass."

He was about to give his committee's explanation for this decision when a pounding, clanging din erupted from the balcony. At least thirty pairs of heavy boots were stamping, stamping, in rhythm, and then came the added sound of jangling metal. Every head on the floor of the House turned. Members saw that the ladies, seated and stomping, had handcuffed themselves to the bar in front of them. The handcuffs rattled, the boots stomped, little children started to cry, and the gavel kept up its banging. There seemed no way to restore order and get about the business of the state. Patsy's heart was pounding, caught up in the strong drama of which she was a part. This was very elemental democracy.

She didn't care for the Speaker, feeling he was tyrannical, power-hungry, and often unfair, but she acknowledged his brilliance. How would he handle this? He was known to be inordinately proud of the reputation "his" House had for decorum. Nothing would be worse than calling in Capitol security or city police to restore order. No politician in his right mind would demand, or even allow, women and children to be evicted from their State House.

These women were determined and firm. They truly believed that the health of their families was threatened by spraying's effect on water and on vegetable crops. What good to them were the dollars brought in by the industry if better blueberry crops proved fatal?

Bang, bang, crack! The gavel actually splintered on that last one and the head flew into the air. Not unusual, but for once no one laughed. But the room did become quiet, for just an instant. And in that instant the Speaker, stony-faced, adjourned the House for the day and weekend, left the podium, and strode imperiously down the aisle, out into the hall, and to his office.

There was a stunned silence, then a few frustrated boos from the balcony. They had failed; it was over.

Following the Speaker's lead, grateful for his skilled leadership in avoiding a nasty showdown, members of the House, even the backers of the bill, picked up their briefcases and quietly filed out of the Chamber. Taking the elevator down to their lockers, without their usual end-of-the week ribbing, they put on their boots and coats and, going to their snow-covered cars, headed for home.

Patsy's reactions were mixed; she was impressed by the handling of the situation, yet heartbroken for those women left in the balcony with nothing to show for their efforts.

Rather than following her fellows, she took a seat on a bench in the Rotunda and waited. Soon a few of the women appeared on the stairs, and she moved toward them, a bright cardinal, in her red blazer, approaching sparrows. She smiled and held out her hands, palms upward, in friendship.

"I just wanted to thank you for coming, and would be glad to answer any questions." Some, spotting the name tag and position on her lapel, kept on moving, antagonistic, but several stopped.

"There was no discussion, no discussion at all. We thought there would be that, at least." The speaker was small, wiry, with intense brown eyes. Hearing her, more women, with their children, joined the group. Patsy wanted to give a good answer, and possibly restore their faith, if not hope.

A large hearing room near the stairs was vacant and she decided to act. "If you ladies will follow me, we can go somewhere quiet and talk." Then she thought of their long trip, and the children. "If any of you need the Ladies Room, it is over there on the right," pointing it out. Some thanked her for that.

Soon they were all seated in the committee room, and Patsy stood.

"To answer your question about discussion. If a Committee's report is unanimously Ought Not to Pass there is hardly ever discussion. If every bill, good, bad and indifferent, had to be debated on the floor of the House, it would take all year. That is one of the purposes of the Committee system, to study the bills and weed out those that are poorly written, unnecessary, frivolous, unenforceable, etc."

"What was wrong with our bill?" This mother was a tall, slender blonde.

"To be honest with you, I haven't studied it in detail," admitted Patsy, "but I heard from several sources that it needed much more work. I heard that many sprays, in the amounts used, are not hazardous, but the bill wanted to eliminate all. There was also a lack of solid evidence, with figures, of health problems due to sprays. Quite a number of bills that are based on good ideas but not sufficiently documented get turned down only to reappear in the next session, much improved and much more apt to pass. Sometimes a good idea actually takes several sessions to mature and be successful. So don't give up."

She asked if any had attended the initial hearing in committee, when both sides had presented their case, and was told they didn't even know about it. Hearing calendars have to be listed weekly in the Classified Section of larger papers, though few people ever noticed them. The women's ignorance of the system had brought them here only to be disappointed.

A little boy whispered to his mother and then came up to Patsy. He gravely consulted with her, she nodded and took his hand. "We'll be right back" she promised. Here was a really manly little character, not about to share the ladies' facilities.

Patsy walked with him down the deserted hall, seeking in the now almost empty building a male to escort him. To her delight, the Speaker emerged from his office.

"Just the person I'm looking for" she said, beaming, and before he knew what had happened, he had a small boy by the hand and was on his way. Returning in a few minutes, he was actually smiling.

"What's going on here? Where did he come from?"

"He came from the balcony. I'm having a little meeting with those ladies, answering questions, and he needed help. Would you care to join us? I'm trying to restore their faith in the system. You could help, just by acknowledging them." And again the Speaker found himself, the Democratic leader, doing the bidding of this freshman Republican, who was having a hard time believing she'd actually suggested it!

The delegation was polite but not awed, and everyone involved learned quite a bit in the following half hour. Then Patsy led them through the basement tunnel to the cafeteria in the State Office Building. The tunnel sloped downhill and several of the children broke into delighted runs. By the time all had eaten, the snow had ceased, patches of blue sky appeared, and as Patsy headed south and they headed north, all knew a bridge, even though fragile, had been built.

The Speaker, Dan Mulrooney, came from a tiny town in Piscataquis County. Incident after incident proved his leadership, his courage, and his brilliance. His life had been a story of struggle against all odds, and he'd won because of those very characteristics. He was now the third-most important man in the state, and the most feared. Tall, with a rugged Celtic face and a graying windblown mop of red hair, his personal appearance drew as much attention as his almost regal sense of self-importance. But he was, though he would hardly admit it even to himself, a lonely man, one whose ambition had never given him the leisure to make personal friends. Now he was asking himself if it was time after this term to run for Congress, or even the governor's seat. Was his power based more on fear than popularity? He had almost eighteen months in which to find out and organize.

* * * * *

Chicago

Phyllis hated to open her eyes, hated to admit that this new day had begun—and would be dreadful. A board meeting of Jarrett Chemical was being held at 10:00 A.M. and she knew she had to be there to keep an even tenuous control of the business. Since Webb's death the monthly meetings had been postponed but could be put off no longer. She suspected that some of the officers had been doing considerable planning to kick her upstairs and take over the decision making.

After bathing, she deliberately turned the shower handle to COLD, and became thoroughly awake. She decided to wear the most severely businesslike suit she owned; an intimidating appearance might hide the agitation she knew she would suffer. Her cold hands tied a scarf in place, patted the bow controlling her page-boy hairdo, and smoothed her skirt. She pinned a heavy gold pin to her lapel, Webb's last Christmas gift.

Though she had always presided at these meetings, Webb had created the agenda, had lined up the votes, had ensured the company's direction. She had no idea of how votes would fall today, who was friendly and loyal, who was self-seeking. The meeting's agenda seemed harmless, but "new business" was always a threat. She had not one ally on the board she could count on to support her. A grim comment on her leadership.

All the familiar symptoms of panic attacks were emerging as she backed her Caddie from the garage and headed downtown. Her throat tightened up, her vision blurred, and her head became woozy. She parked in her reserved space in the company's garage and, approaching the elevator, she thought "I can turn and run right now." But she stepped in, zombie-like, and pushed the button for the top floor. Palms wet, mouth bone-dry, she smiled graciously at the reception group waiting for her, bowed to those in the background, and proceeded to the boardroom. When handshakes had been exchanged she felt safe in removing her gloves from icy, wet hands.

She had reviewed the agenda, made notes and planned her responses, but could not imagine or control what others might suggest, push, or railroad. The firm's lawyer had briefed her a bit on what he expected, and had promised to guide her, but could she trust him?

As she called the meeting to order and went through the familiar routine, anxiety subsided a bit. The manipulative suggestions were weakly presented, the treasurer's report was assuring, and there was no new business. Finally, it was over.

Phyllis, relieved, felt that this session had been pure luck. Somehow she would have to gain genuine self-confidence and even take initiatives to retain leadership. Remaining in control of this business was all that she had left in life but she must learn first to be in control of herself.

The usual well-catered lunch was served, perfection from tangy jellied consomme to creamy key lime pie. Small talk was not challenging, and she finally felt she could excuse yourself and flee to the safety of her car and home.

But, darn it, this afternoon she had promised the Rev. Morris that she would see him. For several weeks he had attempted to reach her and she had made every excuse possible. Not a regular attendee at church, not having great faith in what help he might suggest, she preferred to lick her wounds in private. But what were her wounds? What she missing Webb the man, or just his support?

Mrs. Johnson had a tea-tray all set for the ordeal. Tweedy, bow-tied, and comfortable, the rector arrived promptly, and conversation was safe and polite. He finally got down to business.

"Mrs. Lewis, I have no idea of your needs right now, but can imagine them, based on experiences with other widows. Most find that sharing emotions and grieving experiences with those in the same situation is really helpful, but because of your age you probably have few friends who have been through this loss."

"You are right," she admitted; she did not add that she really had no friends, widowed or otherwise.

"There is a grieving group that meets each week at the church and you would be most welcome. You might find real comfort in learning that what you are going through is common to many women, no matter how bizarre and frightening you find much of it. Sometimes close friendships are formed, and all involved develop a real faith that there is a new and satisfactory life ahead, though it is hard to imagine now."

Phyllis, private to a fault, could think of nothing worse than weekly cry sessions with a lot of strangers. She was not one bit interested in how they were coping with the loss of men as foreign to her as they were. No thank you. Sensing her lack of interest but wishing to leave her with some sort of lifeline, Mr. Morris reached into his wallet for a card.

"You may not have any need of this, but keep it in case. Dr. Burton is a member of the parish, and is considered a very successful counselor/psychiatrist. He is also a very pleasant, warm person to meet." Putting down his teacup, he rose and shook her hand.

"Please just keep in mind that, though we are all relative strangers, you are not alone. Thank you for letting me come."

After his car disappeared down the drive she cleared away the tea things, changed into comfortable slacks and sweater, and took a stroll around the lawn and gardens. As she walked she thought of the rector's last words: "You are not alone." How wrong he was. She was more aware of her aloneness every day. Gathering up her mail from the hall table, she went into the kitchen, mixed her evening cocktail and took it and her letters into the den. What was the outside world demanding of her today? Sympathy notes had long since stopped coming. Bills, invitations to openings and fashion shows, and the spring fund-raising appeals of many charities. One was about to join the others in the circular file when a picture caught her eye. The letter was from the local Animal Refuge League, generally of no interest to her, but it featured a picture of the ugliest, most raffish, and utterly despondent dog she had ever seen. She actually laughed just looking at it, so she read the accompanying appeal.

"Five years old, well-trained but deserted by a family moving to another city, this nice lab-Airedale and possibly shepherd mix is just plain lonely. Are you? Maybe you could work out your problems together."

Phyllis again chuckled, but threw the mailing into the wastebasket, turned on the evening news, sipped her drink, and took in not one word of the world's disasters and scandals. Listening was simply a habit; it had saved her and Webb from the chore of conversation.

Heating the dinner left for her by Mrs. Johnson, she reviewed the day. She had not only lived through the meeting, she had held her own on some points, and no damage had been done. And she could now cross the Rev. Morris off her list of obligations. Bringing her tray back into the den, she settled again before the TV, not one bit interested but hearing voices was better than silence. As she put the plate on the table next to her she spotted the card the minister had left.

In a continuing war against paper, she threw it away, but then remembered her hell, her panic, her trauma of the morning. She'd gotten over that hurdle, but there were endless hurdles in the future. Life, for her, was just one terrifying steeplechase. Better keep the card, just as she kept aspirin in the medicine closet in case of real need. Dr. Henry Burton. In reaching into the waste basket for it, her fingers touched the animal appeal. Retrieving both she sat for a long time, her thoughts reviewing the words "a pleasant, warm person to meet," "you are not alone," "just plain lonely."

Canned laughter drew her attention, and she realized she was watching an old Lucille Ball rerun, in which Lucy and her pal Ethel Mertz were sharing each other's company on a silly shopping spree.

She had no friend like that, never had had. Lonely? She surely was.

The next morning Phyllis was woken early by the phone. It was Mrs. Johnson calling, breathless and tearful, saying she wouldn't be able to come for at least a week as her sister in Wisconsin had been in an accident, was hospitalized, and someone was needed to take care of her four children. Phyllis made the properly concerned remarks, told the kind lady that she understood the situation. "I'm sure I can manage by myself, in spite of how much you have spoiled me. Take your time and keep me in touch. Good luck to your sister." She put down the phone. "Damn, damn, damn." So now she had a house as well as a business to run, with no feeling of competency in either jobs. And she was due at Mr. Atwater's law office at 10:00 to go over some details of settling Webb's estate. No nice morning greeting or pleasant breakfast was waiting downstairs, no warm presence of her only friend, Mrs. Johnson. No compliments or reassurances.

Mr. Atwater, in spite of the almost forbiddingly plush elegance of his office, was an avuncular type, middle height, with gray hair in a soft fringe around a pink and shining dome, and twinkling eyes above his half-glasses. Phyllis always felt relaxed with him, and safe. The legal matters were taken care of quickly. Then he came around his desk and drew up a chair beside hers.

"I know, dear lady, that Webb took care of all the irritating demands of modern life such as heating oil contracts, snow-plowing service, auto maintenance, insurance policies, etc. Are you at all familiar with those responsibilities?"

"Not really," she answered, losing a bit of the confidence he always instilled in her. "I must go through his desks and checkbooks and try to get on top of all that. Possibly his secretary has the information I need. I suppose there are payments to be made by certain dates?"

The attorney pursed up his lips and thought a moment. "We have a law student helping us out, an intern. Would it help you if he reviewed all of that with you and made out a schedule of when certain things had to be taken care of?"

With gratitude she nodded. What good was it to be such a chemistry expert yet so innocent of practical demands of living?

Even a visit to the supermarket was an unusual experience, as Mrs. Johnson always took care of shopping. The aisles were clogged with elderly couples carefully reading every label and with younger women pushing wagons as full of small children as of groceries. She had no idea where to look for what she wanted and finally gave up, settling for frozen dinners, orange juice, English muffins, and assorted soups. Feeling very inadequate, Phyllis just wanted to get home.

The house was empty, no lights on, no soft radio music from the kitchen. Phyllis unloaded her few groceries, then tried to find a room or view or even a chair that welcomed her. Standing by her desk she looked over the neat piles of notes and bills. That foolish dog picture caught her eye. Dialing the number she realized that her hands were shaking. Maybe no one would answer, and that might save her from a bad mistake.

"Animal Refuge League. May I help you? Yes, that dog is still here. Would you like to drop in and meet him? We're open till 5:00."

She drove quickly to an unfamiliar part of the city. Opening the door of the low building, she immediately smelled disinfectant and heard barking and even howling. Introducing herself to the pleasant but no-nonsense young man in charge, she felt as if she were acting in a play, one set in a far-distant, foreign country, and that the curtain would come down soon and she could return to normal.

But in a minute there he was, that incongruous dog. A wiry rough coat was off-white, with splotches of gray. He had long legs, short ears, a plumed tail and frowsy muzzle. He turned his head and, unbelieving, she saw he had just one eye! His head and tail hung down, and seemed to say "What you sees is what you gets. This is all there is." He had no more self-confidence or self-esteem than she did. Phyllis, without thinking, let one hand drop, near his nose, and he lifted his head a little, sniffed her fingers, and licked them, without enthusiasm. But his tongue had been warm. It was a contact.

"Is he healthy? And how old do you think he is?"

"Except for the loss of his eye he's perfectly healthy, and we've given him all the necessary shots. From all appearances he's about five, housebroken, and obeys simple commands. We've named him Jack. You know, he's a one-eyed Jack, like in a pack of cards." The young man chuckled, and ran his hand over Jack's back in a friendly way. The tail moved slowly from side to side, then dropped again.

"What are adoption procedures?" she asked, hooked.

In fifteen minutes Phyllis and Jack were headed home, she in the front seat, he in the back, looking mournfully out the rear window.

She stopped in her driveway, attached the rope they had given her to his collar and invited him to descend. She slowly walked him around the lawn, inspecting the property, bushes and trees together. One caught his fancy and he relieved himself, then looked up at her as if to say "OK, that's taken care of, what next?"

Indoors, in the kitchen, she filled a bowl with water and put it on the floor, then offered him one of the doggy treats provided by the agency. He accepted gravely. Dispensing with the temporary leash, she led him through the dining room and living room to the den, then sat in her favorite chair, interested to see what he would do, though she felt as nervous as he probably did.

For the first time in a long time, Phyllis was acutely conscious of the needs of another being. If she and Jack were to share this house he must feel free to move around. Jack stared at her for a short while, saw her pick up a book and leaf through it, so considered himself dismissed and on his own. He left the room. After a while she heard the click-click of his nails as he came down the stairs and back across the hall. Entering the den, he came to her chair, looked her straight in the eye, again licked her fingers and, with a yawn, sank down on the floor beside her chair, his head on his paws, his one eye shut. He slept, and Phyllis smiled a little and closed her eyes too. Such as her companion was, he had breached the wall of loneliness.

* * * * *

Harding's Corner

Gradually, the back of winter was broken. The warm blue of the sky and the texture of the clouds held little threat of more serious snow. The spring thaw set in and one day they left the truck parked out on the main road, planning to backpack supplies in to the farm for a few weeks rather than risk losing the truck in the deep mud soon to develop. A small roadside tree was felled to lie across the lane as a reminder to others till it was passable again. Very faint greens appeared on some trees, a welcome sight.

On April Fool's Day, before they sat down to dinner, Stan wandered over to the old Victrola cabinet, cranked it up, and selected a record. Soon they were enjoying their food to the music of Glen Gray and his Casa Loma band. By dessert they were listening to Benny Goodman. Stan and Susan danced around the room like pros and finally Webb got to his feet and cut in. He and Susan, old enough to be his mother, flung themselves into "Stomping at the Savoy." Stan applauded them as, breathless, they came back to the table, Webb bowed to Susan, beautiful in her enjoyment, and they were seated again. It reminded them all of dancing-school manners.

But over coffee Stan went on a fishing expedition. He queried Webb skillfully and oh so innocently on his opinions on some of the few subjects not yet thoroughly exhausted as they'd worked together. Arms control, defense spending, federal involvement with education. What did he think of the current welfare picture, did the U.S. have a real foreign policy, were special interests or the elected representatives running our state? What about the press, unelected as was the bureaucracy but wooed by every candidate because of its enormous influence over the average voter? Had he been a hippy himself? Why or why not?

Susan sighed. This was a playback of those suburban years when Stan's soapbox was as much part of any dinner party as the centerpiece. But she knew he had missed this kind of talk, and she also knew he was sounding out their guest. And why.

And Webb, hardly stupid and realizing that a lot might be hanging in the balance, was perfectly candid in his answers, though he knew many were quite at odds with what Stan believed. Stan seemed ready to go on all evening but Webb, sensing where this was leading, forced the issue. He moved from general topics to his own problems.

"No matter who or what I was, where I am, no matter what I do, I have to have a name. Some day soon I'll ride into town with you in the boat or the truck and you'll have to introduce me to someone. Any ideas?"

Silence. He continued. "How about me being 'somebody' Harding? You found me at Harding's Corner. Maybe I was looking up my roots. Aren't you tired of saying 'Hey, you?' And another thing, a big thing. I'm obviously not your responsibility, and I've been here over two months. It's time I moved on, and I'm well enough to take care of myself. I hope we'll stay in touch though; you'll never know what you've done for me." His voice had grown shaky. Damn, he'd hoped to sound so cool.

Stan interrupted. "OK. Time for biting the bullet, all cards on the table." He fiddled with his coffee cup, and leaning forward, stretched both hands out flat. Webb noticed once again the long fingers and fine shape, not the hands of most farm workers. Firelight danced dramatically over Stan's strong face.

Susan and Webb held their breaths as Stan got ready to deliver his opinion.

"I picked up a miserable, cold, beat-up piece of humanity some weeks ago, and brought him home like a half- drowned kitten, no use to anybody. We warmed him up, fed him, left him alone, which is what we would have done for anybody, or almost anybody.

"Then we started to know each other, to respect, to learn what skills each had. But most important was the studying and discussion of our personal philosophies, what makes us tick, what governs our decisions, what we think important, and why. And I don't know when I've been so pleased to get to know a feller, though we certainly don't agree on everything.

"There's plenty of work here to go around, I know you have some new ideas of improvements of your own and I'm not getting any younger."

He stood and knocked his pipe against the andirons, slowly refilled and lit it. Standing with his back to the flames he continued.

"If you'd like to stay here for board and room and a little cash to buy your own booze and new socks, I'd be glad to have you, as long as you'd like to stay. And I know Susan agrees." He cocked his eye in her direction and a radiant smile was the answer. He looked at Webb, who had been studying the pattern on his empty plate, but at this offer had looked up in surprise.

"Stan, Susan. I don't know where to begin, because I am moved beyond anything I ever imagined." He took a deep breath and plunged on. "You two are among the finest people I have ever known, and you're willing to take me in, no references, no name?"

Though he'd known for weeks that this moment must come, his throat tightened up and he wondered if he could go on.

"Because of my respect for you, before I can possibly accept this offer to share your home and your lives, I've got to level with you."

Stan showed no surprise, but Susan held her breath. Webb's hands grasped his coffee mug to hide their trembling, but there was nothing that could control his voice or chin. By leveling he would probably ruin his chances for a life he'd begun to love, and lose the trust of people he loved even more. He made eye contact with each of them, in turn, steadily.

"My name is Webb Lewis. I'm thirty-five years old, raised in upper New York State by my mom, who was widowed by the Korean War. I'm a '72 graduate of Harvard College and then Harvard Business School. I'm married, live near Chicago, and have no children. I am, or was, president and CEO of a successful chemical manufacturing plant, which my father-in-law started. My wife has advanced degrees in chemical engineering and together we have developed the company so that it is now a significant member of that industry.

"My wife is a good person, but very insecure. Her parents never gave her support or confidence in the areas that really mattered to her, either as a child or as an adult. Several years ago my wife miscarried a child, our first, and was told she could have no more. The fetus was also terribly deformed. This just about finished her. Searching for a solution she could live with, she took refuge in putting the entire blame on me, genetically and any other way she could think of. She would accept no responsibility for the miscarriage, or admit that it might have been a natural accident. Her one weapon, to keep her sanity, was to keep putting me down, trying to destroy me in our home, at work, socially, in the community. I became, to her, a worthless individual. She would not hear of any psychiatric help, and

I wanted so desperately to save her that I allowed this behavior to continue till it became a pattern, our way of life. A mistake, possibly, but I'm better at support than confrontation."

Stan and Susan, white-faced, exchanged glances, and reached for each other's hands. A tale so similar, so heartbreakingly similar.

"'We had had little social life, she had always been too shy, unsure. I began to get into community affairs a bit where at least I could help people in worse situations and possibly hang on to sanity myself. She had no interest in where I was or what I was doing, putting her energies into the business, particularly research. Divorce was unthinkable, she was too fragile. And, for the record, I have never cheated on her. Never wanted to.

"I was at that Cairo conference, discussing not only the possible pollution of the Nile by chemical fertilizers made necessary by the Aswan Dam, but also the chances of chemical warfare, not just in the mid-East, but worldwide. I learned, once and for all, that I am not in a pretty business.

"Flying home I was heartsick, seeing no happy future for Phyllis and me, or for the business. Yes, I was on that plane. For some reason known only to the Man Upstairs I was ejected from the emergency door, thrown clear, and was absolutely the only survivor. I sought for others till I lost hope."

He rose and refilled his coffee mug from the pot on the stove. Continuing, he looked over their heads, addressing nothing in particular.

"Then this crazy idea came to me. I threw my wallet, with all my ID, into the snow near the plane, which gas that was now leaking out of. Then I grabbed a blanket and made a new record for staggering through deep snow.

"Am I a sadist, killing off Phyllis's whipping boy and enabler, leaving her on her own? Am I a coward, unable to confront people and work things out? I know I can come back from the dead, resurrect miraculously, but is that best for anyone concerned? Phyllis is brilliant. I honestly feel that, without me, she may grow up, take the bit in her teeth, and Lord only knows where she'll end up.

"For her sake, I'm going to stay dead as a mackerel, unless she really folds and needs me. And I hope I have the intelligence, the education, and the will to recover fully from this, and then find some way to make a real difference in this town, or state, or world."

He took his seat at the table again and his voice became softer, almost a whisper.

"For some reason I have been given a second chance and, without sounding noble, it is important to me to do better this time, a lot better, to express my gratitude in a significant way. Gradually the horrors of that accident have been buried in my mind, just as the wreckage was buried by clean white snow. I feel that I have a new sense of hope and purpose.

"I'm not a fighter but a peacemaker, a compromiser at the table. I've been praised for this, and pilloried." His voice became strong again, full of hope and determination.

"Maybe someday I will be lucky enough to find a cause or person I honor so much that I will be willing to give my life for it. I want to truly live.

"Thank you for listening, and feel free to throw me out in the morning if that is your pleasure." He didn't embarrass them by meeting their eyes now, but put his face in his hands, and waited.

It wasn't a long wait. Susan and Stan, holding hands, tears in Susan's eyes, looked at him with empathy and understanding. Then Susan rose, taking the dinner dishes to the sink. Behind Webb's back she motioned to Stan to come to her. They held a short, whispered conversation, with Susan obviously making demands, not requests. Stan's face was a study of surprise at this novelty, yet he finally nodded agreement enthusiastically and they returned to the table.

Stan spoke.

"The night you arrived I refolded that blanket you brought with you, and recognized it as one from the plane. In the pocket of your jacket was a map you must have found in the cabin where you stayed. It was clearly marked. So we've known from the beginning where you came from, and only wondered why. And you've had a tough one; you certainly have.

"OK. Let's plan ahead." He paused, and Webb barely dared breathe.

"You really can be valuable to us; you have a lot of ideas applicable to the farm and even to this region. Particularly in the field of economic development. I think you're honest and seem to have real integrity. You are still welcome here as long as you want to stay and put in a day's work for a day's pay."

Webb's shoulders were shaking, and embarrassing tears slipped between his fingers, ran down his hands and wrists. He knew he was still weak from his experience, but this was touching other vulnerable spots, deep ones.

Stan continued. "You lost a child, a nameless little bundle of tissues that were so precious. Your wife reacted in her way, and it was devastating. We lost a child, as you may have guessed, a splendid redheaded eight-year-old into whom we both put all the riches we had. A tragic accident, and my wife reacted in her way, denial. You and I, we each had not only the loss but a new challenge."

Susan sucked in her breath. She had not expected this; it had never been discussed in all those years. She too began to tremble. Stan's big hand reached across the table and covered hers.

"I went along with Susan on that, playing the same game, just as you did under different circumstances; each play was different. Oh that heart-breaking game, which often kept us apart when we needed each other's arms so much. And good Susan, when she finally accepted his loss, has let me continue to play the game, as she knows it's my cloddish way of saying I'm sorry for being such a chauvinist bastard. And she's right." Such an admission from him was a first.

He looked into her eyes, deeply, humbly, and neither wavered. Slowly rich smiles of new trust and gratitude were exchanged. The wall between them was down, unexpectedly, at last.

Stan rose, kissed Susan gently, and went to the liquor cabinet. Producing three dainty glasses he poured a smooth blackberry liqueur of his own making into each and proposed a toast, his leonine head with its magnificent beak and strong bearded jaw tipped skyward. His voice was steady.

"May we three who have been through so much, who have made right and wrong decisions, never lose sight of what is right for us all, and live in such a way that our tragedies become triumphs in the end." They clinked the tiny glasses together, even Stan showing emotion, lips trembling.

"And now I understand that Susan would like to make one more suggestion, to be considered carefully."

Susan stood, shaky but radiant. She spoke slowly and with a certain shyness.

"Stan and I have agreed that we would be honored if our guest, in search of an identity, would take the name of our beloved son, Jerry Warner. We have a bona fide Connecticut birth certificate; you and Jerry were actually born the same year, 1950. There is no record anywhere of Jerry's death or burial. Stan was an only child, my sister died many years ago, and other relatives and old friends long ago gave us up for lost in these woods. It is hardly good manners anymore to ask after children raised in the 60s and 70s; too many have taken off, God knows where. Our few neighbors have supposed he was away at school. If you accept this idea, Webb, I challenge anyone to question the validity or parentage of Jerry Warner."

Stan felt that emotions better be brought down to earth.

"Jerry was a redhead. May I suggest that on my next trip to town I acquire whatever it takes to make you one too? And add a moustache to that beard. Your best friend might have trouble recognizing you." They all laughingly agreed.

Under the crescent moon hanging in the cold Maine sky that night three released and hopeful people blessed this solution and each other. Each retired feeling finally freed from handicapping deception and fear of hurt, ready to move ahead, trusting and respecting each other and playing no more games of any kind for any reason. Almost.

Now that he had a name, a home, a life, "Jerry" wanted, wih the Warners' permission, to contact Joel. Cutting himself off from Joel permanently would be like cutting a vein and slowly bleeding to death. No more games, particularly with Joel. He must set up some form of communication so that if Phyllis needed him, really needed him, he could be reached. There was stationery in the desk. He pondered over what he would write, something only Joel would understand and that didn't tell him too much at first. Looking around his room for ideas he found his answer. He picked up the pen and printed with his left hand:

"IN WHICH PIGLET PLANS HIS COSTUME:

"Halloween was coming, and little Piglet was unhappy. For several years he had worn a Spider costume, but the WEB had been torn somehow and destroyed. He was such a little pig it would be fun to be something really BIG. He thought of the nearby giant, Paul Bunyan, the legendary woodsman, who had a big black beard, and a fierce look. All Piglet needed was a friend who would be Babe, the Blue Ox of the legend. He would ask Owl, who was Good At Letters, to write a note to the paper, to the Personals. Would anyone answer?"

That would at least let Joel know he was OK. And if Joel was on the ball he'd remember the huge statue of Paul Bunyan in Bangor, Maine, which they used to see when they flew into the airport there every summer for camp. And maybe, just maybe, Joel would think of using the personals in the *Bangor Daily News*. A long shot, but safe. He would start subscribing to the paper tomorrow, as Jerry Warner, MIA for so long. He licked the envelope and addressed it to Joel's office.

He climbed into bed, settled, and the silence of the house was comforting. Then he heard, down the hall, the creaking of a bed, gasps of joy, passion, and release. His eyes stung with tears, happy for Stan and Susan that they were truly together again. More tears came as he thought of what he and Phyllis had lost, and he might never find with anyone again.

* * * * *

Bangor, Maine

March was generally the least flattering time of year for the State of Maine, but this year that drabness had lasted into April. Leafless trees seemed gaunt and spiritless, mud dominated the landscape and decorated salted automobiles, and what little snow still remained on the shady side of the roads was filthy with a mix of oil, salt, and sand. Forsythia, in rare sunny spots, struggled to brighten the scene. On her way to Bangor for a weekend with her daughter and family, Patsy decided that the state needed a good face-washing to remove the winter rime. Get ready, because company's coming!

As she drove, her thoughts turned to that expected "company." Summer people continued to think of Maine as their private and vast vacationland of seaside, lakes, and mountains, with just enough convenient little businesses, amusements, and services to provide the amenities. And, of course, these businesses were owned and managed by such delightfully picturesque "natives" with their endearing accent and dry humor. The "rusticators," as visitors were first called, did not maliciously make fun of those who made their vacations comfortable, but certainly considered them the legitimate and colorful material for amusing vacation tales at Beacon Hill, Main Line Philly or New York dinner parties in the winter. Summer visitors, even those who owned cottages, wanted to think of Maine as a separate place, a refuge from their often stressful "real" world. Though they themselves patronized the good Maine theaters, concerts, and fine dining establishments, they were in deliberate denial about the fact that many residents of Maine regularly attended the Boston Symphony, the Museum of Fine Arts, or Red Sox games. Acknowledging this two-way accessibility and exchange would certainly spoil their illusion, or delusion, of Maine being another world.

Their fantasy was also often jostled when they learned that many of these Maine "characters" were graduates of colleges by which they them-

selves had been turned down, and sojourned in Florida every winter, making their own parochial jokes about southern accents. Why set them straight? They were only underfoot three or four months, and the green of their dollars matched that of the pines for which the state was nicknamed. Tourism was one of the state's greatest income producers. Patsy noted that some visitors who became permanent residents after a few summers soon awoke to the fact that they had not been sent by a Higher Power to straighten Maine out. Many in time actually became quite valuable, contributing new energy and stretching some traditionally hidebound attitudes and aspirations.

Leaving the interstate in Bangor she took Rte lA and, crossing the bridge into Brewer, was soon on a familiar country road. There it was, the homey, middle-aged house Meg and Peter had bought, all lit up for her.

As she parked in the muddy yard, a small figure erupted from the back door. Disregarding the cold, her four-year-old grandson beat on the car door till she could get it open.

"Gramma, Gramma, guess what? I have a new kitten, my very own kitten, and guess what? His name is Tigger." She gave Billy a quick hug, and her purse to carry, while she loaded herself with suitcase and other packages. Meg, holding baby Fannie in her arms, stood in the doorway. A big, friendly dog joined in the welcome, and soon Patsy was inside. Getting rid of coat, boots, and packages she reached for Fannie, and was also handed a warm bottle as a bonus. Settled in the kitchen rocker, she took a deep breath and for a minute or two let it all lap over her. What a change of scene and ambience for her! Meg serenely moved from stove to counter, from counter to sink, automatically avoiding the kaleidoscope of plastic toys, big and little, scattered on the floor.

Patsy directed Billy to bring her one of the packages, suggested he open it and play Santa. Soon Fannie was drooling happily over a big pink bunny, while Billy's head, and that of Tigger, were bent over a Very Scary book about dinosaurs.

A vintage wine and some luxury hors d'oeuvres were put in the fridge for later. Patsy burped the baby expertly, and both children and Tigger were in her lap hearing about the Tyrannosaurus when daddy Peter came in the door. Tall, skinny, bespectacled and starting to have a higher forehead, he was no Robert Redford, but Meg could not have found a dearer husband. They'd met in Virginia while he was working on his CPA degree and Meg was in law school. It was taken for granted that they would

practice in that area, or near New York, but they stunned everyone by moving to Maine, rural Maine. Patsy, with ambitious hopes for Meg's career and future, had had trouble adjusting to their decision to settle in what seemed to her a backwater, but Bill had been tickled to pieces; these kids had done exactly what he had done many years ago and had never regretted. Their values were similar to his: a strong belief in satisfying the precious immaterial qualities of life rather than scrabbling for the more prestigious material.

Peter was employed by one of the huge paper companies, and was well considered. Meg had started out in a fine Bangor law firm but had "retired" just before Fannie arrived. Now she and another woman were building a small firm of their own, compatible with mothering, specializing in family cases close to their hearts.

Children's supper, baths, one last story, goodnight hugs, kisses, and finally lights out completed the familiar nightly ritual. Then mercifully Peter eyed her and asked if she was ready. Peter made the most seductive Manhattans she'd ever tasted; she certainly was ready for one.

During their dinner, she tried to catch up with their lives.

"Mom, I think we're going to make it!" Meg's dark amber eyes and tawny hair made her a golden girl, at least in her mother's mind.

"Three new clients this week, and we're getting nibbles from some of the United Way agencies and programs dealing specifically with domestic violence. Deciding to specialize in helping women and children was a good move." Then her face clouded over. "Mom, I had no idea of the real terror and suffering out there, and it's not all in low-income families."

Patsy nodded, having learned the same lesson herself this winter. How protected by loving parents she too had been. At least Meg was having an earlier start at this form of maturing, the removal of the rose-colored glasses.

Patsy beamed her pride and then turned to her son-in-law. "How about you, Pete? What's new in that world of figures I don't understand?"

"Not much new. I'm always awestruck at the immensity of not only our holdings but those of the other paper companies depending on pulp for survival. From the Maine border at Kittery to Bangor is about a four-hour drive if you step on it. Reaching Bangor, most out-of-staters think they've reached the end of the road, and that their front bumper is in Canada. But they're only halfway there, and there's not much but woods ahead of them. Woods to be harvested, protected, or fought over. The

industrial areas bordering the North-South interstate highway have little in common with the big woods, the coastal barrens and inland lake regions.

"But we're beginning to see in all our activities a constant pressure to catch up with modern technology in order to survive. There's been a real influx of related companies moving in and anxious to expand. Somehow, particularly in the depressed areas, resident aspirations must be heightened and more up-to-date education demanded and provided if Maine young people are to be persuaded to stay, and make a good living here."

These were ideas good for hours of discussion, but it had been a long day and morning would come early. They finished the last duties, the dog was put in the shed, Billy was emptied and Fannie filled. Tigger was placed on Billy's coverlet, and soon all slept.

About six the following morning, Patsy was aware of a presence, very quiet, but one sending out urgent signals. She opened one eye and looked directly into another, brown and warm. In seconds Billy was snuggled up next to her, under the covers. After a while his little voice whispered "Gramma, do you miss Grampy?"

She had been, very much, that same minute, as Billy formerly had always climbed in with Gramp. If there had been no aneurysm he would be here now. "Of course I do, dear, and I think he's very happy you and I have each other now." Silence, but a warm silence.

Meg had planned a little dinner party in her mother's honor. "I think our guests will all be people you'll enjoy, all singles, all doing different, interesting things." She'd planned a menu appealing to people living alone and tired of restaurant food, and Patsy marveled anew at the expertise displayed by this daughter who as a teenager couldn't make a cake mix successfully, much less cook a whole meal. The children were bathed and bedded, adults had time to change and freshen up, a fire was started in the living room, and hors d'oeuvres were placed on small tables. Peter filled the ice bucket, glanced at the clock, and chuckled as he saw headlights come up the drive.

"Here he is, I told you! Mr. Punctuality."

In his early seventies and therefore brought up to be prompt, Amos Wilson, a former legislator himself, climbed out of his vintage sports car. He was soon giving Patsy a chance to talk about what was going on in Augusta. It was fun for her to get his perspective, fueled by one of Peter's martinis. A jeep next crested the rise. The driver was introduced as Harry Woodward, fortyish, somehow involved in power company problems, and a born lobbyist.

Crackers, cheese, pate and chips were passed, conversations began to be easy and relaxed, and the last guest arrived. Almost six feet of breathtaking womanhood slipped into the kitchen. She was dressed simply in well-cut black patio pants and a batik tunic of black and topaz, relieved by a heavy silver necklace. The artistry of her outfit seemed totally unplanned. Heather Hatch, late of Washington newsrooms, had recently come to Maine to prove herself a real reporter and not just a pretty face who read news reports written by others. She was a serious journalist with the handicap of being as beautiful as she was intelligent. Patsy, typical mother, hoped that her bachelor son Charlie might meet this young lady soon.

The lull in conversation following her arrival was almost embarrassing until she turned to Meg, smiling in a warm, unaffected way.

"If that's roast beef I smell, I'm moving right in. My grandmother still tells everyone that all she had to say to get me to meals was 'Meat!' and her dainty little granddaughter would come charging in like a cannibal."

She opted for bourbon and water, moved easily around the room, and Meg knew she had a darn good dinner party on her hands.

* * * * *

Next morning Patsy was the first in the kitchen; she decided on pancakes and got the batter ready, then juice, milk and coffee. Stepping outside she saw a truly spring sky, a warm blue, and fancied she heard bird calls of some sort. Maybe, just maybe, warmer weather was finally on the way.

Accompanied by the dog, she walked down the drive to the mailbox and retrieved the Sunday *New York Times*. She suddenly realized she hadn't even had time to read yesterday's *Bangor Daily News*. Keeping up with all Maine news and op/ed pieces because of their influence, right or wrong, on voters and legislators, was a new responsibility for her.

Returning to the kitchen, she just glanced at the Times' headlines. Then she found yesterday's BDN and quickly leafed through it. Nothing of particular interest. Her hands kept turning pages until she found herself in the classified section. Killing time, she amused herself by reading the Personals. One item caught her eye.

"Pooh delighted to be Babe. Will be at park noon 4/12/87."

That was today! Her interest was whetted and her curiosity in overdrive. It was an absolutely ridiculous message. What Babe? What park?

What Pooh, for that matter? To her, of course, there was only one, "a bear of very little brain." And then a crazy answer popped into her head. At the entrance to Bass Park, Bangor's convention and racetrack center, was a huge statue of Paul Bunyan, a legendary lumberman and owner of Babe, the Blue Ox. No, she was fantasizing. Then everyone showed up for breakfast and such foolishness went out of her mind. She had a meal to produce.

Soon it was time for church and Sunday School, and she took her own car, as Peter had to stay after service to count the offering. When the service drew to a close she glanced at her watch. Almost noon. She knew Meg liked to stay for the socializing, so she offered to take Billy for a drive, then come back for her and the baby. Once on their way, she headed straight for Bass Park and the Bunyan figure. Curiosity had won out.

She cruised up broad Main Street, Sunday empty. As she approached the park, she slowed down a bit to observe, but also to tell the tale of the mythical figure to Billy.

"Paul Bunyan was a giant lumberman, from the Western forests, and Bangor claimed he was born on the very day the city was incorporated. Babe, his ox and partner in bringing tree trunks out of the woods, was so huge that the story claims his horns were 42 ax handles apart! That huge ax slung over Paul's right shoulder is what he used to chop down trees and in his left hand is an enormous peavey, almost his height, with which he moved the logs on snow or in the water."

Billy was impressed. "But where is Babe, Gramma?"

"I don't think the park is really big enough to hold him, do you? He'd need so much room to graze." Gramma fabricated shamelessly, her attention taken by what she'd hoped to find.

Leaning against the statue's base was a bearded man in an unzipped down windbreaker, flannel shirt, jeans, and wool cap. Probably in his mid-thirties, although it was hard to tell because of the beard. A modern Paul Bunyan cut down to size? In dress and build he could have served as the statue's model. A taxi pulled up. Another man, dressed in citified gray flannels and camel-hair overcoat, got out eagerly, hesitated a few seconds, then ran toward the first, who moved to greet him. To her they certainly bore no resemblance to Pooh or Piglet, but she felt she'd never seen a more heartfelt or enthusiastic meeting. It was almost too personal to watch and she felt like what she was, an intruder. A lump was in her throat from sharing their obvious joy at reunion, almost as if one had returned from the dead. They were totally un-self-conscious, and she was happy for them. A relative loner herself, she was even envious.

Returning to Augusta in the late afternoon she reviewed the weekend. It was ridiculous not to come up more often, when it took just a little longer than returning to Portland in the opposite direction, but she also remembered her resolution not to move into her children's lives now that she was alone. Then she realized how refreshing the change of scene, pace, and personalities had been, and promised herself to avoid becoming too comfortable in her new routines and challenges. Snuggling with Billy was better medicine than anything Augusta had to offer.

* * * * *

Joel's heart was pounding as his taxi neared the Paul Bunyan statue. Was he all wet about interpreting that strange note he'd received? If not, would Webb have even seen his answer? As the statue came in sight, he could hardly breathe. And then, though there was a car with a woman and little kid in the way, he could see a figure waiting, and it looked a helluva lot like one he'd known for a long time.

As the cab stopped he handed the driver a crumpled wad of bills, jumped out and almost ran toward the other man. But as he got close he hesitated, tilting his head and looking at the other carefully. A lot was right, but something was different too.

"C'mon, Pooh, what's a broken nose and a red beard between friends?" Jerry asked, laughing. He hadn't realized that his appearance had changed so much. Probably a good thing.

Joel whooped "It really is you, old Piglet!"

Neither gave any thought as to what the proper, Sunday downeast rules were for such a meeting, they just held on to each other hard, so as never to lose each other again. But they were a little slow in making eye contact, each a bit loath to let the other see tears and wobbly chin.

Finally Jerry said in a rather shaky voice, "My borrowed truck is across the street. Let's head for the Pilot's Grille for lunch, and I hope you have all day." He gave his old friend his well-remembered grin and they both whooped, laughed, and actually ran for the truck.

Settled in a booth at the busy restaurant, pretending to study the huge menu, each began to simmer down; when their beers arrived their tongues were loosened. They felt muscles and nerve endings relaxing, then melt into total euphoria.

"I can't believe it really worked, and that you're here. Thanks, Joel. Oh God, it's wonderful to be me again, with you, even for a few hours. 'Sing Ho for the life of a Bear'."

Though wild with curiosity about Webb's "resurrection," Joel hastened to speak first of his latest talks with Phyllis, in case that subject was uppermost in his friend's mind.

"She's really doing OK, I think. She sounds more sure of herself every time I call, and I think she's honestly trying to understand and take control of the company. Possibly a much needed ego trip. She may even have a new interest. She let the name 'Jack' drop into our conversation. Something about a dinner date!"

Jerry was surprised that that news gave him no pangs of jealousy.

"She refused to go south with her parents, so at least they're not on her back, and she's winging it on her own. She practically never calls me." Joel didn't want to say that she practically never mentioned Webb either.

"But now I've got to hear your tale, because it must be a doozy. Who are you, what are you, why are you, and where are you headed?"

Jerry chuckled. Impetuous Joel had to have it all at once, in one sentence, with historic accuracy and a neat list of explanations. Thank goodness, he thought, I've done my homework and gotten it all in order to present, or he'll go nuts.

"Well, first and foremost, I have a new name and identity. Try very hard to get used to calling me and thinking of me as Jerry Warner, about-to-be legally adopted son of an Eli, Stan Warner, and his wife Susan, two wonderful people you've got to meet somehow. I'm absolutely legit, but it'd take too long to go into that now."

"Glad to meetcha, Jerry," and Joel extended his hand.

"Right now I'm their handyman, working on a subsistence farm way the hell off in the woods. Besides what this city slicker is learning about farm life, he's also studying the conditions and problems of this part of Maine. I hope to slowly emerge, when I think it is safe, and do my share constructively in the community or state or whatever. You know how much I love this state."

Joel moved the salt shaker, the ketchup bottle, the sugar bowl around on the table, to give himself poise for whatever was coming.

"We'll get back to all that, but I know you want to first hear the how and why of this situation. I think you'll find it hard to believe, and impossible to understand."

Jerry went into satisfying detail about the plane crash, his woozy decision to start afresh, his wilderness experience and what the Warners had done for him. To Joel's relief he was finally candid about what had been off limits for so long, his relationship with Phyllis and his future; he made no excuses. Now there were no walls between them.

Joel listened with keen sympathy, even empathy where possible, and began to realize that this was a new Webb—Jerry—talking, a more decisive, positive, and committed man than the one he had known. Even if he had been half out of his head at the time, it had taken great courage to cut himself off so completely from a whole life. Unbelievably he seemed happy and at peace, full of energy and real self-confidence.

"So that's the story; thanks for listening. Now, enough about me. How are you, Carol, and the kids? Your family is so important to me that I want to keep current, even if I can't actually be with you."

Joel filled him in, with enthusiasm and pride, but then came back to what Jerry's future might be.

"OK, you've asked for it. Listen goo-ood. The Maine we were shown as teenagers for three or four woodsy summers was marvelously primal and unspoiled, peopled by clear-eyed, honest, and endearing characters. Actually, even then there was a Maine far more sophisticated than we ever saw, in the southern part of the state and along the interstate. Now that is more true than ever.

"Technology, computers, visionaries, and MBA immigrants have made their places. There are more lawyers per capita in Portland than in any city but Washington. Several teaching medical centers are nationally respected, as are the university, which has campuses all over the state, and at least three private colleges. Companies such as Bath Iron Works, the paper mills, and the tourist industry employ thousands. The armed services have several bases that pump money into the economy.

"But there are at least two Maines. Appalling poverty, country slums, illiteracy, and the dirty little secrets of drugs, incest, and all kinds of abuse were hardly featured in the Namakant brochures or tourist material.

"In between these extremes are the solid-as-a-rock small businesses, fishing, papermaking and agricultural populations trying to keep it all in balance. Some mills still exist. An amazing number of out-of-state entrepreneurs, big and little, have moved up here with creative ideas and made them fly. I haven't seen these things firsthand, hiding out as I am, but I've read a helluva lot."

Joel, intrigued, realizing how little they had really understood of the state, urged Jerry to continue.

"I foresee a pretty big confrontation between the liberals—who are predominantly pro-labor, environmentalists, or elitists 'from away'—and the small businessmen and native-born conservatives who still hope to keep the state's economy based on traditional agriculture, fishing, lumbering, and the offshoots thereof. State and federal regulations are literally choking many businesses of all sizes to death, largely because of rules dreamed up by bureaucrats who've never left Washington or their desks in Augusta. Workman's comp rates, taxes, and environmental nitpicking discourage new businesses from moving in.

"Education, particularly technical stuff, is in trouble, as is rural medicine. For too long there has been a brain drain of good students moving out. Will a part of Maine become just a big vacationland for the world, at miserable income for most, or can Yankee ingenuity and work ethic lick the out-of-state land speculators? State government is clean as far as corruption goes, but it sure loves to tie things up with partisan power plays. I could go on and on about federal involvement, too."

Neither had eaten much breakfast because of their excitement over the meeting. Now they plowed into their steaks, french fries, and salads like starving men. With huge portions of apple pie for dessert they were finally satisfied.

It was Joel's turn to take the floor.

"Do you want to hear about your funeral? It was great, if I do say so."

He suddenly realized he might reasonably be just a bit irritated at having gone through what he had experienced emotionally to stage such a tribute to a perfectly healthy "corpse." He took from his pocket a copy of the program of the service and told in detail of the speeches, songs, and reactions. They both laughed at the plight of good Rev. Morris when he recognized he'd lost to amateurs. Jerry really wished he'd been there, hidden away like a church mouse under a pew or like Tom Sawyer at his funeral, though Tom had, at the right moment, emerged.

Then Jerry sobered, overwhelmed by the effect his life and so-called death had had on so many. Was this really what some people thought of him? Maybe he had something to live up to now. Would new self esteem give him the confidence he needed to move on?

"That kid, the paperboy. Have you kept in touch with him?" Joel admitted that he hadn't, and Jerry asked him to try, even if just by phone. "He's a hard worker, has lots of ambition, and if his values are kept straight he should have a real future. But he's at the age when his values need support. Having been without a dad myself it was easy to understand what he was missing, and I'd hate to have left him in the lurch."

They discussed news of old friends and swapped some amusing tales, particularly of Jerry's new lifestyle which was as foreign to Joel as life on the moon.

Now that Joel had a name and address for him, an exchange of letters should be simple, as long as there was no leak. They decided that Joel should rent a box at a post office so that none of Jerry's letters could fall into the wrong hands. Secrecy was still vital; it might always be. Jerry impressed upon his ally that he would emerge any time that Phyllis might really need him, but that giving her this chance to have a new life was possibly the best gift he could give her. He would appreciate Joel's keeping in touch with her and reporting to him.

Joel promised to help in any way he could, both on that assignment and when Jerry decided on a course of action. Isolated as the Warners were, it was difficult to get information on many subjects, and Jerry wanted to jump into whatever it was he decided to pursue fairly well-armed with information. Solutions would be found.

Their waitress poured yet another cup of coffee for each and wondered if they'd ever leave.

Getting back to one subject he had touched on earlier, Jerry said, "One of the chief stumbling-blocks here—and not confined to Maine—is the partisanship that keeps everything at a standstill. Republicans ruled the roost for so long that they became complacent. Democrats, under Muskie's leadership and taking advantage of the old adage of nature abhorring a vacuum, got back on the map and now are glorying in being in the saddle at last.

"The Republicans have retrenched, found new blood to challenge their unimaginative Old Guard, and are fighting back. Both parties piously proclaim that their differences and infighting are simply philosophical. That's hogwash. It's just a question of wanting power and even revenge. I know this is an old story for as long as there have been politics and several parties, but it still isn't right, and just because it's habit doesn't mean it is cast in cement. Hell, change is possible, and two wrongs don't make a right.

"Maybe what I should really do is fight this political gridlock rather than concentrating on any one problem. I believe the future of the state of Maine, even of the country, depends entirely on everyone learning to pull together for common objectives. Voter apathy and cynicism are the real enemy now and appallingly powerful. They scare me, and yet they are not surprising.

"Maine is stuck up here in the northeastern corner of the nation, with so-so rail, road, and plane services, but a helluva lot of coastline, rivers, and good harbors. If both parties would jointly focus on both the assets and the problems, then jointly seek solutions, we just might get somewhere. Now each comes up with bills that are simply short-term bromides, with nobody thinking of actually curing the festering wound. Some good legislation gets enacted, but party too often comes first."

Joel interrupted with real excitement. "Let me try this idea on for size. It's actually an idea I've been playing with since you 'died.' Whatever you decide to do will take bucks. How about a Webb Lewis Fund? A lot of people still ask about what you'd have liked as a memorial. We could word the purpose of it loosely enough so it would be pretty flexible, from camp scholarships to saving endangered species to angeling some campaign for a Good Cause. Think about it. You'd just have to stay dead, but I gather you're planning to anyway."

He looked at his watch and rose to his feet. "Gotta go. I've a flight back to Boston for 3:10. Where the hell's the airport and can we make it? and whaddya think of becoming a faceless executive director, broken nose, red beard, and all?"

Laughing, Jerry reassured him. "We're practically on the runway, Joel, so calm your body. You'll make it." He reached for his jacket and continued with earnest gravity, almost in a whisper.

"Pooh, I'm perhaps the luckiest guy alive—or dead, whichever way you want to think about it. I've been given a second chance, by a series of miracles. Because of that I'm dedicated to investing this new life soundly, finding some goal that will make a real and positive difference. I have a colossal debt to repay to someone or something. Let's see what I find, how legal it would be considering I'm still embarrassingly warm and breathing. What fairly universal appeal would such a fund have to have? My friends were of many shades and types of political and philosophical persuasions."

Jerry picked up the check. "I owe you that much, Pooh. Gotta keep your hunny-pots full." Two very happy men climbed into the truck.

"By the way," added Jerry, "do your Carol and the girls know where you are and what you're doing today? If not, let's keep it a secret still, if you don't mind." Joel agreed, though he'd had no secrets from Carol before.

With hearty slaps on the back and firm handshakes, they parted at the airport, more lighthearted than they'd been in months. Life was almost back to normal again in some ways, and it felt good. The hemorrhages were under control, the wounds would heal. They were in touch again, and both recognized that their mutual trust was still strong, their future, as a team, exciting.

The restaurants and the airport had seemed so crowded, so noisy, so active even on a Sunday that Jerry's head was tired. He realized for the first time how isolated and quiet his life for almost three months had been. Not even bothering to turn on the TV in his motel room, he climbed contentedly into bed, but before sleep came he just lay there, warmed not only by Joel's friendship but by the unbelievable news of what he'd meant to so many.

* * * * *

Augusta

In the morning he sought out the Bangor library, a beautiful and dignified building in the heart of the business district, and made a quick survey of its research potential. As Maine's largest public library it would be a fine resource.

Getting back on I-95, and feeling like a kid playing hooky, he drove south in Stan's truck to Waterville, checked out the Colby College library, and went on to Augusta.

After finally locating a parking space behind the Capitol, he visited the building housing the State Archives and the State Museum, and had a hard time tearing himself away from both the library and the exhibits. Expertly created reproductions of the industries and resources of the past showed the state as an example of hardiness, ingenuity, and strong work ethic. Were those traits still strong, strong enough to support a renaissance affecting the whole state? He could pray.

Next he investigated the library in the State House, with shelf after shelf of documents, reports, and books dealing with legislative history. Comfortable in the knowledge that he could put his hands on any information he needed in his search for a cause, he went out onto the third-floor balcony, enjoying the pattern of the Maine Arboretum, and looking across the broad Kennebec to the State Mental Hospital. He wondered wryly, as hundreds had wondered before him, if the patients there were as interested in watching the screwy activities in the Capitol as the legislators were concerned with the inmates' sometimes weird antics. Not much choice, sometimes.

He checked the daily legislative calendar to see if there were any committee hearings on situations that particularly interested him, found there weren't, and took an elevator down to the first floor. It might have been an ordinary enough end to a visit, but sharing the elevator with him was one of the most attractive women he had seen in a long, long time.

Tall and slim, she was dressed in baggy OD's but wore a lively orange and gold scarf knotted loosely around her neck. Everything about her appearance was casual and gave the impression of naturalness. There were golden glints in loose wavy hair, a rosy skin glowing without benefit of makeup, and amazing blue eyes that met his own with candor. He was favored with a friendly, brief smile that was utterly unaffected. On the floor by her feet were a backpack and a small TV camera and equipment. Possibly from one of the networks, she seemed to be on her own, with no crew as backup. Hooray, she might appreciate a hand.

When the car reached the ground floor and the doors opened, she expertly scooped up her gear with both hands, donned the backpack with a twist of her shoulders, and was out and going down the hall almost before Jerry realized the ride was over.

He caught up with her at the door to the parking lot, opened and held it, grinning foolishly. He was trying to think of something not totally inane to say when she gave a brisk "thank you. Have to make the six o'clock news" and plunged down the steps to a network van. At least he got the logo of that in his head just before she swept out of the lot and headed for Western Avenue and I-95.

His pickup was way on the other side of thc lot, so that was that. It was kind of a nice feeling, though, to react like a college kid to a gorgeous gal. And he knew what his favorite channel was from now on but TV had not yet invaded the castle of Stan and Susan. Shit. He pulled their shopping lists from his pocket, decided to take care of them in Bangor, and headed north.

Several hours later, with the back of the pickup boasting lumpy bagfuls of groceries, supplies for all the animals, necessities for the garden and house, and a few little gifts he had painstakingly chosen for his "family," he relished memories of these past two days. He felt at last a real melding of "Jerry" and "Webb," some problems that had tormented him now seemed problems no longer, and he felt all of a piece.

He'd found Joel was still his best friend with generous ideas and no criticism, that a wealth of material was available to him courtesy of the state he now called his, and a knockout female had proved to him that all systems were still in working order. Add in supporters like Stan and Susan, and a soft, starlit spring night; all seemed to sing in his heart as he headed home. Home, at last—what a wonderful word.

* * * * *

Harding's Corner

It was a late Easter, very late, April 19, and because of the long winter it was doubly welcome, everywhere. People of many religions could join together wholeheartedly this year in celebrating the renewal of life that comes each spring. In New York's Central Park, around the Tidal Basin in Washington, and through the woods of Valley Forge the tender green leaves, the pink cherry blossoms, and the fairy lights of dogwood renewed faith in at least one system that was beyond the control of Wall Street, presidents, lobbyists, or special interests.

Though snow was still deep on Mt. Washington in New Hampshire, and spring skiing on the "corn snow" was popular as ever, baby lambs finally frolicked in the fields below and learned that green grass was delicious. And finally the ice was out on Maine's Moosehead Lake, now a sapphire expanse.

Susan awoke early Easter morning, pulled on her shapeless wool bathrobe, peeked out the window, and gasped. A soft last snow had once again fallen during the night, just enough to coat every leaf and twig with an almost translucent frosting.

The clear bright greens of yesterday were now chalky greens, an effect she had never seen before. What did it remind her of? And then she could almost see, in her little-girl hand, a piece of a green ginger-ale bottle, trash glass that had been tossed and ground and whirled by the tide and sands and stormy waves till all edges were softened and the surface glaze scrubbed. Sea glass, she was told. A treasure she'd found on the beach. So does nature often improve upon itself as a gift to those with eyes to see. A miracle.

She poked Stan gently, whispered orders to look out the window and then go back to sleep and, going to Jerry's door, knocked and gave the same message.

Two of her lambs were still on bottles and living in the shed off the kitchen, so she warmed milk for them, and soon a grateful pair was busy filling empty bellies. Pancake batter enhanced with diced bits of apple and last summer's blueberries stood in a pitcher ready for the griddle. A few crocuses had bloomed bravely in the shelter of the house, and she produced a small bouquet for a centerpiece. How long had it been since there had been real joy for Easter, or any other holiday, in this house?

Stan and Jerry appeared almost at the same time. Each saluted her with a kiss, and thanked her for alerting them to the snow scene before the morning sun destroyed it. The kitchen table, a deep honey-colored maple, was set with yellow place mats and napkins, and patterned by the early morning sun shining in the window. Green stoneware was at each place, and Susan's precious but rarely used little Wedgwood pitcher held the maple syrup. But what caught the men's eyes was the exquisitely decorated egg each found at his place.

Nestled and supported in soft, real hay, each egg stood on its broad end, glowing with bright colors. No decals or bunny designs on these, they were genuine pysankys, made in the ancient Ukrainian style with delicately waxed motifs dyed in sequence, a complicated batik. Against black backgrounds, multicolored geometries and patterns glowed. Each was different, obviously designed as a personal offering. Completely taken by surprise, each man had the sense to appreciate and study his egg in silence, inspect the other's, then reward a beaming Susan with beams of his own.

Jerry's egg at first glance was like paisley, covered with amoeba-like shapes and wiggly worms, all very colorful and vibrant. But a closer inspection showed that the shapes were like pieces of a jigsaw puzzle, possibly the answer to his future if put together. And the worms were simply question marks. An egg, the symbol of life and containing life, held the answer? How would the pieces fall together?

He looked over at Stan's, a design of strong lines both horizontally and vertically, a tight design, black, white, and brilliant red. But, as he studied it, he saw more. Very fine threadlike lines, like cracks in the eggshell, hinted at vulnerability, change? A mind opening to new ideas? An inner secret to be revealed?

Susan's egg was glorious. No real design or motifs, just pure color, the colors of Easter, of new life, of energy. One did not need daffodils, chickens, lambs, or bunnies to get that message. She was once more joyously alive; the wall was down. In her sixties, with hair a stranger to a salon, weatherbeaten skin, and her body enveloped in that shapeless bathrobe, she was breathtakingly beautiful to both men.

She broke the silence. "How many pancakes are you good for, Dad?"

They pulled out their chairs, tucked in their napkins. Coffee was poured, pancakes were on each plate, and syrup waited in the treasured little pitcher. Jerry couldn't contain himself, so deep was his happiness and faith in whatever the jigsaw of his life might produce. He stretched out his arms, reaching for their hands on either side of him. With all hands joined, he flung their arms into the air, crying from an old hymn, "Welcome happy morning, age to age shall say!" and all three shouted "Halleluhah!"

Later that Easter day, positioning his beautiful egg on his bureau, Jerry mused to himself, "It is too heavy to have been blown and is therefore not empty, fragile. That is a comfort. But is it hard-boiled, rigid, unchangeable, or is it still in almost liquid form, full of promise and richness?"

As he lay in bed, rethinking the day, he added up the score. Jerry followed the local and state news carefully on the radio, particularly the activities of the Legislature, now within a month or so of winding up this session. Many questions were being debated that he had paid no attention to before, ranging from education to environment to labor disputes and welfare programs. All were now interesting to him and seen in an entirely new light. And almost all of those already passed by the Legislature were dependent for funding on the decisions of the Appropriations Committee. By law the state had to stay within the budget.

If he was to continue to live in Maine, in his present role, he wanted to be a real part of what went on. But how to choose a cause or interest? Would he be limited by having to keep a low profile? How much, and how soon, would he dare to mingle with people? Were there local needs that would benefit from what he might have to offer? This region was so sparsely settled, and so poor, what decision might make a difference in a positive way? What suggestions from him would be acceptable?

Stan had always kept out of area affairs, consciously nurturing self-sufficiency and independence. Did he not care under what conditions his neighbors lived, be they one mile or ten miles away? Maybe this attitude and lifestyle should be talked out. Jerry was too young, too restless and energetic, to settle for just handyman activity. He and Stan had had different reasons for their departures from the rat race. Did they have the same ideals of personal satisfaction and community responsibility, or different ones? Stan was governed by the seasons, the natural laws of growth and harvest, and the challenge to produce while not upsetting nature's rules. It was a full-time job worthy of respect, but the days of the subsistence farmer were numbered, and all Jerry's training and expertise were aimed at finding alternatives or solutions to just this type of adapting to change.

Sparsely inhabited Northern Maine was rich in beauty, freedom (so far), and modest opportunities to live unbothered by the feds or power pressures typical of the urban areas. But, in spite of dreams, would and could this life last? And did these people really want it to? Those with TVs saw other lifestyles. How many of those living in poorer areas were there because they chose to be, like the Warners? Were welfare handouts preferable to admitting that their traditional occupations of fishing, farming, or lumbering were outdated and unproductive? Why did so many of the promising youth leave the state? How many were simply the chronically poor, uneducated, malnourished product of lethargy? Mere survival is not an objective of choice but a necessity. How to help aspirationless human beings aim higher, higher than the animals with whom they shared the wilds, and give them ambition based on hope and self-confidence? Jerry's mind whirled as he lay in bed, looking at the stars in the clear night sky, and accepted his own present ignorance and lack of direction.

That Easter night he made his re-birthday in terms of seeking a purpose, to step by step find a path to making not only a rewarding life for himself but a positive difference to those in whom a spark still burned. Jerry Warner was on his way at last.

Chapter 3: Summer 1987

Portland

April had turned into May, and May to June. The legislative session was duty-bound to adjourn in June, though many bills still waited for review and decision. The Appropriations Committee had sharpened its fiscally responsible knives in order to wind up with expenses that could be met. Legislators from the northern counties drank in the alien beauty of the azaleas and even forsythia that surrounded Blaine House, the governor's mansion. Everyone lived for weekends and family preparations for summer. The Legislature was anxious to adjourn.

Days in which the House was not actually in session did not count as legislative days, so on into June the committees worked. Bills that had been deliberately held back for partisan reasons were given short shrift, just as the committee chairmen had planned. Strategists knew few members would draw out the session by protesting and thus infuriating even their own party; those bills would just reappear next session. Committees worked late into the afternoons and many evenings; the building was not air-conditioned, and tempers grew short. On the days they did sit, the House rules of decorum forbade the removal of ties and coats by the gentlemen, no matter what the temperature. They had to count on some kindhearted or politically motivated female legislator to make a motion that such flagrant informality be allowed. Patsy had shrewdly taken her turn in this.

Final bills were presented, argued over, and sent to the printers for amending. Wait, wait, wait. Funny stories were told, to kill time. Sentimental speeches were delivered. Lunch hours became quite lengthy and often picnics sprouted up with the dandelions on the State House lawn. One restaurant known for its May wine, complete with a floating strawberry, did much to appease the impatient members, or unleash their tongues.

And, finally, the session was over. It had produced little new, good or bad, but had kept the state moving without embarrassing headlines and without scandals, personal or otherwise. Some perennial bills had finally been passed, others buried forever. New ideas had surfaced that needed more study. Taxes had not risen. The Ship of State was pretty seaworthy, in spite of partisanship in the bilges.

As it was his prerogative by long tradition, on that last day the most elderly member, who had actually not said a word on the floor during the entire session, stood shakily. "Mr. Speaker, Ladies and Gentlemen of the House. I move we adjourn, sine die."

And with cheers everyone went forward to the rostrum to receive their final paycheck, then carried their dog-eared and bulging blue notebooks to the rear and dumped them in a trash bin. They shook hands with anybody, friend or foe, promised to keep in touch, and headed for home, to relax with their families or to reap the most they could from fertile fields, ice-cold waters, laden orchards, and spendthrift tourists.

Patsy's mind was working on two levels as she drove south. Considering herself now a professional, she was determined to prove it to fellow legislators come January, 1988, and was already planning. Being a pawn on the board was no fun; she was going to become a piece in the back row.

Dreading the aloneness of this first widowed summer, she had booked a Mediterranean cruise for late August. To test herself and to learn how to travel as a single, she had deliberately chosen to go alone. Bill had taken her on one trip to England, for business, but now, if she wanted to see something of the world, it was up to her to take the initiative. But first she would oversee some necessary repairs to her house, visit her children and catch up with friends. She would lose, possibly, the ten pounds she had put on by living on restaurant meals with no exercise, and read, read, read about the Near East, Greek Islands, and Venice.

Singing all the way down I-95, she gloried in the beauty of Maine in June. Lilacs were a thing of the past, but stately lupines were massed on every banking, and the fields were strewn with daisies and buttercups. Cows were grazing outdoors once more, and it seemed to her that every shop and house was sporting fresh paint, prepared for visitors. Boatyards were emptying of their winter fleets. Canvas and plastic shrouds had been removed from yachts, caulking, painting, and varnishing had kept owners busy over weekends, and one by one the graceful craft had been launched for yet another season, joining the working boats up and down the coast.

Traffic had increased noticeably on I-95, with many northbound autos carrying bicycles, canoes, or kayaks on the roof, or hauling larger boats or campers. Lumbering RV's slowed the flow considerably. July 4th was still two weeks away, but "they" had arrived.

As she approached Portland on Rte 295 she was rewarded by a vista of the city, her city, silhouetted against the soft blue sky. High-rises on the eastern end of the peninsula did not dwarf the sturdy old Observatory, a tower built early in the city's history and from which owners and wives had spotted returning sailing vessels that might have been gone for years. The spire of the Catholic Cathedral, the massive shape of a residence for the elderly, new bank buildings, the cupola and weathervane of City Hall, the monumental majesty of Maine Medical Center, gave her a sense of pride in an adopted city that advertised its values by its skyline. Portland put faith, care of the less fortunate, government, and health care center stage, with pride.

She skirted Back Cove, an almost inland body. Wind-surfers dotted the water, fitness buffs jogged with determination, and families, lovers, seniors and, of course, countless leashed dogs took advantage of this unique area of the city. But soon, pulling into her driveway, she giggled. "Forget the grandiose dreams, the headlines, the glory, kid. Forget Greece and Istanbul. Get busy and mow that lawn. You're back in the real world, and the grass is a foot high."

* * * * *

Donato Vassalo, Esq. looked out his office window, over rooftops, to the ever-changing activity of Portland Harbor, and daydreamed. Just admitted as a very minor partner to one of Portland's largest law firms, he felt he was one step closer to a plan he had made almost a dozen years ago.

During the summer before his senior year at Portland's Jesuit High School he had worked as a volunteer on a gubernatorial campaign. In those ten weeks he had become a dedicated political junkie, loving the game, the organizing, and the feeling of participating in a very small way in history. Meeting party leaders gave him role models and advisors for the future.

That fall every minute he could take from school was spent at Democratic gubernatorial campaign headquarters, or on the road, delivering brochures, putting up signs, decorating halls, and stuffing endless envelopes. To everyone's surprise an Independent had won in that election of 1974, but the "disease" of politics was well established in the young man's veins. There would be other campaigns.

Don was ambitious and capable; so far he had succeeded at everything he'd tackled. Smart, personable, athletic, he was voted Most Likely to Succeed at high school, and walked off the graduation platform with several awards and the comfortable knowledge that he had been accepted at Holy Cross. During the next vacations he deliberately worked at a variety of jobs, to experience firsthand the reality of mass transportation, tourism, and papermaking. In one of those summers, as a treat to himself and as a rite of passage, he joined a friend and crossed the country in a dilapidated old van, the epitome of irresponsibly cheerful hippies. By way of contrast, the summer of his senior year he landed an internship in Washington, working in a senator's office, another heady experience.

After graduation it was on to Boston and the the B.U. law school, where he made the Law Review and met and married Marilyn LaPierre of Lewiston, Maine, a Mt. Holyoke graduate working for her M.S.W. at Simmons. They both graduated in 1981.

So much for the preliminaries. From that point all his energies were directed toward just one goal . . . the governorship or a seat in Congress by 1994, at the very latest. Twelve years to do so much! He chose as his mentor a behind-the-scenes politician, Patrick O'Flynn, a man who had never sought office, had few ideological or political hang-ups, but was exceedingly well-versed in how to create a winning Democratic candidate or campaign. No fancy titles or party positions handicapped this man, but he was known statewide in the smoke-filled rooms of Democratic strategists. He earned his livelihood as a wholesale grocer with connections all over Maine. He was as Irish as Don was Italian.

"Donny, m'boy, you probably know that there are just three keys to winning political office: name recognition, reliable sources of campaign funds, and, most important, having a platform that keeps a fire in your belly burning night and day. Candidates only seeking personal power are spotted right away, unless, of course, they have expensive and talented image-makers."

They were meeting on a bench in Portland's Monument Square the week after Don graduated from law school. Pat took a few minutes to enjoy the summer lunch-hour crowds of strollers, street musicians, and shoppers passing by, while Don digested those words of wisdom.

"You come from a big, close, well-respected Italian family from working-class Munjoy Hill, and you were brought up in the suburban Deering area. That's a great start. You're a native through and through; no one can ever label you a carpetbagger and today that's a big plus. Your background is like solid gold.

"As a first assignment, I want you to make 3 x 5 cards or enter into a computer the names of everyone you know on the Hill, Irish, Italians, and the rest. Everyone you ever went to school with, from grammar school through Lincoln Jr. High to Cheverus. Who was in your Cub Scout den, your Little League team, your Sunday School class, served with you as an acolyte? Those cute girls you dated. Then ask your wife to do the same. You're lucky to have her as a key to the French vote. Boys and girls, men and women. Jews, Protestants, black, white, and khaki. Democrats, Republicans, and Independent. Neighbors, cops, teachers, employers. Everybody you know who would vote for you or could be persuaded to. Then add the friends you made at college and law school. They may not vote in Maine but they'll send in campaign contributions. Names, addresses, phones, occupations, anything else you know about them. You get the picture?

"Next, start writing short, meaty and memorable letters to the editor, raising questions, espousing causes, battling the bad guys, and being the cool new voice of reason. Establish your name and positions in reader's minds. Don't limit yourself to the Portland papers. Hit the weeklies, the *Sunday Telegram* and the *Bangor Daily News*, on issues important to their regions. Just don't overdo it. And get visibly involved in the community. Go to meetings on sensitive issues. Speak up."

The older man looked him straight in the eye now, dead serious. "There's a lot of hype in the world today. Candidates are just like soap or any other product; an image has to be created that makes people want to buy, or vote. But if the soap doesn't get junior's jeans clean, forget it. Build your image but make sure it's the real you. Phoneys don't last long; the not-so-dumb public doesn't like being taken. A lot of voters are tired of being manipulated by false promises and Madison Avenue image-makers. They're wising up. So keep your nose clean. Negative campaigns aren't very nice but what is dug up is not easily forgotten. No dirty laundry, I hope?" Don had smiled easily as he shook his head. That same old question.

O'Flynn shifted his position on the bench and studied the sky a minute.

"Now that you've moved back to Maine, what are your own immediate plans? Other than eventually running the state, of course."

Don had answered honestly. "I've applied for a job in the Attorney General's office. Even starting off at the bottom of that ladder would give me statewide experience as well as exposure. It would look great on my resume or campaign brochure. Then I would try to find a spot in a good Portland firm, possibly getting lobbying assignments, which would make me familiar to legislators and would teach me the fine points of how it all works up there."

"Donny boy, you're almost ahead of me in planning. What else?"

"I was active in the Cheverus Key Club, so the Kiwanis might take me in. Volunteering for United Way campaigns as a Loaned Executive, if my firm would allow it. Seeking membership on boards of nonprofit agencies that are making a real difference. Coaching Little League teams or kids' basketball, but also improving my own golf game at a nice middle-income country club. And certainly getting on to the Portland Democratic City Committee, and then the County Committee, working on every election. By 1988 I should run for the Maine House, or even Senate."

"And when do you plan to practice law, have good times with your wife and friends?" Pat's eyes were smiling, but his voice a bit sarcastic. "You haven't even left enough time in there to start a family!"

Donny had chuckled. "That's all taken care of, due in November."

Now it was 1987. During the last five years all had worked out as planned. He was representing several of the firm's smaller clients as a lobbyist, he had made a good name for himself in the AG's office, the other activities took a great deal of his time, but not so much that he was robbed of the pleasures of young Don Jr. and Sam. Their lively faces smiled out at him from the pictures frame on his desk.

He looked at his watch. Time to walk over to Congress St, follow it up the Hill, past the Observatory, and then turn off to where his grandmother lived on the top floor of an old frame three-decker, just a block or so from the Eastern Promenade and Casco Bay. He had a standing date for lunch with her every Tuesday and he was always nourished in many ways.

She was waiting in her doorway for him. Held close to her formidable bosom, he felt just as safe and loved as he had when sitting in her lap as a little boy. She was a large woman, tall, heavy, and solid. Iron-gray hair was pulled back in a bun, doing nothing to soften her rugged features. Dark smudges under her eyes accentuated their brown depths, her nose was beak-like, and her mouth was strong, unsoftened by laugh lines. In repose her face was almost forbidding, hinting at the tough peasant stock from which she came, but at the sight or sound of family the eyes glowed with warmth and her smile crumbled what had seemed a rigid structure.

"You look well, my Donato, except maybe a little tired. How is the fine Marilyn, and my bambinos?" Assured they were all well, she led him into the living room.

It glowed with rich wine velvet upholstery and draperies, shining carved mahogany chairs and tables, luxuriant plants, and touches of brass and gilt decoration. Framed family photos stood on every flat surface, and on the walls hung more, competing for space with religious scenes, a crucifix, large prints of St. Peter's, the Coliseum, and a small village on the coast near Anzio.

"I know you never can take all the time I hope for, so let's eat and talk right now. What's going on in that world at the foot of my hill?"

Don sat where he always did at the table. She knew he loved to look out over the Eastern Promenade and Casco Bay as he ate, and her dining room had a view most Portlanders would die for. French doors led out onto a small porch, and one could count on cool breezes there in summer heat. Studded with islands and enlivened with passing ships and sails, the bay was a sight far more beautiful than that of the oil tanks, railroad bridges, and warehouses that met the eyes of residents on the more fashionable Western Promenade.

Colorful antipasto was waiting for them, firm crusty bread, and then the pasta with pesto sauce, one of his favorite lunches. Then Gramma asked a question that had been bothering her for a long time.

"They do such crazy things in Washington, even in Augusta. Why, my Donato, do you want to join them?"

He looked at her seriously.

"Because of what you just said. Not about doing crazy things, but because you used the word 'they' to describe our Congress and our Legislature. I believe, Gramma, that when people in this country use that word, in that way, they no longer see those legislators, or governors, as individuals, elected by themselves. Those voters see them as faceless and nameless, remote beings wielding a power that the voter can no longer control. It's as if 'they' were the enemy. And when our nation, or any nation, reaches that point of disillusion or hopelessness, it is frightening.

"Do you know the sentence everyone uses when they try out a new typewriter? 'Now is the time for all good men to come to the aid of the party'." He pushed his chair back and placed his napkin on the table. "That's my answer, Gramma. Think about it, and give me your opinion next week."

He bent to kiss her, loved the feel of her cheek, hugged her, and went down the stairs.

* * * * *

Harding's Corner

Jerry was surprised that nothing had been done to prepare the little farm stand for summer. Stan had his own ideas about that and, true to form, it never occurred to him to share them. He had heard that a new Farmer's Market was opening up on Saturdays just outside Millinocket and, giving Susan and Jerry little warning, he put them to work the last Friday evening in June. Peas and asparagus, lettuces, spinach, beet greens, strawberries and rhubarb were garnered and prepared for not only the townsfolk but for campers already pouring into Baxter State Park.

On the early morning drive over, Stan was unusually quiet except when addressed, at which times he was downright testy. Susan caught Jerry's eye and winked, mouthing the word "nervous." Stan Warner was rejoining the human race! Like the produce in his truck, he had finally pushed his way up out of the cold and dark and was seeking warmth and sunshine.

The Farmer's Market was a great success. About twelve other families showed up, some with few items, others with much, and all friendly, all new at this game. Most were sold out by noon.

After that, on Friday evenings the Happy Hour was moved outdoors to the big picnic table and, cocktail glasses within easy reach, both men and Susan washed, weighed, and bundled vegetables and berries. Susan contributed breads with real character and flavor, huge sticky cinnamon buns, and wonderfully flaky sugar cookies. Firewood lined the bottom of the truck; then the produce and baked goods were put in place and covered with a plastic drop cloth. Scales, cash box, and early flowers made up the load. By six on Saturday mornings they were on their way.

All over the state these markets had emerged, providing not only fresh vegetables and fruits to a public learning to discriminate, but a bit of extra income and socializing to these farm men and women who often lived quite isolated lives.

Susan had been a bit nervous about how Jerry would be received, but she had nothing to fear. Introduced as their son lately returned from business ventures overseas, he was politely looked over the first week, then accepted. Quiet, often deferential, and unfailingly friendly, he became one of the group. People's day-to-day lives held enough uncertainties without wasting energy poking into the backgrounds of each newcomer who crossed their paths.

The new Jerry Warner was experiencing another rebirth into the great basic of humanity's world, its sustenance. He was both humbled and awestruck by all he was learning. Like the burgeoning gardens, he felt himself growing in a new way, closer to people as well as closer to the earth that supported him and to the air that gave him life. Always a city boy, he had never been introduced to the mystery of how food appeared on his table. Its history before it showed up in the supermarket had been of no interest or concern; his only agricultural education had been the study of corn futures and the like at business school,

Since Stan's peas went into the ground in April, followed by all the other vegetable at the proper times, Jerry had marveled at the new to him homely miracles. How did that tiny brown speck in his palm have the knowledge to become a bright orange carrot, while another of the same size produced a cheerful red radish? Seed catalogues were the farmers' classic literature as they decided which strains to gamble on this season. He had been in the chemical business, but had given little thought to what produced the green in spinach.

Susan's creativity came into play. She brought a card table one week and covered it with a gay cloth, her baked goods, and bouquets. On the truck's tail she arranged the greens and fruits with a professional eye to color, and sprayed them gently with fresh water. A bright ribbon was braided into her hair. Other wives took note and politely complimented her, but a friendly war was on. Someone thought of providing lemonade for thirsty shoppers. A few craft items competed for attention, and undiscovered talents were brought to light. More and more newcomers could be spotted each week by their white legs and sunburned noses.

One Friday night while Stan was relaxing after his preparations, Susan, passing, patted him on the top of his head and bent to kiss him, "What's all this about, woman? You want something?"

"Sure do," she laughed, and the next morning there was an extra passenger in the truck, the friskiest and whitest little lamb of her flock.

Tethered to their truck, it had such appeal that before noon the Warners were sold out and on their way home, the lamb snuggled in Susan's lap, exhausted from petting.

After that kittens, puppies, piglets and even a nanny-goat were displayed. Beets, broccoli, zucchini, and carrots soon added more color and variety as the summer ripened, and they were tied in neater, more appealing bundles. Berries were favorites.

Jerry realized that, given a few new ideas and encouraged, many of these families could pull themselves out of the ruts they had settled into. A bit of recognition just might do it. The old confidence and incentive he had had in the corporate world of international trade were actually coming back in terms of, unbelievably, berries, beans, and bread.

At the *Bangor Daily News* the features editor next Monday read and reread a letter from a Jerry Warner, then called for one of his writers. On the following Saturday that writer and a photographer arrived, still sleepy, at the market site as the farm trucks backed into their accustomed spots.

By the next weekend half the state of Maine knew all about the emergence of this innovative vegetable stand on the edge of the wilderness. It became a destination in itself, not just a local convenience. Saturdays on Rt. 11 resembled old English market days.

Spurred on by this success, gaining his own self-confidence and direction, Jerry began investigating other fields, not of vegetables, but of ideas, problems, and possible solutions. One fine day, following the purloined map, he retraced his way to Kidney Pond and the camp that really saved his life. Nothing had changed; the owners had not yet returned. On the table he left a case of B&M baked beans, a bottle of fine Scotch, a box of cigars, and the can-opener, sporting a newly gilded handle. The owners might feel a miracle had taken place, but they would be in ignorance as to what miracle.

He wrote Joel frequently, throwing him questions, testing out plans, asking for advice. Additional trips to libraries in Bangor and the State University in Orono resulted in many late nights of reading and note-taking. If Joel's idea of a memorial fund was put into motion, what should the cause be? Based on what information? Jerry didn't dream of just one more fund created to simply be another Band-Aid. Nor did he want to raise money for yet another report on Maine's future, to take its place beside the many dusty ones preceding it.

Joel's last letter would have been funny if it wasn't so serious. "I don't know how to go about starting up a fund to memorialize an old buddy who is actually enjoying an outdoor summer in Maine while we toil in our steel and cement air-conditioned beehives.

"Meanwhile, it is fun making first drafts of a fund-raising letter, playing on all the poetry in my Brahmin soul. When one of these comes anywhere near close I'll shoot it up to you. We've got to make the recipients feel damn lucky to even be on our list, so we'll have to be fairly specific as to goals.

"Your research sounds great and none of it will ever be wasted. I can't keep Carol in the dark much longer as she often remarks on how amazingly I've recovered from your death. I'm either guilty of being a lousy friend or of not telling her the good news. Hey, just had an idea. How about letting us camp on the farm, out of your way but giving us all an opportunity for a long, uninterrupted powwow? Lemme know!"

So on a warm weekend Joel and Carol drove into the Warners' yard towing a rented camper with a small boat lashed on top. Joel had prepared Carol for Jerry's resurrection, as he knew she wouldn't handle a miracle of that magnitude with much aplomb otherwise.

Carol was small but not petite, no French doll, and in good shape. Her brown curls were short, her makeup was minimal, and her shorts and shirt had seen service in her garden as well as on the tennis courts. There were more calluses on her hands than nail polish; her hazel eyes glowed with friendship, common sense, and fun.

After her initial squeals, tears, and hugs there were introductions all around. Soon the trailer was towed down through the field to a level, shorefront site and the boat launched and moored. The Warners watched with amusement as the McLeans transformed a metal box into a good-sized home; folding chairs, a grill, and bikes all found places outside.

Dusty and hot from the trip, the McLeans changed into bathing suits. Jerry simply handed his watch to Stan, took off his shirt and shoes, and plunged with his friends into the water, all whooping and splashing like teenagers.

Later, with the two extra pairs of hands, preparations for market next day went quickly. Then the picnic table assumed its natural role of bar and buffet, coals were lit in the old rusting grill, and drinks were handed around. For a little while there was just a contented silence, created by the euphoria of sharing a magnificent sunset over the mountains and lake with thoroughly congenial companions.

Practical Susan broke the spell by suggesting that the first corn of the season be picked before dark. Stan let Joel and Jerry have a chance to talk while picking, and Carol went inside to help Susan with the rest of dinner. She stood beside her hostess at the counter for a minute as Susan tossed the potato salad, then just opened her arms and held her close. "I don't know who or what brings these things about, but aren't we all lucky? I just hope you and Stan have needed us as much as we three have needed you."

Quietly Susan, such a loner for so long, replied, "You'll never know how much. And I'll admit to being very nervous about this visit, a country mouse wanting so much to have you both understand and accept us, for Jerry's sake. I was terrified you were going to be a sophisticated suburban clotheshorse, Sak's or Bonwit's, and bored to death with me, my faded jeans and pigtail. I'm particularly happy for Jerry as he sees us all really enjoying each other. We four are all the family he has."

"Coals are ready, ladies," called Stan. Out went the marinated lamb shanks, salad, and dessert fruit. The corn pickers were back, shucking, and Susan made sure boiling water was ready in a big pot on the stove. Places were set and a last round of drinks provided while the lamb sputtered over the coals.

When they were seated, Jerry said quietly, "I'm not going to get maudlin, but even if the calendar says August, I'm feeling very Thanksgivingy. Praise God from whom all blessings flow,"

The McLeans thoroughly enjoyed the Farmer's Market stint the next morning, and Joel marveled at how easily Jerry mingled with a very mixed group of people with whom he himself could not spin a thread. Recently, on the rare occasions when he was in alien gatherings such as this, he was beginning to feel less comfortable, realizing that his own society was limited to a relatively small number and was based, more often than not, on birth rather than accomplishment. Had he really had a "privileged" childhood, or had he actually been deprived?

That afternoon the three men climbed up the little hill to the blue spruce, settled themselves carefully to enjoy the view, and got down to work. Jerry had kept Stan current with his and Joel's thinking and had sought his opinions. Stan's marketing skills of many years ago were basically as sound as ever, though innocent of the latest technological aids or lingo.

"Marketing boils down to just one premise: making the other guy want something you have and be willing to pay for it, and that's a skill gadgets can't do for you," he stated. The younger men agreed with him.

Jerry reported, "My study has been devoted to Maine, not just because we all love it and want to help it if, where, and when help is needed, but because of its rich diversity. It seems a perfect lab for a pilot program. Agreed?

"Southern Maine is prosperous, moving, and definitely 'with it' as far as technology and services are concerned. It is very attractive to well-trained yuppies with MBA's, electronic skills, or law degrees. Portland, the state's largest city, is situated on a good harbor about fifty miles from the New Hampshire border and then a hop, skip, and a jump to Boston. It's booming.

" Real estate is climbing, service industries are growing, art and music are well served, and fine new restaurants are opening every week. Portland is drawing more and more conventions. Medical facilities have national reputations. A fast-developing branch of the State University provides good graduate degree programs, including a Law School. It's retiree heaven.

"The coast up as far as Camden, or even Ellsworth, is doing OK too. Real estate prices have never been better there either, based on location, location, location. Entrepreneurial businesses do well, whether manufacturing, handcrafts, or technical. Again, retirees or yuppies seeking quality of life are moving in every day.

"Routes 495 and 95 are the main arteries of economic growth, sort of what Rte 128 proved to be in Massachusetts. Route 1 goes through some nice older towns and is the favorite of tourists looking for atmosphere and antiques.

"Bangor is beginning to bloom again since its days as the Queen City of the lumber trade, but that's about it. The counties to the west and those in the northeast need help. They are based on an agricultural economy that is passing on, or a fishing economy that is suffering from both overfishing and mindless Washington regulations. There are some woodworking plants and mills still, but little interest in or money for new methods, expansion, or new products. Lotsa tourist centers, but they are seasonal. Roads go north and south, with little connecting them, through thousands of acres of woods and interrupted by hundreds of lakes and ponds, largely owned by paper companies.

"So you can see there are at least two Maines. The Southern section is almost part of the Northeast's prosperous megalopolis, though still with a much better quality of life. West, north, and northeast of Augusta will have to work hard to catch up. However, those are *exactly* the areas having the image in most out-of-staters' minds of what Maine is and what they like about it: lakes, big woods, mountains, moose, rugged individuals who talk funny, quaint small towns, like Christmas cards, and good harbors and coves for gunk-holing yachters.

"Stan, you're the only resident here. How much of this would you agree with?"

"Pretty much on the button, though I've had little personal experience with much of it. There's a lot of money in these woods, the paper companies' woods, but precious little of that stays in Maine. There are a lot of outsiders investing in ski and hunting facilities, too, so right now that potential is in other hands. However, there's a couple of things you haven't mentioned.

"Time and again we hear or read of the great reputation Maine workers have. Their work ethic and ability to learn new skills while hanging on to the old ones are famous. But too many of our young people, untrained here, are leaving the state for better training and jobs elsewhere, while companies depending on trained technologists can't find 'em here and so decide to expand out of state.

"It's sort of a chicken and egg situation . . . what comes first, aspirations or education? Some poor we'll always have, just as every state does, but we have a lot of good people just needing a little push of hope and a helping mentor to find 'there's no place like home.'"

Joel had learned much from Jerry's letters, but still had questions.

"What about small businesses? Is there much support for entrepreneurs from either private capital or the state? What percent of the state's economy is small business, and what percent of the population does that section employ? Skilled or unskilled labor? Opportunities for employees to buy in? Has the virus of overregulation hit here yet? How about insurance rates and taxes?"

"Good questions, Joel." Jerry rummaged through his papers. "It's a much larger percent than you'd think, and a lot of these little businesses have imaginative, creative owners with hopes of worldwide distribution. Don't forget, Maine slippers have gone to the moon, patchwork skirts go to Fifth Avenue, and the lobster eaten today in Chicago slept last night in Penobscot Bay. Damn, I can't find those figures, but I'll get them to you both.

"I have a list of topics I want to do more study on, so if it's OK with you, I'll finish those up and send you a report. Each is on a subject vital to Maine's image and welfare and each strongly affects the others. I'll have the latest statistics and plans for each of them. And, though I know it is vulgar to talk about money, we'll need some start-up cash pretty soon. I can't go on borrowing Stan's truck forever, and there's got to be an available phone. Now think about this." He was so pleased with what he was about to propose that they began to grin too.

"We need an accessible office, as I think Susan would poison the lot of us if we took over her kitchen, which is hardly on the beaten track anyway. Not far from here is a little building that played a big part in this story. How about taking over that beat-up little store at Harding's Corner? Power and phone lines go by there, and even an occasional mail truck."

Stan boomed with excitement. "Great idea. I guess I'm sentimental too. Another question. What are we going to call this enterprise? As we've been shooting the breeze a name has occurred to me. Try it out." He paused and held his breath; he wanted so much for them to like it.

"Well?" Joel teased.

"So far Jerry or Webb or whatever you want to call him has come back to life, and by that I mean really living. And damned if he isn't bringing me back too, after playing hermit for so long. We may just hit on a project that will reactivate the thinking and attitudes of many others."

Jerry laughed. "My God, what an optimist. C'mon, what's the name?"

Joel held his breath, hoping it wasn't too corny.

"I suggest we name it 'Phoenix Associates'."

Into Jerry's mind flashed the memory of that burning plane, once so full of laughter and hope, reported later to be nothing but ashes. This project, so named, might offer him redemption. He met Joel's eyes and knew they were seeing right into him, understanding completely. Jerry nodded and let Joel be the one to tell Stan that it couldn't be a better title.

After Joel said he'd find some money, starting with a visit to Phyllis, down the hill they went, deciding to try out the McLeans' little sailboat.

The women had spent the time exploring each others' interests, hopes, worries and pastimes. They were just as compatible as they'd hoped to be. Carol knew that Susan was artistic and asked to see some paintings, so she was led to the "studio".

"Do you know how very, very good these are?" Carol asked, overwhelmed by what she was shown. "I work part-time in a gallery outside

Boston, in Wellesley, and we've had nothing as exciting, as sensitive or finished as these. Would you ever consider letting us exhibit them for you?"

Susan was more than surprised. Stan had always told her that everything she created was perfect, because that is what a husband is meant to say. Jerry's enthusiasm was probably the same and, being Susan, she didn't believe either of them. But this was different.

"Oh my, I would have to think about that. How many would you want? Are these frames Stan made OK?" Her head was dithering inside.

"Tell you what. Why don't you come down for a fall visit, look at the gallery, experience a few days of life in the big city, 'shop till you drop,' and then make up your mind? Maybe it could be our Christmas show if you come early enough."

Life was turning from familiar reality to a dream world for Susan this summer. Why not extend it into the fall before she woke up?

When the men came down from the hill they agreed with the plan wholeheartedly, sorry Jerry couldn't join them for fear of being recognized. The great mission of the brand-new Phoenix Associates could not be jeopardized by even something as splendid as Susan's one-woman show.

* * * * *

Chicago

Driving to meet Joel at the airport, Phyllis reviewed the events of the six months since the crash. She felt that an accounting was due good, faithful Joel, and was quite proud of what she would tell him. There had been no great accomplishments, no dragons slain, but she seemed to be inching forward, every day, in a direction that would please him. His approval surprisingly meant a lot to her. Father figure?

Jack, seated like royalty beside her in the front seat, had been responsible for much. He had unerringly found little cracks in her defenses and had wagged, slobbered, and demanded his way in. Jack would seldom take "no" for an answer, so her lifelong talent for making up excuses to avoid situations fell on deaf doggy ears. Neurotic women were definitely not his bag, or bone. In fair weather or foul he insisted on long walks, and he sometimes led her into strange territory, causing her to observe her surroundings more closely and often to thank him for his curiosity. It had been fun discovering her neighborhood. So many lovely gardens; so many friendly children. Why had Webb never suggested such a thing? Would she have assented if he had?

One late afternoon, in a strange new area, Jack had been threatened and almost attacked by a territory-conscious dog larger and younger than he. Phyllis routed the stranger with firm orders and a stick. As they departed with some semblance of dignity, she realized that she had not panicked, was not shaking, and was actually pleased with her handling of the incident. Was it because she had thought of Jack's safety rather than her own? Or because there had been no one else to cope if she hadn't? No matter, she'd done it.

Jarrett Enterprises had settled down to her liking, and the board had found a man to replace Webb as CEO. Roger Milliken, originally from the cattle country of Montana, knew and understood the business, respected the company, and quickly earned the admiration of the board and staff. Firm but fair, he was actually taking control quickly without being perceived as a threat. Almost intuitively, he avoided falling into the trap of being compared to Webb in style or methods. Phyllis admired his quiet decisiveness and his focus.

She had invited him to dinner tonight. Divorced many years earlier, he had moved into an apartment overlooking the lake, not far from the office, and seemed to enjoy getting out of the city when given the opportunity. Phyllis wanted Joel to meet him and give her his opinion. Depending on how this visit worked out, she would perhaps also share with Joel what she was learning from her shrink. That was still a very private experience, but perhaps the most important of the last six months. Picking up the phone and making her first appointment had taken more courage than she'd given herself credit for; mental illness carried a stigma that the common cold did not. Now she actually looked forward to each meeting and had learned that there was nothing demeaning in seeking such help. Actually, it probably was dumb not to, and maybe, just maybe, she should have done it years and years ago.

One Sunday morning she had decided to go to church for the express purpose of getting someone to point out the suggested doctor to her, so she could look him over. At the coffee hour after the service she had been about to put her plan into action when a round and very cheery gentleman offered her a doughnut and introduced himself.

"Mrs. Lewis, I'm Dr. Henry Burton, a friend of Webb's. I make a point of butting into people's lives and helping if they are willing. How about it? Give me a call." No deep-set, searching eyes, no beard, no long words and, she discovered, no couch.

The kindly doctor was teaching her to look at herself, past and present, and guiding her very gently into options and solutions. She was slowly learning not to blame others, but to take responsibility for herself, and to look ahead, not back. She relied less and less on the "panic" pills he had initially prescribed.

Now Joel was waiting at the baggage carousel and felt, as he hugged her, that this was a more relaxed, warm Phyllis than he had seen for years. Having been led to believe, through mail and phone, that "Jack" was a new two-legged male interest in her life, he broke into roars of laughter upon meeting the mutt. Jack, a bit grudgingly, found him acceptable and relinquished the front seat. So far so good.

Midsummer heat blanketed the area, and Phyllis's invitation to have a swim sounded great. Seated on the edge of her pool, feet dangling in the water, he brought her up to date on Carol, the kids, and harmless gossip about their few mutual friends. They still had an hour or so till Milliken was due, so Joel approached the business that had brought him so that Phyllis could have time to think it over thoroughly before he left the next day. He needed her endorsement as well as financial support..

"From time to time since your tragedy I have had calls and letters from old friends of Webb's asking if there was to be a memorial fund or if perhaps you had named some charity as a suggestion for gifts. You have probably had the same experience?"

She nodded, truly relieved that finally the subject was opened up. Knowing something was expected, she felt at least that much was owed to Webb. "What ideas do you have, Joel?"

He answered slowly. "Very often people, in their lives, have been connected strongly to one specific charity, institution, or cause. However, Webb was too young to have made such a decision, and, I feel, was still testing and probing various fields. The more I've thought about this the more I've felt we might possibly do something quite splendid, quite significant. If his tragedy had not brought such a strong reaction from so many, I would suggest some social agency right here and let it go at that. But the dramatic shock of the crash and the depth of feeling evidenced by the crowd at his service makes me feel there is a rich lode really asking to be tapped. Webb obviously made a real difference, and I think a lot of people want to continue to do that work in some way, and in his name."

The old irritation she still harbored threatened to become obvious. She was not ever going to let Joel or anyone else know how their admiration for Webb distressed and confused her. Why couldn't they remember him as she often did, an ineffective wimp? How could they be so blind?

Joel continued. "I am not talking about yet another Band-Aid of help for local education, child care, or low-income elderly, as examples. Nor am I thinking of financing some study of a major problem, a study that would end up on a dusty shelf with those preceding it. First I'd like to set up a mailing to discover the major concerns of Webb's friends and associates. This would mean contributors would have a sense of being given some say in the use and direction of their gifts and that these initial gifts in his honor might be simply seed money. If that research defines or suggests a program that is truly popular, exciting, and feasible, a permanent foundation in honor of Webb and many others in the future could be established. Annual pledges rather than just the one gift at the beginning would keep it going and growing. What's your reaction to that?"

Phyllis shook her head with real amusement. "You certainly do think big, Joel. And you've given me the feeling that you have a plan all set to go. Am I right?"

"Am I that obvious?" He chuckled. "You don't think I'd come all the way out here carrying just one idea, do you?" Glancing at her, he hoped to see some real interest. Not yet.

"Try this on for size. How about putting together a list of Webb's close friends from camp, college, and business and approaching them by mail, phone, or personal visits? We would ask them for initial donations to set up a simply equipped office, to hire an executive director, and possibly provide a car. We'd need your endorsement and help with names. This director would actually have three jobs. The first two would be to raise the seed money while also polling donors by questionnaire for ideas as to the purpose of the eventual fund. The third job, more important and time-consuming, would be to then evaluate the most interesting of those ideas as to their practicality and need. The bigger, more exciting the goal, the more enthusiasm we'll engender. Each donor will feel actively part of the adventure and decision making." He did not add that a certain someone was already studying many possible fields.

Phyllis looked a little puzzled. "Can you be more specific? Here I was thinking in terms of establishing a home for one-eyed mutts and you may be talking about changing the world."

"You've got it," crowed Joel. "What I have in mind is querying these friends to let us know what really disturbs them most about today's world, their children's' future, and changing values. And then ask what remedies they would suggest to improve things. We want to choose a really sensational course with a broad base of support. To keep their interest up we would send them newsletters of our research and reports of plans in action. Make 'em feel like knights setting up a new Round Table."

He was almost squirming with excitement and his restless feet were making great splashes in the cool water. Phyllis felt his energy and could have sworn that the leaves on the trees around the pool were giving up their listlessness and beginning to move in a new breeze. An intensity came into his eyes and voice. He continued, speaking more slowly and emphasizing every word.

"If in some little corner of this world a pilot program was tried that proved truly effective in solving local ills, the news might just get out, and the idea might be copied. Who knows?" and his arms made a huge circle. "With the use of modern communications technology, this program might move into hearts and minds all over the world! And even if it didn't, but managed to do some little good somewhere, it would be worth it. I guess I would rather 'light one candle than curse the darkness'."

At cocktails, and later at dinner, Joel sounded out a completely surprised Roger Milliken, whom he had liked immediately. Though well-trained in his field, and obviously capable, Milliken still maintained the clear-eyed freshness of his prairie boyhood. No world-weary patina clung to his manner; his speech, though very articulate, lacked phony polish. While hardly a diamond in the rough, he would never be taken for an Ivy League club man, and Joel drew him out a bit about his boyhood.

The oldest child of a cattle rancher, he had been tutored at home till old enough to drive himself to the nearest high school, twenty miles from the ranch. There he found his love and concern for nature in competition with what opened up to him in labs, and determined to combine the two. A degree in chemical engineering at the state university was followed by an MBA from Northwestern.

"Don't you miss the ranch life, the wide open spaces and good bone-tiredness at the end of the day?" queried Joel, who had spent one idyllic summer as a "dude."

"You bet I do. Since leaving home I have somehow managed to get back for a cattle drive or rodeo every year, just to keep me humble and in shape. And I always feel a bit hemmed in, want to stretch my vision beyond the big buildings and see the big mountains instead."

Joel was not so wrapped up in his great idea that he missed interesting signs of interplay between his companions. Roger didn't walk on tiptoe in discussions with Phyllis, who was long used to Webb's careful and protective handling. Occasionally this seemed to unsettle her, but Joel noted that she often looked to Roger for approval. There were no reminders of the manipulative or whining woman he'd known so long.

Good salesman that Joel was, he leapt from idea to idea, each one larger than the last. They began to make lists of projects, lists of names, and a budget for a reasonable amount of money to use as a goal for start-up.

The next day Joel kept his promise to Jerry and looked up Tommy and his mother. The boy had shot up during the past months and seemed even more mature and focused. He would be a high school freshman in the fall, and his personality was so appealing that Joel decided to keep more closely in touch and try to serve in Jerry's place.

He had been encouraged by a large personal check for Webb's memorial from Phyllis, and the promise of an even larger one from Jarrett Enterprises. She had also given permission to start looking for an executive director, location, etc., and had promised to help in any way she could, including a strong endorsement statement. If she had been even a little more enthusiastic Joel would have felt really guilty.

The trip had been more successful than he'd thought possible. Starting out with an idea of simply giving her a perfunctory explanation, he had expected almost total lack of interest, if not resistance. How to keep Webb dead? She must never meet Jerry. This was going to be a knife-edge trail to walk, with a good lawyer right beside him on the mountain.

A few days later Jerry received a letter from Joel describing the whole visit, though he held back a bit about Phyllis' changes and her reactions to Milliken.

"I never used the word dead, deceased, or anything that final. This fund is in your 'honor,' and I'm going to get a damn good lawyer on it so we'll never be charged with out-and-out misrepresentation. Here I am planning a good and noble thing yet feeling like a crook. Am I one?"

Jerry chuckled as he read that. Joel a crook? Never, unless they were all crooks. Were they?

"Also, be on the lookout for some good public relations person. We can do the original appeal letters if we have to, but sooner or later we're going to need real savvy. Someone with great talent and knowhow. Old

Piglet, we're in business, and Pooh is dreaming of very full hunny-pots."

* * * * *

Eastport, Maine

After putting her house and affairs in order and catching up with friends she had had to neglect all winter, Patsy took off to visit her son Charlie near Eastport. Though he telephoned frequently, she had not seen him since he came down to Augusta for her swearing-in back in January. A biologist specializing in marine life, he was employed by a small Atlantic Salmon farm. Aquaculture was just taking hold, hoping to prove its worth in Maine waters, as overfishing was threatening naturally produced fish such as haddock and cod and even lobster. With his landlord's permission he was also restoring and furnishing an old but sound cottage, once a fish-house, right on the water. Patsy was excited about seeing that too, as he was imaginative and his taste was faultless.

Even with its slow summer traffic, Patsy chose to drive up Rte 1. Much less tiring, really, than constant high speed on I-95. Beyond Bath and its mammoth shipyard Rte. 1 crossed marshes, visited picture postcard towns, accepted strips of small service shops as inevitable, and served as the spine from which ribs led inland or to seacoast villages.

Today she felt less touristy herself than in past trips up the coast. Now as she passed through each town she felt a new bonding as she knew exactly who served as that town's representative in Augusta. Partisanship reigned in the capitol, but once away from it the members of the Legislature became almost extended family, a nice feeling.

She was grateful for the perfect weather, warm and clear, as that meant her favorite view in all of Maine would be at its best. Approaching Lincolnville Beach she slowed down a bit to savor what was coming, There it was! Her eye swept down a long pasture, dotted with a few trees and grazing cows, on to the blue infinity of Penobscot Bay. Capable of many moods, marked with rocky, tree-clad islands of all sizes, most of them uninhabited, it swept majestically out to join the broad Atlantic.

To Patsy this was the absolute essence of the state, prepared to meet whatever challenges nature might hand out. The granite against which the surf often pounded spoke of indomitable strength, the hardy firs proved the tenacity of life, and the inhabited islands were communities going it alone without feeling the need for artificial support. With a bite to the clear air and a chill to the water, nothing was easy here, even at best. Strength, tenacity, and independence were the qualities of Maine's people, too. They could count on the sun rising each morning, seen or unseen, and the seasons and tide changing with regularity, period. The rest was up to them. Some people need the inspiration of towering mountain scenery, others find strength in the great cathedrals of the world or in Nature's generosity in tropical areas. Penobscot Bay, Maine gave Patsy an indispensable, overwhelming sense of awe, reverence, and support.

"Don't change" she prayed, and continued on her way.

Searsport, home of many sea captains in the past and now a charming antique center, was a bottleneck of browsing tourists. Past Bucksport with its huge paper mill, the road led through blueberry barrens to Ellsworth , the area's service center. Milbridge and Cherryfield were sites of not only a few magnificent old houses but of the state's Christmas wreath industry and production and processing of wild blueberries. Now she was truly downeast. She'd jump off for Eastport.

How she would have loved to see that town at its best, many years ago, a shipping port outranking even Boston and later home to the long departed sardine industry. Isolated geographically from the rest of the nation it was now a gallant community trying to stay alive. Fine old Federal-style houses still stood, though unable to hide their nakedness. No paint, shutters, or anything passing for a lawn covered their condition.

Aquaculture might just be the start of a renaissance. Hard-working people need something to work at and these people were hopeful, though aware of the challenges of Chilean and other foreign fisheries. Japanese markets were encouraging.

Driving along the coastal road a few more miles, Patsy followed directions and pulled into Charlie's yard. Respecting her children's' privacy as they respected hers, she knocked on the door of the cottage. Surprisingly it was opened by a tall, handsome man, black-haired, and dusky-skinned.

"Hello, I'm Charlie's mother." She put warmth into her voice, a smile in her eyes, hoping to cover this unforeseen situation graciously. Who was this man?

"Oh, I know, Mrs. Hudson. We're looking forward so much to having you here, and Charlie will be home anytime. I'm Hank, Hank Longbow." He put out his hand to shake hers, then took her suitcase from her, held the door, and ushered her inside.

She stepped into the living room and was drawn immediately to a large bay window at the far end. The view, though not as far-reaching, rivaled her favorite back at Lincolnville Beach, and had the advantage of being very close to the water. Fingers of land and small islands gave life to the surface of Cobscook Bay, and beyond was the silhouette of southern New Brunswick and the waters of the Bay of Fundy. As Patsy was turning to inspect the rest of the room she heard Charlie's cheerful "Hi, Mom" and his arms were around her. How good it was to get a strong male hug. Pulling back, they grinned at one another.

"How's that for a million-dollar view?"

"You, or the one out the window?" she countered.

One reason she loved being with her son was that he was almost a carbon copy of his dad. Just under six feet, and solid, with broad shoulders, he had a slim enough waist; most of his height was in his legs. His hair just missed being red and he was deeply tanned, not having the fair skin or blue eyes of many redheads. "Oh, you're still my best-looking son," and they laughed at their old joke.

"You and Hank have met, I see." Hank was pulling on a light jacket, preparing to go out. "I tried to get him to stay for supper, but he has other plans. We'll see him later."

The house had just one floor, with two bedrooms and bath off the living room. Patsy could see a reasonably sized kitchen on the other side. What looked like a fairly new and certainly dramatic fieldstone fireplace and chimney dominated one wall of the living room. Some of her own furniture, given to Charlie when he left home, seemed to welcome her as an old friend.

Satisfied that he was living in decent comfort, she settled into what had been his grandmother's wing chair and asked about his work. "I hope I'll be given a tour as I'm really interested but woefully ignorant." Though it was of little concern to her own constituents, it was important that she understand the statewide implications of this relatively new field.

"All planned for tomorrow or Sunday, plus a trip to the Roosevelt house on Campobello, if a good Republican like you would be interested in seeing how 'that man' lived. Now, mother mine, I judge the sun to be over the yardarm, so what is your pleasure?" Like his father, he made the accepted ritual an occasion, with a courtly flourish.

Settled with their drinks and a veggie dip, they talked about Meg and the children, about Patsy's forthcoming trip to Greece, about some of the hatchery problems and accomplishments. From time to time Charlie popped into the kitchen, refusing all offers of help. "I'm a helluva cook, woman."

During her second round, curiosity overcame her.

"I didn't know you had a housemate, and I'm glad you do. Being alone isn't much fun, is it? I hate it. Tell me about him."

Charlie was sitting on the floor in front of her, his back resting on her legs, just as he used to as a child.

"Hank is about my age, a graduate of the University and the University Law School. As you may have guessed, he's an Indian, a Passamaquoddy, raised on the reservation. His parents had real aspirations for him and saw to it that he could and would make it in the white world. He worked with the Indians' lawyer on the Land Settlement case a few years back. Now he specializes as an ombudsman for the tribes in matters of discrimination, welfare settlements, and any dealings with the government. He's damn good at it too."

"I'm looking forward to knowing him better. I like what I've seen. Have you known him long?"

"Yeah. Since late fall. Actually we met on the basketball court at the high school. Pickup game, something to do of an evening. We started going out for a beer afterwards, and became friends." Patsy felt his spine stiffening against her knees. "Good friends."

A little bell that had been ringing in her head began to really clang. She wished, oh so much, that her Bill was here with her. Or did she really, right now? Bill had been a "black or white" guy. A thing was either right or wrong, and situational ethics had been beyond his comprehension, as had permissive child rearing. Bad behavior was paid for, good behavior was taken for granted.

Why was she afraid? Of what?

Charlie continued, almost in a whisper. "So eventually I asked him to share this house."

There was a long silence, uncomfortably long. Patsy swallowed hard.

"And your bed?" She made her voice as light and loving as she could, having a hard time believing this conversation was happening but refusing to pretend it wasn't. She had never believed in sweeping upsetting facts under the rug.

Charlie slowly swiveled round, so he was facing her. His face was white beneath the tan, but his brown eyes, tear-filled, looked right into hers. He reached for her hands, held them tight, and said gently "Yes, Ma, and it's so right for us."

She freed her hands and put her arms around him, hoping he hadn't caught the matching tears in her eyes. Her mind was racing. She was desperately hoping to be able to say the words that were the wisest and most loving, but also totally honest. Whatever she said, right this minute, would never be forgotten by either. He had obviously been waiting weeks, if not months, for this. The ball was now in her court. Though certainly found off guard, she mustn't send it into the net.

Patsy took a long breath. "Thank you for leveling with me, son. This is obviously a surprise, something I never expected, so it's hard to grasp. I'll need time. Amazingly, right now I'm both sad and happy, for us both. I am sad because I know you have had a hard time coming to this decision, learning about yourself, and what this means. You may have already faced cruelty and unpleasantness. Mothers hate to know their children are being hurt, physically or mentally. And you won't know the joy of fatherhood, which is my loss too.

"I am happy because you obviously are. Homosexuality is something I know little about, but I don't think it is a lifestyle many deliberately choose, no matter what their hormones are telling them. No one likes to be different, and you probably had no idea what ailed you. For years you must have wondered why you weren't feeling what the other boys were. Now that is resolved and you feel you are a whole person, a satisfied person. Am I right?"

Charlie nodded, eyes showing gratitude and relief.

"Now that you know, I am. You have had a tough enough year and new life of your own to adjust to, Ma. News like this wouldn't have been much of a Christmas present. Then you went to Augusta and all that was new. So I've waited till now, when you had a break and we could really talk it out."

He shifted around into a more comfortable position.

"It was pretty scary in the beginning, as it is a first for both of us. We are not ashamed of our lifestyle, but we are discreet. The Indians are far more broadminded than we are, sometimes feeling a kind of reverence for what may be a supernatural situation. This part of Maine is very conservative, with many fundamentalist churches strongly against gays. But we've talked to a minister, an Episcopalian, and he is willing to hear our vows and bless our relationship, though of course he can't marry us.

Then he became almost shy. Patsy wondered what more he could possibly have to tell her. "Don't laugh, but we're thinking of adopting a kid, probably an Indian, if it becomes legal in this state."

How could she laugh when her son had practically handed her another baby! Hooray!

But how would this community accept that step? What were really the feelings and traditions of Hank's tribe? So many problems and decisions, so few guideposts.

They sat silently a while, each recovering. Then Charlie leapt to his feet, "Oh my God, dinner!"

As he pulled out her chair, he leaned over and kissed the top of her head. "Where did you get your smarts? You and Dad were always so strict and traditional with us, for our own good, that I have really dreaded this talk. You particularly have always been so very conscious of image, of what 'people would say' and pride in family. Thank you, Ma, for being so understanding, for refraining from an explosion, fireworks, or, worst of all, tears."

"We may have been strict, Charlie, but we always tried to be fair." She would not let him see how surprised and even hurt she was by his portrait of her. Now wasn't the time to discuss that, but she certainly would examine the charges in her own mind and weigh their truth. So she chuckled convincingly.

"Do you remember, for instance, when you broke Mr. Davis' cellar window with a baseball? You came to me very honestly and told me about it, and I suggested you go and tell him; then you paid for the new glass out of your allowance, and Dad helped you install it.

"You did not break the glass on purpose, later you did not smash up my old red Ford on purpose, now you are not gay on purpose. These things happen, and honesty, courage, and fairness are what build mutual trust and real love, which are the most precious things. And this dinner looks delicious."

As they were cleaning up Hank came in, caught Charlie's eye, and saw him nod in the affirmative, grinning. Patsy followed with a grin of her own, not quite as relaxed as Charlie's, but genuine. The day ended on a positive note.

As she lay in bed the wonderful smell of damp salt air drifted in her open window, or was it a mixture of salt, seaweed, and maybe a soupcon of dead fish? Whatever, it should be bottled and sold worldwide. Then later, just after dawn, she became half-awake and heard in the distance an almost forgotten sound of the girlhood summers when she had visited in

Maine. It was the rhythmic putt-putt-putt of a lobster boat leaving the harbor. Not the "one-lunger" putt-putt she remembered, but comfortably close enough. With a smile she turned over and went back to sleep. Maine air and memories, serving so well as anesthetics.

Hank was with them off and on, at breakfast, for a picnic after her tour of the salmon farm, and again in the evening, when it was his turn to cook dinner. Hoping she would appreciate it, he defrosted a delicious venison stew made in the fall and produced homemade rolls. Patsy did not disappoint him.

She tried very hard to be as natural as they were, and put up a good front. Hank was a good storyteller, and often very funny. There was a lot of laughter, but she found herself watching for behavior she didn't want to see. This situation was easier to accept intellectually than emotionally. Was her uneasiness built on small-minded bigotry, which is learned, or an instinctive dislike of aberrations of nature? How was this situation going to affect her relationship with her son, the family as a whole, or even, very importantly, her political career? Time would tell. For Patsy to accept having her son, her splendid child, referred to as a pansy, a fairy, a queer was an appalling idea. Was this truly an act of nature, or had she herself gone wrong somehow?

And down deep, so deep that she hated to even acknowledge it was there, was a feeling of betrayal. She had put so much thought for so many years into giving her children the highest standards of behavior and what she had felt were the best values. Now, for the first time, she had been put in a position that was almost defensive, quite different from her usual proud complacency. Oh Charlie, Charlie. And Bill, how you are needed now. Still, she knew that it was going to be possible to accept it and live with it, even with most of the old pride. He was still her Charlie and she loved him.

* * * * *

The Mediterranean

In late August Patsy joined thirty-five strangers at Logan Airport and flew with them to Venice where they boarded the ship *Navarino* for a two-week Mediterranean cruise. A mixed bag of rather attractive people made up the group. She soon discovered that though there were other singles, each was traveling with a companion and, having opted for a single stateroom, she was very much on her own. Mistake? Bonus?

Promising herself not to become a leech, for the first few days she was friendly but deliberately sat by herself on the sunny deck or on bus excursions. When it was obvious she was not a parasitic threat she began to be included in small groups and make pleasant acquaintances.

Few had known each other before this trip, which gave them all a type of anonymity. Some, almost compulsively, made sure that their fellow-passengers heard all about their children and their own importance in the 'home town" structure. Others seemed to relish freedom from status or responsibilities. She learned that while a few thoroughly enjoyed just being away from their routines and problems, with little curiosity in what they were seeing or even where they were, others made study a fetish, as if preparing for an exam, taking notes on everything. Lectures given on board were well done, as were the guided land tours. Patsy, while listening with interest to talks on ancient history and art, surprisingly found herself more intrigued with each country's current social and economic problems and their governmental solutions.

During the earlier part of the summer, at home, she had discovered that her attitude toward the activities of her circle of old friends had changed. Their lives had always seemed busy and satisfying, but now appeared to her almost humdrum, without interesting goals or purpose. She was sometimes impatient at their lack of interest in her new work and even worse, at the fact that many ridiculed politics, putting her on the defensive about something of which she was increasingly proud. But, in fairness, she was the one who had broken ranks, wasn't she? Now drawn to expanding and enriching this new interest rather than just relaxing, she was gratified to recognize that she had chosen a satisfying career, one that not only meant a great deal to her but that was also a constant challenge, a future.

Athens was more bustling and modern than she had expected, though dominated by the antique majesty of the Acropolis. Visible from almost every viewpoint, it daily reminded Greeks and visitors alike of the glory of its ancient past. At Olympia she learned how the Games, beyond their entertainment and competitive character, reflected the fabric of city-state philosophy. For the period of the contests all skirmishes and battles between them were put on hold and they joined sincerely in paying homage to their gods by the feats of their bodies.

Istanbul, one crossroad of East and West, was in the throes of an election and she found they took their politics seriously. Muslim fundamentalists were challenging the more liberal establishment, a condition prevalent in many Mid-Eastern states. Armed soldiers were on most corners, and military weapons carriers were much in evidence near where rallies were scheduled.

Though facing a modern dilemma, Turkey presented to her the greatest culture shock in terms of its language, dress, and general customs. The bazaar, the mosques, even the people on the street, were of another world and time, though possibly a force soon to affect the Western world.

In Israel, landing at Haifa, they found security very tight with nothing subtle about it. Passports were examined regularly and the Stars and Stripes fluttering from the stern of small Navy vessels in Haifa harbor were a very reassuring sight. Israel was a country under constant siege, mentally if not actually.

She had a continuing interest in modern Israel, generated first by Uris' book *Exodus*. She daily secured a seat up front in the bus so she could question the very knowledgeable guide. Flattered by Patsy's interest in more than ancient and biblical history, he satisfied her questions concerning political parties, current peace, and the economy. He even included, at her request, a visit to a kibbutz, which had not been on the schedule.

Much of Israel was rocky and desolate wasteland but, like real estate everywhere in the world, location, location, location had caused the terrible struggles over the centuries. It was still the main crossroad of European, African, and Asian trade routes, as well as their religions and cultures. Now, due to the pride, energy and perseverance of the dedicated, even desperate post-WW II settlers, orchards, forest, fields, and cities flourished in many places. A true miracle, accomplished by Jews from many nations and of varied forms of worship. Israel was another vibrant melting pot of true pioneers 350 years after the American experiment began, with many similarities.

More skeptical than some of her shipmates about the authenticity of many of the "biblical sites," Patsy did however respect the religious importance of the area to Jews, Christians, and Muslims. For the first time she truly understood how hard establishing a real peace would be, considering those centuries of religious conflict.

Back in Greek waters, Mykonos and other small islands were like white meringues on a blue plate and she wished those visits could have been longer. Though tourist-oriented, they were much less Americanized than the cities. Fewer T-shirts, jeans, and rock musicians. Ancient landmarks on treeless hillsides cropped bare by long-gone goats were exactly what, theoretically, she had come to see, but by the end of the first week the ubiquitous fallen columns, headless figures, and marble dust made her feel dry as a potato chip.

Then blessedly came Rhodes, robust, medieval, and green, with glorious flowers, both in the city and in the countryside. She was now not a chip but a juicy and tasty Greek olive.

From the harbor they went by bus to Lindos, a little seaside town built at the foot of a mountain. Most of her friends rode donkeys up to yet another acropolis, in the clouds, to acquire yet more facts, but the Mediterranean summoned Patsy. She had not come this far to pass up the opportunity of a swim in that cobalt sea, and had packed her bathing suit in her large shoulder bag. The group was to meet for lunch at the restaurant on the beach and she'd asked friends to make sure she was on board before the bus left.

Down the steep little street she went, past displays of delicately embroidered blouses, pottery, and souvenirs. She inquired about a dressing room and was shown a rough hut in the bushes by the service entrance to the restaurant. The door of the structure had but one hinge. Nothing ventured.......

Soon she was in her suit and packed her clothes in the bag, leaving it in the hut. Her toes wiggled happily in the sand as she neared the water. This was IT! Patsy Hudson, for so long a provincial all-American hometown girl, was about to plunge into the Mediterranean, the sea so familiar to the Romans, the Carthaginians, Cleopatra, and the glorious Sophia!

The water was just the right temperature, not too warm for a girl from Maine. It was amazingly clear, and the bottom was clean. She swam, she floated lazily, she went underwater, blew bubbles and splashed. Only a mother and young child shared the water with her. Out in the bay a few fishing boats were moored, and closer to shore a man was trying to conquer, with little luck, the art of windsurfing, often going backwards or falling off. Joining the other woman in laughter, she swam a bit more, then regretfully and slowly made her way back to the beach and her dressing hut.

When about fifty feet away from it she saw, to her horror, a dog emerging from the hut, triumphantly carrying her bag in its mouth. Clothes, camera, passport, money! She yelled and ran although she knew it was hopeless, swearing, sobbing, and soon panting. Behind her she heard other running feet; someone flew past her and up the path the dog had taken. In a short while a man reappeared, waving her bag happily over his head.

"How can I ever thank you?" she cried. She wasn't even sure he spoke English, but he'd know she was pleased..

Six feet plus, lean, with a very amused expression on his tan face, he said "Just never, never laugh at a beginning windsurfer again, young lady."

She put on a show of vast humility and shame, laughing with him this time.

"To make up for your sins, how about joining me, my sister, and my niece for lunch?" Because he looked a bit like Vice President Bush, Maine's noted Republican summer resident, she accepted. Why not?

They met on the inn's outdoor terrace, enjoyed a light wine, established where they were all from. He was from Virginia and his sister was taking a short break from the heat of Athens, where her husband was attached to the U.S. embassy. Cold calamari salad, olives, and delicious Greek pastry were just finished when the bus driver blew his horn, and Patsy rose, said that she'd expect to see him windsurfing on Casco Bay like a pro, another thank you, and she ran to catch the bus.

Not until she was seated did she realize that they had not even exchanged names or addresses. Oh well, they would never meet again, but it had been fun. Attractive men really improved one's day, and the potato chip feeling was gone. All olive now, rich and tasty. She'd even forgotten for a few hours to feel like a politician.

Late on the last night at sea, she stood alone in the bow as the *Navarino* made its way north through the Adriatic. Italian Alps were on her port side and the rugged mountains of Yugoslavia to starboard, black against a dark blue sky. No lights shone from either shore, and no other ships were in evidence. She realized that what she was seeing must have appeared exactly the same to Phoenicians and Carthaginians sailing this very route centuries before. Finally, thank goodness, she felt part of it all, physically and emotionally, not just a spectator loaded with facts she might soon forget.

In reviewing her trip later she realized that even thousands of miles from Augusta, Maine, she had not neglected her present occupation and was grateful for what she had learned. Ancient solons and modern pols had much in common, and in her own mind was the reaffirmation that the U.S. system, though not perfect, was by far the best. Highlights? The monuments and geography of ancient cultures were just as she'd thought they'd be, and so what stood out was the unexpected, particularly the human contacts. No travel books or National Geographic specials had prepared her for these quite special events, which made the trip so personal.

She would never forget crouching, in fun, on the starting line in the original Olympic setting. The impish little Turkish boys in a truck next to their bus in Istanbul traffic, waggling their fingers and making funny faces, forged an East-West connection as she waggled and grimaced back, more memorable than the Topkapi Palace or the Blue Mosque. She still refused to admit to herself that the Greek dance with the stunning captain of their ship was part of his job. The waiter in a Cretan restaurant who had a head as classic as those of any statue she'd studied, and yes, quite definitely, the little lunch date at Lindos would all be remembered longer than any historical dates she'd been given.

She was ready to plan for the next session, broadened and definitely refreshed. Not only was she bringing back a pleasant memory, but problems had been left at home for a while or considered in such interesting settings that they seemed diminished in magnitude. Even Charlie's situation had somehow become part of reality, to be accepted, absorbed, lived with, not constantly worried like a bone.

This first year alone, in retrospect, had been one of unexpected growth. Projects to lessen or anesthetize her pain had proved to be keys to attitudes, insights, and much more intimate knowledge of herself, some of which was embarrassing and some pleasantly surprising. What next?

* * * * *

Portland, Maine

Metaphorically, Heather Hatch thought of herself as standing again on the edge of a beach she had once visited on the coast of Israel. Tempting white sand had stretched down to the blue, blue sea, but both sand and sea had been inaccessible because of a high barbed-wire fence. She hadn't been able to even get her feet wet in that beautiful Mediterranean, much less fully enjoy its waters. So it was with her job-hunting now. Very dry feet. Dreams of becoming part of TV news production were still nothing but dreams. She had recently moved from Bangor to Portland where there might be more opportunities. Various stations had taken her name, filed her resume, and then obviously forgotten about her. There seemed to be an "If it ain't broke, don't fix it" attitude. So much for Big City experience. One station had suggested she call back during the summer when they occasionally used newcomers on weekends or to cover reporters on vacation.

She had independently shot a few short stories, concentrating on the legislative scene, and had learned all about rejection. She could now understand poor old Van Gogh's depression, never selling a painting in his whole life! Her money was running out and she was afraid she'd have to give up her goal of doing more than just decorating the screen. Maybe she wasn't all that great after all.

She was also concerned today by a letter from her grandmother. Theirs was a close, uncluttered relationship, but she had not yet admitted to her most loyal fan that all was not going well. Silly thing, pride. The dear lady was in her eighties, sharp as a tack and generally considered healthy unless pressed for details. She lived in an attractive retirement community in Wisconsin, near where she and Heather's grand-dad had made their home for many years, and so was close to those few old friends still alive. Independent, thanks to a comfortable income and an unsullied driver's license, she was generally on the crest, with few voiced complaints.

But events of the last weeks had forced her spirits down and her blood pressure up. She had had sad news of her three closest friends. One had died, though not unexpectedly; the healthiest had had a slight stroke; and the third was diagnosed with terminal cancer.

> All of us 'sprung chickens' at this Old Folks Home try to be upbeat, to keep our minds off what's ahead and to make each day as rich as possible. But the Big Clock on the wall keeps ticking, and there's not one darn thing we can do about it. We take all those fool vitamins and cures we hear about on TV, and to keep our doctors happy we walk around the condo grounds three times a day cause that's a mile, and just about as exciting as watching grass grow. Hooray for us.
>
> Sometimes I brighten things up by starting outrageously false juicy rumors, or by pretending to cheat at bridge. Last week, for excitement, I hid two pieces of the jigsaw puzzle we all were working on. Most of the TV programs are lousy, and good books too heavy to hold unless you read in bed. We will probably have more time in bed than we ever wanted soon enough.

Mostly, I fight becoming 'institutionalized,' as many here have. So much is done for us that it's awfully easy to lose initiative, to attend all the events mindlessly, to forget we were once responsible enough to manage homes and bring up children.

After a bit of Attitude Adjustment (aka the happy hour before dinner), the 'girls' and I occasionally talk about the Big End. (Sometimes we can even capture one the 'boys' to join us in these chitchats. Big deal). Philosophically we're not afraid. We've had good lives, some even have the satisfaction of having made a real difference. But right now we feel useless and unneeded; our only activity is to stay as well as possible so we'll be no burden to our families. No one expects much of us so we don't want to disappoint them. Show up for breakfast warm and breathing every day and you've won a gold star. Two stars if you know what day it is! All we hope for is to just sleep away, neat and tidy, no aches and pains, no months in bed or wheelchairs, and please God, with all our marbles. Fat chance!

Forgive me for being so negative; it's a rotten rainy day, the third in a row. Drip, drip, drip. I've got to blow my stack to someone sometime, and who else but you? Give my love and hugs and kisses to anyone I might know up there in your Maine woods. It might even be fun to hug a lonely bear, if you see one around. .

I won't say good-bye. I've been saying that too often to too many things.

All my love, dear girl, Nana

How Heather herself would love a hug from that wonderful old gal, right this minute.

Grampa and Nana Delano had brought her up, at least since the horrible accident when she was orphaned at five. Her dad, in the U.S. Air Force, had been stationed in Germany. They had lived happily on the base, surrounded by other Americans but also enjoying weekends in the countryside, poking around small villages, seeking out the unusual, picnicking in enchanted places.

One Sunday night, returning to base in a downpour, whole bunches of headlights came together with terrible screeching of brakes, crumpling of metal, then silence, except for the car radio that still played lovely waltzes as if nothing had happened.

Heather remembered being able to sit up, remembered Mummy and Daddy lying in very peculiar positions and very quiet. Feeling alone and forsaken, she remembered opening her mouth and letting out a monstrous wail she was sure someone who loved her would hear. And someone did. Her next memory, from a hospital bed, was seeing Nana's face, all round and pink and teary, trying to look happy for her.

Heather's mom's family lived somewhere in New England; those grandparents were quite old and not very well. She had visited them once when she was three or four and remembered them a little, particularly her Gramma, who brought out a lot of pretty little treasures for her to play with, one of which she had let fall on the floor. She still felt guilty about that, she hadn't meant to do it.

Dad's parents, however, had come over to Germany for a visit just last summer, so they were her good buddies, and they wanted her, how they did want her!

Soon Heather and Nana were flying home over the Atlantic to Wisconsin, USA, with very precious memories and pictures packed in their luggage and their hearts. Heather missed having a mother and particularly her own special mother, every day of her life. But she certainly had been lucky in grandparents. Grampa had died three years ago, but his wisdom still lived in her, as did his humor. Nana was still her very best friend.

They had never said "I told you so" when her brief and miserable marriage to Si Hatch, campus idol, burnt itself out. He'd evidently needed to collect affairs as much as athletic trophies. Two golden kids had had to grow up the hard way, and Heather had kept his name as a reminder of the lessons she had learned. She was still, seven years later, so low in self-confidence in her judgments, that being absorbed by a job was important.

Now, looking around her little studio apartment in Portland, furnished courtesy of an obviously colorblind landlord, she knew she had to get out, for dinner at least. Something had to cheer her up. She plunged down the ill-lit stairs and out onto the street. Rain poured down, a cold late summer rain.

Heather stood for a moment making the decision of turning right or left. Right would lead her to the Old Port section, a lively mixture of boutiques, good restaurants, and bars. Often fun, but pricey. So she turned left and in a few minutes was on Congress Street, formerly the nerve center of downtown Portland but a victim of mall development, parking woes, and the economy. Now it was home to rather second-rate stores and several small, almost hole-:in-the-wall restaurants, generally serving hearty soups and sandwiches. One even provided fairly good reading matter for lonely diners like herself.

Turning to go in there she collided with someone obviously in a hurry.

"For God's sake, f —— bitch, look where you're going." The young man snarled and gave her a shove into the bargain. Down she went, caught unprepared. He continued on his way, outraged.

Heather Hatch, homecoming queen, bright girl reporter, the gal who was going to take this state by storm, was lying in the puddles on a wet sidewalk, in tears.

A splendid primal rage seemed to start in her toes and creep up her body, into her chest, her arms, and finally her head. She pounded the sidewalk with her fists, got to her feet, and furiously brushed off her raincoat as best she could. Squaring her shoulders, she took a deep breath, counted to ten, and entered the little restaurant.

It was half empty, but the only waitress took her own sweet time coming to Heather's table and handing her a menu, tapping her foot impatiently while waiting for the order. Heather's rage came back, but ice-cold this time, not hot and burning. A really nasty, cutting remark would put this little floozie in her place. But while she waited for just the right put-down to come to her, she heard instead a voice from the past.

"Heather Delano, I never want to hear you talk like that again. You must learn to always keep a civil tongue in your head. Civility may not be as much fun as the rough stuff, but it is the only effective way to deal with people. A famous writer, Mr. Ralph Waldo Emerson, once said 'Life is not so short but there is always time enough for courtesy.' Remember that. Now let's get you on your feet and see what the damage is."

Grampa had been nearby when the neighborhood show-off had forced the little girl and her bike off the sidewalk and into a tree, so many years ago, and she had reacted saltily.

Civility, what had happened to it? Were so many people so angry that they felt a need to express that anger in their treatment of others? Or had they never been taught manners, that code of courtesy based on simply making others feel comfortable ? Were parents and teachers too busy and harried themselves to serve as role models? Anger only produced more anger. At this minute she was the perfect example.

She ordered the vegetable beef soup and coffee, smiled warmly though hypocritically at the waitress, and continued her train of thought,.

For whom had she always been on her best behavior? Her grandparents, not because she was afraid of them but because she loved them and it made them happy to be proud of her. They had taught, not the phony little curtsies, or just the mechanical thank-yous and I'm sorry's, but the real thing, to think of others, to be genuinely courteous. These warm, fun, but respected elders seemed to have time for her and made the lessons a privilege, not a criticism. She had always liked herself better when she followed their example and rules and discovered it made a real difference to others..

She hardly noticed when the soup arrived, slopping into the saucer, and her "thank you" was automatic. Her mind was on Nana's letter and a wonderful idea was forming in her head. "We feel so useless" the old lady had written.

"Not any more, my gal" thought Heather, "not any more." Her idea would take work and study and genius, but now she had a purpose. She gulped down the soup and hurried back to her room, her word processor, her dreams, and to Nana and Grampa, still there for her. She was almost grateful to the boor who had knocked her down because the incident had changed her direction. "Career" was put on hold and "cause" took her full attention.

Chapter 4: Fall 1987

Harding's Corner

Labor Day came and went, and with it the summer people, or most of them. Their exodus, as usual, rivalled that of the Bible, but the Israelites hadn't had to cope with toll booths, exhaust fumes, and overloaded automobiles topped by or towing every known vacation device. Mainers waved good-bye from porches and overpasses, then quietly and happily estimated the season's take. Many then confirmed their Florida condo reservations for the winter. Most agreed on having had a good season.

Garnering crops before the first killing frost was keeping all the Warners busy. Customers still clamored for more of everything at the market, including Susan's preserves and dried flowers. She almost prayed for that frost as zucchini and tomatoes kept endlessly appearing by the basketful on her kitchen counter. She couldn't NOT can or freeze them, but "how many more, O Lord, how many?" Tougher vegetables would linger on, and many were already in the freezer or lined up in jars in the cellar. She loved parsnips, just loved 'em. They stayed in the ground all winter, no bother at all, being at their sweetest when dug up in the early spring. A last haying was complete, potatoes were dug, onions were drying, and Brussels sprouts finally had the garden to themselves.

Jerry was discovering that wearing two hats at once was a tough trick to pull off. Whenever possible he drove to Orono, Bangor, or Augusta, trying to finish his research and to produce for the Warners and Joel the promised material on which to base their campaign for funds and support. He made a point, on each of these excursions, of visiting with men and women at their places of work to informally chat and discover their attitudes and concerns. He met with game wardens, paper mill workers, fishermen and policemen, day care providers and hospital workers. The list was inexhaustible. Each week he tried to add the opinions of yet another wage-earning group to his list. And, he reasoned, if nothing ever came of all this, he had at least met some damned fine people.

Joel had added a generous check to the project, Stan was in the process of tracking down the owners of the little building at Harding's Corner, and power, TV, and telephone lines had insinuated their presence into the Warner lifestyle. An "experienced" pickup truck had joined Stan's in the dooryard.

These changes would have seemed appalling if there were not such a compelling reason for them, and Susan and Stan were trying to adjust, with Stan having the hardest time. Working at being "primitive" for thirty years was a hard act to forget.

At the State House Jerry became friendly with one of the freelance reporters and picked his brains for sources more interesting than reference books filled with statistics and tables. They lunched together occasionally in the basement cafeteria, and on one such occasion Jerry happened to think of the very attractive young woman he had seen in the building months before.

"We've just acquired a TV, up in our boonies, and I've been keeping my eye out for a real knockout gal perhaps connected with a Portland news channel. No luck." And he described her briefly from memory.

Mark Lowell looked puzzled for a moment, then his face cleared. "That's probably Heather Hatch. She wants to be more than just a pretty face reading wire service reports and is hoping to do her own documentaries and reporting. Lots of experience in Washington, well trained, but I've heard she's having problems finding her niche. Rumor has it that right now she's all fired up about encouraging old folks out of retirement to teach kids what parents evidently haven't time for—a little civility and respect. Good luck to her with the little monsters."

Hearing the words "civility and respect," Jerry almost choked on his Pepsi, recovered, and asked how one could get in touch with the young lady.

Amused, Mark allowed that he was not a dating service.

"Damn it, I really want to meet her, but not for the reasons you're thinking. My father is looking for someone with PR or journalistic experience to take on a really novel job. He wants someone with no baggage, no local lobbying reputation or image. Someone who can write really good copy, sell ideas, and help move money from the wallets of good people to the coffers of a good cause. From what you've said she might be just the person to fill the bill."

Jerry suddenly shut up. His own skills were certainly rusty. He had just tipped off one of the best reporters in the state to the fact that Stan was not a guileless old hayseed but was up to something more interesting than potatoes and broccoli. A certain professional curiosity glinted in Mark's eyes, and Jerry knew he had to make a deal.

"OK, there may be a story here, in time. If you can give me the info and then forget this conversation for a while, you'll get the scoop when there is one. I mean that."

Mark had suspected all along that this obviously well-educated character, doing research on many facets of Maine's economy and culture, was working on something worth checking into. Smoke may be hard to grab by the handful, but it generally means there's a fire to locate.

"That's a deal, Jerry. Give me your number, and I'll fax her address and phone number up to you."

Heather Hatch soon met with Jerry, Stan, and Joel for lunch. She was just as lovely and refreshing as Jerry had remembered. When they were seated, Joel opened the proceedings.

"Thank you, Miss Hatch, for sending your very impressive resume. We have all studied it, and feel that we have an advantage over you as you know nothing of us. Why don't we each fill you in?" And they did, with Jerry being necessarily brief, vague, but somehow convincing. She listened carefully.

"Jerry, it's your turn now to explain the project," offered Joel, but Jerry turned the task back to him, unwilling to have to blow his own trumpet so deviously. Joel accepted the assignment happily.

"To put it simply, we are setting up a fund to celebrate and honor the life of one particular friend, as well as the lives of others. To be quite frank, we do not yet know the purpose of the fund, but we want it to be something that will really mirror the concerns of these honorees. If we catch the imagination of the people on our donor list, and on other donor lists, we may possibly affect something that badly needs changing."

He went on to explain the plan of requesting ideas by questionnaire, reviewing the results, then presenting a program to the contributors for their approval.

"Depending on the goal we choose, we may start very quietly and then patiently grow, or we may start out with a bang, a real attention-getter. As you have heard, we all have business experience, we are pretty well educated, we are used to making decisions. In other words, we aren't naive do-gooders. Our philosophies vary quite a bit so you needn't worry about getting caught up in some wild-eyed very liberal or very conservative crusade.

"We would ask you to be responsible for our public relations campaign, getting out fund-raising letters, newsletters, and press releases. Evaluating responses to our questionnaire is something we'll all work on. There may be TV spots later on.

"As you can tell, we all see ourselves as idea people. Sometimes we're sensible, sometimes completely mad. You would have to serve as ringmaster of that circus, adding your own ideas and yet cracking the whip when necessary. Now, young lady, the floor is yours."

Heather was saved from an immediate reply by a waiter ready to take their orders. Once that was done, she took a sip of her Bloody Mary, gathered her resources, and then grinned with delight, eyes glowing.

"If I were writing a novel," she said slowly "about a poor but honest news-hen who, for the sake of principles, left a cushy, meaningless job in the big city and came to the almost unspoiled forests of Maine, our conversation today would be the very first chapter. Word for word. Were there ever any lady knights on quests, looking for nasty problems to impale upon their pink lances? Or am I the first?

"To be honest with you, I've been pretty discouraged so far. No dragons have appeared on this quest, just skunks and woodchucks. A few weekend gigs covering for TV newspeople on vacation have just about paid my rent, and I'm not living in an oceanfront condo, believe me. But I am still holding out for what I described in my resume, a challenge, to use what skills I have to make a difference."

At this, the men all sought each other's feet under the table to express, with well-placed kicks, their approval. By sheer luck, no one kicked Heather. "To make a difference" was the phrase that did it. Their goal entirely. Now down to details.

"You probably wonder in what Maine metropolis we are located." Joel teased. "Portland, no. Augusta, no. Bangor, no. Our office is in an old, almost-restored country store, complete now with indoor plumbing, heat, power, and phone, at a spot called Harding's Corner. I use the word 'spot' advisedly. There's nothing else there. Nothing. This totally un-historic landmark is kinda between Millinocket and Lincoln, in an Unorganized Territory. The offices are on the ground floor of this proud edifice and an apartment is being carved out upstairs for whoever dares take the job. All the amenities, basic furniture, and one whale of a view are provided, including about a thousand acres in which to park your car."

"And from November first for about a month you dare not go out the door without wearing blaze orange vest and hat. You don't really look like a deer, but anything that moves is in deadly peril. When Stan used to keep cows he even painted the word COW on their sides each fall, but this huntin' crowd loses all power to think, to read, to reason. The only part of them that moves according to plan is that trigger finger."

"In the winter the snowplow comes through pretty regular. And the Warner farm is about six miles as the crow flies, a bit more in mud season, when you'd get there by water."

Stan, relaxed and enjoying every minute of this, had to put in his oar.

With an exaggerated Maine accent he added, "Don't know what newfangled gadgets you're used to, but we want you to know we've actually graduated from smoke signals and carrier pigeons. Besides the phone, we now boast something called a fax machine, a stuck-up typewriter called a word processor, and," he couldn't restrain himself, "one of them gol-darned snotty machines giving us old folks inferiority complexes, a computer. Spits out labels, budgets, and bios like crazy, when we got power. No damn good after a thunderstorm."

Jerry took over then. "Slight matter of salary to discuss. We have absolutely no idea of what the response to our appeal will be. Send us an idea of your figure, taking in perks, mileage, free rent, etc. We'll review it and keep terms flexible, depending on the effect of our poetry, excuse me, your poetry, in fund-raising letters."

"Fair enough." Heather cut into her lunch. "And I'm so happy I don't know whether to purr or explode."

They shook hands all around; Heather was on board.

During the ride home Stan looked over at Jerry. "You've got an awfully silly smile on your puss. And I don't blame you."

With Carol's head on his shoulder that night, Joel ended his day with "Old Webb's life is getting better and better, but 'complicateder.' He's still married to Phyllis. You'll like Heather a lot, but we all agreed to keep her in the dark as to who Jerry-Webb is. We had to draw the line somewhere.."

* * * * *

Two weeks later Heather moved into her Harding's Corner apartment. Susan had helped her repaint secondhand tables and chairs with bright clear colors, wash the windows, and sand and polish the floor. The two women had formed an unusually comfortable friendship from the start.

One crisp October morning Heather telephoned the farm, begging Susan to come over immediately, her voice charged with excitement. The UPS truck had just delivered a footlocker sent, upon request, by her grandmother, and the event simply had to be shared.

Opening it had been like discovering a casket of priceless gems. Colors leaped out at the two women, and Heather plunged both arms deep into the contents, as if to hug and welcome what was there. Wall hangings, shawls, pillows, and mats were wrapped in yards of fabric, all blazing in patterns created on the other side of the earth. The materials ranged from sturdy peasant rugs to silken scarves light as a whisper. Some served as wrappings for pottery, brass, and carved wood mementoes. Small boxes held jade and ivory figurines, dolls richly dressed, fine filigree jewelry. Oriental prints and posters of exotic scenes were unrolled. And from it all came an almost musty but attractive odor of sandalwood and spices.

Turning to ask for an explanation, Susan saw happy tears running down Heather's cheeks. The younger woman sniffled, grinned, and exclaimed, "Finally, the important pieces of Heather Hatch have come together. I'm home, at last."

Little by little, as each treasure was inspected and its history given, Susan heard, for the first time, the story of Heather's life after her divorce at twenty-two. She had suffered the embarrassment and insecurity of not knowing which friends were in Si's camp and which were in hers. Few of their contemporaries had yet experienced how devastating a divorce can be. She felt vulnerable and unsure of her own judgment. To make matters worse, when word had spread that the marriage was over, she was bombarded with the attention of, as Nana put it, every eligible rooster in the barnyard.

Rather than jump from the frying pan into the fire, she joined the Peace Corps and went to Southeast Asia. She fell in love with Thailand, the people with whom she worked, the culture and philosophy by which they lived. The meditative and peaceful life was the best medicine she could have found.

When her tour was over she did not come home, but put a pack on her back, hiking boots on her feet and set out to see more, much more. At the start she banked enough money to ensure a flight home; from then on she had to be self-supporting. When she ran low on cash she would stop and find work, be it in the rice fields, as a nanny, a waitress, or a teacher of English. She had even coached Javanese cheerleaders!

It was fascinating to find how many young, single women like herself from the West were on the road, backpacking as she was, sponging up information. Sometimes they travelled together for a while, international nomads. When the time seemed right they would probably return home, wherever that was, find a career, marry and settle down like their stay-at-home sisters. But they would have had their grand adventure and earned graduate degrees given by no university. An unthinkable adventure in their mothers' generation.

One steamy spring day, when she had finally made it to Australia, she stopped at the US Consulate in Brisbane hoping to find some mail. A sign on the door announced "Due to our annual national celebration of Thanksgiving today, the office is closed." Thanksgiving! She looked upward and watched the Stars and Stripes fluttering lazily over the building in the warm breeze. At home there might be snow on the ground, football games, cold noses and warm mittens. She could almost smell the roasting turkeys and sense the clans gathering. Nana and Grampa, for want of their own, would be sharing family with neighbors, possibly wondering where their girl was. She needed them, yearned for them, right this minute. After four years it was time to go home.

Occasionally in her wanderings she had written short articles of her experiences and sent them to her home town paper. Not only had they been received graciously, but she had been offered a job when she returned. A new career was waiting.

Sitting spellbound through this recital, Susan shook her head, then laughed with glee. "I wonder if Harding's Corner will ever recover? Its only inhabitant is hardly a nondescript little brown partridge, but another phoenix of glorious plumage." How all this bright beauty was satisfying her own artistic thirst!

Together they hung bright curtains, put mats on the floor, tossed pillows everywhere, decided shelves were needed to display her collection. Very unexotic peanut butter sandwiches were made for lunch and then the work downstairs could no longer be ignored.

Packed neatly into boxes were now 500 Susan-addressed envelopes, ready for stuffing. At Joel's request Miss Hewins, Jerry's former secretary, had sent up list after list from his personal files, yearbook data, camp lists, college reports, and club rosters. Phyllis had contributed their Christmas card list and family addresses. It was hard for isolated Susan to believe one person could know so many others.

The letter itself was a team product, having been faxed back and forth with new ideas or phraseology, but always in Joel's personal idiom. The whole project depended on the strength of this appeal. They had been very careful in the letter to avoid the use of "memorial" stating instead that gifts would be "in honor of Webb Lewis and, later, others." Because of the range and diversity of his friendships it was clearly stated that whatever the fund did would be carefully secular, nonpartisan, and nondiscriminatory. An endorsement from Phyllis was included, surprisingly supportive. Wives were encouraged to send in answers of their own.

Stan's marketing skills were steadily coming back, rusty machinery now well-oiled by his appreciative crew, and he seemed to be enjoying his changed life, though grudgingly at times.

"We ought to point out that it's not very often one gets a fund-raising letter that gives the recipient the opportunity of choosing, or helping to choose, how his or her money will be spent."

Joel, remembering all that was said at Webb's services, and the phrase that had sold the men on employing Heather, had inserted "We can't all be heroes but this program may let each of us make a difference, a difference of our own choosing and one we couldn't possibly afford to do individually."

Finally, they were all satisfied.

For tax purposes, they knew it should be sent out before New Year's, but they also knew the competition at that time from other holiday requests would be enormous. What could they do to guarantee that their mailing would live to be opened and read, not dropped stillborn into a "round file?"

"Too bad this isn't an inaugural year," Heather had mused. "We could dress it up like a personal ball invitation from the incoming president."

Stan's eyes had opened wide with delight, his bushy eyebrows high.

"Hey, we can still do that, inaugural ball or not. Everyone likes to be invited to a party, any party. Really classy stationery, invitation size, hand-addressed, with the Phoenix logo embossed discreetly on the back flap of the envelope should do the trick. I guarantee each will be opened.

"The letter, a pledge card, and return envelope will be enclosed, as well as that dynamite questionnaire. That's the real bait. Most people just can't resist a chance to give their opinions. Each letter can be personalized by Joel, with correct nicknames, wives' names, and references to old friends and memories. Ego-boosting always works. Both political parties have pulled this trick for years, and most recipients are so flattered they don't see through it."

It was finally done, every letter proofread meticulously, and signed by Joel. Now, with the questionnaires and return envelopes, they were ready to be placed in the handsome envelopes. The boxes were moved to the Warners. Carol and Joel had come up from Boston to help stuff and stamp, then take the finished product back with them so there would be a convincing Boston postmark.

Seated around Susan's dining table all looked with pride at the pile of sealed envelopes. At one end of the table were sheets of stamps and some small sponges in saucers. Stan stared at them with irritation, then looked down at his big hands. Pushing his chair back, he rose.

"Gentlemen," he barked. "I'm calling a special meeting of the Firewood Committee in the barn right this minute. Long overdue."

Jerry caught on first and kept a straight face. Joel followed them out into the cold, bewildered but optimistic.

Susan hooted. "It's just as well. No way would I let those clumsy oafs spoil my gorgeous envelopes with crooked or smudged stamps. Let's just take our time, have a cup of tea, swap some silly stories, and get the job done. Unless he's got a bottle hidden out there they'll be back when the chill gets to them, and they better bring in armfuls of wood for my stove."

He did and they didn't. But they did bring something else. Planned for later in the evening, now seemed a better time for a presentation.

Though there had been few recent crimes in the area, the little building at Harding's Corner was certainly not only isolated but conspicuous in that isolation. The out-of-state deer hunters weren't all necessarily choirboys, and the Phoenix team had misgivings about Heather's safety. She had refused to accept a firearm of any kind. Stan entered the kitchen first and stood before her.

"Up in these parts we're not very sophisticated about security; we react pretty basically to meddlesome strangers. Electronic gadgets are great if the nearest sheriff is a quarter mile away, but we haven't even got a sheriff. For a couple centuries man has relied on just one thing to give the alarm and hold the fort." He swung around to let Joel and Jerry carry in a big cardboard box. "Miss Heather, here's your Security System, fresh from the factory."

She approached the box warily, knowing that if the men looked that pleased with themselves it was an especially suspect occasion. Carefully she lifted the lid and luckily stepped back as a huge mature German shepherd vaulted out into the room. He ran from one to another, sniffing, wagging, introducing himself, then came back to where Heather stood, giving a paw to shake hands. On his collar was pinned a tin sheriff's badge. Matt Dillon had entered their lives, trained and ready.

* * * * *

Boston

Susan accompanied the McLeans back to Boston at Carol's insistence. Because her best paintings now hung in the Phoenix office, the gallery show had been put on hold for another time. But Carol felt the time was now right to uproot the newly blossoming Susan and transplant her temporarily into the urban world of the present. She also wanted to get to know her better, sensing that Susan's old-fashioned wisdom would help her as a modern parent.

Familiar with the New York of thirty years ago but almost a stranger to Boston at any time, Susan made a list of places to see and things to do. For starters they shopped for wardrobe additions that would be suitable for the visit but useful at home too. Her quiet world up there in the woods was being extensively altered. Naturally faded denims no longer sufficed. A corduroy suit, soft knit tops, and a jumper made a good start, plus a silky, jewel-toned dress. Shirts and a sports coat of current tailoring were found for Stan. Who knew, he might wear them!

On the second day Susan came down for breakfast wearing one of her new outfits, eyes dancing yet a stubborn set to her chin.

"Because Stan isn't here to talk me out of it, let's eat fast and get to a beauty parlor right away before I change my mind. Off with the pigtail, on with a new Susan!

Soft, silver-gray curls soon framed her face and emphasized her tan complexion. She was lovely.

First on the tour was a visit to the Boston Museum of Fine Arts. The MFA's extensive collections covered art from all over the world and over many centuries, and she knew just what her priorities were.

Shyly she explained her choices to Carol. "Many years ago I promised a very special little boy that someday we would visit the Egyptian mummies here, and then the room of medieval armor." She could almost feel that little hand in hers as she and Carol walked through those exhibits, and Carol felt that perhaps this was the beginning of the confidences she hoped for.

Susan's chin had stopped wobbling by the time they found the Impressionists, which she studied carefully and professionally, then acknowledged that she'd had enough stimulation for one visit. They lunched in the pleasant upstairs restaurant and picked up cards and gifts in the Museum shop. Carol, watching her friend almost reverently make selections, realized how many Boston natives take this treasure-chest for granted.

Good walkers that they were, they continued along Huntington Avenue past Symphony Hall to the Prudential Building. Carol had chosen this site for the view from the top that gave the best introduction to the topography of the city. Susan moved from window to window, fascinated. What intellectual giants had built this city, called once by some the Hub of the Universe. Statesmen, writers, artists, and scholars had used political liberation to explore with freedom new philosophical boundaries. Did their like exist today? History would judge. How could the amateur Phoenix program dream of making an impression on the home of such rich history?

The week flew by. Susan became accustomed to the noise, the sirens of emergency vehicles in the night even in the McLeans' suburb, exhaust fumes and crowds. She had a chronic case of "museum feet" and didn't care. She loved the patina of the old and the shine of the new.

And they also explored each other, with rewarding results. Carol proved to be the nonthreatening stimulant Susan needed to seek more contemporary attitudes, while in return Carol received a refresher course in the values of simplicity. A sensible person in an often foolish society, she valued the older woman's less trampled-upon opinions. She shared with her guest the stresses of modern parenting, the threat of peer pressures., drugs, too early sex. Joel was a thoroughly old-fashioned father, referring endlessly to the way things were in his day, so Carol was the one who had to listen, weigh, and advise in this new world. She realized that young people no longer aimed at being accepted by adults but were making their own rules and challenging adults to respect those reasons and their differences. Susan found herself responding more and more to the younger woman's warmth and candor, finding herself articulating confidences she'd long considered too private to share. She felt inner walls of reserve crumbling, and the sensation was good.

"Carol, visiting with you is like coming home after a long day in Bangor all gussied up and uncomfy, getting my shoes off and letting my toes wiggle free. Better yet," and she giggled, "taking off the darn girdle I'd really outgrown years ago and being able to take a good deep breath. Freedom. Or, to use another metaphor, this experience has been like spring housecleaning. I've sorted through the closets and drawers of my mind and hauled a lot to the dump, making space for new ideas. I've also recognized the true worth of some ideas that have been stored away too long. Bless you and your magic."

Laughing, and very pleased, Carol replied, "My dear mother taught me one of her best lessons at the time of my father's death. Instead of being nobly brave and private, as taught, she shared her grief and really important feelings with friends and family, and gloried in the way they responded. New and precious intimacies and respect truly enriched these relationships. I think her philosophy of true candor at all times in our lives was the most valuable thing she left me."

Meeting some of the McLeans' friends gave Susan a new perspective on her own life. Most had kind but almost patronizing things to say of Maine. Some had gone to summer camps in Maine as children, or visited grandparents at the grand "cottages" of York Harbor, Kennebunkport, Prout's Neck or Mt. Desert. Many had cruised along the coast and knew the state only as a series of moorings off Portland, Boothbay, Camden, or the islands. The idea of actually living in her world of hidden lakes and wooded mountains, of lumber roads and white-water brooks was unknown, unimagined. Had she and others like her even existed in their minds, or had they been unimagined too?

Susan had loved every minute of every day, but she itched to return to her sewing machine, her loom, the kiln and brushes. Her creativity had always been productive, but now she realized that it was for her a continuing oasis of limitless refreshment.

Watching her absorbing so much. Carol likened the visit to the change a brighter bulb makes in the atmosphere of a room. A brighter bulb burned in Susan, a new energy and joy. If nothing at all came of the letter and its requests, a new and glowing phoenix hen was well out of the ashes, and preening with confidence.

Saying good-bye at Logan they clung to each other. Then Susan, as if it were something she did every day, marched sturdily to the gate and on board the first plane she had ever graced.

Disembarking in Bangor, Susan took in deep lungfuls of cold Maine air only slightly polluted in comparison to Boston's. She found herself relaxing from not just the flight, but the past week. She inspected with appreciation the people meeting the plane. Some, to sophisticated eyes, were possibly quaint or unbelievably dowdy, but to her eyes they were woodsy, warm and familiar. Not a purple Mohawk in the bunch, or miniskirts giving no protection to bare thighs. These were Mainers being their down-to-earth selves.

Stan and Jerry put on a great show of at first not recognizing her, but their hugs told her she'd been missed, a lot.

"Guess we're stuck with taking this glamour girl out for dinner, Jerry," Stan muttered. "She'd probably turn her nose up at those sardine sandwiches, pickles, and hard-boiled eggs we'd planned on eating in the car."

Susan laughed at this fairy tale and announced that she really needed a "fix" such as an honest-to-God Maine fish chowder with no frills. Before they'd even reached the car she was begging for news of the farm and the Phoenix project. "How is Matt Dillon adjusting to the life of a lawman? Any snow yet? Have any answers come to the mailing?"

She was assured that Matt and Mr. Howard, the mailman, had come to a mutual understanding of their respective responsibilities, with Heather acting as referee and providing dog yummies, hot coffee, and a Frisbee as treats. Yes, there had finally been a killing frost, but no snow yet. Replies to the letter and questionnaire were coming in much sooner and in greater quantity than they had expected. Both men seemed not altogether surprised that most were eruptions of strong feelings finally given an outlet, feelings of dissatisfaction, anger, and even fear.

"And most of them contain checks, sizeable checks, as the idea of having a chance to participate in the creation of an experimental and constructive program seems really appealing." Jerry's voice expressed his pleasure and almost disbelief.

Arriving at a busy seafood restaurant they were fortunate in getting a table near the fireplace, and quickly ordered celebration drinks. Jerry continued his analysis of the response.

"I haven't had much time to think this out, but I wonder if most of the responders, including ourselves, have felt a loss of control over their own lives because we all, somewhere down the line and for various reasons, abdicated our roles as decision makers. It may have always been like this, particularly in times of vast social and cultural changes, such as the Industrial Revolution, the American and French Revolutions, the results of our Civil War and the opening up of the West. Confusion about the rights and wrongs of old and familiar values is so upsetting that perhaps they often get swept under the rug, too troublesome and complex to handle or try to answer right then. So the opportunity to stay in charge, to protect at least those things worth protecting, is not only postponed but possibly lost for good and all."

He stirred his Manhattan with a swizzle stick and sucked off the cherry.

"In these letters I read of insecurity and the resulting fear and anger. Familiar guideposts have disappeared, familiar institutions are gone or unrecognizable; it's like trying to navigate in fog. New specialists tell us not to worry, they will take care of us, they will determine the needs of our families and children and communities, and they say it using words and terms we hardly understand.

"Financial needs of those answering seem to be met, though strained by insatiable consumerism. Maybe the best way to describe what we've seen so far is a debilitating lack of real honest-to-God old-fashioned satisfaction, no matter what has been achieved materially, possibly because goals are so uncertain. Annual incomes and security today are based on paper, Dow Jones, the GNP, etc., all intangibles and not worth a hoot in hell if there's a depression. Most of our forefathers had the genuine satisfaction of owning land or ships and being in charge of their destinies. Do our quests seem worth the effort? Do Holy Grails turn out to be only plastic or what plastic can buy? In all fairness, we did ask for what were the greatest concerns, disappointments, and fears. We certainly have been sent that sort of material, and that's what we're after, isn't it?"

Through this soliloquy Stan seemed about to erupt. The arrival of steaming bowls of chowder gave him the break he wanted. As spoons plunged into the soup, he plunged into the discussion.

"Damn it, the answer is clear as the nose on your face. This 'confusion' all started when that man, and you know who I mean, moved into the White House. He gave us the welfare state and big government, and was saved from having to pay for it by getting us into a dandy war, creating jobs a-plenty and sounding the death knell of private enterprise and initiative."

Sensing that she and Jerry were in for a long evening, Susan interrupted with unusual assurance.

"But Stan, with this 'welfare state' came badly needed social programs for those really unable to help themselves. The technological advances caused by war-created research made this country the world leader. A lot of other good things have happened too. The GI Bill brought new energy and a very different middle class emerged, while the lowest on the social ladder began their climb for rights. Wars always change society. Some wars go on and on, like the Cold War, influencing decisions more than we realize."

With that, Susan innocently crumbled her crackers into her chowder and continued her supper. With fascination Jerry watched Stan's face during this little speech and saw confusion, a touch of anger, but mostly shock. Had this thinking always been hidden beneath his wife's gentle, almost subservient demeanor? Did he see her as a stranger? Was she changing?

"OK, hear, hear, etc. Until we really catalog and analyze the answers we can't jump to conclusions," Jerry tactfully interrupted. "What I'd like to jump to is the tale of our pilgrim, and what she found in Beantown." Stan rather grumpily agreed. Tension evaporated.

It had been many years since Susan had had the opportunity to recount an experience not shared by Stan. She made good use of this freedom, mischievously presenting a tale of adventures and luxurious living that had both men wondering just where truth stopped and imagination kicked in. Talking and gesturing, she glowed with pleasure, warming the hearts of both listeners. Quite deliberately, hoping this was but the first of many trips, she set a standard of travel amenities that Stan would not be allowed to forget.

* * * * *

Portland

The Hudson attic was a mess. Twenty-five years of family life had found its way up there, and no amount of scolding, threats or promise of rewards could motivate Meg or Charlie to tackle their share and get most of it out, much less to the dump. Why should they when their parents' college textbooks and even term papers were still also up there, in piles? Letters, old photo albums, athletic awards, even Bill's father's footlocker, with WWII uniforms at the ready. One lonely fall Saturday Patsy mounted the steep stairs and, groping, found the long cord reaching the one light in the rafters. Here was a project to fill that day and many others, if she had the will.

As she worked, making a very small pile of books to throw away and a larger pile of those considered precious, she found herself occasionally near tears, moved by the memories being brought back. She looked through the album from her wedding. How young she and Bill looked, but they had certainly made the right choices. She had met young men more clever, from more prominent families, or handsomer, but none as fine as Bill Hudson, none so just right for her. Wrapped up in achieving, she had never made many close friends, and even with them had maintained a protective wall around her innermost spirit. This warm, decent, and loving man from Kittery, Maine, a student at nearby Amherst, had broken down most of that wall. She had given him all she knew how to give. Life with Bill was comfortable and happy. Bill was a lousy dancer but a whale of a diaper changer. He was often late to events but always on hand when she needed him. Too outspoken to ever win elective office, he was still active in community affairs and volunteer leadership. He didn't have an exciting imagination but was a completely truthful person, never afraid to stand up and be counted. She had never ceased feeling honored to be Mrs. William Hudson and tried to make him as happy and secure as he made her.

Fighting a corporate life, he built up a small but successful heating oil business of his own in Portland, content to sell an honest product for a fair price with good service. He was, above all else, a man of principle, and, most importantly, he loved her with absolutely no reservations, accepting her exactly as she was. It was a fine, solid marriage. Her competitive spirit had concentrated on preparing their children for success, based on her definitions of same.

Now the years of happy security had ended with Bill's death. For the first time, it was important to Patsy to prove something to herself and to others. "I hope it's more than just superficial personal image, Charlie, much more," she had mused. "I see a troubled world out there and I'm honestly in the race to find solutions. Republican solutions." This trip to the attic, bringing back the past, spurred her into really planning her future.

Looking ahead to reelection, Patsy searched for an issue that would not only excite and affect her own constituency but would also generate interest from Kittery to Fort Kent. She was intent on making a name for herself; eventually, she wanted to move on from representing just one fraction of Portland to Republican statewide office. So far the search had proved how much she had absorbed in this first year and how much she still had to learn. She had begun to understand how the legislature worked. Now she must discover how to make it work for her.

Health, education, and welfare concerns were the topics most candidates always beat to death, but fruitlessly, tied up as they were with federal largesse and red tape. Tax relief was popular, but beyond any one legislator to deliver and voters were tired of those empty campaign promises. They hoped for creative but practical ideas and laws that were enforceable, not just pie-in-the-sky oratory.

Racial discrimination in a state that was ninety-eight percent white was hardly a problem except to the few people of color involved. While Southeast Asian, Hispanic, and black populations were growing fast, particularly in Portland, the schools and churches were doing an acceptable job so far on integration and respect for diversity. Environmental issues, except for harbor spills and controlling industrial waste, did not yet directly excite Portlanders enough to be the center of a campaign .

One fine October day, Patsy took a favorite walk through the beautiful cemetery near her home. Designed to be more like an arboretum than just a burial ground, it was where her children had learned to skate, to drive, and, she was sure, even to "park" after dates. And it was where her Bill was buried.

Now she found much of its peace and dignity shattered by vandalism. Headstones were toppled, vaults were painted with foul graffiti, healthy shrubs were ripped out of the ground. Who would do such things? She knew this was not the first of such offenses here, but it was the first she'd seen personally. It made her furious. Marching immediately to the superintendent's office she found little satisfaction, just polite and hopeless frustration.

"Sorry, madam? Of course we're sorry. We have over two hundred acres to supervise and tend, lawns to keep mowed, trees and shrubs pruned, roads kept in decent condition. And we are about dead bottom, no joke intended, on the city's priority list when it comes to budgeting. Every year we can hire less help, so we cut corners and do our best. Yet people go right on dying, you know.

"I don't like to put the blame on any one group, but facts speak for themselves. This cemetery is smack in the middle of a residential area that contains three grammar schools, one junior high, and three high schools. That's a lot of kids let loose every afternoon by three o'clock, good kids and not so good. Many of the older ones have jobs, but most go home to empty houses or hang out around the stores or here in the cemetery. Believe me, in here, they're not on nature walks. But what can we do? We have a business to run, grounds to keep neat. We're not security cops. You say you're in the legislature? Find us an answer there. Find out what happened to respect."

For several weeks Patsy combed through the newspaper more carefully and found too many stories dealing with minor juvenile crimes. She discovered that, by Maine law, the names of juveniles guilty of minor crimes were never published, only the crimes and occasionally the victim. No neighborhood seemed immune, which was the worst shock of all. This was not just an inner-city, low-income situation. There were good kids everywhere, and also the others.

Armed with facts and outrage she called on the chief of police, known for his tough attitudes. She visited the schools and talked with the principals and guidance counselors; she stopped in at the county courtrooms and at the Boys' Training Center. Everywhere, she heard the same story. Too many turned off, unmotivated kids, too many indifferent or overwhelmed parents. Even good students with aspirations, worried parents doing conscientious jobs, and tired teachers willing to give extra time and effort had a hard time not being dragged down into this quagmire of disrespect. Worst of all, much of the public lumped all teens together as problem kids.

Was it possible to turn back the clock, to promote accountability, restore respect? At least Maine was forward-thinking enough to keep juveniles separated from adult prisoners in the county jails, but the Boys Training School was woefully crowded and understaffed. Effective rehab was nothing but a dream. In a world full of fine opportunities for the kids who were plugged in in time, too many young people with but one life to live were messed up already.

One evening, listening to a City Council's broadcast discussion on proposed curfew and loitering laws for troublesome juveniles downtown, Patsy was impressed by a recently elected young councilor who seemed to be on the same track as she was. Vassalo, Don Vassalo. A Democrat. She remembered the name from campaign posters but it was familiar in some other connection. What was it?

She called Vassalo the next day and he agreed to meet for lunch, any day but Tuesday. "Oh? Something special?" she kiddingly asked.

"You bet. That's the day my grandmother fills me up with good Italian food, support, and common sense, and I never miss that date." Patsy liked him right away, Democrat though he was.

Thursday was chosen and he suggested the Cumberland Club, where they could talk in relative quiet.

"Oho," thought Patsy. The prestigious and exclusive Cumberland Club, long the bastion of Portland's WASP social and business leaders, had certainly become more elastic in its membership. Formerly very few from once working-class Munjoy Hill backgrounds were accepted as members; now WASP Patsy was to be the guest of one. Portland was growing up.

Vassalo was waiting in the reception room of the fine old Federal mansion on High Street, and she recognized him instantly. No wonder the name had been familiar. Don had been in her Cub Scout den over twenty years ago, and the twinkle was still in his eye and the warmth in his manner. He'd been no angel, but was a favorite, and she was sorry she hadn't kept in touch. He was equally glad to see her.

That lunch led to other meetings. Her research and his legal background and volunteer work with kids gave them both more material in which to seek answers. They agreed that getting funded remedies for these obnoxious minor crimes of mixed-up juveniles was currently about as prioritized as immediate treatment for a sprained ankle in a hospital emergency room. A similar triage system was in place, called a bureaucratic budget.

The public could be divided into two groups concerning criminals: the Bleeding Hearts and the Lock the Bums Ups. Liberals seemed more concerned with helping the perpetrator than the victim, finding society at fault. Conservatives touted accountability and retribution, but balked at paying for more prisons. Average citizens didn't give wrongdoers much thought unless they personally were robbed or molested. Some prayed for the culprits and victims each Sunday, often not listening with their hearts to the words their mouths were saying. Others felt that annual contributions to

United Way exonerated them of any further social responsibility. A very few gave precious time and thought to serving on boards of agencies trying to staunch the hemorrhages, and a handful actually served on the rescue squads, the recreational programs, or labored in the prison cells.

Was there some innovative deal the courts could make offering a constructive second chance? Should the full responsibility fall on the juveniles, or was there a meaningful way to include parents in a rehab program?

Patsy found her answer one late afternoon in the checkout line of the supermarket. Two boys, about thirteen, stood behind her, chatting as they waited their turn to pay for chips and sodas.

"Saw your big brother's name in the Society Column last week," kidded one. "Your family must have been plenty pissed off."

"You'd better believe it. Jeez, even if he's legally an adult he's been grounded for a month and has to pay his own fine. I don't think they were half as mad about his getting the ticket as they were about seeing his name in the paper. It's our name too, ya know."

Patsy almost turned and hugged them, but the clerk had bagged her order and was impatiently waiting for payment. Arms full, she practically ran to her car. Ideas raced through her head as she drove home, carried the groceries into her house, and put them away. Later she found some in very odd places, but heck, genius was at work! She chuckled when marmalade showed up later with her cleaning supplies under the sink.

Who would have thought the District Court Report was read by anyone? Or that it was called the "Society Column?" Mentally she was transported to back to Olympia, Greece, home of the first Games. Last summer she had been particularly intrigued by what the guide had said about statues originally at the entrance to the arena. Not glorifying winners, they were monuments to shame for all to see, portraying those athletes who had cheated in some way and thus brought dishonor to their families and villages. Ancient history wasn't so dead!

She called Don. Without preamble she burst out, "How about this? A kid gets caught for a first minor crime and has to appear in court with his parents. The judge, depending on the severity of the case, sets a fine and possibly some community service, as per usual. But then, here we go, Hizzoner announces that he never wants to see the kid before his bench again, but if he does the kid and the parents will have two choices. Option Number One is a much stiffer fine and possibly a trip to the Training

School *plus* publication in the paper of the kid's name and address. Option Number Two is an agreement by the parents as well as the offender to go through a series of counseling sessions together, period."

There was silence on the other end of the line, and Patsy's throat tightened with disappointment. Then over the wire came "Wow!" Patsy could breathe again.

"There are lots of details to work out, of course, but it will bring the family into it as a unit. They will all learn more about one another's stresses."

They met for lunch the next day, this time at a small seafood place on Commercial Street, near the docks, part of real no-nonsense Portland though bordering on the chi-chi Old Port boutiques.

"Here's something else about it that I like." Patsy was sitting on the edge of her stool, face alight. "Counseling could bring all the principal actors in the drama together, even the victims, to sit down and talk things out with a positive goal rather a punitive one. The anger of each, including that of the police, could be vented with all sides listening to the other. Trained counselors can bring out feelings of fear, loneliness, and insecurity that judges aren't trained to do nor do they have the time to handle. Such supervised collaboration isn't a bad idea."

"Collaboration is a darned good remedy no matter what the problem," Don replied, "one I think we're going to hear more of. In this case, volunteers might act as mediators or even mentors. Put your political thinking cap on and consider this as a bill. It might even be used in just a few counties as a pilot. Try to find out what would it cost? Or save?"

"Have you ever thought of running for the legislature?" Patsy asked. Even though they were in different camps, she felt he was the kind of man who could make a difference, the right kind of difference.

Don laughed, a bit ruefully. "Funny you should ask. Since high school I have dreamed of doing just that, but lately it just doesn't seem to have the same appeal."

Grinning shyly, he continued. "To serve as a representative of my neighbors or my city has always sounded like a great position to aim for, but recently I've felt that it has lost its prestige and desirability. Politicians are rated pretty near the bottom of the ladder of respectability, along with horse traders and carnival shills. If I do run some day, it will be with reservations, and if I don't it may be with regrets." His voice drifted off and he didn't meet her eye.

"All the more reason for you to do it," Patsy almost shouted. "I feel that way lots of nights. But then the next morning, on the way to work, I look at that magnificent dome symbolizing the dignity of our state, and I walk proudly to my desk. On Mondays our sessions are opened by the Star Spangled Banner being played by an invited high school band that has been up before dawn to make the most of this honor. We transact the people's business in orderly fashion in the morning, and then in the afternoon, in committee, listen to the people of our state testify as to the effect proposed bills would have on their lives. We have the responsibility of making a decision. That makes our job important, not second-class, doesn't it? Don't listen to the sneerers. Go for it!"

Don actually whistled his way back to the office. He was reenergized, and intrigued by the plans they had for juvenile lawbreakers. What a challenge for all ages, for his own grandmother! What a ready-made mentor she'd be!

The Legislature would reconvene in January, giving Patsy about eight weeks to get her bill put together and ready for the hopper. She decided that she would also market it from the start, testing its appeal and building interest. With a presidential election coming up in just about a year she realized that there would be a lot of competition for the voters' attention and support. But she had also learned that most voters care more about issues they can identify with than they do about foreign policies or the national debt. This just might be one of those!

Lists. Constituent lists, lobbyist lists, media lists, etc. Patsy's 3 x 5 card filing system, of which she had been so proud, was proving inadequate for the twin campaigns of her bill and, later on, her reelection.

"Mom, what you need is a computer" came from both Bangor and Eastport. Hell's bells, she couldn't even really type, just hunt and peck. Her familiarity with the electronic and digital revolutions was minimal, to say the least. Sometimes she wished she was older, old enough to say it was too late to teach this old dog anything but play dead. But she was only in her mid-fifties and saw the handwriting on the wall. Get with it!

So a computer took possession of the dining-room table, and guests had to learn to eat around it. A crash course taught her the fundamentals of the monster, and both children repeated ad nauseam on the phone, "Think of it as a toy and play games with it." Pretty expensive and humiliating toy.

But once she had entered the information, darned if it couldn't spit out labels faster than she could peel them off and put them on envelopes.

A strong believer in personalizing all letters, she learned to write a form letter and with a certain amount of diddling around make each copy very personal indeed.

So off went a letter to her constituents of all parties and persuasions reminding them that she existed and asking for their opinions ASAP on this juvenile crime bill, very positively described. The darned computer did everything but lick the stamp. Welcome, Patsy Hudson, to cybernetics.

One morning as she pulled on jeans and a sweatshirt she caught sight of herself in the full-length mirror. Just a year ago that day she had been, by election, committed to a job she had sought but knew little about. She had partially moved to a strange city, prepared to learn, hoping to make friends, and taking herself off her children's worry list. All done without the support and advice from Bill she had taken for granted for so many years. She studied her image and decided this was a woman she knew, and liked, but quite different from last year's model. Her figure hadn't broadened, but her mind certainly had.

" Keep it up, old girl" she whispered, "you're doing OK."

Chapter 5: Winter 1987

Harding's Corner

Snow had fallen midweek, but the meteorologists promised clear and seasonable weather for Thanksgiving weekend. The annual gathering of families was well under way nationally. In the waiting room of Bangor International Airport, Heather positioned herself to catch the first possible glimpse of her grandmother debarking from the Chicago plane. Finally, there she was, petite, perfectly groomed, and exchanging holiday wishes with total strangers as she came into the reception area, while scanning every area for her granddaughter. In no time they were holding up traffic and not caring a bit; they were together.

Heather had taken a motel room for the afternoon so they could rest, freshen up, and be ready for dinner and an evening concert with the Warners. Soon they were enjoying thermos bottle tea and Heather-made cookies, gabbling like two schoolgirls, except for quite frequent pauses when they just stared at the other and beamed.

Finally Heather said, "I had a long drive and we'll have a long one back tonight. You can go for a hike if you want, Nana, but I'm going to catch some Z's." Soon Nana, grateful, was snoring peacefully and Heather, wrapped in a blanket, was happily gazing at the ceiling and whispering to herself, "My life has finally come together."

At six the three Warners appeared. No introductions were necessary, and they all enjoyed what Stan had brought along for a Happy Hour. As the concert was at the University in Orono, they drove to a fine Oriental restaurant there.

Heather was dressed in one of her Thai silk dresses, bright and beautifully draped. Nana wore a suit that just matched her extraordinary blue eyes, and Susan, glowing in her Boston finery, was happy to see that both men were sporting the ties she had brought them. Not a hayseed in the bunch!

The concert, featuring a South American dance group and chorus, was exceptionally good, and Nana seemed impressed to find such cosmopolitan quality in what she considered wilderness. During the intermission Heather waved at two women in the lobby, who came over to join them. Rep. Patsy Hudson, R, of Portland, was spending the holiday with her lawyer daughter Meg, a Brewer resident. Patsy was glad to see Heather again and hear that she was doing public relations work with the Warners, having evidently put TV journalism on hold.

"Since seeing you I moved to Portland, found a cause I wanted to do a documentary on, but then was lured from that back up here with the Warners on a wonderful job. There are rumors, Mrs. Hudson, that you are working on a bill very similar to my cause, juveniles."

Patsy would have loved to pursue that subject but knew this wasn't the time or place. Actually she was even more interested in the younger Warner, as she knew she had met him somewhere. Never mind, it would come to her some time; but why did Piglet enter her mind? The lights blinked and they all returned to their seats.

Much later Heather parked her car beside the little office building. She'd left lights on when she took off in the morning, those upstairs carefully placed to make every treasure glow. Nana caught her breath, enchanted by the beauty of this little nest, for that is how she saw her granddaughter's home, a shelter from a world that hadn't always been kind to her.

But now she wouldn't even sit down. "I haven't had to say this to you for a long, long time, child, but I'm saying it now. Beddy-bye time, for both of us, because this is one Thanksgiving on which I'm going to be truly thankful, given a decent sleep."

Next morning, the little living room was just as lovely in the daylight as at night, and Nana loved hearing again the story of each of the treasures, brought together actually for the first time.

Over a second cup of coffee Heather became pensive, a bit shy. "Well, what do you think of him?"

Nana was caught off guard. Think of whom? Stan, Jerry, Matt? It must be Jerry, as neither of the other two would evoke the dreamy look in the girl's eyes. None of Heather's letters had forewarned her of this.

"Jerry? From what little I've seen of him I like him. Nice looking in spite of the skewgee face. Did he meet up with a moose? And really nice laugh lines around his eyes. By the way, he couldn't take those eyes off you last night." From the little intake of Heather's breath Nana knew this was serious.

"Nana, I think this is it. Really. I feel so utterly comfortable with him, and we seem to operate on the same wavelength and at the same tempo. Though I've only known him a few weeks, and have little idea of his past life and what he hopes for a future, I've total faith in his integrity and respect for his values. Something tells me he has been through something big and hurtful, but I know in my heart it is something I can accept, even help him handle, given the opportunity."

She put her mug down and walked over to the window, looking out over the snowy fields. Very softly "And I sometimes believe I mean something to him, but then he'll suddenly turn off and I'm left hanging, in the dark. He'll be so happy, so warm, and then he seems to hear alarm bells. I'm not that scary, am I?"

Nana laughed gently. "'Scary' is never a word I'd apply to you, dear. You're new to each other. It's been several years since you were badly hurt yourself. Maybe he needs more time."

"OK, wise one. But let's help him along. He gets the full treatment today. My gold ultra-suede is going to war!"

Soon they were on the way to the Warners, a basket of nuts, candies, olives, and crackers tucked out of Matt's way. Nana had had little concept of how really uninhabited this area was, noting now that the only buildings they passed were obviously deserted, the fields untended. A few cars were parked near occasional wooded areas.

"This is the last weekend of the deer-hunting season, Nana, and then even these visitors will be gone."

Though Heather had written her of the charm of the Warner home, Nana was not prepared for the warmth produced by hospitality, colors, cooking odors, and the old stove itself, doing a herculean task on this special day. Susan, shy as always about showing off her artistry, let Heather do the honors with a tour, then all three women set to work peeling potatoes, dicing squash, basting the sputtering turkey, and slipping gemlike jellies onto saucers.

Today was too special for even faultless Susan-made pottery; nothing but fine porcelain would do, with heirloom crystal, silver, and damask also brought from storage. The chill of the little-used dining room was chased by a fire in the huge fireplace. Shining apples, mixed gourds, and nuts formed a centerpiece. Several wine glasses were at each place.

Heather, idly inspecting the china set out on the kitchen counters, caught sight of a delicate little Wedgwood pitcher, and her heart unexpectedly flipped. Her hand went out, picked it up, and turned it over and around. Susan was passing by and saw her interest.

"Lovely, isn't it? Sort of an heirloom, even though a little the worse for wear." She referred to cracks expertly mended.

She was surprised at the intensity of Heather's reply. "How did it get broken, and when?"

"My sister, who has since died, was visiting my mother with her little girl, and the child seemed to like the little figures on the pitcher. Unfortunately, it slipped out of her hand and broke, but so cleanly that it was easily mended later. When we lost my mother it came to me, with all her other things. I've always hoped that my little niece knew it was mended and still in use."

"Your sister, when did she die, and where?" Heather's voice was strained and tight. Nana heard this and she moved gently, to hold Heather's hand and squeeze it.

"About twenty, no, about twenty-five years ago. She and her husband and the little girl were in a terrible accident in Germany, where her husband was stationed in the Army. Sara and Bob were killed, and the little girl was raised by her dad's parents in the Midwest. For many sad reasons, we lost touch. But I have this reminder."

Heather was very white, her eyes huge. Nana spoke softly, still holding Heather's hand and reaching for Susan's.

"I think we all have more, unbelievably, to be thankful for today than we could possibly imagine. From your story I believe that your sister's husband was my son, Bob Delano. Heather is that little pitcher-breaker. You've probably have never had reason to hear my last name; I'm not just Nana, but Nana Delano."

For just a second the three women were almost rigid, then Susan's arms enveloped Heather, and Nana did her best to hug both.

Across the room, noting an unaccustomed female silence, Stan was about to make some kidding remark but realized, for once, that the timing might be very bad indeed. There was something in that tableau of the three women reminiscent of Greek drama, Greek tragedy.

Susan recovered first, though sobbing. "Stan, Jerry, we have just become a bigger, a most wonderful family. Heather, our new treasure, is also my sister Sara's child! Oh my darling girl, welcome, welcome."

As Susan's arms went around her again, Heather felt a warm rush of joy greater than she had ever known. Susan, dear, loving Susan was her aunt; now she had part of her mother back. Still in Susan's embrace she looked over that soft shoulder and saw Jerry grinning at her. Suddenly she turned ice-cold inside. Jerry was her cousin, her first cousin! Damn, damn,damn. Calling on lifelong poise and training she crossed the room to hug her new uncle and his son. She stiffened as Jerry's arms at last went around her and his lips brushed her cheek.

Surprised by this reaction, but alerted by what he saw in her eyes, Jerry automatically shifted into his accustomed role of warding off trouble, preventing drama. "The sun may not be quite over the yardarm yet, but this calls for immediate celebration. Give me a hand, coz?" And with a wink he led her off to the bar area, where, as she filled glasses, she could take a few good deep breaths and start mending whatever had been broken—a heart this time, not a little pitcher.

Everything went well after that. The toasts were not only amusing and clever, but permissibly sentimental. The meal, almost all of which had been produced on the farm, was splendid; the dishes were done in no time by the men anxious to watch their promised ball game. This was a Thanksgiving first for Stan, and even better than listening to the Harvard-Yale game with Jerry last week, though Yale had won.

Later, Heather could not recall one minute of it all. However Nana assured her, on the way home, that acting was always a talent she could fall back on, so well had she hidden her heartbreak. The one thing she would always remember was Jerry's immediate sensitivity and kindness though he had no idea why it was needed. But damn, that was like finally being anchor for your own TV show, even noting celebrities in the studio, and then having the power fail, permanently! Do all dreams have to die?

Now she would have the almost daily opportunities to be with him, get to know him better, to love him more, but right across that dear "skewgee" face she would always read the word "NO!" She was going to be like a diabetic in a candy shop.

* * * * *

Friday and Saturday were spent finishing the tabulation of the questionnaires, enjoying Thanksgiving leftovers, and reintroducing Nana to a lifestyle that was extraordinarily similar to hers fifty years ago as far as amenities and simplicity were concerned. She purred.

Sunday afternoon was set aside for business, and they all met in the little office, crowded around a long table.

"December first was the date we asked for responses, and this is close enough." Jerry was in charge. He asked Heather to turn on a tape recorder so that absent Joel and Carol could have a verbatim report.

"On the table behind me are large envelopes, one for each of us. They contain digests of the research I have been doing for over six months, research on Maine, its pluses and minuses, its needs, its gifts, and mainly its people and how they think. It has been a fun project and a humbling one. What a great place! Many, many thanks to Heather for putting all my scribbles and notes and photocopies together.

"On the table before me are the answers we've received to our questionnaire, an amazingly high sixty-two percent response rate. Heather and I have separated them according to what problem each person believes needs the most attention, why, and sometimes what to do about it. As you can see, these piles are labeled by subject matter. If they strike you as negative, even whiny, don't forget that we asked for what was most troubling in today's culture."

Stan interrupted. "What's that biggest one, labeled Umbrella? All the miscellaneous stuff that didn't fit in anywhere else?"

"Not quite, Stan. That pile contains letters suggesting a generalized program, one that actually deals with all the others, but based on a single philosophy or common attitude rather than specifics. There are some amazing plans in it, well thought out, and plans that with a little adjustment or tailoring would be as applicable, for instance, to education as to small business,

"In your big envelopes is a review of all these replies and letters. There is a whale of a lot of work ahead for us all. By the way, Nana, will you honor us and come on board as senior consultant ? You represent a generation we need to hear more from."

She nodded happily, excitement shining from her eyes. A new interest, or career, just when she thought she was done.

Susan spoke up. "You can't leave us hanging in suspense this way. Is there any common thread to the Umbrella suggestions? Wouldn't it make it easier for all of us if we learned of it now and discussed it a little, rather than each going it alone when we separate?"

Jerry laughed and, moving over to her, patted her lovingly on the shoulder. "I thought no one would ever ask, and I'm just bursting with it. Thanks, Mom." It was the first time he had called her that. A "mom" and "cousin" all in one weekend!

"Yes, there is a very definite similarity in all these solutions, something that caused me weeks of extra work and research. Prepare to be as surprised as I was. Here goes."

He pushed the piles off to one side, refilled his mug, and looked at each of the board to be sure he had their full attention.

"There are five major religions in the world: Islam, Judaism, Christianity, Buddhism, and Hinduism, and many other branches or sects of these. They are all based on the revelations of founders, on the voices of prophets, or on the results of mystic experiences. Some have books of laws and of history. Some worship in churches, with formal services. Others use temples and shrines just for individual worship and guidance. Each looks on life on this earth and in the hereafter quite differently. These five involve most of the people of this planet. But different as they may seem to us, they all have as their cornerstones, one basic tenet. In Christianity, we call it the Golden Rule."

He rose and walked around the table to where the Umbrella pile lay. He put his hand on it.

"In each and every one of these letters is that same theme, expressed in individual ways. Each writer cries out for some way to make respect, mutual trust, and caring for one another our prime concern. A great many of them start out wistfully with the words 'if only.' They go on to paint a world of civility, integrity, respect of rights and one in which progress can be made because of faith in the existence of all these conditions. Very, very few of them mention God, organized religion, even spirituality, and they all blame the 'other guy."

He laughed, albeit a little hollowly. "It's as if each thought they'd invented the idea themselves."

The others joined him in laughing, but a little nervously, wondering what was coming next.

He sensed that nervousness. "Don't worry. I have no idea of asking you to become televangelists, or to run around in orange robes and shaven heads, begging. But if you agree, after study, that this is their message and plea, then we have an even bigger job than we'd imagined, much bigger. My religious education and feelings are a bit unorthodox, typical probably of my generation. I am definitely not a fundamentalist believing each and every word of the Good Book literally. To me the Bible is a wonderful history of the Jewish people, a combination of magnificent prose and poetry, and a textbook using marvelously crafted stories and parables to teach what even in those ancient times were already age-old and proven truths. Myths can be more powerful than truth sometimes. Moses probably existed, may have led the Exodus, and may possibly have gone to a mountain for a long period, returning with laws of how to live with God and one another, mysteriously cut into stone tablets. On the other hand, maybe a group of wise old Hebrews, sitting under a palm tree one hot day, tried to think of a way to pass on the wisdom of their years and history to their heirs. They made a list of the do's and dont's of successful communal and spiritual living and gave the hero role to a leader who had actually existed, in order to keep that list in peoples' minds. It's lasted almost three thousand years.

"Other bodies of religious law have been written later to fine-tune the so-called Commandments as populations expanded, urban living became prevalent, and restless young questioned their elders' authority. Sound familiar? So there had to be rewards for good behavior, not material, but spiritual. The Beatitudes were one such, promising a lot. I truly doubt that anyone was sitting there on that hillside taking them down in some Greek, Hebrew, or even cuneiform shorthand. No, it was probably a new bunch of wise old men, and maybe women, under a different palm tree, creating them, possibly with divine guidance. And new, stronger creeds were written when the old ones were ready to be recycled.

"But sadly, little by little, with vast cultural changes, the message of those old sages on the road out of Egypt has been so watered down and reinterpreted that many of us now apply the rules only when convenient. The awesome authority of many religions has weakened. We've twisted the rules to our advantage, adopted situational ethics, and now have a tough time personally accepting disciplines of any kind, though deploring the flaccidity of manners and mores of our times, And that's just the history of Judaism and Christianity."

Throat dry, but eyes shining with excitement, Jerry poured another mug of coffee and looked around the room. His friends were silent, whether shocked out of their socks or spellbound he didn't know. Certainly not bored.

Patting the Umbrella pile again, he resumed.

"Many of the responses we've received list small complaints that add up to huge annoyances and very real stress. Traffic gridlock daily, hands too quick on the horn, road rage. The lure of the nearest bar on the way from office to train to home in suburbs, only to find the children already fed and wife waiting with another drink ready. They cite rudeness from people as stressed-out as they are and truth frighteningly twisted for personal advantage. They underline that competition for things, for status cars and designer jeans and sneakers, takes the place of knightly tournaments or the title of Mighty Hunter. Big deals are being made of a lot of little nothings because maybe there aren't any satisfying Big Somethings in view.

"They write of lives cluttered up with therapists, self-improvement books, and sweat-till-you-drop exercise clubs, created because your lawn is so big you either hire someone to cut it or buy a riding mower. Churches clinging to fear-of-God Puritanism seem to have no message of joy and are out of touch except when they act as social agencies. Many other denominations are getting closer and closer to becoming entertainment centers with feel-good hallelujahs but not much meat.

"And they write of narrow-minded suspicion and friction between even the Christian sects, let alone acceptance or validity of Judaism, Islam, or Eastern faiths. Look at history and you see a lot of blood shed in the name of a religion or a certain deity, though most of the founders preached peace. The magnitude of crime, of the drug problem, and of homelessness is frightening, but seems too big to tackle. Discrimination and violence poison society. Families are breaking up or need a new definition.

"So, you get the idea. Frustrated, angry, and empty, our friends out there really want to come to terms with their fellowman, sharing trust, respect and even purpose with him.

"Ladies and gentleman, the next months are busy. Can we study this material and meet again on Presidents' Weekend, full of ideas, answers, and the energy to formulate an attractive plan? Can we then choose either some specific area, or just one for this general condition? OK? What time is it?"

Nana looked at the wall clock. "Five-thirty, and where I live that is Attitude Adjustment time!" They all roared approval, then Heather's voice rose above the others.

"That's it. That's what we'll call this general program, Attitude Adjustment. Nice modern sound to that, yet it's right on the mark. Or, think about this. How about Altitude Adjustment, to tie it into Phoenix rising up, up from the ashes?" Cheers.

The bottles were brought forth, ice began to clink in glasses, but the excitement over what had been said fired up the hour more than the bottled spirits did.

That evening, their last together for a while, Heather and Nana discussed the weekend. They would, as always, keep in close touch by mail and phone, and Nana's shoulder was always figuratively ready when the Jerry problem got too upsetting. Now Nana cocked her head and asked, "What else is on your mind that we haven't talked about? I know there's something."

"You always do." And Heather finally told her of being pushed down on the sidewalk, her rage and the resulting determination to somehow replace anger with courtesy and fear with trust.

"This happened the day I'd received your letter about being useless and unneeded. Wrong, wrong. Yours is the first generation to live longer than charts say you should. When you were born it was estimated you would live to fifty. Ha!. It's wonderful, but probably frightening for you in many ways, as you have no role models to turn to. You can't think back to what your mother, at eighty-three, would have done in certain circumstances, because she never reached that age. You're on your own in a new, confusing world, and want to find a place for yourselves and niches to fill, if I'm not mistaken."

Nana nodded, touched that her granddaughter was so perceptive.

"Since the Industrial Revolution older people have been considered more and more useless as they generally have not kept up with technology. Rural families may still count on them to help with the children, chores, and housework, but in the cities there is less and less room for them and too many are actually being warehoused. Now perhaps the computer is actually doing the same thing again: enlarging or even creating another tremendous generation gap.

"Few of us take into consideration your years of rich living experience or of acquiring wisdom. You clutter up the supermarket aisles as you carefully read labels. You have discounts on a great deal, though our payments into Social Security go up and up. There is precious little sympathy for you as your crises are magnified by politicians dependent on delivering your perceived lifelines in exchange for your vote.

"But," and her eyes glowed with love and conviction, "older people have the gift of seeing things in long-range perspective. Stored in your memories are the anecdotes and histories of many of life's challenges and how they have been met by friends and relatives. You all have an objectivity it takes years to develop. Maybe seniors grouse about change because the guideposts by which they were raised and lived not only seem to be threatened but may have disappeared entirely. Some are frightened. I'm sure some feel entitled to all they can get for free.

"However, Foster Grandparents, tutors, mentors, are all needed by young people aching for seasoned advice, for someone who will truly listen, set them straight and love them. Kids are so very knowledgeable about so much that impressed adults don't realize how naive they really are about a lot. My generation needs you too, to help face the problems you faced and licked."

She stared at her grandmother, excited and hopeful.

Nana's face grew serious. "I agree with almost all of that, dear. So now let's talk about what to do. You and I haven't much time before I leave, so let's face facts. Your grandfather was in advertising, and I learned a bit from him. A good campaign is a must, as pervasive as those of Cabbage Patch Doll, the Pet Rock, or Barbie. You've got to suck people in and then let them find out that what they've fallen for is for real, and actually worth something."

"All the talk this afternoon sounds great, but I believe that what has been suggested is going to take superb marketing. It cannot smack of the old answers that have lost their appeal, but will need classy, imaginative presentation as well as fantastic logos and slogans. Right now perhaps the cynicism and apathy are so great that you will even have to sell the idea on 'what's in it for me' terms in the beginning, rather than idealism. Frankly, I wish your Grandpa was here to help"

Heather gave a whoop of pure joy. "I think you've got it, I think you've got it," she sang, and leaping to her feet she whirled around the room. Grabbing her grandmother she spun her around too, and into the bedroom where they both fell on the bed, laughing.

Next morning Nana looked down on Maine from hundreds of feet up in a clear blue sky. In her bag was the big envelope full of work to be studied, and in her heart was the feeling that she might just be needed again. In addition to her concern for a good public relations plan, her mind was racing. What could one old lady do to help mixed-up, unhappy young people? She didn't even know any. The only ones she could think of were the high school girls and boys who served in the dining room at her residence. So, what's to lose?

* * * * *

Christmas music had been playing in the stores since Halloween, truckloads of Christmas trees rolled south and west along Maine highways, and in Washington and Hancock counties millions of balsam tips were gathered and fashioned into fragrant wreaths to be shipped all over the world. In most towns, after the football season was history and as soon as the United Way campaign was over, all energies of the community-minded were devoted to the church fairs, the school plays, the Salvation Army toy drive or the choral society's concert. Letters to Santa were mailed, presents secretly wrapped and hidden. Just as in years past, commercialism actually ran a poor second to the excitement of giving.

Many ancient rituals, myths and legends, generally based on the season's solstice, had combined over the ages to welcome once again the coming of new life with the renewal of light. It would be interesting, in centuries to come, to read a history of this great holiday, its roots, development and universality, its magic that answered a basic human need.

Joel and Carol were busy shopping, addressing and mailing packages and cards, attending a round of neighborhood and business parties, and ferrying their young to other parties and rehearsals. Their suburban home glowed with lovely lighting, ingenious decorations, and a tree trimmed almost entirely with precious objects made by the family over the years.

Yet every night, before turning out their lights, they disciplined themselves to read and discuss the material Jerry and Heather had so painstakingly collected. Both were impressed by the lengths Jerry had gone to give accurate and unbiased facts. He had sought facts for facts' sake and not to prove any particular points. His own training made possible expert analysis, based on laborious studies from every source obtainable and including many personal interviews. And every night the McLeans' lights burned later and their discussions became more excited. If this Phoenix thing really worked, it would be the best gift they had ever had a hand in donating.

Nana spent her days making an extra effort to contact friends more housebound than she, bringing them brightly colored little gifts and spreading her new message of their own importance. Little by little she drew them out, finding slots of meaningful activities into which they could fit. A few already were serving as mentors, and were planning a Christmas party for the teens with whom they had connected. Rather than finding her own pleasure in nostalgic memories, for the first time in quite a while Nana reveled in the current excitement. She felt part of it again, no longer a useless spectator but a doer with responsibilities.

In addition, every night after dinner with friends in the center's dining room, she scurried upstairs to her own apartment, found her glasses, and settled down for a good evening's study of Jerry's material. What an education for an old lady! She'd had no idea that graphs of such things as commercial fish catches, population data, or hunting licenses sold to outta-staters could be so interesting. She was particularly intrigued to see how each fitted into a general picture, like a jigsaw puzzle. Her calls to Heather became more frequent as she just had to talk some of the subjects over with someone. To save her energies for February she planned to stay put for Christmas and pep things up at the home.

After many, many years of shying away from all that the season meant, Susan woke one morning with the splendid idea of having a real Christmas party, inviting their few neighbors, the new friends they had made at the Farmers' Market and anyone else she could think of. Introducing her "son" and niece to them would be a joy, and her mind went back many years to the childhood Christmases shared with Heather's mother. She would try to recreate those celebrations for the girl; already she was putting together a scrapbook of yellowing snapshots and faded letters, to introduce Heather to her heritage. Jerry's arrival, the healing of her marriage, Heather and the exciting broadening of her own thinking: all needed expression. Christmas, with its message, was just the vehicle.

Surprisingly, Stan went right along with her plans, particularly interested in finding the best possible tree and mixing the most impossibly splendid punch. They chose the Saturday before Christmas, and Susan designed and mailed invitations that would be hard to resist. "Open House, Open Hearts, Open Mouths; come, enjoy each other and sing, eat and drink all your old favorites. Get the chores done by five and pray for good driving weather."

Lots of work to do as one splendid idea led to another. Susan became fascinated by the new-to-her Christmas TV programs suggesting recipes, decorations, and handmade gifts, not to mention scenes of the holiday preparations from 5th Avenue to Hong Kong. But as cookies baked, candies cooled, and little painted decorations and gifts dried, both Stan and Susan also pored over those pages and pages of Jerry's research. They were amazed that a newcomer could have discovered so much about their adopted state in such a short time, and presented it so fairly. It was an exciting world out there, much of it a surprise to them, ready to be explored.

Of course Heather helped with party plans, and was busy making surprise gifts for her new family. During her traveling years she had collected little objects that she'd always wanted to put on a Christmas tree. Made from clay, metal, leather, fabric, or straw, they had a wonderful variety of colors and shapes. These were placed on and around the Warner tree. On a small table was her favorite Christmas treasure, a crèche from Africa, carved in mahogany and telling the wonderful story most dramatically. They all were reminders that the Gift belonged to the whole world and to every race.

Christmas, with its warmth, love, and joy, was going to be blessed in another way, as she'd never had so many she loved together. But that was also a quandary. Jerry was more and more the gift she wanted in the toe of her stocking, the angel she wanted to put on the top of the tree, the Santa who brought nothing but good things. He was going to be there every minute, off limits. Good old cousin Jerry. Bah, humbug.

In the office, working together almost daily, she had learned to concentrate on professionalism, on the business at hand. But how could she be coolly professional in the smashing red dress she'd found, with Christmas music swirling around her, with love the message of the day? Why, oh why, had this joke been played on her? In the past few years she had met, and coped with, lovesick young men in London, Paris, New York, on the equator, and on all seven continents. Now, in an unnamed township in the wilds of the most remote of the Lower 48 states, she had found what she'd been seeking, the prince of her dreams—and he was her first cousin! Very funny, very haha. She tried hard to switch her mind to the Phoenix report, reevaluating those pages and pages she had typed.

The amount of mail continued to amaze Jerry, but most of it was supportive. Some people had written not once but several times, as they had time to absorb what Joel's letter had suggested. More and more Jerry was convinced that going for Altitude Adjustment rather than one specific field was almost inevitable, but he felt honor-bound to leave this decision to the committee. Doing that would also tell him who was really interested in what, and where they should be placed in whatever program they chose. His mind was so full of it that he wondered if he slept at night at all.

But the program didn't command all his attention. Since Thanksgiving Heather had cooled off a lot, which puzzled him, but it did make things a bit easier. If she had continued the warmth and friendliness he'd been so grateful for, they might be in a real mess. Until he could find a solution to the Phyllis problem he refused to make a move. Heather was too precious for just an affair. He could not cheapen her that way, even if she was willing. So he concentrated on the party plans when Phoenix didn't demand his attention.

Finally Susan's Saturday came. Enough snow had fallen the night before to make a good plowing job necessary for adequate parking in the yard. A huge wreath hung from the barn door. Candles placed in short paper bags lit the guests' way to the seldom-used front walk, while other candles twinkled from every window. Sporting bright red ribbon collars, the dogs greeted all enthusiastically while Grandma Moses, similarly bedecked, watched with feigned boredom from a perch atop the refrigerator.

Most of the guests brought gifts, from practical household necessities such as fresh potholders, to jams, pickles, mincemeat and cookies. Some decorations were added quietly. One giggling spinster presented Susan with a large mistletoe kissing ball to be hung over a busy doorway. Stan quickly put it in place, genuinely amazed at how much he was enjoying everything. What had happened to the crusty old codger he had worked so long to create?

Isolated as most of the guests' homes were, a party was a real event. Everyone knew someone else, but new acquaintances were made too. Most were making their first visit to the Warner home, so the sharing of pleasure in their surroundings brought strangers together: the mailman in civilian clothes, the garage mechanic magically free of grease, and a group from the power company looking unfamiliar without hard hats. Women who had only seen each other in jeans, shirts, and bandannas exclaimed over pretty skirts, blouses, and holiday accessories. There were few young people, a fact not lost on Jerry. Had they emigrated, discouraged?

Native Mainers mixed well with the outta-staters, as all of this group lived under similar conditions. A few of the Back-to-the-Land-Trust-Fund-Babies took occasional winter trips to Florida to visit vacationing parents, but were generally quiet about these. Weather conditions ruled more lives than did the stock market. Frozen pipes were more familiar than frozen assets.

Susan had decided to have this an old-fashioned party, so instead of music coming from the new stereo or tapes, it came from the old windup record player. All rooms were lit by candles and lamps, and that soft lighting was complimentary to even the weathered and bearded men.

True to form, Stan's punch was the center of mingling, then the tables laden with chips, small sandwiches, and raw vegetables and dips. Time for snacking first, but all knew a real meal lay ahead. Nobody was expected to drive this far in the dead of winter for just peanuts or pretzels. As the level of the punch bowl went down, the noise level rose.

Susan opened the shed door occasionally to cool off the kitchen, where most people gathered. The windows steamed up. Heather kept her eye on the few shy guests and drew them into chatting groups. She'd lost track of Jerry early in the evening as he also moved from group to group. Probably it was best.

Standing in the dining room, she heard a cheer come from the kitchen, a big deep "ho, ho, ho." Running to the door, she saw Santa come in from the yard, carrying a huge sack over his shoulder. Even the pillows, white beard and exaggerated deep voice did not fool her.

"So that's where he's been," she said to herself. When her heart stopped beating outrageously she leaned against the doorframe and joined the others in laughter.

Santa sat down in Stan's rocking chair, pack on the floor beside him. As he called out names each person had to come forward, receive some kindly personal kidding and a gift, and perform in some way. The jokes, little songs, sleight-of-hand, and even imitations that followed were all greeted with enthusiasm; some were surprisingly good.

Jerry left his family to the last and Stan and Susan knew what was expected of them. As their names were called Stan walked over to the old record player, gave it a good windup, and took Susan in his arms. Off they danced to "A White Christmas."

Santa stood up and moved over to where Heather was, his arms outstretched. Her face was flaming, but as he gathered her to him and started to dance, she felt she could melt into his body, padded though it was. This dance must last forever.

Soon the floor was covered with dancing couples, just as Stan had intended. Records were changed when necessary, old favorites found, and everyone was involved when Susan called out "Come and get it!"

Reluctantly Jerry let his arms drop and those two just stood and looked at each other. People moved past them to where the food was served. Soon they were alone, standing in the doorway. Heather could hardly breathe. Jerry looked over her head and spotted the mistletoe.

"Thank God," he whispered, "we can't not." As their lips met, the pillows, fake beard, and mustache made no difference. Mouths opened eagerly, little gasps of more than casual pleasure escaped them both. As they pressed closer together she could feel his excitement, and wanted so much to respond. Then voices and laughter broke into the room and Jerry stepped back, gave her his love with his eyes, and disappeared up the front stairs to change back into his jacket and slacks. Heather was limp, almost faint, but knew she had an act to play. Shaking her head waggishly, but really to clear it, she pointed at the mistletoe and giggled, then went to the dining room to fill her plate.

When all had had enough to eat, or more than enough, to everyone's surprise Mr. Howard, the mailman, went out to his car and brought back an accordion. Starting with "Jingle Bells" he led them through most of the loved old carols and Christmas songs. There were enough good voices to inspire the others. It was quite late when he paused and gave them time to relax. Then slowly and gently all the guests joined in "Silent Night." As the last notes were sung, people moved, sought their coats and boots, wished each other well. A new neighborliness had been given birth that night; just what Christmas was all about.

Finally the dishes were done, all things put away, and Heather went in to the hall for her coat. Jerry followed.

"I'd like to drive you home, if I may. There's something I have to tell you," he pleaded.

"As long as you don't make me hike back here tomorrow. My car isn't trained to drive itself, you know." She tried to make her voice light and went to find the Warners for a Christmas kiss.

Heather knew that Jerry was very serious about something. This was a time for her to keep her cool. She needed to listen with her head as well as her heart, yet not spoil in any way the moments they had clung together. That precious Christmas gift.

He drove silently for a while and she waited, almost not breathing. When he spoke he tried to keep his voice cool.

"Heather, I think you know that you mean a great deal to me. But, without going into a long song and dance, it's time you knew," and he paused, his voice now trembling. "I'm married."

Heather stiffened. If he had opened a window and let in the icy air, she would have had the same sense of shock. No talk about cousinhood, for which she had prepared herself. Married! This was completely unexpected.

"I guess that does make a difference. Do you want to tell me more?" She couldn't believe that her voice was so controlled.

"Just that we've been separated for almost a year actually, but for many years emotionally. There are two sides to everything. But I believe my wife is a very fine but disturbed woman. I did all I knew how to do to help her. Leaving her was my final remedy for her, and for me. From what I hear, she may improve. But a divorce would be the monster blow of all to her, and she doesn't deserve that treatment."

He looked out across the snow-covered moonlit fields, up into the clear night sky. "I don't feel I can ask you to wait till this all works out. I don't want to cheapen what I feel for you by having an affair with no acceptable end in sight." He chuckled grimly. "Here I am doing all the talking, saying what I want. What do you feel? What do you want?"

Heather looked out her window at the fields on her side of the road, and at the sky that covered them both.

"First, I thank you for telling me. And I thank you for the respect you are showing me. But I have a problem too, one that also keeps us apart. So let's drive on to my little nest, give each other chaste little Christmas kisses, and hope by the time this works out, if it ever does," she forced a laugh, "we won't be too old to make a go of it."

She was disappointed in what she'd said. It came out coldly, which she hadn't intended. She wanted to cry out, saying "I don't really mean all that," but was that fair? She mustn't start what he felt he mustn't finish.

Climbing alone up the narrow stairs to her apartment she realized how exhausted she was. The beautiful red dress was thrown on a chair, the tired but comfy flannel nightie embraced her, and as she put her head on the pillow she thought about "Oh Come All Ye Faithful." But why does this one have to be so darned faithful?" In her heart she was glad he was. If only her problem with him could be solved, like his, by patient waiting.

Chapter 6: Late Winter, 1988

Augusta

Choosing the most effective legislators to be cosponsors for her bill had tested Patsy's developing political savvy. As a relative newcomer, it was important to establish credibility by exhibiting strong, solid support. She wanted workers who were willing to put their political names on the line for an idea they believed in. She needed people who could bring in votes from all shades of legislators, yet she must keep in mind that she would owe them for their support and should be comfortable returning the favor. A good balance of both parties, Houses, sexes, and districts was only sensible. That was the way the game was played.

She finally chose four legislators: a teacher, a social worker, a retired police chief, and a factory worker—two from each party. As well as their experience in the field of juvenile problems, all four had reputations for effective and broadminded legislating. Patsy sent them a rough draft of the bill with a letter asking for their help and inviting them to lunch the opening day of the session. By formalizing her request for support in this way and on this day she hoped to earn their attention, if not their respect. All had accepted.

She reserved a small private dining room at the Senator, where there would be no interruptions. At each place she put a packet containing photocopied news stories of minor juvenile crimes which had taken place recently in their own districts. This should indicate that they were not dealing with just a Portland problem, a kiss of death to many bills. Results of her own constituent poll were also enclosed, as they had been very positive.

Not only because he deserved it, but because his presence would underline the bipartisan quality of the bill, she had invited Don Vassalo. Newsman Mark Lowell had caught wind of the meeting and had asked to attend. "It sounds interesting and I will keep it under my hat until you give me an OK to go further." Flattering.

When her guests had finished their fruit cup and the entree was being served, Patsy tapped on her glass for attention.

"Thank you for coming, and I hope that it was more than curiosity about this unorthodox approach that brought you. Today is a busy one and many of you have meetings after this, so let's get started.

"I need you, or rather this bill needs you, very badly. In my research I have found that juvenile petty crime is not just an urban or a rural problem, nor is it peculiar only to southern Maine, Downeast, or the western mountains." She smiled. "It isn't even endemic to one party more than the other. Strictly bipartisan."

Her guests nodded agreement, appreciating her humor.

"I hope you would all agree that what we are seeing is not only an increasing statewide and even nationwide breakdown of respect for others and their property, but also of family responsibility. Tragically, there also seems to be a lessening of youthful aspirations and self-confidence. These attitudes are puzzling and frightening.

"In this bill parents get help, the public feels less threatened, and the juvenile, while disciplined, may believe that at last he or she has the interest and possible support of both family and caring mentors. The first counseling session of those juveniles involved for a second time in minor crime, and whose parents have chosen this option, will include the victims, the parents, police, and the kids themselves. This approach may bring results. I call it Collaboration. It admits and defines the problem and throws it open to constructive solution, with input from all involved. Each case is given the dignity of being unique and solvable.

"You've all read the rough draft. Now I'd like comments and questions."

The retired police chief raised his hand.

"I'm sorry to say, some few kids will probably never stay out of trouble long. But many I've seen just need positive support, particularly from parents who need it also. I still believe most kids would rather steal second base than an automobile. If kids don't get support and confidence from their families they may seek and find for themselves an alternative, a gang situation which, for all the wrong reasons, does support them.

"Having said that," he continued, "in order to work, the program would have to be compassionate, but without sentimentality. A lot of families live precariously from day to day. We'll have to learn to walk in their shoes, and show them we care. I suggest that a bit of flexibility be included, possibly giving the judge on the case some leeway in sentencing, depending on the family situation? Mrs. Hudson, I'd be glad to sign on. We can't afford to just go on as we are and this just might work."

Don sent Patsy a discreet wink of congratulations.

Speaking up next, a factory worker from a town just outside Bangor represented semirural life but also small manufacturing business, unions, and a belief in activism.

"As a mother from a household in which both parents work, I see this from the other side of the coin. Like all families, we have problems, but on the whole we are fairly functional. Though sometimes I'd like to send my dog to summer camp and the kids to obedience school. Our biggest challenge right now, as parents, is the peer pressure our kids feel. It's one thing to get your name in the paper as high scorer for a basketball game, but another as a kid who is a neighborhoood troublemaker, a menace. That isn't 'cool,' or shouldn't be. Just knowing that this bill is law might stop a lot of the mostly mindless, disturbing activity. Parents would be challenged to accept more responsibility, even just in self-defense. A good name is sometimes all that some families have, and it's worth working to keep." She chuckled. "I know."

Patsy warmed to this woman immediately, a sharp and honest human being. Nodding with understanding, she recalled Meg and Charlie's teenage years and the code worked out jointly by parents and young people. It had made "but everybody else can do it" a useless plea, but just for a while. More was called for than a booklet of rules handed out the first day of school and then forgotten.

Active in administration of shelters for teens in Cumberland County, the social worker had been listening with interest, nodding often in agreement, but sometimes shaking her head.

"We all seem to agree that too many of these kids in trouble are acting out because of little support or interest at home. It's their way to get the attention they crave. Being yelled at, or even grounded, is sometimes better than being ignored. They are given 'things,' but come home after school to an empty house. 'Things' are no substitute for loving encouragement and standards of behavior, none of which cost a cent. Sometimes the crimes are just thoughtless, showing disrespect of the rights of others. Sometimes they are deliberate, expressing pain and anger.

"Families of professional or business leaders can be just as dysfunctional as low-income families, due to too few hours in a day and lack of communication. More money does not buy greater happiness, only more expensive toys. This program could grease the skids for improvements in all sorts of families, launching new relationships, if you'll excuse the pun."

"A good line to use," mused Mark.

"I see not only petty vandalism and shoplifting. From heartbreaking experience I know that the vast majority of runaways and kids living on the street have been victims of alcoholic, physical, and even sexual abuse at home. The chance for this bill causing further child abuse is therefore pretty real. Still, with judicial options written into it, as has been suggested, I feel your approach is certainly worth trying. It can reach both the mixed-up suburban vandal and the battered little addict or prostitute. There's lots of room for volunteer mentors in this. Good ideas may also show up in the hearings or in committee. Count me in."

Patsy was truly surprised that at least three seemed so willing, with little criticism and really good suggestions. She turned to the teacher, whose body language was signalling at the least boredom, at worst rejection. She was anxious to hear his views.

"You see more of these young people in their day-to-day lives than the rest of us. What is your reaction ?"

He shifted position, uncrossed his legs and leaned forward, toyed with the salt shaker, sat back again.

"In theory it sounds great, Rep. Hudson, and I agree with everything said so far. But I'm going to be practical. Where and when are these counseling sessions? Are they case by case, or with a group of kids and parents? Could parents actually get to them? And I'd like to make a suggestion on another angle. Including a kid's teacher is as important as having the police, the victim, and the family. In school we see kids interacting with one another, we know who their friends are, how often they're absent and why, what some of their interests and even dreams are. We know which parents attend parent-teacher conferences, games or concerts. The loners, the nerds, the geeks, the jocks, preppies, and cheerleaders all need help at some time, as well as the hoods. But, and it's a big but. Do you have any idea of how many hours teachers put in on outside programs like this in addition to a full day's schedule? You need us, but can you get us?

"I'll do what I can to sell it, but," and his voice rose with enthusiasm, "let's also find the means to provide not just a few token sessions. Demand enough help to do the job right. The suggestion of mentors is not enough; make it a must. I agree also that we are reaching a crisis stage. This country is in no danger of being invaded, our juveniles are too well armed."

It was all Patsy could do to keep from walking over to that tired but cooperative man and hugging him.

One o'clock, and time to return to the State House. Patsy realized that she had not only put together a good team, but that they all seemed interested in the challenges.

"Again, I can't thank you enough for coming, for being so candid, and for signing on. I am enormously encouraged. Can we meet again quite soon to go over these changes that I'll get written?

"Now I have an admission to make." She tried to avoid sounding coy. "I've never presented a bill before, and you will have to teach me the ropes, though I may add a few of my own."

She gathered up her papers and added, "We have some leisure now, at the beginning of the session, so let's talk this up with fellow legislators as well as in our districts and in the local media. Let's treat the problem as an emergency, and do it right."

As the new sponsors left they were still exchanging ideas. Don and Mark didn't need to be invited for their opinions.

"Your batting average was great," commented Don, "but let's see if they really move beyond first base. It's going to take real needling to keep even positive people working the crowds. It always does, as they have their own fish to fry. But for a beginner you couldn't have chosen a better combination of sponsors."

Mark agreed and promised himself to sit in on more Juvenile Court proceedings. It was a field to which he had given little thought, but juveniles were tomorrow's adults; hopefully they would behave accordingly.,

That very afternoon Patsy took herself to the Revisor of Statutes Office which reviews all drafts and edits them to make them conform to proper style and usage. She knew full well that bills in the second session were limited to budgetary matters, governor's legislation, and emergency legislation approved by the Legislative Council or legislation submitted by initiative petition. Hers met none of those requirements, but that didn't faze her one little bit.

* * * * *

Harding's Corner

Sitting at his bedroom desk, Jerry stared out at the winter night. There was no wind, and the stars shone brightly down on this farm that had become his world. Moonlight on the unbroken crust of snow contrasted sharply with black forms of lofty pines at the edge of the field. Even the silence was serene.

Just a year ago he had been flung from a huge, impersonal piece of machinery into a culture of relative simplicity. The novel *A Connecticut Yankee in King Arthur's Court* came back to him, not for the first time. What a fantastic world in which the Stan Warners and NASA shared space.

As years go, 1987 had been routine to many, but for Jerry it had been historic. The Cairo conference and his final loss of innocence as to his career, the crash and the decision he'd made, his rescue and acceptance by the Warners—all were dramatic. In addition there was the excitement of finding a real commitment, supported by the refreshing down-to-earth values of the Warners and their neighbors.

The self-enforced withdrawal from the busy life he'd known had allowed him to study that world from an objective distance. He'd developed a compulsion to alleviate what he saw as the stresses undermining the lives of decent people. Best of all, this project had the moral and financial support of his friends, a group much larger than he had dreamed. Privately, of course, was the joy of discovering Heather, inaccessible at present, but so precious that he truly believed that no matter how long the wait, they somehow had a future.

So now, because of this second chance at life and the confidence-building support of Joel and the Warners, he hoped to present what he considered a desperately needed revival of mutual respect, trust, and good-fellowship—in a word, civility.

This idea dated back to his "funeral." He was even yet overwhelmed both by the number of people who had attended and by the reasons they gave for being there. All his life he had tried to do what was right. He had avoided confrontation and conflict, preferring to rely on quiet reasoning and a respect for other people's opinions—even when he disagreed with those opinions. Still, he had often privately questioned this approach: was it cowardly, or almost worse, passionless? He found the comments of his friends and neighbors in that packed church a supportive tribute to this consideration of others, consideration that went far beyond just good manners. Slowly, over the last year, he had found real self-confidence and, hopefully, a ruling passion and mission.

He was occasionally troubled by twinges of conscience, even fear. By unspoken but common assent neither he nor the Warners or McLeans ever discussed his double identity or the doubtful legality of their positions. Project Phoenix meant so much to them all that they refused to acknowledge that black cloud just over the horizon. They reasoned that no one was being hurt by the deception and much good might come from it.

Religious only to a point and often impatient with institutionalized theologies, Jerry did firmly believe that what others might often call happy coincidences must be proof of a caring Being. There must have been a reason for the miracle of his survival, not just luck. So each time the doubts assailed him he concentrated on that thought. Never in his life had he been so excited about a plan, so sure of its importance, or less sure of success.

Joel and Carol were due to arrive tomorrow, with their daughters and ski equipment in tow. Nana had flown to Bangor today and was settling in with Heather. Susan was cooking up a storm, and Stan had the tractor talked into behaving well for snow-plowing if necessary. This weekend would tell the tale. Jerry was too honest, too fair, and too naturally compliant to go against any majority decisions of his committee. He had tried to be totally objective in the material he had given them to study, subject by subject, and expected and actually hoped for diversity of opinions. Now all the facts and figures were available, all the documentation on file. He gathered up the last few papers in piles and came as close to formal prayer as he ever did. "Please, oh please, let them see it my way and decide to go full steam ahead."

The next evening, in spite of overburdened air and highway holiday traffic, all committee members were gathered in the Warners' big kitchen for supper. The two McLean girls were delighted to see Susan again, and curious about meeting the others. Everyone was so wrapped up in the purpose of the meeting that no one had considered whether the girls would recognize Jerry; it had been several years since they had seen him as Webb. However, as Carol showed them around the barn, the eldest spoke up.

"I like Jerry, and I can see why Pop does. Though I haven't seen Uncle Webb for ages, Jerry reminds me of him. They even look alike. But Jerry's such a happy person, and Uncle Webb always seemed so sad."

Carol blinked, appalled at the chance they had unwittingly taken, but delighted at the results. A warning, however.

Because they knew that fresh seafood was a treat to the Warners, the McLeans had brought with them the makings of a huge lobster stew. With Susan's corn bread, and a George Washington pie for dessert, this real State of Maine soul food got the weekend off to a positive start.

* * * * *

Before nine next morning, Heather heard the squeaky crunching of tires and footsteps on the frozen snow. Soon the little office was filled with people. The phone was switched to the answering machine, the stove was stoked, and good coffee smells filled the air. Matt Dillon was the perfect host, thrilled with the unaccustomed company. The girls took off for cross-country skiing and the adults were soon seated around the table on an eclectic variety of chairs, stools and boxes.

There was no gavel, so Jerry rang a Thai temple bell Heather provided, and all got down to business.

"First, I think we should have a treasurer's report. Joel?"

The figures Joel read were a surprise, and a pleasant one. Even without further immediate requests for gifts or pledges, Phoenix was in a position to cover its overhead for at least three months.

"Second order of business. Has each of you had the opportunity to study in full the material given to you in November? All of you? Great." Jerry was genuinely pleased, but would have been tempted to wring the neck of anyone who hadn't done the assignment.

"A report on your reactions to the material is in order. Be as specific or as general as you wish, just don't be phony. Feel free to disagree. No decisions will be made as to our course of action without a candid airing of our various opinions. Agreed? OK, Stan, will you start off?"

Susan, knowing her man of old and having heard his stump speeches for decades, held her breath as he stood up. She'd loved him for so long for what he was, but now she prayed that maybe he had joined the times in which they lived, constructively.

"Your Honor," and Stan bowed to Jerry, "it has been most humbling to both Susan and me to learn so much about our state from our lately returned prodigal son. For years I've been so intent on hewing out a living from these woods, fields, and streams that I've bothered very little about the problems of others." One eyebrow went up quizzically. "OK, I was a self-centered b______________, but look at what all this talk has done for me already! I've finally figured out why the good Lord gave me two ears and just one mouth."

His audience laughed, and loved him all the more for his accuracy.

"I left Megalopolis to escape grey-flannel-suitism, status seeking, bureaucracies and their red tapes. I have tried to live a self-sufficient, independent life, albeit it a somewhat antisocial one. The only red tape I'll put up with comes wrapped around Christmas presents. Now I discover, thanks to all of you, that we are all actually interconnected, in many subtle relationships. I've gone about my various farming tasks in the last months chewing and cogitating and weighing ideas. I've decided that, basically, no progress is possible if we can't count on one another, a fairly revolutionary attitude for me." He toyed with his pipe, needing time to collect further thoughts.

"Every one of the separate subjects brought up for study is important, no question about it. But I feel that an overall campaign to alter approaches would be the most effective. Incidentally, there's one category that was omitted, and that's the media. Protected by the Bill of Rights we can't take 'em on, but let's not forget them. Getting too big for their britches and getting away with it."

He chuckled and looked around the room.

"Education would rank second with me, not in terms of formal education, such as what should be taught in second grade, but making sure the public is trained and then constantly reminded to seek out and listen to all sides of an issue before making decisions. Everyone may not be able to go to college, but schools could certainly give students the skill and appreciation of objectivity, in personal as well as political decisions.

"Students should be educated, not by the faction with the most money to spend on propaganda, but by a fair process supported by neutral communicators, independent of media ratings and all that hype. Understanding issues is a lifelong study, and goes way beyond K–12."

Talked out for once, he sat down, his bottom hitting the chair seat decisively.

Susan's body relaxed, and her eyes were shining as she grinned at him. No harangues, no pontificating. He'd been magnificent. Phoenix success No. l. Jerry called on her next.

She didn't stand, but sat at the table with hands clasped in front of her.

"As a former teacher I naturally, early on, veered toward investment in education, formal education, K–12,. But as I read on, I found that too often the approaches of our unions, administrators, and teachers seemed to reflect almost as much self-interest as student-interest.

"This may not be a fair assessment and perhaps, even if true, is quite natural in light of teachers' status in the past. But why have test scores here and nationally gone down so dramatically? Is there a correlation between that and government involvement? And why have so many parents backed away from their own responsibilities, expecting schools to do more and more of what are really family jobs, such as values, morals, manners, and aspirations, to name a few.

"I would like to see education the subject of a statewide discussion led by parents, students, teachers, taxpayers, and social workers, in a setting completely independent of the government and unions.

"This could be used as an example of how to deal with the other subjects, too. Collaboration by all interested parties involved in each of Jerry's categories could result in an across-the-board exchange of ideas and goals. This might help get rid of the 'us vs. them' atmosphere. Trust and respect might be resurrected.

"Actually, doesn't the whole Phoenix idea boil down to constant and informal education? The more people learn about all sides of what's bugging them on all these subjects, the better decisions they're in a position to make, with greater tolerance."

"Thank you, Susan. You've given us a lot to think about. Let's hear from our suburban friends, the McLeans. One of you has the floor."

Joel deferred to Carol and she stood, intense and excited.

"In spite of all you wrote, Jerry, all you handed us, I still feel a stranger to Maine, with no feeling of really belonging here. So forgive me if I speak out of line. How many of you have been to Disneyworld in Florida?"

Only Heather's and Jerry's hands went up. Jerry had been there briefly on a business trip. Heather had wallowed in it as a college student, entranced by such displays of imagination.

"Why do I ask? Because I believe that to many outsiders Maine is essentially an unorganized theme park, a never-never land, underlined by the word Vacationland on its license plates. Tourism is a screen behind which lives the real Maine, but only true Mainers know that. Phoenix needs support from outside the state for financing. We will need to overcome that theme-park notion. Mainers are not costumed players like Mickey Mouse and Goofy, trying to earn a living in three months each year. It isn't a play with a curtain coming down on their everyday problems by Labor

Day. Mainers work year-round in mills and offices; they catch and process fish, dig potatoes, rake blueberries. Others harvest trees for paper-mills and toothpicks. Insurance is sold, banks lend and invest, doctors, lawyers, and accountants are all busy. All these Mainers have education costs, health expenses, college tuition, taxes and car payments, just like the rest of us.

"Sure, right now the southern counties are almost an annex to Massachusetts' megalopolis, technically advanced and prosperous, with exciting spinoffs in an artistic and sophisticated lifestyle. New mansions are common and marinas are crowded. However, this lifestyle is common to only one quarter of Maine's counties and is not a true portrait of the state as a whole. I gather that the two Maines are not always in sync with each other."

She was running out of breath, so excited was her delivery.

"I vote to put every bit of energy into a pilot program encouraging greater understanding, respect, and accountability between Mainers, north and south, their seasonal guests, and the rest of the country because we will need the support of all. Starting with Maine's natural advantages we could be an example of what can be done anywhere by dedicated individuals if we do it before the virus hits here."

Joel stood, just shaking his head in wonder at this firecracker of a wife. He stood.

"Wow, that's a tough act to follow. Here goes anyway." He consulted notes he'd made.

"I'd thought the environmental program was pretty important, as I believe that respect for every living thing, not just homo sapiens, is vital. However, I've learned that plans for the state in that area are already plentiful and with enough controversies to keep the subject active. One more pressure group on that subject is not needed.

"We all know that a healthy economy solves a lot of other problems. Maine's small businesses, we have learned, employ by far the largest percentage of Mainers and are what keep the state going. They could certainly benefit from help, smothered as they are with regulations, state and federal. These figures bear me out."

He waved his notes. "Too often people I meet in other parts of the country say, 'Oh yes, I went to camp in Maine' or 'I've cruised the coast often,' but I never hear them say 'I'd like to move my business there.' Regulation-heavy environmental agencies, hefty workman's compensation rates, and the lack of an east-west highway all discourage businesses that could otherwise be lured by Maine's work ethic and quality of life, and by the mystique of the words 'Made in Maine' stamped on their product."

"But are we concentrating too much on solutions for Maine as an end in itself, rather than thinking of the state as our lab, the proving ground for an overall program? Also, if we choose the umbrella plan, concentrating on our philosophy, I am concerned about how we would sell Altitude Adjustment, without sounding preachy, impractical or just plain bonkers."

Susan nodded in agreement but Jerry grinned. This was just what he'd hoped for from Joel. A good, down-to-earth, dollars-and-cents question, typical of a Boston financier and providing room for discussion. He spoke up.

"After Thanksgiving, when we missed having the McLeans with us, a conversation was reported that gave me all sorts of confidence. One of our members recognized that a modern, sophisticated, 'what's in it for me' PR campaign was essential. It should be fueled by an angle that would catch the imagination of the movers, shakers, and contributors. Many thanks to you, Nana. Maybe you have more to add?" Jerry gave her the floor.

Her face was unusually pink with embarrassment, but her eyes were sparkling and she was obviously pleased at being recognized. She stood and beamed at them.

"I was born near the beginning of this century and remember World War I well, with all its propaganda and slogans and patriotism. Ancient history to most of you. I remember the Roaring Twenties, Clara Bow and Rudolf Valentino and the Charleston and Prohibition. The crash in 1929, the Dust Bowl and bread lines in the depths of the Depression were frightening to a young bride starting to raise a family. Then came Roosevelt, NRA, the CCC, World War II and rationing, blackout curtains, casualty lists, the bomb and peace, fragile as it has been. The Cold War, Vietnam, and the terrible events of the 1960s shook the nation. For the first time we saw it all happen in our living rooms, on TV.

"The years from 1918 to 1988 have obviously not been easy ones. Still, each time our national character was tested it was not found wanting. Sadly, I'm not so sure about now. Looking back on all those times I recall that as each crisis arose so did commitment, nurtured by slogans, images, or songs introduced to keep us going, with faith and pride and teamwork. You may still sing some of those songs around campfires: 'Pack up Your Troubles' 'Happy Days are Here Again,' 'There'll be Bluebirds over the White Cliffs of Dover.'

"While men like Roosevelt and Churchill were certainly great, it was PR that helped them get chosen as our leaders. They were helped by Madison Avenue, mass media, and instant news coverage, eventually TV. Even 'Camelot' and 'America's Royal Family' were really media creations.

"I've gone on too long, but I'm trying to point out how important it is for us to take a page from history. Whatever we do, we need to have a convincing PR campaign. Rather than selling idealism and sentiment, we need to convince individuals that our program is in their best interests. People aren't ready for the Golden Rule as a cause. Make it a sound investment—a necessity."

Several nodded in agreement.

Thanking Nana for her contribution, Jerry stood.

"So, to recap. Susan opted at first for an education program but switched to collaboration. Joel was interested in luring small business and developing marketing. Carol suggested sort of a reverse tourism pilot plan. Nana stressed how to market our programs. All good and valid ideas. You were all magnificent, and I thank you. Any more?"

Joel raised his hand.

"May I add another two cents? Nana's history lesson brought back memories to me, including the Volstead Act, or Prohibition, which made the sale and enjoyment of alcoholic beverages illegal. Thank God it was repealed before I was born."

Stan interrupted. "Getting rid of that nonsense was the only thing Roosevelt did right."

Joel continued, grinning, but very serious. "That proved you cannot legislate good behavior; you can only make bad behavior uncomfortable. You cannot even buy genuine good behavior; the carrot approach doesn't work for long. Nana has hit the nail right on the head. Our job is to sell our program, whichever we choose, using every trick in the book. We've got to make it a top priority on everyone's wish list,"

Stan rose again, resolution on his face. He squared his shoulders as he had while in uniform so many years ago. He was dead serious.

"Though we all chose different subjects, I feel we all shared a general thought. As Susan put it, teaching the value of collaboration of all the interested parties involved in each separate subject is our common goal. It could lead to overall understanding and mutual respect, possibly a new way of thinking across the board. I suggest we take it on, by Altitude Adjustment, subject by subject. It is a positive, not negative, approach. Let's get busy and start eliminating that virus Carol spoke of before it gets here."

"Thank you, Dad. Good point, and what a challenge! Any more ideas?"

Jerry almost held his breath, but all had had their say. "OK, let's put it to a vote. All now in favor for General Altitude Adjustment ?"

It was unanimous; he tried hard to hide his pleasure.

When they were seated again, relaxed, Jerry picked up a sheaf of papers from the table and tore it into small pieces. "These are the plans I'd worked out in case you guys decided on any one specific subject." And he happily stuffed the scraps into the stove.

A thicker pile lay by his elbow. "This is what I've put together as a program for what you've chosen. It's just a rough draft and I urge you to interrupt, add, delete, argue. I've had the leisure to do this groundwork. Now you become the architects, the engineers and salesmen. Take it home with you and work on it."

"All our study in these months has headed for this moment. Now we're in business, we have a commitment, and it is up to us all to form a plan. If we don't get anything else done this morning, let's at least compose a statement of purpose, never an easy job."

Heather passed around pencils and paper and Jerry asked each person the write a short statement. "I think it's easier to edit existing material than to try, as a group, to create from scratch.

"We may have quite different viewpoints too, and now is the time to discover them." He stood up. "Matt needs fresh air. We'll be right back." He didn't want to cramp their style.

Extraordinarily, discussion was centered more on semantics than ideas. Heather's thesaurus was put into action. They knew that this statement would provide the foundation for all their undertakings, and they could not afford to make mistakes. By noon they were satisfied. The statement finally read:

"The Phoenix Association, supported by private subscription, is dedicated to the renewal of mutual trust, civility, and respect for differences between all parties involved in decision making that affects the lives of fellow-citizens. It is believed that sincere Collaboration, replacing Confrontation, will prove advantageous to all, and create a safer and happier world for us and for our children."

Next morning Jerry called for one last meeting. He felt it was important to report some action to those friends who had already contributed.

"From the letters and comments we've studied, it strikes me that the chief scapegoat seems to be government, or more specifically, politics. As a youth I loved the small slice of Maine I saw. I have talked to people here in Maine, and I've felt I was finally tasting the whole pie. But I found that each slice of the pie—be it health, education, transportation, recreation, crime, or the environment—had as its base the same crust: government. No matter what field I was exploring, no matter how many private organizations I found involved, there was always the presence of Augusta or Washington. It might be as helpmate, regulator, or brick wall, but it was there."

He let that sink in a moment. "I've had a crazy idea. This is an election year and here in Maine we will vote on our entire Legislature, two congressional representatives, and the president. Interest is low, cynicism high. It's no fun to dedicate, as politicians do, all one's energies, reputation, and time into an activity considered suspect if not almost sleazy."

He hesitated, for effect, then took a deep breath and looked piercingly into each face.

"How about inviting, from all parties, the legislative leaders, cabinet members, party chairmen of the state and county committees, national committee members and, of course, the governor, to a strictly nonpartisan weekend workshop aimed at changing that image of themselves? Through lectures, debates, and exercises involving collaborative techniques, this might just result in less gridlock and a more tolerant atmosphere. Civility, respect, and trust might be proven to actually have practical value. Needless to say, party affiliations would be checked at the door."

The committee had been courteously receptive to each other's opinions earlier. Now they were spellbound.

"The two Maines and all political parties might come to think of each other in a new way, recognizing that differences can be positive, even energizing. All would have the opportunity to work together on campaign ethics, fund-raising methods, and particularly how to renew voter interest and trust. Participants could be given the opportunity to create a nonpartisan statement of campaign rules with which they would agree to comply, and could incorporate this into their brochures and speeches.

"These politicians might go home with the hope that, with some elbow grease on their parts and good press, politics might be made a respectable avocation again. Administrators can be hired, but political leaders must be inspired, in order to move others. Such leaders could truly lead their parties and candidates into new thought patterns. Anyway, what have they actually got to lose? Nothing."

He grinned, almost impishly. "My head is so full of this I could go on all night with the details. But," and he drew a long breath, "what do you guys think?"

Heather almost soared to her feet. "I didn't speak up before, but I'm sure going to now. I think this plan answers all our questions. First, the results would affect every citizen of Maine. Measurable results, such as voter turnout, would be grand material for the politicians and for our future programs.

"My experience tells me that with a little imagination the workshop could be a real news story, possibly nationally, describing the exercises, the personalities, etc. This plan is hitting the softest, most vulnerable spot, and if it works the other worrisome subjects will be a piece of cake. Phoenix is not a political movement, but politics would be a perfect pilot program, with results that would be immediately evident and convincing."

She looked around, almost begging for support, and got it. Joel, Susan, and Carol agreed with excitement. Nana beamed. Stan muttered something about it taking longer than one weekend to make a politician honest, but Susan shushed him. It was agreed. Jerry would start looking into leadership courses; the others were asked to start composing a letter of invitation that the invitees could not or would not dare refuse. Joel would find a location. The detail work would be tremendous but, because it was innovative, it would be fun.

Heather spoke up again, this time showing real concern.

"As I look around this table I see only one honest-to-God Maine native, and he spent only his childhood here. We're doing exactly what we fault other newcomers for, moving up here and then trying to change everything to their way of thinking. I think we've got to get the endorsement or sponsorship of some very well-known and respected native Mainers representing many interests, or we won't move from square one."

Stan looked at her for a moment, then laughed.

"That was probably the smartest thing anyone's said today. As they say here in these boonies, 'that gal sure knows where the fish are biting.'" Loud claps from all.

Time for lunch and farewells. As he went out the door Jerry turned to Heather, mouthed the word "Thank you," and blew her a kiss.

* * * * *

Having put it off as long as he could, Jerry reluctantly dialed Mark Lowell's office at the State House.

"Hi, this is Jerry Warner. Haven't seen you for a bit. How are things?" He forced himself get to the point.

"Do you remember that when you gave me Heather Hatch's phone number I promised that you would be the first to know what I'm up to? Well, I need your help again, but this time you get the story too, exclusively."

There, he'd said it and the die was cast. Phoenix wasn't an exclusive, independent little club any more. Their dreams and plans were now open to scrutiny, praise, or ridicule.

"How would you like to come up here soon for a weekend, meet my family, and get a feel for our operation? And let us pick your brains."

"Hold on, chum. Where is here? How soon? What brains? What story?"

It was arranged, a few incivilities were jovially exchanged, and Jerry hung up, giving Heather a wry grin. Following her earlier suggestion concerning the need for valid native-born supporters, the committee had decided that Mark Lowell probably understood the hierarchy of movers and shakers in the state as well as anyone, without being part of it. He could also probably be objective, representing no special interest.

"Now I know how an author feels when he turns over his precious manuscript to an editor," muttered Jerry. "Or how a legislator feels when he puts his carefully crafted bill into the hopper, to be mauled by hearings, amendments, and financial restraints."

Ten days later the usual peace of the Warners' farm was shattered by a motorcycle roaring up the lane. Stan's eyes grew steely. The sheep lost what little minds sheep have; Susan threw her apron over her head and pretended this wasn't happening.

Well over six feet tall, heavy and clad in shiny black leather, with a helmet from outer space, Mark himself would have been an event even if he'd arrived on foot. Jerry cheered up. This visit might be fun.

Though Maine roads in early March are hardly dusty, Stan insisted that Mark wet his whistle. Since, as host, Stan needed to keep him company in that activity, the weekend started off well. Heather arrived for supper all gussied up, hoping the presence of another appreciative single male would give Jerry some troubled moments.

During this Happy Hour the phone rang, Joel calling Jerry.

"Hi. You what? You talked to who? He said what? That is fantastic, perfect. Time, size, cost, all as planned? I will indeed, and they all send their best to you. Mark is here with us now. Kiss Carol and the girls for me. Ya done goo-oo-d, Bayuh, real goo-oo-d." He carefully put the phone down and thrust both thumbs up.

"We've got Camp Namakant for free the last weekend in August. They can sleep about sixty, just our size. All we do is bring ourselves, 'campers,' bedrolls, vittles, towels, and a damn good curriculum. Yippee!"

Susan couldn't believe that this ecstatic man dancing around the room was the woebegone stray who'd arrived a little over a year ago.

At dinner the group finally got down to business, first giving Mark more detailed introductions to themselves and to Joel, in absentia. This was done after stressing confidentiality until the time was right to go public. Joel was described as the instigator, wanting to honor a friend; Jerry Warner and dad had been suggested by mutual acquaintances to administer the project.

Jerry's background, for Heather's information as well as Mark's, was skimmed over as vaguely as possible, with emphasis on out-of-state and even European schooling and employment. Home to recuperate from a bad auto accident in the Netherlands, this job was just what Jerry had needed, they were told. Stan's former business connections were impressive, as was Heather's PR expertise. Susan, and Nana and Carol in absentia, were introduced as the only ones with any common sense.

The evening was spent in describing the project so far, in detail, and nervously. Mark was the first outsider to hear it; he was their guinea pig, and they watched him carefully for reactions. As a good reporter he had to seem unopinionated, but often he dug deeper into a detail or point than they would have expected. He certainly did not seem bored or restless.

"What's to be the initial program of Altitude Adjustment?" he asked. When he heard it was to be a weekend workshop for legislative and party leaders of both sides his eyes lit up with more than amusement. They waited for a comment, but what they got was a wonderful deep roll of laughter, joyous and free.

"This I've got to be in on," he gasped. "Oh, my God, I wouldn't miss it for the world." And he began to mutter and chuckle as he named individuals he'd watched bicker for years and now would see in a different relationship, even as potential bunkmates.

"Have you thought of including all the candidates for both Houses? That would really be a show, but would involve over 400 people—302 for the House and 70 for the Senate, plus all these other jokers you mentioned."

Jerry admitted that the thought had crossed his mind, too. It had boiled down to a choice between too many people trying to absorb too much into just one day or, more practically, deliberately infecting the political leadership with a very lively virus over a period of several days. It just might spread, given a little strategic help.

"What would you think of a mailing afterwards to all those uninvited candidates, covering the whole shooting match, for their study and inspiration?"

It was agreed that he had the only answer.

Getting up from his old rocker, Stan stretched and announced he was through for the day. But Jerry asked Mark to hear him out on one last point, a major one.

"Here we are, concentrating on Maine as the setting for a pilot program for a much larger arena, though of course hoping to help Maine too in many ways. But there's not an honest-to-God Maine native in the bunch of us! Even I came as an infant, not the genuine article. None of us have even been active enough in the state to know who the real leaders are. As you know, since WWII so many out-of-staters have moved in and done so much that many are in real leadership and executive positions, a fact many 'natives' find hard to overlook.

"Mark, now that you know what we're planning, can you can help us? I'd like a list with names of outstanding men and women from all over the state who were born here, some possibly to families who have been here for generations. We're not just looking for politicians, but lawyers, educators, business people, or cultural bigwigs.

"Without people like that on board and endorsing us we will be just one more little group of newcomers moving in and telling Mainers how to live. A lot of the 'imports' have brought great ideas and expertise, but too often the locals have felt pushed out or considered a bit second-rate. Give this some thought overnight."

Heather went on her way, Rousseau was let out, and Stan and Mark stood outside for a moment, looking up at the stars.

"You people have not been idle. I don't know when I've enjoyed an evening more; stimulating but comfortable. Handled the right way I really think this may make quite a story, possibly a big difference." Mark turned to go inside.

Stan quietly added, "Even if nothing comes of it you'd be amazed how much good it has done already."

Mark's Saturday mornings were generally dedicated to staying in the sack, a holdover from his teenage years, but on this day he was down at the lakeshore by six, watching the sun rise. A mist hung over the water as the gray of the sky gave way to pink streaks, reminding him of the nacre interior of a mussel shell. The silence was profound, but as beautiful to him as music.

"Maybe good refreshing ideas need an atmosphere like this for gestation," he thought. Dog-eat-dog stress or having to have eyes in the back of your head while your hands guarded your wallet did not clutter up this setting. Maybe Maine was really the perfect place to launch this drive for civility, respect, and accountability. It became clearer to him than ever before why so many talented and capable out-of-staters had chosen to make their homes and livelihoods here. Few Fortune 500 Companies so far, damn few millionaires, but certainly Maine had precious little of the brittle, ersatz veneer that was the trademark of the big Eastern cities. Hell, he wasn't even a native himself but he wouldn't live anywhere else.

Names had been coming to him ever since he woke, as if a Rolodex in his head was slowly flipping from page to page. It was astonishing how many had to be discarded as recent imports, and he began to think of doing a feature story on what he was discovering. Had the influx since the 1950s been due solely to Maine's quality of life, or was it partly due to an "I can be a big frog in a little pond" attitude? Certainly there wasn't the intensity of competition here.

But these immigrants had had to sell themselves convincingly to Maine people in order to do business and succeed, as not many real Mainers are impressed with signs of conspicuous consumption. The newcomers had had to prove themselves in Maine terms of integrity, craftsmanship, and business sense.

Native Mainers were independent, but also tolerant, and not snoopers. Many artistic characters had recently made their homes there and been accepted, not because their work was necessarily understood but because they were good neighbors. Summer festivals were proof positive of the variety of products successfully produced, ranging from crafts, condiments and boat-building to state-of-the-art technical material.

As he pondered, a bell rang, the sound clear and rich over land and water. Mark didn't take long to realize that breakfast was served.

Walking up to the house through the field just recently freed of snow cover, he found himself looking forward to conversation as wholesome as the oatmeal he hoped would be offered, and vowed not to indulge in the cynical wit for which he was famous. These people were not impractical or starry-eyed idealists; they deserved better than cheap, clever humor.

At the Phoenix office later that morning he was amazed at the reference material Jerry had collected, ranging from the Maine Register to a list of Portland Symphony Board members, from University of Maine donor lists to the Maine Bar Association roster. By noon on Sunday all felt that a good working list of potential endorsers had been put together, well balanced in every way, and all with superb name recognition. Jerry was particularly impressed with the number of women who were making a real difference. Intellectual descendants of Margaret Chase Smith? He also noted that most of the people chosen wore many hats, philanthropic or cultural in addition to professional or business. Impressive.

After lunch everyone went outdoors to see the Black Knight take off. Before climbing aboard his "charger" Mark, the sometimes hard-boiled reporter, swept a very surprised Susan into his arms for a big hug and kiss. Jerry knew they had chosen the right guinea pig.

As he roared down the narrow road, Mark thought about the group he'd just left. He'd wanted to give Heather the same farewell as Susan's, but for quite different reasons. What a dish! There was something between her and Jerry he couldn't put his finger on.

* * * * *

Chicago

After a winter of unprecedented cold and snowfall, the Midwest was welcoming spring with joy. Crocuses and tulips were greeted with the excitement generally reserved for new babies, and even the most stay-at-home oldsters were often seen soaking up the sun on park benches. For Phyllis the winter had been hard in many other ways too. At the anniversary of the plane crash she attempted to tally up her successes and failures in her task of discovering herself and then learning to live with that person. Like the ground outdoors, sometimes she felt frozen and dead; then the drab earth that was her mood would be camouflaged by a glistening white mantle of new resolve or achievement, sparkling.

She referred to the three males in her life as her pillars, and each, wittingly or not, pushed her ahead in her quest. Jack gave the companionship and loyalty she had taken for granted from Webb, but now appreciated so much. Sessions with Dr. Burton proved increasingly productive as he gently placed in her thoughts the priority of personal responsibility. The third leg of this support team, Roger Milliken, treated her with respect but allowed no evasions or excuses.

Oddly, she did not resent his management methods. Coming, as he did, so soon after Webb's loss, she had needed someone who would take control. He had done this without pushing her off what she considered her throne. He took care to enquire how Webb had operated but somehow avoided unpleasantness if he did things differently. She received reports on how well he was accepted by staff and others in the plant.

What was most extraordinary was Roger's seeming confidence in her. For many years she had demanded and received the treatment accorded a delicate porcelain figurine. Now, being evidently perceived instead as a well-tooled stainless steel machine was so unexpected that she didn't have time to be shocked. She simply rose to each challenge and performed. Using her office more than before, she had grown aware of what the staff actually did, and began to see it as made up of individuals, with families, problems and ambitions. Possibly as friends.

One late afternoon in January Rog had dropped in with some articles on the commercial chemistry industry he had promised to share with her. Nothing interested her less, still concentrating on the scientific advances as she always done, but she thought it only civil to accept the material. He was so unfailingly courteous it would be unthinkable to be rude.

"Getting late. Shouldn't you be closing up shop?" he asked.

She shrugged. "Jack can't tell time or complain that he's lonely. He will probably forgive me. There were reports I've been checking." A neat pile was on her left, obviously finished work.

"I can tell time, though, and I'm sick of eating dinner alone almost every night." He put on a mock poor-little-me face. "How about joining me tonight? I'd like to talk over this material too."

She liked his candor, mentioning loneliness first, and what he could have used as an excuse for the invitation second.

From her window the city below looked inviting, hundreds of little lights signifying hundreds of people eating, playing, doing things together. Not hundreds. Thousands. Why not add two more?

Webb had stopped suggesting this kind of evening after her many refusals. That was before she'd discovered loneliness, when her energy was concentrated on self-interest and self-protection.

"Thank you, I'd like that," she heard herself saying, and she experienced only a tiny quiver of nervous anxiety as they left the building.

The restaurant Rog chose was quiet, making no attempt at trendiness, with a menu of traditional food, no nouvelle cuisine or self-conscious ethnicity. Service was unobtrusive, their dinners excellently cooked and attractively presented.

Over dessert, he brought up the articles he was lending her.

"You once mentioned that your late husband had attended the Cairo conference just before his death. These are some of the papers read at those meetings, and they are causing quite a stir in our industry, a stir that may lead us all into some pretty important decision making. I think you should be aware of them."

That made a certain amount of sense, though the business end of the company had been Webb's province exclusively by mutual agreement.

"I'd be glad to look them over, Rog. What sort of concerns do they cover?"

"Actually, it is one big concern. What is the responsibility of companies like ours that produce powerful chemical materials? It is not only felt, but proven, that much of what we make and sell abroad as fertilizer can be used irresponsibly and therefore has the potential of a great deal of harm. Is it OK for us to continue to sell to countries we suspect of putting our product into the manufacture of deadly gases or dangerous fertilizers? And if it is not OK what do we do about it?"

Phyllis, for long years, had had little interest in predicaments other than her own. She wrote checks to charities to ease her conscience, but was very happy to slip awareness of conditions calling for reform under the rug. International chemical warfare had been under the rug a long time.

Rog had watched for a reaction, hoping for her interest. She did not, however, lean forward with excitement and curiosity. She looked down at her coffee, toyed with her spoon and stiffened her back against the chair.

Finally, knowing she had to respond, she said in flat tones, "I'll take them home and may read them soon. And speaking of home, that poor dog must feel abandoned." She then picked up her purse, Rog motioned for the waiter and check, and the evening was over.

Living alone as he did, with few acquaintances other than business contacts, Roger had fallen into the habit of studying those with whom he worked, guessing about their lives and joys. He even sought ways he could improve their lot while enriching his own with their friendship. He had heard quite a bit about both Webb and Phyllis. He saw a potentially attractive woman, with a mind capable of a lot more than it was being used for, but also a desperately insecure person. With all the material things she could want, and evidently a decent man for a husband, what had gone wrong?

Like the unbroken horses he'd tamed as a kid, she offered a challenge, to be understood, and gentled. Early on he had decided to attempt to build her self-confidence by asking more of her than she had felt capable of handling. It seemed to be working, so far. She had been fairly good company at dinner that evening till after dessert and the business discussion. He'd decided to try again but next time concentrate on entertainment or just relaxed companionship. Her only friend seemed to be that ridiculous dog. Maybe he could ask to accompany them on walks, and draw her out as they slipped and slid on icy paths.

Now, weeks later, they were on one of those walks, though the ice and snow had vanished except in the middle of the huge lake. Locals were betting, as usual, on the date when the last rotten and massive chunk of ice would slip beneath the surface. Trees had fuzzy green sprouts of leaves, some shrubs were flowering, and Jack was wild with springy smells leading him from one spot to another.

Once she felt confident that Roger would not bring up business problems Phyllis had relaxed They discovered a few mutual interests. On this day they were keeping track of the species of birds they spotted, migrating north. As a lonely child Phyllis had enjoyed watching birds, and introduced him to those of this area.

Talk of birds led to the work of Rachel Carson and her fight against DDT. What a difference that book had made; springs were no longer so silent.

To Rog's surprise, Phyllis hesitatingly asked, "What do you know of something called 'endocrine disruptions'? In one of those Cairo reports you gave me to read there is mention of them and how they affect the hormones of embryos. Yet it was pointed out that the chemicals suspected are important to industry and there is also some question as to how the data has been interpreted."

He couldn't have been more surprised and prayed that he'd answer satisfactorily. What a turnaround! And she'd read the reports!

"I don't know much beyond what you do, except that in some areas where certain chemicals have been used as fertilizers, there seems to be an unusual instance of deformed living species, such as frogs. DES is also possibly an example. I believe there is a book *Our Stolen Future* by Coburn. More evidence is being sought before we can be sure if there is truly cause and effect."

"Thank you." And changing the subject she said, "Jack will now show you his favorite mudhole. He rolls in it, comes up to let you have a glorious whiff, and then shakes. You're warned."

In the following weeks much of Phyllis' spare time was spent in new research. It brought back her work in college, took her into the city's great library, and even into telephone contact with former professors. At times she was happy to have returned to that world, but as she came closer and closer to the answer she sought the more miserable she was. The last source of information took the most courage to contact, yet with that interview the search was over. Old Dr. Gibbons' records of her pregnancy, submitted to modern evaluation, told the tale.

The March board meeting was almost ready to adjourn. The loose ends were tied up, financial reports healthy, and nothing else of much interest seemed to exist. Then Phyllis, as chairwoman, announced that she wished to introduce some new business. Even Rog was taken by surprise.

Without delay she got to the point, poised and no-nonsense..

"I have been doing a great deal of research in the past months on the effects of some of the products we manufacture and sell. We have run tests, of course, on their efficacy as weed-killers, pest controls, and fertilizers. We have also tested them for qualities dangerous to good environmental practices. We are a company with a good reputation. After today it will be better.

"Several years ago I did the original lab work on one of our products, and was justly proud of my results. But they were based on the limited, obtainable knowledge of the time. Since then I have found that dreadful side-effects, under certain conditions, can occur due to use of our product and others like it.

"Therefore, as majority stockholder, I am moving that we take this product, Greengro, immediately from the market, even though this action will have unfavorable financial results. Objections? Hearing none, it is done." And she banged the gavel. "Meeting adjourned."

As she turned to pick up her briefcase, she heard mutterings in the room. Quickly she retrieved the gavel and used it. "I know this comes as a surprise and not a happy one. There may be more like it in the future. If anyone wishes to speak to me about it, I will be in my office. If anyone is seriously against this decision, I am sure their resignation will be accepted. Good afternoon."

Back straight and chin up, she walked through the now silent room to the hall and down its lonely length to her office. She closed the door, went to her desk, and sat down with her head on her arms. Finally, at long last, she began crying uncontrollably for the deformed little foetus that had aborted so many years ago.

Darkness had fallen when exhaustion overtook her and she raised her head. The only light came through her now open door from the hall, and at first she did not see him. How long Rog had been sitting across the desk from her she had no idea, but she was strangely glad to have him there. She also was aware of a sense of liberation, though from what she was unsure.

He broke the silence. "I couldn't leave without tendering my very sincere congratulations. Anyone on that board who thought of you just as a figurehead must be doing some solid reconsidering tonight. Not enough boards have the privilege of strong leadership, and certainly few have leaders who advocate loss of revenue. Hooray for you, boss. A commendable beginning, a brave first step."

Phyllis wiped her eyes with the back of one hand, found a hanky, blew her nose and took a long, quivering breath.

"Some day I may tell you the whole story of why and how. Right now, though, for the first time in a long time, I feel like echoing you. Hooray for me."

She opened a desk drawer, removed her purse, and stood.

"And now, Mr. Milliken, would you be kind enough to take me out to eat? Not some fancy place, but one that can give me the best, biggest and juiciest hamburger in town, with the works."

Later, as she sought sleep, she went over the events of the afternoon. Using courage she'd never known she had, she taken her stand. It had felt good, and Roger had seamed impressed. But what had he meant by "commendable beginning" and "first step?" What else must one do to lead?

And Rog, looking out his apartment window toward the West of his boyhood, recalled a spooked little mare afraid not only of people, but of the herd. He thought back on how he had brought her out of her corner of the field and eventually to leadership in the corral. Smiling, he turned and climbed into bed.

Chapter 7: Spring 1988

Augusta

One morning later in April, when the sun was actually shining again and faces were cheerful, Patsy walked down the House aisle, ready for the day's work. She slid behind chairs to her own and saw on her desk, as on that of every other legislator, a copy of her bill, new and shiny, LD 2365. The pertinent facts of date, sponsor, selected committee, cosponsors, title, and text were there, including the Statement of Fact, that invaluable explanation of every Bill in plain English, provided by the Revisor's office. She decided that she would frame the document to keep forever, and reviewed in her mind the course that had brought it this far.

The early winter had been an open one, rather gloomy, with little snow, moderate temperatures, and generally overcast skies. Commuters were delighted, town budget offices rejoiced in the savings on road maintenance and snow removal, and school superintendents were grateful daily for being spared the decision of whether to call off classes. Skiing, skating, and snowmobiling were nonexistent. Children and teens not involved in basketball were bored, bored, bored.

However, election year fever had begun to build up, not only in Augusta but in every city and town. Democrats and Republicans caucused to elect delegates to their respective state conventions and to rebuild party enthusiasm. Except for funerals and basketball games there were never many winter get-togethers in country areas, so caucuses were often well attended. Almost as entertaining as Town Meetings

These caucus selections were the formal, old-fashioned, grassroots beginning of the process of each party to eventually choose a presidential candidate at the August National Conventions. Workers for the various presidential hopefuls of both parties had actively recruited supporters for months to procure from each town a majority of committed delegates, and the field was large.

Not one to ignore any gatherings of Republicans, Patsy had tried to attend every caucus within a reasonable evening's drive. Often, if the House member representing that town was Republican, she could count on introductions. Handing out brochures describing her bill gave her a contact that often led to conversations. At the end of each such evening she had had the satisfaction of noticing that few of these brochures were left behind on the floor.

Most newspapers, daily and weekly, had given her first press release at least a little space. Some radio talk shows had given her air time. But best of all were the number of favorable responses arriving in her mail every day. She had talked with the Office of Policy and Legal Analysis and that of Fiscal and Program Review, and had been given a green light by both, as to content and form. Still, everyone had reminded her that the Legislative Council would probably turn her bill down. It just didn't qualify as emergency material. She had been advised to wait for the following term.

February school vacation had begun on a particularly foul, rainy weekend, with all planned activities washed out. No better weather was forecast for the near future. Parents dreaded the next ten days.

On Monday *The Portland Press Herald* reported, in headlines, that Sunday morning worshippers had arrived at several churches in both the city and suburbs to find unbelievable destruction of their sanctuaries. Hymnals, prayer books, and bibles were thrown around, sacred vessels on the altars smashed, some stained glass windows lay in smithereens. In some cases the vandals had proceeded to the parish houses and continued their rampage, indiscriminately hurling eggs and milk they found in refrigerators.

Residents over a large area had been appalled, and not only churchgoers. There were no clues. All that could be done was to clean up the mess and hope the police had some luck. Nothing had been stolen. It was just mindless vandalism, probably by kids. The following weekend there were similar incidents farther afield. No particular sect or denomination seemed to be the target. Was this second week the work of copycats, or was it proof of an organized gang?

Hating to benefit from such monstrous events but more convinced than ever that her bill had value, Patsy immediately requested a meeting with the Legislative Council to ask that her bill now be considered emergency legislation. The Council had agreed wholeheartedly and the bill was accepted. By the end of that week the Revisor of Statutes Office had cleared it for form, the Bill was duly signed by all sponsors and sent to the Clerk of the House for printing. Now it lay on her desk, and on every desk in the entire Legislature!

Almost automatically LD 2365 was voted by the House and later the Senate to be assigned to the Judiciary Committee for review and discussion and was placed on the House Calendar for public hearing. Voters were screaming for action and the Council had responded. Because it was considered emergency legislation, obviously bipartisan and therefore not a political issue, the House and Senate co-chairs of the Judiciary Committee set an early date for the hearing. This information was published, by law, in all Maine's major newspapers, and available at the State House.

Was this the end or just the beginning? The bill was now out of Patsy's hands, except for the presentation she would make to the Committee. It might be amended, cut to ribbons, or passed to become law.

On the afternoon of the hearing, in mid-March, Patsy and the sponsors arrived together at the committee room. They were astonished to see the number of people already seated. In addition to the expected social agency personnel and some members of the legal profession, citizens of all ages and economic strata filled the room. Several clergymen were scattered through the crowd, Scout leaders were there in uniform, and PTA members carried placards identifying their schools. Patsy and her team were pleased to see that the whole committee was, for once, in attendance, already seated at the horseshoe-shaped table. Several reporters, including Mark Lowell, were there, as well as network TV. A public nerve had been touched.

The Senate Chairwoman was a Republican, because of the majority in that house, and the House Chairman a Democrat. The Senator presided and as usual made all attendees comfortable with a little welcoming speech.

"We are always glad to see members of the public interested in what their Legislature does. Making the trip to Augusta isn't always convenient but today if there had been many more of you we would have had to move to larger quarters.

"To those of you who are not familiar with the process I will explain that first we will hear from the sponsor of the bill, who will explain its purpose. She will be followed by the cosponsors and other proponents, including any of you who wish to speak and who have so indicated. Opponents testify next, and then anyone who is neither for nor against. At the end of each testimony, committee members may ask questions of the sponsors. No decisions will be made until after our work sessions, later in the week, at which times amendments may be made or compromises suggested. We ask that all speakers be brief so we can adjourn at a reasonable hour. Representative Hudson, please present L.D. 2365."

Patsy approached the lectern at the open end of the table. She had testified before a few committees, but always for other people's bills. Placing her papers carefully before her, she adjusted the mike and smiled at the members of the Committee, most of whom she knew, at least slightly. Her heart was pounding. This hearing might affect her entire political future.

"Senator Howe, Representative Wilson, ladies and gentlemen of the Committee and guests, I feel today like someone who has been hiking for months along the Appalachian Trail and who has finally reached the foot of Mt. Katahdin. This presentation is the last leg of that long journey for me. I hope I do justice to all those who helped me along the way."

She only occasionally glanced at her notes, knowing the familiar arguments by heart. The Committee members seemed intensely interested, though many were already somewhat familiar with the bill. She could not tell how others in the room were reacting as they were seated behind her. She was soon relaxed and felt clearheaded and capable. A good sign?

There were no questions, as committee members knew that the cosponsors would fill in the gaps she had purposely left for them.

Next to come to the lectern was the Senate social worker from Portland, carrying a gift-wrapped box.

"Madam Chairman, members of the Committee and honored guests. Before I begin I wish to carry out a tradition of this Maine Legislature.

"Last term I was a member of this Committee. This is my first visit back, and it is the custom for returnees to present the current members with a gift. It could have been fruit, but I know many of you well enough to have chosen absolutely sinful chocolates."

She stepped forward and handed her gift to the Chairman. Spontaneous laughter and clapping destroyed any tension there might have been in the chamber.

From then on the hearing went smoothly, with only a few easily answered questions. A conservative felt the bill provided even more government interference in private lives. Several liberal opponents brought up exactly what was expected: possible child abuse, loss of self-esteem, cost, and the frailty of many families.

Patsy muttered to herself "They still don't get it! They see this only as punitive, not positive. Are they afraid that if it goes through and is proved effective all their wishy-washy, permissive philosophy will be stove up?"

The police chief answered one question of this type quite bluntly, directed to him by a well-known espouser of liberal causes.

"Sir, I've been working with kids on the wrong side of the law since you were a kid yourself. I've listened to all the modern theories of parenting, such as permissiveness, freedom to express oneself, self-esteem, and so forth, and we've all seen the results.

"My old man used to say, 'I don't care if my kids love me, but damn it, I want them to respect me.' He set us a fine example of behavior, he carried out his promises of discipline, he was consistent, and we always knew it was because he loved us. We had the security of knowing very well what our boundaries were, and why. It's called tough love, standing up against your kids and saying 'no' when you have to, for their own good.

"My parents had high standards for our behavior. If we slipped, we hadn't fallen too far. Somewhere along the line since then parents have decided to become their kids' buddies instead of being parents, and have erased the words accountability and respect from their vocabulary. Mine didn't and I still am grateful."

The Chairman had to pound with her gavel to stop the applause.

As the hearing broke up Patsy kept her ears tuned for any grumblings from either the committee members or the crowd. She could hear none, and as she walked out many gave her broad smiles and even a few pats. Reporters waited for her in the hall, though she had little left to say. Then it dawned on her that these were her first interviews actually sought by the press. She had been so anxious to get the bill on its way that she'd almost forgotten about her personal ambitions. Quite a day, Patsy. What next?

She looked at her watch, went to the nearest phone, and dialed. "Meg, my bill just had its hearing. Yes, pretty well. I'm so wheed up that I want to watch the 6:00 o'clock news with family. May I come up for the night? If I leave right now I'll be up in time for baths and stories. Thank you." She felt like a little kid who just had to share her spelling paper's gold star.

At the Senator she threw a few things into a bag and headed for Brewer. The only vehicle that passed her on the road was a big black motorcycle; she was surprised to find it, or its twin, parked in Meg's drive. Meg hadn't told her that she was having guests tonight. Heather and Jerry were going to be in Bangor on business and had not only invited themselves for supper but suggested including Mark as well, so the party had grown.

As Patsy entered the kitchen, Billy ran to greet her and she was delighted to see little Fanny tottering along on her own two feet, an art she had learned since Christmas.

Meg started to introduce Mark, but he assured her he already knew her mother, had actually spent the afternoon with her. "Which means," he stated, "that I can give you an absolutely objective review of her performance this afternoon. Terrific."

A young woman who looked a bit familiar came up and reminded Patsy that she had been one of the mothers fighting the spraying of the blueberry barrens.

"My group are clients of your daughter's, and we feel we're making headway, even nationally. Just recently Jarrett's, a large midwestern chemical firm, took one of their fertilizers off the market, and others followed suit because of the documentation. Incidentally, the former president of that company was one of the passengers lost last year in that plane crash near here. Webb Lewis, his name was. I remembered that because the newspapers said, at that time, he had been a camper in Maine years ago."

Pleased that she'd been remembered, but only half listening to what the woman said, Patsy swooped up Fannie and took her to the window to admire the sunset. The little girl wriggled with pleasure at seeing a truck come up the drive, and all moved out to greet Heather and Jerry, with Billy carrying the fully grown Tigger draped over one shoulder. Jerry was soon introduced to Peter and the children.

"And this is Tigger, my very own cat," piped up Billy.

"Of course it is," said Jerry. "Are you really Christopher Robin?"

Delighted, Billy giggled and countered, "If I'm Christopher Robin, you could be . . . Piglet?"

Jerry's face softened, and he asked in almost a whisper "How did you ever guess? I've been Piglet for a long, long time."

Everyone laughed but Patsy. Pooh, Piglet, Paul Bunyan statue.

Now she knew why Jerry had looked familiar the night of the Thanksgiving concert. Who was Pooh?

Peter had been keeping track of the clock. "Almost time for the news.

Let's see if our heroine is featured."

Patsy sat on the floor with both children in her lap. Suffering through the commercials and the story of a local Bangor robbery, the viewers were finally treated to Augusta and their Legislature.

The news reporter was as usual shown speaking from the lawn below the State House.

"Acting swiftly is not one of the characteristics of legislatures, for which we may generally be duly grateful. Today, however, Maine's Judiciary Committee heard the pros and cons of a bill that was pushed through at record speed in the wake of the appalling vandalism of the past weeks. If enacted, the sponsors feel it may help curb juvenile crime.

"The chief sponsor, Rep. Patsy Hudson of Portland," and at this point the camera moved to the scene of Patsy presenting her case, "spoke movingly of the necessity and possible means to nip the epidemic of minor but disturbing juvenile crime in the bud."

As Patsy spoke the camera panned around the committee room, showing the crowd.

"This bill I am presenting is not punitive as much as it is corrective, or even therapeutic. It provides a way to reopen family communication lines, to discuss family values, to create respect between members. Parents who may have lost their skills or are overwhelmed by today's problems are first given a gentle nudge toward reacceptance of their responsibilities, and then presented with the tools with which to pull the family together."

Fannie wiggled her little bottom around so that she was facing Patsy. "Gamma here? Gamma there?" pointing at the TV. "Where Gamma?"

She got a big hug, and a kiss in the magic place just under her ear, and became very sure of Gamma's location.

Even Mark was impressed by the amount of time the station gave the story, presenting all sides. And, to top it all off, the following segment of the news included interviews with the state attorney general and Portland's police chief, both positive.

When time came for more commercials and the weather report, all in Meg's kitchen stood up, clapped, and one by one hugged Patsy, who was almost in tears, tears of excitement. She shuddered to think of having had to watch that show alone in her motel room. Thank God for family supporters,

Later, helping Meg clear the dishes, Mark whispered, his eyes dancing, "Your Mom's just started on what I predict will be a very interesting road.

When she moves to the White House, you can tell people where and when that prediction was made, and don't forget to include who made it."

LD 2365 was voted on by both Houses and passed in each by large majorities. Signed immediately by the governor, it became law.

* * * * *

Bangor

Later, in April, Republicans from the sixteen Maine counties came to Bangor on the wide Penobscot. Cabin fever no longer threatened. Winter chores had been completed and summer ones were not yet due. Uncle Sam had just been paid for his favors, and it was time to take matters of state and nation to task. This biennial flushing out of accumulated mental outrage was healthy, and there was no more effective way than to politick.

The huge Bangor auditorium was decorated with miles of red, white, and blue crepe paper streamers, hundreds of candidate posters, and bobbing balloons of all colors. Volunteers for the major candidates had booths dispensing brochures, position papers, and lollipops; Republican clubs and organizations were selling memorabilia, gadgets, and anything else that might raise money for their local campaign coffers. Those delegates who had served in earlier legislatures or as party officials sought out old friends, newcomers were confused but excited, and candidates at all levels sought hands to shake and backs to slap. The presence of local TV increased the sense of self-importance, of being part of a happening.

It was like a big family reunion, even with an inevitable share of black sheep and ne'er-do-wells. Fat or thin, urbane or hayseed, rich or poor, praise be, they were all Republican. No two thought just alike and on some issues they were sharply divided, but they had one goal in common—beat the Democrats. They would follow their political Golden Rule: Do unto Democrats as they would do unto you, but do it first.

Having attended the convention two years ago, Patsy was somewhat familiar with the goings-on; she certainly knew more people this time. She was pleased when strangers, reading her name tag, introduced themselves and congratulated her on the just-passed juvenile bill. The Portland diehards, a loyal and ever-hopeful group from that Democratic stronghold, were again proud to have her in their delegation.

People dribbled in all day Friday. Little new was brought out in keynote speeches at the gala opening night banquet. There are just so many ways to say "This time we're going to win," and most of the delegates had heard them all in the past. The big-name politicos sent up by the National Committee to serve as cheerleaders were effective, but the real activity began after the banquet. Then, delegates began visiting the motel and hotel hospitality suites hosted by major candidates.

Inexhaustible supplies of wine, beer, and stronger offerings, kept chilled in ice-packed bathtubs, kept enthusiasm up. Elevators were jammed, staircases crowded, and lines into each suite slow, but this was why the delegates had come. They could return home to their towns or cities with the memory of shaking candidates' hands, exchanging a few words, and possibly even making an impression themselves. "Sure, I met him, had a good talk. Y'know, he listened real good to my idea on fishin' rights. Might send him a few bucks later on." Or "Yeah, I talked to that guy. Didn't believe a word; he's a real hairpin." Such was the very essence of the gathering, with satisfaction on both sides.

As she had met them only a few times, in large crowds, Patsy was impressed that both the governor and Sen. Snowe called her by name, and at last she met Sen. Bill Cohen. Seeing Jerry Warner and Heather at one reception was a surprise; Patsy had no idea they were so interested in politics. And it was fun spotting David Broder as he interviewed the vice president's son, Neal.

Having dealt with almost paranoid partisanship for so many months she found herself relaxing in this one hundred percent Republican atmosphere. There were good delegates, and not so good, but all Republicans.

On Saturday, at the Cumberland County caucus, Patsy was delighted to be elected to a seat on the State Committee. She had wanted it not only for the prestige but because she felt there was too little communication between that Committee and the legislators it worked so hard to elect.

There were speeches by the party's congressional members, and the platform committee made its report. The real excitement, other than the rallies for all congressional hopefuls from both First and Second Districts, was choosing delegates to the national convention. County caucuses, made up of those delegates elected from towns, now chose delegates to vie for the state's representation at the national convention. This was actually the chief responsibility of the biennial gathering. The results of all those midwinter meetings now came into play, and slates were drawn up for each presidential hopeful. Vice president Bush was the clear winner, and the entire Maine delegation was eventually pledged to vote for him at the national convention in August. The convention ended on a positive note.

Victory was in sight, you could almost smell it.

Heather and Jerry, as absolute newcomers, had enjoyed admittance courtesy of Heather's press pass. This was the largest public gathering Jerry had attended in his new role, and he kept his eyes open for familiar faces to avoid. In the York County delegation he spotted a man who had been a few years behind him at Harvard, an acquaintance, not a close friend. Taking a chance, needing to know how recognizable he was, he managed to make eye contact, even smiled, but received no reaction at all from the other. A weight, though a small one, slid off his shoulders.

Driving home he and Heather picked each other's brains for reactions to the weekend. Heather was obviously troubled and a little cynical.

"How many of those hundreds of people do you think feel they made any difference by being there? Did most have a clue about how much had already been decided without them, weeks before? And by whom? Does it make any sense for them to come?"

Jerry laughed. "Of course it makes sense. They're more important than the candidates and they know it. Who do you think gets out the vote, stuffs and licks and mails fund-raising appeals, and sends thousands of their own dollars to a combination of campaigns? They were the honored guests, not the cabinet member or prominent senators.

"No, they may not feel they personally made history, but they'll be back again in 1990, win or lose this year, because they also had a whale of a good time. They weren't even conscious of what we used to call the smoke-filled rooms because they were politicking themselves with anyone who'd listen. Getting things off their chests and mingling with like thinkers. We'll see exactly the same thing at the Democrat's powwow.

"I think that's what a convention is all about. It is an ingathering, a mustering, an adult pep rally. Lots of people, little and big, made to feel part of something important, something that is actually counting on them. In many communities Republicans are in the minority, and they find it easy to lose heart. Tonight they all feel like Charles Atlas. If they can keep that enthusiasm till November they *will* make history, in a way."

"Mark said to keep an eye on Rep. Hudson, that she's going places. Smart, nothing else demands her time, and she has a real knack for politics. Think back on how she got that juvenile bill passed. She'd done her homework, and used her imagination. Most of all, Mark says she is extremely ambitious."

Heather waited for Jerry's comments.

"From what I've seen I'd agree with Mark but she may have two problems: her kids. Her son, I've heard, is gay, involved with a Passamaquoddy. Her daughter, a lawyer, specializes in women's issues and rights, and is definitely pro-choice. All of that plays OK in the southern counties, but rural voters are a conservative bunch. The Christian Right didn't win anything big this weekend, but it is obviously gaining strength at the grassroots level, particularly on the questions of abortion, homosexual rights, and prayer in schools. Patsy might have to make some tough decisions if she ever decides to run for a First District office, much less one statewide. Party loyalty vs. family. Moderate Republican candidates really have to count on that conservative vote, though they do attract Independents too."

"You're probably right, oh Man of Wisdom. Let's change the subject for now. A lot of thought and expertise went into some of the speeches we heard, those given by pros," mused Heather. "I took notes on techniques, use of images, how they built excitement. We're going to write some of the best letters and make some of the best speeches you ever heard."

"You never stop, do you, young lady?" said Jerry kiddingly.

He continued, "I wasn't idle either, keeping my eyes open for catchy logos, slogans and gimmickry. We heard a lot of regional accents, even local idioms, but at no time were they considered joke material or worthy of mention. This state has a lot of well-earned dignity. Nana's right; we've got to have a carefully thought-out, sensitive marketing program."

Heather's head was nodding; it had been a long day. Soon it drooped even further, and she slept. Jerry looked over at her lovely profile, so relaxed. His hand went out to pat her on the knee, but stopped. Too bad to wake her up. And if he did, what then? But how he'd love to have that head on his pillow every morning.

Chapter 8: Summer 1988

"Harry, what the tunket is in that letter? I don't know when I've seen you so taken in. Obviously it isn't junk mail."

The York County bank president looked over his glasses at his wife and grinned. "Just when. I was beginning to think of cutting down on activities, along comes an idea that's wicked interesting. Here, read it for yourself.'" He passed a letter across the breakfast table.

Finishing it, she beamed. "While it is really just a dinner invitation to learn more of a plan, I don't see how you can refuse. From what is said here," and she waved the paper, "they are going to tackle a mess of the things I listen to you grumble about every evening. And I like their explaining why they need Maine-born support. Most of our 'saviors' from away think they are heaven-sent, until, of course, we put them straight." She chuckled.

"Well, keep it under your belt as they ask, and I'll check my calendar at the office and reply today."

Further north a well-used but still serviceable pickup truck fought its way over a road well chowdered by winter's tire chains and still awaiting its annual scraping. Making it to the state road the vehicle finally, almost triumphantly, pulled into a post-office parking lot. Taking his time going up the porch steps, waving at a few acquaintances on the "Liars bench," a lanky man in worn overalls opened the door and went to his mailbox, twisting the dials automatically.

"Morning, Governor, any fish biting up your way?" The postmistress had a bit of chat for everyone.

"Not yet, Eldena, but any day now. I'll bring you one if I'm lucky."

He regained his truck, slid behind the wheel, gave his canine passenger a pat, and looked over his mail. Though he'd been retired for several years from his law practice, and longer than that from serving as governor, he still received requests, reports, and political comments almost daily. A bother to read some days, but it kept him from feeling useless. He often read his mail in the parked truck as that put off going right home and receiving his orders for the day from his wife. She wasn't exactly bossy, but she did hate to see a man inactive; didn't think it was healthy—or moral.

One envelope seemed of interest, addressed in a fine hand, and of good quality paper. He certainly found it different from the run-of-the-mill correspondence he was used to. It presented solid ideas and didn't seem to be the work of idealistic nuts or political cranks. An invitation to consider. He liked particularly its goal to lessen, if not actually eliminate, the bitter and crippling partisanship in Augusta. That partisanship had taken most of the pleasure out of his terms as governor. No question about it, he'd be there, spend the night in Augusta, look up old friends, and find out what this was all about. He had a late case of cabin fever anyway.

On the top floor of a Bangor office building a middle-aged, well-dressed woman accepted her mail from a secretary. As the heiress to a large lumber company owning thousands of acres due north, she was not only active in that enterprise, but on the board of many nonprofit agencies as well as that of a large bank. Wasting time was a luxury she could not afford, so she glanced hurriedly at the letters, anxious to make a few phone calls before leaving the building for a meeting. However, one envelope caught her eye and she opened it. After reading the first few sentences she sat back comfortably in her chair and gave the remainder her full and relaxed attention.

Twelve other such letters reached their destinations that day, delivered to city homes, rural mail boxes, and offices large and small. All were read, and if it had been possible for anyone to be present at each reading, they could have honestly reported that interest was immediate, and positive.

Ten nights later all fifteen recipients gathered for dinner in a Waterville hotel, meeting with Stan and Jerry Warner, Joel McLean, and Heather Hatch. Many of the guests knew each other; actually, most of them were privately flattered to be included in such a blue-ribbon gathering. In addition, they were all Maine born, bred, and proud of it. An unusual occasion these days.

As their acceptances had come in to the office, Heather had sent out packets with more information, so the guests were already somewhat familiar with the plans.

At dinner their questions were answered easily; good preparation and thinking had gone into the presentation. The philosophy was sound and the goal almost too good to be true. A number of valuable suggestions were made. What interested the guests most was this kickoff, the legislative workshop. Mark Lowell was not alone in being enchanted with the colorful possibilities of give and take there. "That'll be some powwow, even a turkey shoot," said one gentleman, a blueberry processor from Washington County.

As the meeting was breaking up, one man took out his checkbook. "I appreciate the fact there has been no tin cup passed around, but I have always believed in one-hundred percent support of anything to which I lend my name. I'd like to help grease the skids," and he wrote a check. Others followed. Then goodnights were said and the company scattered for, in most cases, long drives home.

Joel was spending a few days with the Warners to work out more details. On the long ride back to the farm the talk was excited and happy. They certainly were grateful to Mark for helping to bring together such a group; they'd liked and respected them all. Heather, ever practical, finally blurted out that she had to know what the evenings "take" was, and the rest admitted they'd been itching to add it up too. Stopping at a gas station in the last little town that had such an amenity, Joel added up the total.

"Wow, have we ever done something right?" gasped Heather. Each check was generous and they were all in the same range, real confidence builders. Jerry grinned and said he had an errand in the store.

Replaying his Santa Claus role he soon reappeared with a Snickers Bar for each of them, and one for Susan into the bargain. "I know this is reckless spending but, gang, again we've 'done real goo-oo-d," said he. "Of course, now we gotta work our butts off."

* * * * *

Harding's Corner

In June, the Maine political primaries took center stage, and then they too were history. Each major party had fielded an almost full, though not exciting, slate for the legislature, but the congressional contests promised to be lively.

Though Patsy had been unopposed by any Republican hopeful, she had still put up lawn signs, sent out a mailing, and in general kept her name in front of her district. Pretty sure she would win reelection, she had nevertheless taken no chances. She wanted to win by a landslide, a real headliner. Her Democratic challenger was an older man, bored with retirement. Though he was a loyal activist, he had never run for office. He would probably be well funded, but didn't seem to have the prerequisites of name recognition or a real passion.

Don Vassalo had also considered running for the Maine House but decided that devoting his energies to the Dukakis presidential campaign in Maine would introduce him to the party bigwigs. He also believed that it would be best to take his plunge in 1990, when there would be no presidential campaign to divert supporters.

The Phoenix group settled down to finalizing plans for the August seminar. The detail was infinite, but Heather took it all in stride as if conferences were her stock in trade.

Jerry had found a number of leadership courses and counselors available, many specialized to an almost ridiculous degree. Were there more leadership openings than qualified people to fill them? Or did most people lack the confidence to try anything new without training? Had a new breed of "experts" sprung up as advisors, preying on ambitions?

As he studied their material he was startled to discover that some people needed to learn skills he had taken for granted from birth. He began to realize that many, if not most, people never thought of themselves as leaders but as worker bees who contentedly followed orders. Did they never think to light one candle or to even curse the darkness? Most of his own life had been spent with other aspiring chiefs, few Indians. From Cub Scouts to Little League and then on to class offices and SAT scores, under the guidance of supportive or ambitious parents, his friends had also been ambitious and competitive. Leadership was as natural as breathing to those who had been made self-confident from birth.

A simile came to his mind. Of all the millions of acorns that fall to the forest floor annually, how many grow to be oaks? What determines which ones will germinate and survive, which ones will be Thanksgiving dinner to a squirrel? Was it the warmth of sunshine? Some just lie there in the shade till they rot and give new nourishment to the soil. Each category certainly plays a role in the balance of nature and deserved respect. He had had sunshine.

Harding's Corner was scarcely in competition with Times Square as a traffic nightmare, but meetings of psychologists, teachers, and sociologists were conducted there frequently during the early summer. All guests were pledged to secrecy, and intrigued enough to come to that remote laboratory to share their thoughts on Altitude Adjustment. They agreed with Jerry that his list of invitees was almost bizarre but not really unique. Like many international summit meeting participants, these men and women were actually leaders already who had simply been given the opportunity to form bad habits. How had they gotten away with this? Who was to blame for the apathy and abuse of power and cynicism—the politicians, or the electorate?

"Entering the political arena at any level, no matter how dedicated to your own ideals, takes courage and self-confidence. No other profession goes under such scrutiny. Each candidate puts himself or herself on the block, to be inspected and judged. I'm always interested in how each handles that personal drive, and in what it eventually does to them."

Professor Charles Archibald, political science chair of a respected Massachusetts college, stared out Jerry's office window at the green and flowery fields.

"Look at these fields. Once they supported healthy crops of vegetables, field corn, or even just good hay. They were taken care of, fertilized, kept as clean and pest-free as possible by good farmers. Now, though they get the same sun and rain and seasons, there is no nurturing. They've gone to wild grasses and weeds, pretty as some such weeds may be. The owners' neglect, for one reason or another, is responsible. I believe that politicians need nurturing also, fertilized by trust and respect. If neglected or overlooked, they become second-rate and of little interest. They blow their own horns during campaigns, but after that little positive is said of them.

"Our great leaders rose to the top because the times demanded greatness. Survival hasn't been an issue for a long time, so now the litmus test is 'state of the pocketbook'; greatness doesn't count, just dollar signs. Voters, uninterested in keeping up with the complicated details, have chosen legislators almost solely on the basis of two things, and those two are incompatible. Voters want their taxes lowered, yet they want the government to pay for more services. Legislators get blamed either way it goes.

Jerry laughed, but not because the situation was funny. It was absurd.

"I've learned that legislators take themselves very seriously, perhaps because no one else does. They love having their own license plates, being on TV occasionally, being asked to address local organizations hard up for weekly speakers. They like having their mail addressed to the Hon. John Doe for the rest of their lives. Sadly, however, most of them could drop dead on their own Main Street and it would be some time before anyone came along who knew where to ship the body.

"Top-of-the ticket candidates are on TV of course, ad nauseam, but the poor little guy, running for the legislature or county office, full of noble plans, can't afford that. No one is at home any more if a candidate goes door-to-door, so the best exposure opportunities are the 4th of July parade, the county fairs, and other big summer crowd-gatherers. And who gets to see him? Out-of-state tourists. The expense of TV time leads to questionable campaign financing or dependency on pressure groups."

Jerry took up the discussion.

"There must be better ways to get close to the voter, and I don't mean coffee parties, talking to half a dozen ladies who'll twitter over a candidate and probably vote as their husbands suggest. Yes, I agree, we should not only stroke legislators but show sincere respect if we want respectable results."

Nodding agreement, Archibald added, "In politics there are no runner-ups, it's win or lose, period. Why do they do it ?"

"Dunno. I love this theorizing and asking the whys, but time's a-wasting. Let's get down to work."

Jerry navigated a path to his desk between the shoals of boxes of envelopes, piles of books, and the surf of unfiled manila folders. Heather's desk had been moved around a corner so that she could work in comparative calm.

"The seminar invitations should go out next week. I want your frank opinion of the draft, because the whole shooting match depends on it."

Archibald turned from the window and sat down in an almost empty chair to read. Jerry watched nervously, as this man had the reputation of being able to get inside the minds of those in public office. He knew what buttons to push and when to push them, he knew danger signs, and knew how to sprinkle flowers along dangerous pathways.

The professor read in silence, finished the first page and concentrated on the second. After a few moments he lifted his head and Jerry saw that his eyes were twinkling.

"Couldn't have done better myself. This opening, asking them if they are concerned about the esteem in which politicians are held, is great. No one likes to admit, even to themselves, that their career choice is deemed less than honorable, or that they themselves are either stupid or self-serving. You make no bones about assuming they agree with you, probably with grateful relief because someone understands. That simpatico 'ally' approach sucks 'em right in every time. The 'good cop' routine.

"Then you build the poor bastards up, stressing the real courage they have shown in seeking public office or in holding office in the party organization. The challenges they have accepted and the stamina they have often exhibited in holding to positions have proved the commitment they feel. Now their heads come up, their chests swell, and they read on with curiosity and excitement.

"I quote, 'You took a chance when you became a candidate or an organizer. You still take chances on many of the hard decisions you make. We are offering you yet another gamble, a chance to improve, or possibly correct, your image.' This challenge is made exciting, a bit mysterious, even a little dangerous, but one they cannot afford to reject, knowing their absence would be noticed by both sides.

"Your description of what Phoenix is and why you're doing this is straightforward and clear. The team of sponsors is balanced and prestigious enough to allay any fears they might have of scam. You list who is being invited, you are specific as to what they're expected to bring both in their heads and on their backs, and best of all, you stress that it won't cost them a cent.

"You ask that they not mention this event to other invitees, and assure them that the press will be represented by only one member. The only requisite is that they leave partisanship at the gate, as cowboys in the olden days were asked to park their six-shooters before entering a bar. May I make one suggestion?"

"Only one?" Jerry's voice showed his relief.

"There is no mention of tangible reward. No gold star paper to bring home and put on the refrigerator. Do you have anything in mind?"

"Rewards? We've certainly discussed them, and have some ideas. One is that they receive, at the end of the course, a certificate of graduation that describes the purpose and curriculum of the course they have completed. A copy of their voluntary agreement to follow certain :rules during the life of this campaign would be included. They would then have the opportunity to insert reprints of that certificate and contract in the body of their brochures if they are candidates. There might even be a pin to wear or, heaven forbid, a T-shirt or cap, proving they arrived as suspicious rivals and left as a solid team, in uniform."

Alexander thought over these suggestions

"What about all the candidates who could not be invited? Can the material of this course trickle down to them? While they could not have a certificate, could they sign the pledge and use it in their own leaflets, plus their comments on the spirit of the program?"

Jerry clapped his hands with enthusiasm.

"At first we wanted to invite all candidates, but that was out of the question because of sheer numbers. Part of the course will cover how those who attend can teach other candidates of their party what they have learned. But your idea of giving all a chance to sign and display the pledge is terrific. If this all works as planned, no candidate would dare not sign up.

"Have you chosen a slogan or logo to help sell the Phoenix plan as a whole, later on, or at least this segment of it? I can see a real marketing challenge."

Jerry shook his head. "That is about the toughest assignment. We're torn between so many ideas, some great, some ridiculous. I'm personally hoping we can come up with some doohickey that appeals to kids, as they're great salespeople. We want something they scream and whine for, maybe something that has variables leading to a collecting rage, like Barbie doll outfits. We need something that suggests our overall purpose and will not be limited to just this political venture. Ideas? The Phoenix name is great to indicate rebirth, second chances, etc., but who the hell wants to collect dead birds?"

Alexander laughed. "It's a tough one, but I'll bet with a lot of crazy minds like yours working you'll find a doozy. After all, now that I think of it, Maine probably has more creative minds per capita than any other state."

"Now that the invitations have your approval, plus your suggestions, we'll have them run off this week so they'll be in the mail just after July 4th. A second letter with specific details will go out to those who accept. OK?"

"You're right on target, and I wish you luck. If this works there'll be a lot of grateful people in this state. We hear about how wonderful Maine air is and what a fortune could be made in bottling it. This program is going to make it a helluva lot better. Too bad the prevailing wind is downeast instead of due west or south, where it'd do a lot of good."

After Alexander's departure, Jerry peered around the corner to see if

Heather had comments. Her chair was empty, so she was probably upstairs. Disappointed, Jerry went back to the farm; chores still had to be done.

Heather was on her knees beside one of her chests, pawing through the contents. Finally, in triumph, she pulled out a small, bright box, sank back on her heels and held it to her heart, beaming. The sight of her treasure brought back the sounds and smells of a market square on the other side of the world. She could almost hear the laughter of the children as they watched a toy merchant demonstrate his wares.

"'Who the hell wants to collect dead birds?' says he," she muttered. "This little box and I are going to Portland on Saturday."

* * * * *

What a culture shock Portland was! Heather's present abode was so isolated that even Bangor now seemed 'big-city' to her, and here she was in Portland at the height of the tourist season. Monument Square was the site of the Saturday Farmer's Market, a sophisticated version of the one upstate she sometimes attended with the Warners. A band, equipped with amplifiers, filled the air with rhythm, balloons floated aloft from the heartbroken grasp of chubby little hands, and the smell of vendors' hot dogs tickled hungry noses. Tourists wandered leisurely, enjoying the vacation tempo, studying shop windows, or seeking just the right restaurant for their mood. Some sat on benches under the shade trees, people-watching. The passengers from a huge cruise ship had guidebooks in hand, and commented on the scene in many languages.

Heather had to park in a garage on Fore Street. She headed on foot through the Old Port, past the colorful Exchange Street boutiques and restaurants to a small Asian shop displaying native crafts. As she entered there was a happy greeting.

"Oh Heather, you are back! We miss you, much.!" The tiny woman came around the counter and hugged the girl who towered over her. "What brings you? Where you living? What you do?"

During her short stay in the city a year ago Heather had become connected with many of the Southeast Asians who had recently settled in Portland. She wanted to repay the kindness and hospitality she had received in their countries, and her times with them brought back great memories. Now she knew that before she could mention why she was here, she would have to satisfy Nga's curiosity.

Over tea, in the back of the shop, she told her tale, then took the little treasure from her bag. “Have you ever seen anything like this?” she asked, holding her breath.

Face wreathed in smiles, Nga took the box in her hands and pulled a string on the bottom. The lid sprang open and a small, very colorful bird was released to soar to the ceiling, wings actually flapping. Nga reeled it in again by the string, laughing.

“Yes, yes, these very popular at home. An old toy, but the children never get tired of it. You have them here, in USA?”

With a happy grin Heather answered, “No, but we're going to have them, hundreds and hundreds if, dear Nga, you can tell me if there is anyone here who knows how to make them.,”

Little Nga, like a small, bright bird herself, cocked her head. “My cousin's husband, he makes toys for his grandchildren. Maybe he know.” She rose and went, to the phone. For the next few minutes there was rapid Vietnamese conversation; after courtesies had been exchanged, the all-important question was asked. Nga listened intently, wrote down a name and number, and finally, after long and polite farewells, hung up.

“He has never made any, but say there's a man in Gorham, an old man, who still makes them. He speak a little English, too. You want to see him?”

Heather certainly did. Soon she was on her way west of Portland to the lovely college town. Her conversation with the old gentleman was slow, but effective, and he agreed to make several of the birds for her. They would serve as models for a manufacturer to copy. A business arrangement would be made, and even plans for a patent.

That night Heather visited with Portland friends, had a hard time choosing a place to dine, and finally opted for a fine Indian restaurant by the docks. Portland was a fun place, under the right conditions. Getting to sleep on the friend's sofa-bed was almost impossible not only because of her excitement but because of city sounds. Fire engines, sirens of ambulances and police, endless auto noises and the foghorn at Portland Head Light were her unfamiliar lullaby. She really believed she'd hit on what was needed by Phoenix. Now to sell it to the others. Packaging, message, name, and marketing all lay ahead. Maybe even a new Maine industry. How long would it take to get into production? Finally sleep came.

Though she'd planned to lollygag her way home in the morning, now she couldn't get there fast enough. A real presentation had to be prepared, as professional as possible, before she shared this. It was going to be hours of work, but it would certainly be fun.

With only about six weeks to go before the seminar the work in the little office expanded like bread dough on a warm day, filling the lives of the workers, creeping into every little interstice of their routines. Responses had been very positive so far, which made the work satisfying. There were interesting questions and comments every day in the mail. One day there was even a little package for Heather, which puzzled her at first. Then she saw the Gorham postmark and had the wrappings off in seconds.

Inside were two of the little bird-boxes. There was also another with box and bird in separate pieces, ready to be assembled, wrapped in paper covered with delicate writing and clear illustrations.

"That dear, dear man," crowed Heather. Hiding it all, she finished her morning's work, then took her package upstairs, even closing the door at the top of the stairs for security.

Reading slowly and studying the various parts, she finally had a good understanding of how to put the mechanism together, and also of how and why it worked. The strings and springs that controlled the lid and ejected the bird were examples of clever engineering, but possible to copy. She was absolutely delighted to see that assembly was also fairly simple, with the bright materials of the bird the only possible challenge to reproduce. Her basket of colorful fabrics had found a use at last. They were in business!

On Friday she insisted that the Warners come for drinks that evening. Susan reminded her that Joel and Carol were even then en route for the weekend and Heather exclaimed, "So much the better!"

To complement the planned demonstration, she dressed in her most exotic Thai garments, swept her hair up, held by ivory pins, and tried to duplicate some of the delicate hors d'oeuvres she had enjoyed so far away. Spring rolls and potstickers at Harding's Corner, Maine!

Office chairs were carried out to the little lawn she had created behind the building. Late-afternoon clouds promised a spectacular sunset, the perfect setting for her little drama. Stubbornly, she wanted her guests to be in an agony of curiosity, so she waited till the second round of drinks before giving her exhibition.

Going into the office, she removed a drab little box from a desk drawer and took it out to the cocktail table. Shiny, as if lacquered, but a dead ashen color, it created absolutely no excitement. Carol politely reached for it and Heather let her examine it.

"Now, hold it up in one hand, and put one finger of the other hand into the ring at the bottom. Pull gently but steadily."

Carol stood, raised the box shoulder-high, and pulled. Smoothly the lid opened and out whirled a brightly colored bird, chickadee-sized. Not like a child's pet parakeet, but like a miniature falcon, resolute and fearless.

"Pull the other ring in short, up-and-down strokes with another finger." The wings began to flap as the bird continued to rise and actually float on the little evening breeze.

Her guests were like children viewing a magic stage production, holding their breaths and watching every flap and twist. As the bird finally began to return to earth, Heather showed Carol the tiny crank by which she could rewind the strings for the next flight. As it was tucked away in its nest again, there was a babbling of excited questions and appreciation.

Heather produced the second bird, identical except for plumage, and the directions. As they examined these she went into her office and emerged with an armful of Heather-made posters. Presenting them to her friends, the chuckles turned to guffaws and cries of delight. "Phoenix Phables," "Pheathered Phledglings," "Phunny Phriends," and on and on, all in drab gray and contrasting radiance.

Jerry's curiosity overwhelmed him. "OK, OK, you've done it. Done it in spades. But where the hell did you get the idea?"

"From you, sweet coz." And that was all she would say.

Joel got serious.

"I don't want to be a wet blanket, but we have a busy six weeks till the seminar. Then I hope we'll think we've been loafing so far, as Project Phoenix and As Maine Goes hit the news. Politics will make September and October fly by, and November is too late to get into any kind of production or marketing for Christmas, isn't it?"

"I have looked into production possibilities," Heather answered. "Any woodworking shop can turn out the basic pieces. Assembling the springs and strings would take little practice. So the birds, or rather their wings and feathers, are the only stumbling-block, and I can provide those fabrics myself. Now don't laugh at me or at this next idea." She was dead serious.

They waited, still not quite used to her bursts of imagination.

"Yesterday, at lunchtime, I made a sandwich, a sardine sandwich, and a very good one." She paused, letting that humdrum statement sink in.

"And I looked with fresh appreciation at those perfect little fish packed so neatly and with such precision into the relatively small can. Whose nimble fingers did that? Those of the good ladies of Eastport, of Lubec, of the coastal towns of Washington and Hancock counties. Those women are begging for new ideas, for interesting work. Mightn't they jump at the chance to create, with those clever fingers, exotic birds from beautiful fabrics, no two alike? It's something they could do at home, no day care problems, and a lot nicer smelling than dead fish."

Practical Carol broke in, with excitement. "Wouldn't the Southeast Asian immigrant ladies like to help too? They need all the support they can get."

Heather nodded happily and continued.

"I'm afraid Joel is right about this Christmas. There's no sense in biting off more than we can chew and making fools of ourselves. By next year we'll be able to flood the country. Now here is Idea #2. These are a lot prettier than Cabbage Patch dolls or pet rocks, and they have a message, an ideal to support! Renewal, rebirth, a second chance for all, built on attitudes. We're not proselytizing a religion, morals, or ethics. Our message is just good common sense, isn't it, a plan for successful living? Altitude Adjustment, higher sights.

"I'd like to take time to have written, or to collect, stories and poems for children, classic or modern, based on such things as respect, integrity, courtesy. One booklet would be packaged with each bird and the others could be collected like Barbie outfits or Lego sets."

Happy cries of "Hear, hear." She waited for arguments, wisecracks or pessimism, but none were forthcoming.

Joel, ever the businessman, added "We could build up a good supply, ready for the 1989 summer fairs and nice gift shops. The big Christmas craft shows would be a perfect spot for them. We'd probably need a marketing agent to help us, because we'll have many other irons in the fire by then, I hope."

Stan broke in, his former talents well stimulated.

"Well-made treasures copied faithfully from ancient Oriental art could command a good price for the women, and what a logo for us. These little birds are a specialty item, not to be hawked along with T-shirts and fried dough, but not too expensive either. A great teaching tool."

By the time darkness had fallen and the moon was white and bright in the heavens, all of their imaginations had soared like the little bird and were tucked away, exhausted, in whatever container imaginations call home.

Heather's surprise had been a triumph, and one more Phoenix hurdle had been cleared. Her call to Nana later that night was extravagant beyond belief—and worth every penny.

* * * * *

Piscataquis County, Maine

Camp Namakant, hidden in the deep woods of Piscataquis County, was originally a paper company's sporting camp. Business associates, influential members of Congress, even presidents of the United States were flown in to enjoy the beautiful spot on the shores of a mountain-girded lake.

Just after World War II it had been acquired by a group of old-money Philadelphia and Boston men. With careful planning, they had transformed it into a summer camp for boys. Staffed by teachers and coaches from prestigious boarding schools and serving largely the teenage sons of the eastern elite, it had soon taken its place among other, older camps known for far more than swimming, tennis and overnight hikes.

The old school tie was still an influential scrap of fabric in the society into which these boys had been born. The choice of summer camp was often handed down from father to son as a legacy, unearned, unquestioned, but treasured. The camp founders recognized that these boys were apt to inherit not only wealth but, in many cases, the powerful corporate positions of tomorrow. The main focus of the camp was to reinforce the values and leadership skills the boys were given at school, but by example and physical challenges rather than bookwork. Mutual respect and trust were key. Most of the work around camp was done by the boys; a Campfire Council provided self-government. Honesty, integrity, and kindness were simply taken for granted.

Every summer each board member sponsored, as his guest, a boy from a different background, socially, ethnically, or financially. These campers, carefully chosen because for their own strengths, were introduced as examples of the ideal Namakant boy, models to follow, never patronized as tokens. It wasn't unusual for a Namakant boy to choose former cabinmates as ushers at his wedding or to serve as godfather to his sons. Namakant friendships were strong and treasured.

Now, due to a pair of dedicated "graduates," the political leaders of the State of Maine were wending their way along miles of back roads, headed for a condensed but rigorous Namakant experience. Unbelievably, all invitees had accepted.

The Phoenix board had moved in on Wednesday, and everything was ready. Sleeping assignments had been made with no regard to party, and kitchen work crews had been chosen. The women board members had agreed that good communicating is more apt to take place drying dishes or peeling potatoes than in a structured atmosphere, but had volunteered to provide Friday's dinner themselves, turning the jobs over to campers on Saturday.

The first "camper" to arrive was a loved and admired State Committee woman from western York County. She probably had the longest drive, but also a reputation for never being late, ever. Included in her baggage was her cat. The governor, complete with tennis racquet and his security officer, brought up a carful; Jerry was pleased to see that it was a nonpartisan group.

As each person checked in he or she was given an envelope containing instructions and a program. The weekend would open officially at dinner, and all were urged to glance through the packet before that time. Cabins for six lined the shore, and others were scattered through the woods.

A cooling breeze rose in the late afternoon, and soon the waterfront drew swimmers. All noted with anticipation the canoes and sailboats pulled up on the beach. There was a lodge, originally built for paper company guests but now used as office space, small conference rooms, and bedrooms for visiting parents. A long screened porch stretched the length of the lodge, with a glorious view of the lake and mountains. What impressed them most was the Great Hall, almost baronial in size, with a huge fieldstone fireplace. It was here they would eat and hold many of the meetings. They would, however, experience little use of the recreational attractions they had been admiring.

After a brief discussion some weeks earlier, Stan had won out on having a "happy hour" each evening. By six almost everyone had gathered on the lodge porch, paper cup in hand, and the group proceeded to mellow and meld. Jerry went to get more ice and whispered to Heather, "They're not a bad-looking bunch when you get 'em in shorts. But there are some beer bellies that are going to be a helluva lot flatter by Sunday night."

Joel, a stranger to all of them, moved around noting a great deal. Few 'campers' were his familiar Harvard, Boston, or Somerset Club types, and he really envied Jerry's ability to mix easily. He recognized the gap between his Brooks Brothers wardrobe and that of the Army-Navy store garb of many of the attendees. This weekend might prove a challenge and attitude adjustment for him, too. He was particularly interested in the Speaker, who was standing by himself at the porch railing. Would he wrap himself in his prestige or could he be just one of the boys?

Introducing himself, Joel said, "We're awfully glad you came. This meeting may be a flop or a huge success, and I hope you'll express yourselves as we go along. It's an experiment, as you know, and we all have a lot to learn." The Speaker almost smiled, and returned his attention to the lake.

At the Hall, Nana hit the suspended wagon wheel rim with a tire iron. Everyone walked across the pine grove from Lodge to Great Hall and took their places where indicated. After a blessing, they filled their plates with a no-nonsense meat and potatoes supper, complete with fresh corn and salad. Joel stood, tapping on the water pitcher for silence.

"Ladies and gentlemen, you have just inhaled your last unscheduled breath till Sunday night. There's so much to cover that I hope you'll forgive me for breaking in even before you start eating. I am that Joel McLean from who you've received mailings, and chairman of the Phoenix Project. You have all been sent the history and purpose of Phoenix, so I won't waste time repeating that.

"First, thank you for coming. I think I can guarantee you will be different people when you leave, or at least the same people looking at things in a different way. The theme, unannounced till now, is" and he paused for effect, grinning, " 'As Maine Goes.' Not very original, but very apt." Scattered clapping

"As you all know, in the old days, when even November travel could be daunting, Maine was the only state in the Union to vote early in all local and national elections except for the presidency. The results often predicted the national outcome and the phrase was born: 'As Maine goes, so goes the nation.' Let's resurrect it, like the phoenix.

"If, between all of us, with hard work, complete candor, and a real desire for improvement, we can pull off a fresh plan and approach to politics that earns renewed respect and trust, we just might have forty-nine other states following our lead. There are many fine names in Maine's history and few of which to be ashamed. That gives us a good start." More applause.

He took a long pull from his iced tea glass and continued.

"As you drove in here you left party and position behind, out there by the gate. The only thing on your name tag is, by coincidence, your name. As far as the professional counselors who will take over tomorrow are concerned, you're just a nice bunch of guys and gals, and there's no pecking order. This won't be easy for some to remember, but you might just get to like it."

Appreciative laughter followed.

"Many of you have just returned from one or the other of the national conventions, where for almost a week you were reminded at every turn that your party had all the answers and there was little lower on this earth than the opposition. Bands, balloons, and booze make for great conventions. Little was decided that wasn't a foregone conclusion, but you all came home feeling like very fine fellas indeed. Right?" Appreciative clapping from the diners.

"That excitement, that euphoria is going to be hard to forget. But have you noticed how little coverage those conventions got on the tube compared to even a few years ago? Was anything really new said? How many men on the street could tell you which party met in what city? Have your neighbors been begging you for the details? All that noise and hoopla, yet ... who cares?

"You do. And I think that is why you all came here to explore ways to regain the admiration and respect of voters, because you know you're not stupid, you're not crooks, and that you are dedicated to damn serious work for the good of those neighbors. Right?"

This time the applause was much louder.

"That's our challenge, to carve out new approaches, new attitudes and even new rules that will eliminate the gridlock and partisan power plays that are so justifiably criticized. We may learn that politics is not warfare, but is what happens later at the peace table." A good line, but little applause.

Experienced salesman that he was, he recognized that they appreciated his pitch but were holding back on actually signing the contract. A lot was at stake, and Maine people are as careful in accepting new ideas as they are in buying a used car.

"At this point I know very few of you. I have no idea whether the Democrats are all sitting on one side of this room and the Republicans on the other, with smaller parties scattered. If this is so tonight, I hope by the time we break up on Sunday you will have found it interesting, entertaining, and even safe to mix it up a bit.

"I will go 'way out on a limb and suggest, even bet, that there are no two people in this room who think exactly alike on issues or even philosophy. I will also bet that some conservative Democrats are closer to moderate Republicans than to many members of their own party. Same goes, of course for liberal R's and moderate D's. Some of you may agree with me?"

There was some laughter but no great applause at this heresy.

"A few housekeeping details, and then we eat and hit the sack. Today you had a long drive and tomorrow is going to be a real challenge, mentally and physically. A few rules are requested by the camp. No smoking except down on the beach, with butts put in suitable containers. Though you are all experienced Mainers we are asked to go in pairs on any hikes, canoe trips, or even swims. The camp has an excellent record of safety and we don't want to spoil that. We'd like to be invited again.

"Let me introduce the Phoenix staff." He turned and swept his hand in the direction of where they sat.

"Please rise as I name you. Stan Warner, former New York insurance broker and a Maine resident for over thirty years, senior adviser. By the way, if he can leave partisanship out there by the gate, any of you can." Laughter.

"His lovely wife Susan, former teacher and recognized artist and craftswoman, in charge of keeping you all comfortable if you just remember you're not at the Ritz. Their son Jerry, recently returned from a business career overseas, is the guy who really put this together.

"My wife Carol will help Susan in keeping you comfortable, and Heather Hatch, former Washington TV news reporter, will be on hand in the Lodge Office to straighten out any program or supply problems. And from Lewiston, Rep. Jeanette LaPierre, R.N., has offered her services for first aid.

"I've saved the best till last: Nana Delano, Heather's grandmother, who shares her wisdom gracefully and has the knack of making everyone like themselves a little better. She is busy in the Midwest, building up the self-esteem of other seniors and then turning them into mentors. If you have troubles, take them to her; she's a good listener.

"We promised you just one member of the media, but he hasn't arrived yet. This is Mark Lowell, whom many of you see around the State House. He will be sitting in on all meetings and doing interviews whenever he can find you free. If you hear something like a Panzer division approaching in the night, that's Mark on his Harley. Breakfast is at seven and you're ready for work at eight. Get as much homework done tonight as you can." Scattered applause.

Joel sat down to pick at his cold dinner, apparently relaxed on the surface but missing nothing. He caught Jerry's eye and, exchanging winks, they continued surveillance.

He had not thought to describe himself, a product of traditional Boston, brought up with an admirable sense of noblesse oblige but little real understanding of those in the trenches. Would someone else have described him as "nice but a little stuffy?"

Would people truly mingle as they moved outdoors, or would they seek party cohorts? Were legislators getting to know state and county leaders? To whom were the commissioners drawn? He couldn't tell much now, so he carried his plate out to the kitchen, gave Carol, at the sink, a hug, and said dramatically, à la Scarlett "Oh well, tomorrow is another day." A loon cried out on the lake; the sound was exciting.

Next morning the commissioner of mental health was putting together the makings of tuna salad sandwiches for lunch when Stan brought two strangers into the camp kitchen, seeking breakfast.

"We know we're a little late, but these gentlemen arrived well after midnight so we let them sleep. May we help ourselves to what's left?"

The commissioner assented and continued her work, meanwhile clinically inspecting the newcomers who were obviously the speakers for the morning sessions.

The older of the two was round, beige in personality as well as dress, with a carefully put-together look. "He looks just like these onions," she mused. Neat, well-organized, familiar, almost commonplace. Safe, and will probably bore everyone to death. As tasty as stewed overshoe and as exciting as a can of Crisco.

The other was a different veggie altogether. Slim, urbane, and dressed in olive-green shirt and slacks, he brought to mind Bill Moyers, even to the spectacles, with all Moyers' sophisticated and slightly patronizing intellectualism.

"A slick, shiny zucchini, but will he be all show and no substance?" She covered her sandwich mixture with Saran wrap, popped it into the big fridge, and hurried to join the others.

It was exactly eight A.M. A soft mist still hung over the lake, and though in this calm setting no monster was going to rise out of the water, a challenging program was about to surface and possibly change the lives and thinking of all at camp, now gathered in the Great Hall.

Joel greeted them, commending their punctuality and introducing the newcomers.

"Mr. Onion" turned out to be Charles Andrews, a socioeconomics consultant from Boston who would explain the relatively new science of collaborative leadership and illustrate its effectiveness with exercises.

Susan, a pro at studying faces, surveyed the gathering and decided Mr. Andrews had a tough row to hoe. Jaws were set and eyes leaden. The faces had all the warmth of a row of headstones in a cemetery. Had Jerry made a bad mistake? In subject? Presenter?

"Mr. Zucchini" fared no better. He, God help him, was from the Midwest, a foreign country to much of this group, and was named Kurt Volasko, even more foreign. To him would fall the responsibility of teaching the methods of making Andrews' theories work and pay off.

Traditionally wary of ideas "from away," suspicious of differences, and torn away from their families this last weekend of summer, the assemblage was already showing every sign of negativity.

"This is going to be drier than a two-hour August sermon," whispered one senator to another. "Neither of those guys will spin a thread with this bunch. "

"We're going to split into two groups for the first hour, half of you here and the others in the Lodge," Joel directed. "Then you'll swap locations for the next hour, and Charlie and Kurt will repeat their presentations to the new group. OK? Will all the A's through M's please follow Kurt to the Lodge?"

Charlie had brought a tableful of books, pamphlets, and reprints. Kurt was empty-handed. The session got under way, slowly. After checking out the kitchen for lunch arrangements, Stan slid into the almost silent Great Hall. Charlie was just getting into his pitch for collaborative leadership.

"Though we represent different companies, Kurt and I have worked together many times, and we jumped at this opportunity. Generally we work with business or community leaders; we've never had a political group before. We feel challenged, and that's great.

"You may see no similarities, but they're there. Business groups are looking for greater profits, for more satisfied customers and for a more loyal and ambitious workforce. Your profits are the number of votes you receive, produced by a satisfied electorate at the urging of dedicated campaign workers. In other words, by using our suggestions the process may result not only in greater returns, whether dollars or votes, but in greater respect for, and faith in, management. A relaxed atmosphere leads to far greater forward thinking and accomplishment."

Charlie paused, wiped his glasses, and continued, his voice assuming a strong and positive note. "I'm not talking in idealistic terms; this isn't a Sunday school lesson or a scout camporee. What we're investigating is a well-proven though new approach to getting difficult things done, to everyone's benefit. You may ask, 'what's in it for me?' Plenty, believe me, plenty.

"So what is collaborative leadership? Our Constitutional Convention, active over two hundred years ago, is an example of how widely separated interest groups can arrive at a workable solution for a common problem. 'Collaborative leadership,' and I quote," he waved a small book, "' is a shift in the practice of democracy from hostility to civility, from advocacy to conversation, from confrontation to collaboration, from debate to dialogue, and from separation to community.'"

"Each one of you will receive a copy of this book, only about 150 pages, and I would hope you'd at least skim through it sometime today to learn, from examples cited, the effectiveness of the theories. Meanwhile, I'll do my best to block in the main points."

Jerry had joined Stan. Both were nervous, but trying to hide it. Together they studied the faces and body postures before them. Now backs were straightening, heads were coming up, and a few notebooks and pencils were in evidence. Almost everyone had recrossed their legs, made themselves more comfortable and leaned forward.

"He's got 'em, and no ideas have even come up to bat yet! Let's wander over and see what's happening at the Lodge."

They were only about halfway over when they heard roars of laughter and clapping. A few more steps, and it was repeated. Heather caught sight of them and ran out.

"That man is fantastic! He's had them in stitches ever since he started, but he's giving the greatest advice you ever heard. Hurry up, I don't want to miss a word."

Kurt used homely examples familiar to all in political life so that everyone could identify with the situations immediately. However, he had the gift of phrase and gesture to turn each occasion into comedy. That combination of empathy and humor bonded his audience. His listeners had been there, done that. The timing was such that as laughter died down he would quietly and authoritatively point out the solutions employed and why they'd worked. No one would leave that room just remembering the humor; the humor made the points and methods unforgettable.

"Do you remember the cereal ad involving a family with three kids, one named Mikey? The two older kids had Mikey try the new cereal their mom had bought them; they didn't want to try it themselves. When Mikey gobbled the cereal, the older two were impressed. Remember what they said? 'Mikey likes it.' They didn't talk about the nutritional content of the cereal, the vitamins in it. Imagination, warmth, and ordinary family living made the ads a hit. Find the equivalent in political PR by getting your prospect to identify personally with the topic in homely, familiar ways, and you've won."

At nine-thirty the two groups switched locations. Jerry and Joel, putting out the coffee supplies and crackers for the eleven o'clock break, just beamed at each other.

"Can it keep up this pace?" asked Joel. "Or have we peaked in the first hour?"

"Dunno, Pooh. I have an idea that the exercises coming up next may be a letdown, or may pull 'em up higher. People can listen just so long, then they have to participate. And of course I worry about face-to-face confrontations, nasty little digs."

Then he turned and looked out over the lake. "Oh God, isn't it good to be back here, Pooh? I don't want it spoiled."

At the break the air buzzed with excitement. The first hours had flown by. Each group was infected by the enthusiasm of the other. A senator from Rockland muttered to a York County chairman, "I think we've got our bait back," forgetting that the weekend hadn't cost them a cent.

The last session of the morning was in the Great Hall, and the crowd was split into groups of ten. Allowing no time-wasting chitchat, Charlie gave them exercise after exercise. Some were active, some called for paper and pencil; they were based on legislative, bureaucratic, or straight political situations. In each case the group had to define exactly what the problem was rather than what it appeared to be, then discover what had caused it and reach a solution agreeable to and respected by all. These exercises required really listening to the other side, respecting differences and being determined to find solutions—a sharp contrast to the "my team is better than your team" approach they were used to. Occasionally voices rose in argument, and in a few cases individuals had to leave the group to pace around and cool off, but the work was done.

Then it was noon and big platters of sandwiches and fruit appeared, accompanied by gallons of milk and iced tea. Jerry took over.

"This afternoon is not dedicated to nice little sails on the lake, naps, or a swim. It is going to be rugged. So we're magnaminously giving you a fifteen-minute break now. In that time we ask you to do three things. Read the short message I have here for you and stow it somewhere for the future. If necessary change into jeans or their equivalent, and put on lots of bug-juice and really tough walking shoes. Then lie down on your cot and go through every relaxation trick you've ever heard of; you'll need them. See you at one sharp, here."

The rumor had spread earlier that they were to be put through really tough physical activities. At one o'clock, it was a quiet crowd that followed Jerry through the woods to a section of the camp that was almost untouched wilderness. In a clearing they were joined by four members of the Namakant staff who had volunteered their expertise for this part of the program. The eldest, in his mid-twenties and looking as if he'd just finished Green Beret training at the head of his class, took charge.

"Though what you will do is similar to the Outward Bound program, it is our Namakant version, with a slightly different emphasis. My name is Sam, and I'm here to help you. I am not a drill sergeant. No one will be shot at dawn. You will not be told the purpose of any test, but by the end of the afternoon we can guarantee you will know a lot more about yourselves, about trust and respect, and about the strength of teamwork as opposed to individual heroics.

"To be effective we ask that you push yourselves to what you consider your limits and then beyond, but at no time should you feel a sense of failure if you simply can't complete the task. Out here in the woods there are no sissies or chickens, and sometimes it takes more courage to back out than to do something. Whatever your choice, you will be respected. OK, let's go, gang."

Few had noticed, so intent were they on what he was saying, that the clearing was sizeable, about forty feet long and a hundred feet wide. At either end stood a tall, straight tree from which hung rope ladders. About twenty feet off the ground rude platforms about four feet square were built; more ropes ran from one tree to the other, one passing through a pulley.

Sam walked over to the nearest tree, grabbed the rope ladder, and had climbed to the platform before watchers could grasp what this had to do with them. From a branch he plucked a canvas vest, slipped it on, and tied it closed. On its back was a substantial metal ring. He was then joined by one of his crew who attached the rope on the pulley to the ring at Sam's back, then grabbed the other end of that rope. The silence was so profound that the thump of a pinecone hitting the ground startled the watchers. Mosquito bites were unfelt.

"I'm going to demonstrate what you will do, so watch carefully. While you are doing it you will have constant coaching from the platform and the ground. And by the way, we are all trained in CPR and emergency first aid, and have lost no campers."

He sorted out the ropes that went from tree to tree. The watchers on the ground could now see that several of these were braided together, forming a band, or bridge, about six inches wide. Sam reached for one of the two remaining ropes with his right hand and for the last with his left. They were not quite taut, but offered some waist-high support, like banisters.

Holding his arms out as if he had the long balance rod of a high-wire artist, he stepped out away from the platform, putting one foot and then the other on the braided ropes.

He called down to them. "Notice that I am keeping a smooth, steady pace, and that I am looking straight ahead at the far platform, my goal, not at my feet or at the ground. Toby is now climbing up to that platform to receive me, while Joe hangs on to my safety rope and Hank watches from below. A team effort."

In a very short time he had completed the passage.

"See how easy it is?" Hollow laughter from below. "Now I'm going back and will get in trouble, for your benefit."

At about the halfway mark Sam seemed to lose his balance, swayed and fell, caught up almost immediately by Joe's safety rope. He swung back and forth a bit. "This is my Mary Martin number from *Peter Pan*," he crowed, and finally landed in the soft deep pile of hay between the two trees.

"Just remember that Namakant has been in business many years, and not in the business of injuring or killing off little boys. Anyone want to be first? Everybody gets a chance."

To the surprise of all, the governor's security guard volunteered. "I did a bit of this in 'Nam, and I want to know if I still can. Didn't have this pot then, but no one's shooting at me now, either." He patted his belly and went to the ladder.

"While you are waiting your turns, we're going to form teams and do a little wall climbing and take on the obstacle course. Jerry and Joel will help at that. And later there is the Tarzan Trail."

A grandmother from Skowhegan seemed lost in thought. She had all the moral courage in the world but knew she was almost a physical coward, too cautious and too imaginative. This had kept her from being able to launch herself off a diving board, had limited her skiing, had ruled out all the fun rides at amusement parks. More importantly, it had separated her from her children and had been a source of embarrassment all her life, an invisible blemish.

Her head came up and she walked briskly to the rope ladder. Now was the time to make a commitment and to possibly win a lifelong battle. She certainly was in safe hands, wasn't she?

It took some doing to just get her up the ladder, but no one laughed. The vest went on, the rope went through the ring, and as she took hold of the ropes in each hand a wonderful change came over her. She saw herself as an Olympic slalom skier about to hurl herself down an icy slope. One foot went out, then the other, and with chin up and eyes straight ahead, she made it.

A cheer went up from below. She'd had no sense of anyone watching or caring; she'd done it for herself. Several of those who had privately opted not to do it saw the joy on her face, the tilt of her head, and took their places in line.

Some fell, a few froze, but support was there for all.

The obstacle course was not a pretty sight as middle-aged matrons, scrawny or potbellied men, including Joel, and even the younger contestants, wiggled through tubes, crawled on their bellies under wires, ran through carefully laid-out tires, and hit the Berlin Wall. About twenty feet high, with practically no toeholds, it was an exercise in using supportive human bodies as steps. Tall, heavy men held others on their shoulders as those lesser mortals were handed up and over. The excitement was intense.

The Republican Assistant Minority Leader provided the highlight of the afternoon. In her seventies, built like a small tank, she had gotten into politics when the Feds began to monkey around with fishing limits and regulations. Having often served as mate on her late husband's trawler, she knew the business firsthand; she was tough, and no barnacles stuck to her keel. Though rough in speech and colorful in appearance, Maggie was a favorite in Augusta. She was expert at rounding up her party when votes were coming on the floor. She also gave salty resumes of caucus proceedings to anyone who had missed attending. Her smile, when it broke through, revealed a set of teeth that could only be stamped "made in Taiwan." Now, with the single-mindedness of a charging rhinoceros, she rumbled toward the Wall, picking up speed. The two rugged men waiting for her bent their knees and somehow she became firmly planted on them, clawing her way upward. Their shirts were nearly ripped off, their faces made good handholds, and their hair was just a plus. To escape this attack both men worked extra hard to get her to their shoulders. That accomplished, she was still about half a foot below the hands reaching to grab her and pull her up.

"OK, boys," she bellowed, as if into the teeth of a gale. "Let's see some bipartisan effort. Each one of you put a big hand on my fanny, count three, and shove, really shove."

They bent their knees slightly, took deep breaths, and shouted "blastoff!" With that magnificent effort, up she went, her wrists caught by the waiting hands above, and she disappeared over the other side.

"That really was bipartisan effort, gentlemen," said the watching president of the Senate. Trying to pull themselves and their clothes back to normal, the governor of the state and the Speaker of the House, implacable political foes, were laughing helplessly, shaking hands, and a cheer went up.

The Tarzan Trail was a trip through the treetops, swinging on ropes from one branch to another. Such an activity, if it had come first, would have been thought impossible by most. Now, far surer of themselves and of each other, it was pure fun. Once they were loosened up, they let out yells and soared.

Finally the exercises were over and the lake beckoned. Sweat, sand, and bug-juice rolled off the tired bodies. Never had clean clothes seemed like such a treat, and the "happy hour" was happy indeed. Those few who were too physically limited to have gone through the tests at all had taken over the kitchen, and Julia Child would have marveled at what had been done to huge cans of stew, enriched by generous cupfuls of Stan's homemade wine. Thick slabs of black bread sopped up the gravy, and soon the diners were ready for whatever came next.

Carol whispered to Susan, "Look at them! How they're sitting and talking! This morning they were like strangers in a restaurant, barely polite.

Now they're like family, really comfortable with each other. It's working, how it's working."

* * * * *

After dinner, Nana was invited to speak. Tiny and trim, she was such a contrast to the macho leaders of the afternoon that she commanded instant attention.

"Having spent the last months in helping to plan this meeting, and imagining what it would be like with real live people going through these stunts, I find it thrilling to see you doing all the things we'd hoped you'd do, and doing them so well." She laughed. "How's that for a sentence?

"We call ourselves Phoenix, after the mythical bird who rose from the ashes to live again, because we felt that the original essence and vision of our country's culture could and should be brought back to life and given a second chance. A questionnaire we sent out showed that a disturbing lack of satisfaction, direction, and pride was eating at our supposedly content and successful middle class. Apathy, rage, and cynicism don't spell contentment.

"We were trying to decide which major concern to tackle first, be it education, health care, the environment. And then we concluded that the answer and cure for each hinged on one simple thing: Attitude. You were handed a paper at lunch that you may or may not have had time to study. Let me read it to you, as we believe it holds the key to the success of all we've discussed."

She adjusted her glasses, beamed at them, and began.

"The longer I live, the more I realize the impact of attitude on life. Attitude, to me, is more than facts. It is more important than the past, than education, than money, than circumstances, than failures, than successes, than what other people say or do." She stopped to let that sink in.

"It is more important than appearance, giftedness or skills. It will make or break a company ... a church ... a home. The remarkable thing is we have a choice every day regarding the attitude we will embrace for that day. We cannot change our past ... we cannot change the fact that people will act in a certain way. We cannot change the inevitable. The only thing we can do is play the one string we have, and that is our attitude ... I am convinced that life is 10% what happens to me and 90% how I react to it. And so it is with you. We are in charge of our attitudes."

There was silence, quite a profound silence. Then one by one the members of the group stood and started to clap.

Nana waved one hand, asking for quiet.

"Thank you, thank you so much, but I can't lay claim to that wisdom. It was written by one Charles Swindell, reprinted in the paper. I cut it out and have had it on my fridge for years." She acknowledged their applause with, "Then why don't you all take it home and put it on yours?"

Laughter; they sat down, and Joel continued the program.

"Beyond the partisan bickering and infuriating gridlock that turn off so many voters are also the problems of campaign ethics and funding. Your assignment this evening is to come up with ideas for a code that would satisfy the critics and that candidates would be willing to publicly subscribe to.

"Negative campaigning should be carefully defined, sources of acceptable funding discussed, along with the traditional no-no's. You might even find time to explore the methods of luring more of the best minds and leaders of our state into political participation, local, state, and federal."

He paused, studied their faces, and gave them a little time to think. Then, in a low voice, to make them strain to catch every word, he continued.

"It is hoped, most sincerely, that you will apply many of the methods to which you were introduced this morning. Collaborate, test them out. See if these theories work."

"We'll break now into four groups, each of which will choose a reporter, and really go at this assignment till nine. God bless you if you come up with doable bipartisan solutions. We are hoping you can give us enough material to put some kind of mutually agreeable code together before we leave tomorrow."

They began to move from their chairs.

"Oh, there's more. A surprise! Don't think for a minute we're going to tuck you into bed, after a cup of hot cocoa, at nine. Instead you will change into warm clothes, grab a good flashlight, bug juice, and a warm blanket. You will be provided with waterproof groundcloths. You will take no watches or any food with you. Each will be led to a spot not far from here, but well separated from each other. The night will be spent in quiet solitude. How you use that time is up to you, in sleep, in meditation or in planning ahead. Unless there's a real emergency you are asked not to contact each other. The staff will gather you up at 7:00 A.M., and I can promise a very rewarding breakfast.

"Incidentally, but very importantly, I am informed that the governor, in response to reports from Augusta, has just had to declare all fires off-limits to campers, etc., because of explosive fire conditions. In other words, leave your cigarettes back here at the ranch; the NO SMOKING sign is on."

With all these directives to digest it took a little time to form the discussion groups, but they soon became very lively, if sounds were interpreted correctly. Campaign practices were surefire voice and blood pressure raisers, but occasional laughter held the hint of collaboration.

Nine o'clock came surprisingly soon, reports were handed in, and by nine-thirty all campers were en route to their various bivouacs, on foot, by truck, or by boat. To many that day was not over, it was just beginning.

Spread out over almost fifty acres of shorefront, hillside, fields, and the remains of the old quarry, they were far enough apart to feel really isolated. Most were native Mainers or had hunting or camping experience, but being so alone and without equipment was quite a challenge. Some created rude shelters with underbrush or fallen limbs. Others preferred to just lie under the stars. Until the bug juice took effect, the mosquitoes were served a veritable dessert cart of varied and fresh goodies.

Then gradually the silence moved in, broken only by the minute sounds of nature. Occasionally a fish would splash in the lake. Some campers believed they heard even the footfalls of the tiny field mice, and those few who had been placed near the camp vegetable garden swore they could hear the late, last ears of corn rustling their husks as they expanded in the hot, humid night. The lake lapped gently, heat lightning lit the skies from the distance, and darting fireflies punctuated the darkness close by. A slow and gentle breeze blew in over the water.

There had been no time given for these men and women to mentally program or plan these hours. At first many were restless, in the habit of busy people using every moment to full advantage. Thoughts darted around in their heads, only to be discarded for new ones and forgotten. Then an awareness of the relaxation of their bodies absorbed them; some were soon asleep. Others dozed fitfully from the start. And a few were as tense as they could remember ever being, straining for every sound and terrified when they heard one. Moose or mouse? Bird or bobcat?

The little breeze picked up a bit, carrying night sounds and smells. To the nostrils of one camper came the smell of smoke, undeniably cigarette smoke. He raised himself up on an elbow and searched the dark for a telltale red glow. No luck. Quietly he rose to his feet and moved closer to what he considered the source. Respecting the privacy of others he soon stopped, took one last whiff to make sure he wasn't dreaming, and raised both hands to form a megaphone near his mouth.

Deepening his naturally bass voice as much as possible he roared "Hear ye! Hear ye! This is God. Put out that cigarette!"

Thoroughly pleased with himself he found his way back to his blanket. He could sense, if not hear, quiet chuckles in the night. He gave himself a big hug and slept.

The Speaker, Dan Mulrooney, his sharp mind never still, concentrated on what the meeting had proved so far, in personal terms. Here, for a few days, he was just another attendee, not King of the Halls and Chamber. Always a loner by circumstance more than by choice, he now felt a lessening of the dislike and even fear generally directed toward him by his fellow legislators. He was beginning to realize that since childhood he had used people for his own ends, giving little of himself and making little effort to get to know anyone except as they could be useful to him. In these two days he had studied men and women easily sharing warmth and kindnesses with one another and yet still commanding respect and loyalty. They were not necessarily brilliant, or even bright, but invited friendship. Their eyes did not dart around studying each face for motives, as he was sure his did. For some reason he was really enjoying himself; while not euphoric, he was amazed at how at peace he felt.

From the hillside below him he suddenly caught the sounds of hard gasping sobs, muffled cries. Someone was in serious trouble, and probably not of a physical nature. He abhorred scenes, tears, sniveling, and generally just walked away. But this was different. He recognized the sound of desperation. Standing, he made his way softly downward.

Almost hidden beneath bushes he found Nelson Berman, the new commissioner of corrections, curled up in a ball. Sobbing, he dug at the ground with rigid, hooked fingers. In his sixties, of little humor but strong determination, he was turning out to be an excellent executive. Dan found his situation appalling.

Kneeling quietly beside him, the Speaker put a hand on his shoulder. Berman lifted his head, his eyes swollen and his face showing terror. Recognizing his companion seemed to be a last straw and he buried his head again, sobbing "Oh no, oh God, no!"

Dan spoke softly, still touching the hunched-up shoulder.

"I'm here to help you, Nelson. Want to talk it out?"

Silence, sniffling, almost choking, and then the head came up again. Nelson Berman finally rolled over and sat up, putting his head down on bent knees.

"Is it the quiet, or the dark?" Dan racked his brain for ideas, just to keep talking, hoping to throw out a life raft for the man to board.

It was working. Berman swallowed hard, took a long, shuddering breath, and raised his head.

"It is very simple, and very difficult. A long story, since I was eight or nine.."

"Do you want to share it? Can you talk about it?"

Shrugging, as if he had nothing left to lose, Berman admitted that in his twenties he had tried psychotherapy, unsuccessfully. Perhaps his doctors had heard the same story too often. With a shy smile he said, "I'll give it one more try. There is so much I want to do, and it is so hard with this terrible monster always in my head.

"As you may know, I am Jewish, born in Germany. My parents were well educated and had great hopes for my sister and me. You know what happened in Germany. One night, when I was eight, the SS came to our town, you would call it suburbs, and dragged my parents and sister away. I was under a bed, frightened by the noise, and they never looked for me. They closed the front door, I heard a car start and move away, and that was the end of my family, for me. I was left alone in the dark. I have been emotionally alone ever since, but I've always managed to keep lights on, or be with others at night.

"I was lucky. Some neighbors, Lutherans, found and raised me. Finally an uncle in this country located me when I was teenager, and I've been here since.

"It took years, but I eventually learned that my gentle mother and sister were sent to the gas chambers. My father, a skilled doctor, was sent to a work lab far away. From one who also was there I later learned that my father refused to do some of the experiments they demanded and was sent to prison, where he died of filth, starvation, and beatings.

"Those pictures, in my imagination, of my immaculate, handsome strong father reduced by incarceration to the bag of filthy bones he was at the end, gave me my vocation. Prisons can be better, less degrading, no matter what the crime."

In exhaustion his head went down on his knees again, but he was no longer shaking.

Dan made himself comfortable beside him.

"You're not alone in the dark now. You need sleep and so do I. Lie down. I'll stay with you till dawn. Your story is as safe with me as you want it to be, and I would like to help you later on your mission. Good night, friend."

Dan couldn't remember calling anyone "friend" before with real sincerity. He had never bothered to really listen before. As he lay there a memory from his own childhood came back, and he began to softly hum the old Welsh lullaby that had always made him feel safe in the dark. Soon they were both asleep.

Dan was asleep on his own blanket as the sun came up over the lake. He, like many of the others, watched this daily miracle in a slightly different way, with a little more hope, purpose, and respect. Even those who had been at least half-awake all night felt somehow refreshed, and looked forward to whatever this last day offered.

True to their word, the staff provided an unforgettable Sunday breakfast of fruits, cereals, muffins, eggs, bacon, and sausages as starters, with piles of blueberry pancakes to finish.

Before anyone ate, however, Stan asked for silence.

"As probably the senior member present, I'd like to lead us in Sunday thanks to whatever power put us here together, to do this work, enjoy each other, and stretch our minds. I understand that God showed up at at least one site last night, and I'm sure He's up above now, listening in." He lifted his head, that splendid beak pointing straight to Heaven.

"Hello, God, we know you're busy, so we won't keep you too long. The Red Sox need you, just to mention one chore, and there's going to be afternoon gridlock on the turnpike, of course. We have quite a mishmash of people here working on tough problems, too. Thanks again for the weather, for each other, and for guidance in what we're trying to learn, and God, have a nice day."

There were several newcomers at breakfast who had evidently arrived during the night. They were introduced, to those who did not recognize them, as the sponsoring committee of this affair.

"If you people had any idea of the self-restraint we've shown by not sneaking in here for the whole thing, you'd be overwhelmed." The well-known lawyer from Houlton sounded as if he really meant it. "And we've kept it a secret too, counting on the story and pictures Mark will produce to let the world know. Now I'll let you get to work and we'll see you later."

Much of the morning was spent in discussing how best to pass on the messages and methods they'd been given to those who would be working on campaigns. One leader commented, "We've got to get everyone singing from the same page in the hymn book."

Those from the Legislature were assigned to contact and instruct all candidates, standing committee chairmen, and even, where possible, lobbyists. The State Committee people's job was to illuminate county and town committees, in meetings as well as mailings, so that the formal organization of each party heard the same thing. The governor's staff and cabinet members were to educate the bureaucrats so that in the end all those actively engaged in the process of governing would study the same material, very aware that it was a bipartisan effort..

Each State Committee's traditional job was to produce acceptable legislative candidates if none came forth voluntarily, train them, and then raise enough money to help pay for their races. With this machinery already in place, passing on this new information was not an appalling task; selling it might be.

Now the innocent candidates, having been lured into running by the exciting cry of "Let's throw the rascals out," were going to be told "Just fooling; they're really not rascals at all, just a little mixed up. Treat them nicely and they'll do the same. We've got to get the respect of the voters back." Some might rightly feel that their mentors were lost in a fog without a compass.

Mark whispered to Heather. "If you thought selling this outing was a challenge, you ain't seen nothing yet." She smiled and said blithely "That's up to you, pal, you, your word processor, and your camera."

All were assured that the Phoenix staff stood ready to help in any way that might be needed for this educational blitz. Jerry had already privately decided to send an immediate and detailed mailing to all candidates, in preparation for the additional material they should receive from their party. He had learned too often from past experience that good intentions didn't always get put into action.

By some miracle, a code of campaign ethics, based on workshop suggestions, had been hammered out during the night. As Jerry presented it to the group he laughed. "You guys thought you were roughing it outdoors last night. You at least got to lie down and even sleep. Sleep, what's that?"

He proceeded to go over the finished product with them.

The new code tried to generally clean up the campaign process and make the voters feel less manipulated or even cheated. Still, it avoided being an invitation for sanctimonious witch hunts, or so noble it was impossible to follow. Either of these would make it harder to sell a second time around. Too often in the past, reports of campaign finance abuses and outright lies had been set aside till after the election, well after the harm was done. Blatant abuses of all types must be better handled and those laws on the books already enforced immediately and effectively.

Negative campaigning had been tough to define. Was criticizing an incumbent's record in office negative? Isn't that what a campaign is all about, to argue that your plans are better? Is digging up questionable personal behavior in a candidate's past negative campaigning? Very likely, unless it indicates an inherent and serious unfitness for office. To what extend should candidates have control over ads produced for them by State or National Committee, but which the candidates themselves considered embarrassingly biased or negative? No candidate should be refused the right to run unless forbidden by law, but does a State Committee have the right to refuse to support a candidate on moral grounds, or even ask that they withdraw? Should that be up to the voters if they are made aware of the problem? Smears were too often proved untrue, though salty comments such as "crooked as a hairpin" or "he's so damned tight he skims milk at both ends" were generally considered part of the fun.

In the code's final form most of these questions were addressed and worded in acceptable language. Copies were run off; it was a start.

Each participant was very formally handed, at this final morning meeting, a certificate of successful attendance, which explained what had been involved and why. This, and their signature on the ethics code, could be reproduced for their campaign materials.

There was a little time before lunch for comments, reports, and jokes. Mark, busy taking pictures, made a point of looking around for bored, sullen, or even sneering expressions, and found none. The staff did not naively believe that all participants were utterly enthusiastic about everything, but the bait had been taken, and the future would tell. Finally Joel took over. Campers hoped he was going to announce lunch.

"As a last exercise we are finally going on the lake. At my signal you will race down to the shore, get into whatever craft will hold you, and head for Heron Island, the little one just out there. We've figured that there are enough places in the boats for all, and we do hope there's at least one somewhat competent yachtsman in each sailboat. When you get there you'll find a prize."

Stan and Susan opened the doors to the porch, Joel blew his whistle, and off they all went, some grim with determination, others laughing helplessly. Soon the strange armada was afloat, a small powerboat performing Coast Guard surveillance to pick up survivors.

Hitting the beach at Heron wasn't quite like Guadalcanal but certainly competitive, because on the trip over certain splendid and familiar odors had floated out to the mariners. There was a natural clearing just beyond the beach, bordered by long camp tables. As the last stragglers landed, it was announced with enthusiasm, "The bake is open!"

Heavy canvas was pulled off a steaming mound that had been built upon almost red-hot rocks. Under the canvas was a thick layer of seaweed holding, like a nest, bag upon bag of all that makes a Maine bake special. This delivered a perfume that would make a bottler millions of dollars, worldwide. Somebody banged something metal and Joel stood up on a rock where everyone could see him.

"Our sponsoring committee, instead of cheating and attending sessions, went all out and have invited us to be their guests at this gala good-bye party. Line up, get your bag and bib, find a spot to sit and dig in."

In this crowd there wasn't a soul who had to be instructed in the fine arts of clam, lobster, and corn eating. The sponsors circulated with melted butter, salt, and coffee. There was no conversation at all for quite a while. Just when people thought they'd never be able to eat again there was the cry of "seconds," and so it went.

When even the blueberry pies were just a memory old Governor Bronson stood up and the crowd grew silent. As a governor he'd been pretty good; as a person and speaker he was terrific. Mark took out his tape recorder and moved nearer.

"Mr. Bakemaster," and the governor bowed to the expert from the coast who had put this feast together, "ladies and gentlemen. Every one of you is an honored guest so I'm not going to pick on any in particular.

"When I first heard about this affair I was wary as a singed cat. I figured the whole idea was going against human nature and all the fun would go out of politics. It's now our only national entertainment that with a little cleaning up is almost fit to let children hear about or watch.

"I know what I'm talking about as I was governor before some few of you were born, before even Ed Muskie was governor, but I ain't swallowed the anchor yet. So I thought about the falling off of voters, the lack of interest from young people. I chewed on the emergence of those 'experts,' most always outta-staters, whose profession is training other people to run for office, and those other specialists who are called on to raise millions to pay for the electronic manipulation of the public mind. Maybe this idea was better'n nothing.

"I asked my cat one morning what he thought, but he paid me no never mind. So I asked the lathery face in the mirror and that face came right back with 'fish or cut bait.' In my mind I've always thought of this get-together as a clambake, and how right I was, literally and figuratively. Think about this.

"I heard the other day that a woman and a tea bag were a lot alike. How come? 'Cause you can't tell how strong they are till they get in hot water. Hot water is pretty effective stuff."

This crowd was loving every minute of his talk, even sitting in the sun with full bellies and soporific breezes.

He held up a clam, still unopened. "This feller is like our Maine minds, sometimes closed tight to new ideas or to letting one's own ideas out. Put a clam in a little hot water or steam him, and he opens right up."

Searching around on a table near him, he picked up a lobster body, picked clean.

"Now this guy stays down on the bottom, keeping cool and getting nothing done. Curious, up he comes, gets caught and lands in the steamer. He naturally gets some exercised and thrashes around but then gets into the spirit of things by turning bright red with excitement. This enthusiasm makes him the star of the feast."

An ear of shucked corn was produced and the old man looked at it lovingly.

"This here is as sweet as can be only when it's had its bath, like you fellers Saturday night. You bathe this baby in hot water, grease it up with real butter so it'll slide nice, pep it up with a little salt, and your choppers don't have a finer treat.

"And the pies, made of hundreds of little individual berries caught in a pie shell and baked a while, are just right. One or two or even a dozen berries don't amount to shucks, but a lot of berries, even if the picking takes time, win the ribbon at the fair every year.

"So that is a Maine clambake. And what's it got to do with us? I'll make it short 'cause you're not stupid and I also know it's past quitting time.

"Like the tea bags, we don't know our own strength until we give it a try. Like the clam, we gotter open up to communicate with any sense. The lobster shows us how important real enthusiasm is, and the corn and butter are the key, effective buttering up with just a smidgen of salt. It takes a lot of berries to make a good pie, and it takes a lot of people to make progress or effect a change. Putting all these things together, letting 'em steam for a while in each others' juices, that's what does the trick every time.

"This weekend was a real good Downeast clambake. Thank you."

Applause was long and sincere. Finally sated campers started moving, loading the boats and getting back to camp. Once ashore came good-byes, thank-yous, and hugs and back-slapping, even bipartisan. All knew there was a tough two months ahead in which to turn things around enough to make a difference. But they certainly had all the native elements on their side to have a November clambake that might make history.

Driving out the Namakant road Heather looked up in the sky and saw a large bird rising and swirling overhead. She turned to Jerry and asked softly, "Jerry, what does a phoenix look like?"

Chapter 9: Fall 1988

Harding's Corner

Labor Day 1988 came and went, and with it the summer people. Bright leaves began to show on the trees, but this year they had competition from the even brighter political lawn signs and posters decorating the landscape.

From the national headquarters of both parties hundreds of well-trained and zealous young interns were sent all over the country to help direct federal campaigns, though they were often received as intruders rather than saviors. The local hired guns and politically savvy native gurus of top in-state races had a hard time bowing to these peach-fuzz political science majors with little or no practical experience. They tolerated them because their presence also brought promised and fat checks from National, Dem or Rep. The great American political production machine was in full swing, often of interest only to those personally involved, though marketing positions from president to local dogcatcher.

Coming back from Namakant to quiet little Harding's Corner was at first restful, but soon the Phoenix staff began watching for signs, signs of any kind, that the Namakant weekend had not only occurred but had had some effect. They knew it would take Mark several weeks to get his story written and, hopefully, accepted by the Maine papers. They knew it would take time for the various party and legislative leaders to contact and start training those for whom they were responsible.

Finally, during the second week, a few letters from legislative candidates came in, excited, hopeful, and asking for more information. Jerry started making calls to the leaders and to county and town chairmen of both parties, letting them know time was getting short and that Phoenix hadn't gone back to the boonies just to sit on a nest. He asked for results; he wanted those eggs to hatch.

In the middle of the month, the Black Knight once again roared up the Warners' road on his monster. Mark made himself seem deliberate, even nonchalant, as he stripped off his armor.

"Well?" boomed Stan, standing solid as a rock in his dooryard. "Come out with it. You didn't come up here for a cup of tea or to paddle your footsies in the lake."

Mark reached into a saddlebag and brought forth a thick envelope, handing it to Jerry, just to punish Stan. Almost casually he announced, "This will start running in the *Bangor Daily News* on Saturday, to be serialized during the week, and," he paused dramatically, "in the *Maine Sunday Telegram* this weekend, running in its entirety. Believe it or not, I've never known these two papers to agree to simultaneously run the same story by the same author, but I had nothing to lose by asking." His pride of accomplishment came bursting through, yet he was almost embarrassed by it.

His back was slapped, his hand almost crushed, and of course, best yet, he got big hugs and kisses from Heather and Susan.

"It's a bit early to splice the main brace," commented Stan, "and anyway, I want to be dead cold sober when I read this. Susan, we need tremendous glasses of iced tea and some of those ginger cookies I smelled awhile back. Let's sit out here on the hammock and grass and do a little studying."

The Warners and Heather finally started to read, each passing the pages on to the next.

Mark invited Matt Dillon for a walk downhill to the lake. He was tired, dead tired, but he knew it was the best job he'd ever done. As a journalist he'd found it hard to be objective, but he'd managed, and he really believed he'd caught the spirit as well as the significance of the meeting.

He had actually been surprised to find out how much the plan meant to him. It wasn't just another assignment. Now the story was out of his hands and the readers would make their judgments. Sitting on a boulder left by an ancient glacier, he stared out over the quiet water to the great, silent mountains, at peace. Time was no longer a factor. The job was done.

Matt's ears eventually went up, and Mark turned to see Jerry coming down the hill through the tall grass. He rose to meet him, to hear the verdict. The two big men faced each other, one questioning, the other slowly smiling. Then Jerry's arms came up, and he embraced Mark, who was surprised to find his face was wet. Were they his tears or Jerry's, or a mixture? Maybe he wasn't so tough after all.

"Mark, if that superb endeavor doesn't do what we hope for, then it is the fault of the whole plan, or possibly the pigheadedness of the readers, but no one, Thomas Paine or even Thomas Jefferson himself, could have done better than you have."

Slowly they climbed the hill together and the real celebration began.

With the dishes cleared away, and a fire roaring in the stove as the September night fell, the five of them discussed what came next. Heather had previously prepared scripts for immediate release to other papers and to the news services of the radio and TV stations. Enclosed with these would be a full roster of who had attended the course and who had sponsored it, giving the media many names they might want to use in interviews. Press releases were also to be sent to the wire services, which meant the news might become nationwide. Designs for a full-page ad in both the participating papers were constructed in case the response to Mark's series was disappointing. With optimism high, they even discussed the possibility of outgrowing Harding's Corner, at least temporarily, and moving to one of the larger Maine cities to be more accessible.

Portland

Unaware of what was going to break so soon, Patsy Hudson had been working on her routine Portland area door-to-door calls, attending a few coffees in her honor, and giving a lot of time to the First District Congressional campaign, helping in any way she could. This was valuable to her, as she met the local leaders of many towns in the First District, the grassroots people who helped get party members elected. While some town committees were effective, most did just so much as a group and then left a few staunch individuals to handle the long haul. Candidates with experience, dating back even to Margaret Chase Smith, rarely relied on these local committees to any great extent, and took the work they did as a sort of bonus or surprise. Each candidate had to build his or her own devoted personal organizations. Patsy kept notes on each First District town she contacted or visited for the candidate, recording just whom to call on the next time around, possibly for herself.

She had the magic word "reelect" conspicuous on her own posters and lawn signs, and she personalized campaign letters even more than she had two years ago. She went so far as to write the owners of excitable dogs, chained outside their homes, explaining that while she would have liked to make a call, or leave a brochure, she respected the dogs' political opinions almost as much as those of the voters. These notes became a subject of neighborhood political discussion and humor.

One Saturday night, Charlie called from Eastport. "Mom, what do you think of the news? What a whale of an idea! Will it work?"

"Calm your body, boy. What under the sun are you talking about?"

When Charlie finished telling her what he had just read in the *Bangor Daily News*, she was overwhelmed. Would it work? Could the two groups really learn to trust each other? Would the campaigns stay snowwhite? Would voters be brought back, their faith and enthusiasm restored? And would ambitious candidates really stay the course?

When Patsy heard her *Maine Sunday Telegram* thunk against the front door the next morning she was there almost before it hit the porch floor. Across the top of the front page, above the headlines, large letters read "AS MAINE GOES: A NEW APPROACH TO OUR POLITICS STUDIED IN BIPARTISAN SEMINAR."

Her usual Sunday morning rituals were forgotten as she studied and weighed every word of Mark's story. She examined each picture to see just who had been in attendance. A shot of the chairman of Phoenix caught her eye. Joel McLean, from Massachusetts, camper at Namakant years ago, looked familiar. There were no pictures of Jerry, but why did she connect the two men? And then she knew: Joel McLean was Pooh! Interesting, but relevant? A fact to be mentally filed.

She scrabbled through her mail and found Jerry's letter. Signing the enclosed code immediately, she popped it into her mailbox. Phone lines to legislative friends were tied up. The ball had started rolling and was hurtling and bouncing over the state.

Now she knew why Heather and Jerry had been at the convention! How proud she was to know them. It made her feel part of this undertaking already. How could she help? Oh partisanship, oh gridlock, oh mudslinging, may you rest in peace, or in the hot place! Loyal party member that she was she knew the time had come to look at blind partisanship with a leery eye. Too many voters and legislators weren't thinking, they were just casting knee-jerk votes mindlessly, or worse, not at all.

* * * * *

Harding's Corner

Monday morning more phone lines were put in at the Harding's Corner office. Mail was soon no longer placed in the box by the front steps but delivered by bagfuls. Volunteers from nearby towns and even Millinocket and Lincoln were called on regularly, bringing their lunches and working all day. TV reporters and cameramen came up for lengthy interview appointments, and finally the day came when there was a story, short to be sure, going cross-country on the AP wires.

In most Maine papers the Letters to the Editor departments were kept busier than usual. Many of these expressed enthusiastic relief. Some few diehard party stalwarts felt the plan was an outrage against the American way of life, and skeptics felt obliged to pooh-pooh the whole thing. One wrote, "You can put lipstick on a pig but you still have a pig."

Amazingly, though it had not been requested, money poured into the Phoenix coffers. A bookkeeper was brought on board. These gifts were donated specifically to help spread the idea of Altitude Adjustment to other fields of discontent. The public really understood the Phoenix goals.

That all-important first Tuesday in November was approaching fast. The Willie Horton story of supposed Bush racism broke, and national spin doctors made the most of it. Dukakis had the bad luck to look silly, in a huge helmet, riding in a tank. Poll after poll confused everyone, though it seemed impossible to find any person who had ever been questioned.

And then the big day came. When the polling places finally closed at eight PM the real political junkies, the shock troops, volunteers, and usual sycophants, headed for whatever hotel ballroom or conference center their favorites had taken over for victory parties.

Some workers were stationed at the newspaper offices and TV stations to get the most accurate reports. At the offices of congressional hopefuls wall charts were kept current, town by town, as final numbers came in. Experts who had studied these returns for years could sometimes spot a win or loss early in the evening by the way one small town voted.

The Bush victory was assured midevening. Crowds at each headquarters began to swell or thin, depending on the perceived trends of lesser campaigns. Empty soda cans, crushed potato chips, and dried-out cheese snacks littered once neat tables.

Miles away from all this, the Phoenix staff and some local volunteers were gathered quietly around the Warners' TV. Almost empty bowls of popcorn stood on the tables, and Susan's cider supply was ebbing.

"Hush!" called Heather at last. "I think this is it."

A tired but excited reporter was shown speaking from the State House Rotunda.

"It has just come to the attention of our staff here at the State House that a curious phenomenon has taken place in Maine. Though we expected a good turnout because of the presidential election, what has happened has surpassed anything we might have guessed. Not only have many more people from all parties voted this year, but exit polls reveal a heartening increase in the number of young people casting ballots.

"Maine has always had one of the best records in the country for voter participation, generally in the sixty to seventy percent range. This year it may reach over eighty percent! It is felt here at the Capitol that possibly this new Phoenix plan, 'As Maine Goes,' really had some effect. The local campaigns have certainly been cleaner, more to the point. 'As Maine Goes' may be more than just past history and become a truly meaningful phrase again."

Stan turned the sound off and they all looked at each other in silence. Heather's lips began to quiver. Jerry's hand shook as he reached for Stan's, and Susan hid her glowing face to hide the tears.

Jerry stood up and walked over to the kitchen phone, dialed, and waited. "We did it, Bear, we did it!" And he repeated as well as he could the reporter's comments. "We've really made a difference, I think. What? Yeah, give her a hug from me. And Pooh, start thinking what we work on next. This is just the beginning."

Heather, euphoric, didn't know or question what this Bear and Pooh talk was all about. They'd won, and that was all that mattered.

Chapter 10: Winter, Spring, and Summer, 1989

Augusta

Whether because of the popularity of her juvenile bill, her hard campaigning, or the coattail effect of Bush's victory, Patsy had gotten the landslide vote she'd dreamed of. She was now not only an experienced sophomore but one in exceptionally good standing.

In addition to her hope of fostering better communication and understanding between the Republican State Committee and party legislators, Patsy had been studying two other situations. She felt that bills passed by the Legislature were too often changed in emphasis and almost in intention by the bureaucrats who wrote the Rules and Regulations. Simple, straightforward remedies to voters' concerns became quagmires of red tape involving months of processes before any action could be taken. Might these Rules and Regs be brought before the committee again for review and approval before they could take effect? Accountability at work.

Her second concern involved red tape also, but this time in the fields of welfare and human services. Because of client's different needs, their records were often filed in many different departments and bureaus. Now that computers made tracking information so easy, why couldn't all these separate records be combined in one file, accessible to all agencies involved? Agency personnel could see the family situation at a glance, and be better able to make constructive decisions. Welfare fraud and duplication of services would probably be reduced.

But both situations had the same roadblock: turf wars. Both would take time to put into bills with impressive sponsors and foolproof construction.

These ideas, however, took a back seat to her desire to further the Phoenix group's "As Maine Goes" program wherever and whenever possible. Like many fellow legislators of both parties, she was excited by the whole concept of working together, listening and respecting what was said—as long as basic philosophical differences were acknowledged and respected.

As soon as the session opened, a bipartisan group of Namakant Conference alumni from both Senate and House had formed almost spontaneously. They aimed to test collaborative leadership methods, to monitor committee work, and to persuade the unconvinced. It already appeared that bipartisan appreciation of a basic problem and open discussion of solutions were beginning to replace the knee-jerk power plays of the past, but bad habits are hard to break and attitudes hard to change. Perseverance would be the answer.

Amazingly, the Speaker rarely missed these gatherings and listened more than he pontificated. His relationship to House members seemed less rigid; the Namakant alumni agreed that some senseless walls were developing cracks, slowly but visible.

At her House desk one morning in late January, Patsy's train of thought was interrupted by the sound of sirens, very close by. Within minutes a page trotted down the aisle to the rostrum and handed the clerk a note, which he in turn passed to the Speaker.

Reading it quickly, Mulrooney brought his gavel into play.

"Ladies and gentlemen of the House, I am sorry to inform you that a member of the other Chamber has just passed away, while at his desk. Senator John Flanagan is no longer with us. God rest his soul. In respect to his memory, the House stands adjourned." The gavel banged.

House members were stunned. While most legislators were middle-aged or elderly, few had ever before died at work. John Flanagan (D) had been in the Senate four terms, and before that in the House for at least as many. Jovial, pleasant to all, and a hard worker, he would be truly missed. Rarely known to propose bills of any magnitude, or get involved in floor disputes and thus make headlines, the late senator had been a splendid representative of his constituents, a housekeeper aware of the nitty-gritty nuisances and needed improvements in his district. That district was partly in Portland and, curiously, partly in Falmouth, an adjoining town. Flanagan had been Patsy's senator and friend.

Since they were politicians as well as humans, every mind in both chambers speculated on how this would affect the legislature. The Republicans held a slim lead in the Senate and would certainly welcome one more of their own. The Democrats would like to maintain the status quo.

Later in the week, after the Flanagan services and burial, the governor proclaimed a special election, to be held on Tuesday, February 24th. Each party must publicly advertise a senatorial district caucus at which a candidate would be nominated. There would be a short campaign and, unless a miracle took place, probably just a handful would turn out to vote.

Republican party strategists met with Portland and Falmouth leaders and discussed potential candidates. The man who had run against Flanagan in the fall had really just lent his name to fill the slot on the ballot, as Flanagan had been almost guaranteed election as long as he chose to run. There were dedicated party members of senatorial caliber in both communities, but none were in a position to suddenly drop all plans and responsibilities, even for a few months.

A Falmouth resident hesitatingly mentioned Patsy; there was a short silence, then cries of "Why not?" Though she was still a relative beginner, her name recognition, her huge victory and her obvious ambitions made her a natural. All recognized her abilities and believed she was in politics for keeps. Stunned, she accepted the nomination.

Only one Democrat was thirsting for the seat: Donato Vassalo. Win or lose, the campaign would give him a start at getting his name into the minds of voters. He also knew that, no matter who the Republicans named, he had a more than even chance. His caucus handed him the nomination with pleasure. Then he learned that his opposition would be his friend and ally, Rep. Patricia Hudson, R.

Getting home from his meeting, he told his wife the good news, all of it. They laughed, and he called Patsy. They laughed even more and arranged to meet for lunch the next day.

At the Cumberland Club, at this time, they would be too apt to cause a stir, so they met at a student-favored place on Forest Avenue, dark, crowded, and with the most entertaining sandwich menu in town. After laughing again at their situation, Patsy grew serious.

"What made you change your mind about getting into politics? You were pretty turned off the last time we talked about that."

Don hesitated, trying to put into words how he felt.

"Y'know, I think it was this Phoenix thing. It gives me hope, not only that partisanship may cool down and politicians can achieve something, but that campaigns will clean up and candidates' families will be spared the sniping, muckraking, and destructive attacks of the past."

Patsy beamed. "I did a lot of thinking after your call last night and I have some ideas you might consider. We both really want this job, we're good friends, and we also respect the aims of Phoenix. Isn't this a golden opportunity for two relative newcomers to stage a unique, newsworthy campaign that would serve as an example to others? We might prove that campaigns can really cover issues, can be clear about differences but, most of all, can be good, clean fun? More and better candidates might be tempted to try it themselves later on."

Don looked at her in amazement.

"Dear lady, you have almost taken the words out of my mouth."

Neither remembered eating at all, how long they sat at that table, or how many paper napkins served as memo pads. By late afternoon they had laid plans that satisfied them both, and their waiter was finally able to clear. Selling the plans to their respective parties took a bit of real persuasion, but only the diehards were impossible to convince, and they would vote the usual party line anyway. Together, they set up a news conference, promising the media that skipping it would be a grave error. The gist of that conference was that while each candidate would do as much or as little individual coffee-partying or doorbell ringing as he or she chose, the usual lawn sign war would be replaced by signs and other announcements such as "Patsy or Donny? Hear them debate at (place)(date), or on station WCOM live." The three debates would cover taxes, education, and the role of government. Entertainment, refreshments, and transportation would be provided by "As Maine Goes." Radio spots and the live broadcasts of the debates would be arranged, with an absolute minimum of expensive and intrusive TV. The candidates also agreed on a specific budget limit for ads, mailings, and other expenses. February was a dark month, even if a short one, and maybe this type of campaign would lighten things up, give people something to talk about.

They both promised to refuse to accept any negative campaign TV shots or mailings, whether proffered by local special interests or even the National Committees. Just maybe this race would be remembered like Ivory Soap—"99 40/100% pure."

At the first debate, to break the ice, Donny appeared in Cub Scout cap and scarf. Patsy took advantage of her seniority while he kidded about her sometimes unsuccessful den mother efforts, such as overnight hikes in the rain. Then they got down to serious business on taxes vs. new social programs, and the audience finally joined in with questions and comments. Both candidates were careful not to make promises they would not be able to keep, both injected gentle and friendly humor, and the evening was an undoubted success. One member of the press labeled it "The Patsy-Donny Show," and the name stuck. Media coverage was positive.

At the next debate, they exchanged Valentines. At the last debate, before they went out onto the stage, Donny asked Patsy to meet someone in the audience. He led her to an area in the front rows and there, splendid in purple silk, sat his grandmother, radiating both dignity and pride. Patsy had heard much about her and admired her immensely, but was also prepared to be treated frostily, as the enemy, and she was. To challenge Donato was unthinkable.

Election Day was fair and mild, reminder calls were made, and a much larger than usual special election crowd turned out to vote. Most experts had thought it would be a close race, and it was. But in the end Patsy's legislative experience, her name recognition, and the fact that Falmouth voters were largely Republican, won her the seat. She was on her way again!

She and Donny made a joint appearance on the late news, gracious and very friendly. They made a point of reminding the public of "As Maine Goes" and suggested that voters demand the kind of campaigning they had just experienced. The broadcast ended as Donny gently kissed his den mother on the cheek, and received a hug. With her head close to his she whispered "We've made it! I just received a call from *Good Morning America*. They want us and Jerry on next week!"

When they asked him, Jerry, still very wary of public appearances, suggested that Joel or Stan take his place. A coin was tossed, Stan won, and "As Maine Goes" went national.

* * * * *

Waterville

With regret, the Phoenix Board decided in early 1989 to move their headquarters to Waterville. This would be a more accessible location for those politicians and others eagerly seeking information not only about "As Maine Goes" but what future programs would cover. All agreed on the importance of keeping up the "As Maine Goes" momentum, right through the 1990 conventions and elections. Its impact in 1988 must not be allowed to seem just a flash in the pan. To ensure the changes of attitude meant constant and imaginative programming.

Mark's story, the presidential election statistics, and the inquiries following the "Patsy-Donny Show" in February had more than doubled the workload. Questions and suggestions came in from all over the country, and each had to be answered with thought. No "thank you so much" form letter could even be considered. Disciples warranted first-class treatment. Obviously greater space, more personnel, and fewer miles to cover were essential.

"As Maine Goes" was to be the subject of several national network TV shows, and Heather was disappointed that Harding's Corner would no longer be the venue used. That bleak little building in the middle of nowhere gave great credibility to their message that anything is possible if there is commitment, among even a very few.

Because so much of his source material was in Augusta, Jerry accepted Mark's invitation to move in with him. It was a relief, in a way, to put space between himself and Heather; his resolve to keep their relationship on platonic hold had come too close to crumbling many times.

Heather found a studio apartment near the Colby campus for occupancy during the week. When possible, escorted by Matt Dillon, she scurried back to the woods late on Fridays, eager for the Warners' loving support and her treasures. She had had to learn awfully fast how to produce and market the Phoenix Bird in quantity. Manufacturing and assembly groups had been trained, woodworking shops put under contract, good salesmen found.

To keep their Namakant legislators interested in "As Maine Goes" it was suggested that they be given a bird preview, so at a February meeting at the Stat House it was announced that Phoenix had a surprise for them. Heather was reintroduced and came forward with one of the small boxes in hand. They all moved to the Rotunda. She held it up, pulled the string, and a stout-hearted little bird soared toward the top of the dome. The clapping of these legislators was so enthusiastic that the governor, downstairs, heard it and came out of his office to seek the reason.

Heather explained how the toy was going to be used.

"There are now five thousand of these ready for flight. The Phoenix board has decided that, in addition to the explanatory folder for adults about our philosophy and aims, a small storybook for children, the Phoenix Phables and Pholklore, be included in each package. Thus every Phoenix bird will be a messenger of the ideas we hope will appeal to both children and adults.

"Our sales campaign will start soon, though slowly. The Phoenix Phlock is scheduled to hit the wholesalers and gift shows in the early summer, ready for the tourist trade, fairs, and those appallingly organized people who do their Christmas shopping before Labor Day. Wish us luck."

Heather was now seeing very little of Jerry, who was working all over the state to keep the fires of politicians' enthusiasm well stoked with more training sessions. Though she had gone out with Mark a few times since leaving Harding's Corner, she'd done no really independent socializing since joining the Phoenix group in the fall of 1987. A Valentine's party in her apartment building seemed pretty attractive. She would reactivate that red Christmas dress.

Paul Jackson was tall, attractive, and solo, feeling the letdown of an almost snowless, ski-less winter. It was with great pleasure that he spotted a knockout newcomer, seemingly unattached and probably feeling as positive about improving the evening as he did.

After the usual small talk, he discovered that her most pressing current interest was creating little booklets of children's stories. How lucky could he be! Not only might this attractive woman have been something intimidating like a nuclear physicist, but his position as an assistant professor of English at Colby College might fit right into her program. Hans Christian Anderson he was not, but being on speaking terms with *The Wind in the Willows* and *Babar* might qualify.

Responding to his interest, Heather went into enthusiastic and humorous detail about what she had promised to produce for Phoenix Phables and Pholklore, and why. Deciding this very profound subject was far too important to compete with the party babel of their surroundings, they made a graceful exit and soon found a quiet little Italian restaurant, with the pasta and wine of Ovid and Dante to serve as inspiration.

Over dinner they discussed the "Altitude Adjustment" program for kids. Heather was amazed and amused by how different this date was from those of her days in Washington, when brittle, clever exchanges of meaningless chitchat seemed to be inevitable. This evening it was obvious neither one wanted to waste time that way; both were really more interested in getting to know the other than in selling themselves.

Heather explained that one free booklet, based on the Phoenix legend, would be included with each bird and at least a dozen more would be presented gradually, to be collected as a set, each with its own theme. Would the ancient and traditional stories and poems that emphasized the noble qualities of Phoenix's philosophy be most effective, or should new ones be created? In many cases these stories would be read aloud by parents, so they should appeal subtly to that generation too. Heather produced a list of writings ranging from Aesop and Aristotle to Milne, Whitman, and Stevenson. What a wealth of material. She and Paul relived their own childhoods as they recalled these classics, sometimes quoting poetry they'd loved, with gusto.

Finally, tremendously pleased with himself, Paul suggested a solution.

"I'll bet my students would jump at the chance to help, while earning credits. From many different cultural and ethnic backgrounds, they could not only rewrite some traditional folktales but could be challenged to compose new ones."

Heather's eyes shone with excitement, and she pushed the idea further.

"Do you think that the Colby Art Department would encourage its students to volunteer for the illustrative work?" Why not?

So Phoenix was, for the first time, reaching out to the college age, one of the key groups necessary to eventual success, asking for their help rather than preaching to them. What a break!

Later, curled up on the floor with Matt Dillon, running her fingers slowly through his coat, Heather was pleasantly surprised to find she could again really enjoy being with an attractive and interesting male. The evening had been wonderful, in many ways, and possibly just a beginning to more.

* * * * *

Up-country, Stan and Susan were rather relishing peace and quiet after so many months of unaccustomed excitement and change. Susan was doing a little education research for Phoenix and the weekend visits of Heather and occasionally Jerry kept them up to date, though their old familiar routines were the same as ever, even in their much-broadened world. Each day now was filled with new awareness, curiosity, and enthusiasm. They both laughingly admitted to being quite different people from those of two years ago. Older in calendar years, they actually felt younger, much younger.

Susan's paintings were making stronger statements and showed greater perception. After years of working in oils she now experimented with watercolor, loving its translucence and freshness. No matter what medium she used, the trees put down stronger roots, the lake had more sparkle, and the skies were dramas in themselves. Wistfulness had disappeared, joy reigned. She felt almost ready for the promised summer show in Massachusetts.

After years of talking endlessly to himself in the barn, in the fields, or behind the wheel, Stan had begun to honestly evaluate his thoughts and put them on paper. For his own self-respect, he now justified most of his stands rather than just speaking louder, or even roaring. Some research had been necessary, some positions were altered, and once-cherished biases were put on the compost pile to rot.

One surprisingly mild morning in early March he stood in the doorway and stared at the cheerful blue of the sky and the friendly softness of the clouds moving slowly overhead. Bits of snow lay only in deeply shaded spots. Something inside him had also melted, vanished like the snow, and he had no regrets. The anger he had carried for so many years was just a memory, and he was finally free. No longer did he have to make an effort to be pleasant when his cherished negative thinking was interrupted, no longer did he keep his mental soapbox handy from which to harangue those who disagreed with him. He didn't seek troubling news, but enjoyed the few positive items he'd discovered. Just when the melting away had actually taken place he couldn't say, but this morning he knew he would never waste time or energy in such a way again. There was too much good calling on him, demanding his energy and attention.

He opened the door and entered his kitchen. Susan, at the sink, turned and smiled her greeting but certainly wasn't prepared for the enveloping arms that wouldn't let her go.

"Put down whatever you're doing, grab a blanket, and come on up to the spruce tree. Let's just sit there, watch the birds and the lake, then lie back and enjoy one another in the best way I know. Susan, my Susan, life is good."

* * * * *

Augusta

Once she'd settled into her Senate seat, Patsy thoroughly enjoyed her position. She continued on the groundwork of those bills she hoped to introduce at the next session and made a point of attending a variety of local and national workshops, conferences, and symposia on both governmental and social concerns, learning and evaluating. A busy and happy lady. It was an interesting winter, with many bills of a socially divisive nature. Gay rights, teen pregnancy, and drug tests all had champions and foes. Was Maine prepared to handle, on its shores, a disaster such as the oil spills from the Exxon *Valdez* in March? Property tax relief, economic development plans, and a devastating strike at the Jay mills kept the session busy till June.

Just before the adjournment, the president of the Senate invited Sen. Hudson to his office.

"Would you be at all interested in taking part in the White House Conference on Juveniles late this summer? Your bill has evidently impressed some of those planning the conclave and they would like you to lead a short meeting on it, complete, if possible, with the latest figures of results."

She shook her head in disbelief. "Hey, I'm just a beginner who has had some lucky breaks. Me, leading a discussion at the White House? C'mon."

But of course she accepted promptly, changed her vacation plans, and got to work.

Though her bill had been in effect for only a year, there were enough reports from the pilot area to give an exciting early picture. Counselors all agreed that most of the juveniles involved, with their parents, became cooperative after a few meetings and had so far stayed out of further trouble. Parents involved were accepting responsibility and actually feeling good about themselves. Judges had used good common sense deciding in which cases the threat of family publicity would jeopardize a juvenile's already rocky situation, and had sentenced those at-risk kids to rigorous community service projects and special counseling. Patsy was deservedly pleased with what she could report.

* * * * *

Washington, D.C.

Arriving in Washington in mid-August she wondered why, oh why, the founding fathers had chosen a humid swamp as the nation's capital. The city was hot, steamy, swarming with tourists and obscenely expensive, yet Patsy ate up every minute of it. She had been there as a tourist only a few times, and had never even visited her representative's office. Now she was on the inside, part of it, and very well pleased with herself.

To take her mind off her presentation the next day, Patsy spent the afternoon of her arrival at the National Gallery, wandering from room to room, awed at the splendor of her country's collection. Time passed quickly, and she had to rush to get back to her hotel to shower and dress for the evening. Crossing the Mall, she realized that she had a classic case of museum feet, but seeing those paintings had been worth it.

The conference was, of course, not actually in the White House, but the opening reception was, and all the lady conferees had been planning their outfits for this event for months. Patsy was no exception. She was quite satisfied with her well-cut silk cocktail dress of azure blue, with accessories to match. She took the elevator to the lobby, joined the others, and was intrigued by the fashion show they presented. There was everything from prim, tailored suits to gowns fit for a Hollywood opening. Even some mink, in August! Few of the women wore anything on their heads, but those who did were sporting "chapeaux," not to be confused with common hats. Those women had not been spending the afternoon in museums!

The Secret Service had earlier requested and checked the Social Security numbers of all the guests. Bussed from their hotel to a side entrance of the nation's great mansion, they waited while each identification was cleared. The splendidly uniformed Marine Band played softly as the conferees made their way up to the East Room, where President Bush would soon greet and address them. It was a beautiful chamber, airy, decorated in soft colors, with a small platform in the rear, from which the president would speak. Floor-to-ceiling windows gave a sense of space, and all was lit by three magnificent hanging globes. Throughout, the flower arrangements were spectacular.

While few of the conference group yet knew each other, they began to chatter a bit nervously as they waited. Patsy shifted from one sore foot to the other. There were no chairs. She began to pray that the speech would be brief.

All thoughts of her discomfort were brushed aside by the strains of "Hail to the Chief" and President and Mrs. Bush swept into the room and up to the platform, waving and smiling. Cheers and clapping followed, and Patsy felt quite superior to those who were seeing the couple in the flesh for the first time. She had seen them frequently in Maine, even shaken

Barbara's hand. The president called for silence, welcomed them all to his home, then launched into his prepared talk.

Patsy didn't hear a word of it. Her high heels had further set her feet afire and they had reached an agony that required emergency action. She couldn't leave the room, she couldn't sit on the floor, she couldn't continuously hop from one foot to the other. There was just one answer. Off came the offending shoes, and Sen. Patsy Hudson, (R) Maine, stood in her stocking feet on the cool floor of her nation's grandest living room. She wiggled her toes ecstatically and was pleased they still functioned.

Hearing clapping, she realized the speech was over. Though ushers cleared a path for the First Couple, guests surged toward them, eager for a better look and even a possible handshake before the Bushes returned to their private quarters. Patsy stayed put. To her horror, she saw her shoes kicked away by her neighbors as they struggled forward. Would she ever see those pretty little blue shoes again?

The room was emptying as her fellow conferees headed through the series of lovely sitting rooms en route to cocktails in the State Dining Room. When they were all gone maybe she could find her footwear, take a taxi, and flee.

"First it's your clothes and passport, and now it's your shoes. Do you ever keep it all together for very long?"

A kindly voice with a chuckle in it drove the thought of tears from her mind and she looked up. There he was again, her rescuer from the tiny beach at Lindos! And he had not only retrieved her shoes but had recognized her!

"I do very well unless there are knights in shining armor waiting to save me." She grinned at him without affectation. "Now, if you will be good enough to lend me your arm for balance, let's see if we can get these darn things on again."

Once that miracle was accomplished she thanked him, but he held her arm.

"I don't trust you to get to the State Dining Room fully dressed. Out of respect for this house, I feel you need an escort."

They walked arm in arm past the other guests, most of whom were taking pictures of each other with the other's cameras. Patsy was unaware of the priceless paintings, prints, and furniture surrounding them. She was on the arm of a very handsome man, and the Green, Blue and Red rooms would have wait till another time.

The State Dining Room, capable of seating 120 guests comfortably, was magnificent itself; the flowers, linen, glass, and silver made it like fairyland. Long tables were covered with platters of tempting and novel hors d'oeuvres, brimming punchbowls, and wine, all dispensed by liveried waiters.

Patsy edged toward the biggest bowl of ice-cold shrimp she had ever seen. In front of it, on the tablecloth, was a pile of paper cocktail napkins with the presidential seal printed on each. She counted four of these, popped them into her bag, then took one more and turned to her rescuer.

"You may want to pretend you don't know me. I swiped those napkins for my children and grandchildren. And now," with a radiant smile, "I'm going to pig out on shrimp."

What a wonderful laugh he had, and how nicely the laugh lines crinkled around his eyes. He certainly was attractive.

"I'll match you shrimp for shrimp. First, let me get us some drinks." He returned with two glasses of wine.

"My drink would like to introduce himself to your drink. Mine is the drink of one Gordon Abercorn. And yours?"

"That of Patsy Hudson."

"There must be more to it than that or you wouldn't be here. I have your name but not your rank and serial number."

"OK, State Senator Patsy Hudson, Republican, State of Maine, SIR. And you?"

"Undistinguished member of the State Department. Oh, by the way, please go easy on the shrimp." He hesitated a moment, grinned, then continued.

"It's no fun taking a lady to dinner if she hasn't any appetite. Unless you have meetings this evening, I would very much like your company at a seafood restaurant I discovered recently. Will you join me, as you so elegantly put it, in pigging out on more shrimp there?"

Patsy was afraid she'd wake up soon, this was too good to be true. She popped one more pink morsel in her mouth and accepted.

After a delicious dinner they moved on to a small nightclub with an equally small dance floor. Her Bill's arthritis had long ago put a stop to her dancing days, so it was wonderful to be led once again onto the floor, to put her hand in Abercorn's and dance. Her feet had recovered and knew just what to do. The lack of space meant nothing; she felt as if they had a ballroom to themselves. His eyes reflected the admiration in hers.

He was a widower, lived in nearby Virginia, and was with the Far Eastern division of the State Department. She couldn't remember when she had felt as comfortable with a new acquaintance as she did with this man. They seemed to have the same mental tempo, the same points of reference and, on the very few serious subjects they covered, seemed to share the same values. Best of all, he was fun, not with sophisticated, too-too clever humor, poking fun at others, but warm little-boy fun. He had probably driven his third-grade teacher crazy, but she'd undoubtedly loved him the best.

Lying in bed that night, with the memories of the day and particularly the evening swirling in her mind, she let herself wriggle with pleasure. Stretching one last time, and fixing the pillows just right, she almost purred. He had promised to attend her talk tomorrow afternoon and, if she was a very good girl, might buy her dinner again. What had she done to be so lucky? Instead of dreading her upcoming performance, she could hardly wait.

* * * * *

Harding's Corner

Sneezing, sniffling, coughing, Heather pulled into Harding's Corner early one Friday afternoon in mid-August. The public launching of the Phoenix Phlock had taken place a week ago and been so successful that her employers had given her a week's cruise on the *Victory Chimes*, queen of the Penobscot Bay windjammer fleet, with no phones, no TV, no deadlines. This overwhelming summer cold had scuttled those promised days of sea, sky, and superb sustenance as effectively as an iceberg had finished off the *Titanic*.

Her grandfather had always told her, "If you're stuck with a lemon, make lemonade," so she'd decided to have this poorly timed cold in style. She'd stocked up on orange juice, milk, chicken soup, sherbets, Kleenex, and Scotch. Her last purchase was a paperback, purported to have suspense, great characters and enough sex to suit her in this condition. Bleary-eyed and suffering from chills even on this warm summer day, she unloaded the car, let Matt have a few seconds to get comfortable, and struggled up the stairs to her nest.

Groceries away, she heated the kettle. A bag of Red Zinger tea in a mug with steaming water enhanced with a hefty dollop of Glenlivet was the perfect medication. She fell like a rag doll into her big armchair, but a careful doll, not spilling a drop.

Unfortunately, grocery stores don't carry the TLC she most wanted—Jerry's cool male hand on her forehead and his familiar but off-limits shoulder for her plugged-up head. Paul simply did not qualify for the position, any more than Matt did.

Then an almost happy smile crossed her face and she reached into her skirt pocket. On leaving her Waterville apartment she'd found a letter from Nana in her mailbox. Now she could read it in peace. The thick envelope contained several pages in Nana's fine handwriting, and Heather settled down to enjoy every word.

August 17

My dear, dear child,

Not being there right this minute to hug you to pieces ranks high on my lifetime list of frustrations. From the material you sent me I am overwhelmed by the reception your little birdie received, locally, nationally, internationally, and probably in outer space! I should hire a clipping service to be sure. I miss nothing, and personally shall do what they call, I think, "channel surf" for news of it. A new sport for the old girl.

Thank you, thank you for letting me share the event. The tape is magnificent, and I have shown it to everybody here. My "kids" all have birds, compliments of their mentors, and are even selling them for you at school.

The little books are already classics, delightful, to the point, and referred to quite often to as examples of behavior. I particularly like the range of settings, from Scandinavian folklore to African jungle tales, from our wild and woolly West to the dainty exotica of the Orient. I hope those authors and artists are getting the positive feedback they deserve.

Portland Head Light was the perfect location for your demo, lots of space, and a wonderful backdrop of the ocean, gulls, and boats. Oh, it just occurred to me, how did the gulls and Phoenixes get on with each other? Aerial turf wars?

Just where you found someone who could construct that six-

> foot Phoenix is beyond me, and finding others who could make something that big soar from real ashes and fly so high!! Spectacular. What an unforgettable symbol of second chances. So many of the pictures you sent caught the wonder and joy on those hundreds of faces. What an introduction to Altitude Adjustment."

Heather put down the letter, blew her nose once more, and had a big swallow of hot tea. This message was just what she needed, and she felt better already. The Phoenix Phollies of last weekend had been everything she had worked for and had already received wonderful reviews and comments, but Nana's judgment was always required for Heather to be truly satisfied. Nana instinctively knew what parts of a production had demanded the most, and was staunchly reassuring.

> Insisting that each child be accompanied by an adult was smart, a way of ensuring mature interest and possibly the safety of the lovely birdies in excited little hands. But best of all was the absolute lack of preaching, or obvious attempts to take over the children's' minds. You simply presented them with something of value, novel and fun. Now it's up to them to figure it out and react.

> Children out here love them, the skies over our parks seem filled with Phoenix phlocks, and I wouldn't be surprised if McDonald's didn't come up with an 'ash and feather' sandwich to compete with their own cheeseburgers. Yeccch.

> The best part though is the reception by adults. Even national commentators remark that there is already a feeling of waking out of a long nightmare and finding a lovely day at last. One commentator, and I'll have to paraphrase her, said 'there is an enormous relief warming our lives because some few unknown people had the imagination and concern to do for us something we all should have done for ourselves. Altitude Adjustment leading to civility, respect, and integrity can become the lubricant for the friction of our stressful lives.' Now let's see what all these relieved people do about it in their own behavior and lives.

> You wanted to know how this hoopla has affected my buddies

here at Medicare Mansion? Because many of them, thanks to your suggestions, are already active again in the world of volunteer jobs, serving as proxy grandparents, or going back to school, they are very self-important these days. They have the distinction of having been in on something big from the very start, when some of us talked them out of their mental wheelchairs. The days of thinking of themselves as has-beens are over and they actually call themselves The Pioneers. How's that for a positive attitude by octogenarians ? I'm just thrilled! For some it is actually the first time they believe they've truly made a difference, and they're making up for it!

Our mentoring group now has about fifty kids enlisted but the best news is that these kids are forming little clubs of their own, support groups dealing with peer pressure, drugs, family situations, and ambitious hopes for the future. I serve small groups tea every week, very properly, and they are as happy with civility, respect, and integrity as they are with the cookies. Oh my dear one, what you have given me! A new life!

Now, a question. Is this Paul person replacing Jerry in your affections? If so, he must be very special and I look forward to meeting him. What does Matt think of Paul? G-R-R-R-R-R or slobber-slobber? And did you hear that Joel's daughter, valedictorian of her class, spoke on Phoenix, stressing that she knew, from personal experience, how a small group with real commitment can make big changes? Hooray!

I always love talking with you on the phone, hearing your voice and laughter, and I shall call you soon, of course, but when a phone is hung up the voice and message go POOF, and that's that. I wrote this because I wanted you to have one more tangible testament from me of how wonderful you are.

In my top bureau drawer I keep a little stack of support letters from people I love, more therapeutic than anything in my medicine chest, ego-boosters, 'take when needed' stuff. If you have such a pile, add this, if it qualifies.

Love you, love you, Nana

Putting her head back against the chair, Heather let the tears come freely, tears of love and gratitude, sure signs that TLC was working. She got up, blew hard, and went to her bureau. Extracting her own pile of precious support letters, she slipped this latest one under the ribbon.

In the drawer was also a pile of large, soft, snow-white handkerchiefs that once belonged to her grandfather. When she was little he had allowed her to borrow them for extra-specially terrible, awful colds and at his death Nana had given her a few "just in case." One went into her pocket now.

There was a third pile in that drawer, a pile of envelopes addressed to Joel McLean. In each one of them was an unmailed letter of her resignation from the Phoenix staff, written at different times since she had discovered her blood relationship to Jerry. Never had she loved a job so much or felt so lucky just to be on board, but never had she been so frustrated in love, true, adult love. Working day in and day out with the one person with whom she wanted to spend her life and seeing only "No Admittance" signs, she had decided to quit on several occasions. Then some exciting new challenge, some wonderful program would evolve, or need her, and the letter would join the others in her drawer. The Bird's triumph had, for this moment, pushed such thoughts from her mind.

Now, with that problem temporarily tucked away with old hankies and Nana's letters, she concentrated on building a nest of sybaritic comfort on the sofa: pillows, an afghan, her book, the phone, the TV remote, and a virgin box of tissues. Well armed with proven equipment, and mentally turning round and round as Matt would, she finally settled down.

Heather Hatch, star promoter, gave herself up to the art of enjoying ill-health, thoroughly and with panache. She'd earned it. Though laid low herself, her birdies were finally flying high.

Chapter 11: Fall, Winter, and Spring, 1989–1990

Portland and Augusta

Curled up in her big armchair, her bare feet tucked underneath her and the phone cradled on her shoulder, Patsy felt and almost looked like a teenager. Occasionally taking a sip of wine, she listened happily. Gordon Abercorn had become more than just a rescuing knight in her life. Oh, so much more!

"Gordon, cheer up. Tomorrow night you're taking off for Las Vegas, supposedly to an international symposium, but relax, lose some money, and enjoy a desert sunset if you can get far enough away from all the neon lights. Wear your blinders if any showgirls cross your path. As Churchill said 'Up with that I cannot put.' And when, my friend, can I expect you up here for Turkey Day?" Just a few days and he'd be in Maine!

They had not seen each other since August. Still, their friendship had grown steadily on the phone—which, Patsy reluctantly reasoned, was a healthy way for it to grow. His charm came across the wires quite well enough, thank you, and she was being given time to get to know him from a safe distance.

"Barring a revolution on some remote Pacific island or Taiwan attacking mainland China with fighting cocks, I should be in Portland next Wednesday morning, Delta Flight 346, time of arrival 10:17 AM. I will dispense with a brass band, a pink stretch limo and the keys to the city, but may I dare to hope you will be there to meet me?"

"Of course. The reservations you insisted on are all made for you at the Holiday Inn, my kids are looking forward to meeting you, and my grandchildren are totally confused. Unless you have other plans, don't bother with anything dressy; informality is the word. Goodnight, dear friend."

Gordon's responsibilities in his job were filling his days with fruitless conferences, and causing him sleepless nights as well. What he discussed with Patsy was, of course, never top secret, but the minor frustrations that produced major stresses.

He called two or three times a week. Both looked forward to these exchanges of ideas and shared feelings. Losing one's spouse meant, in most cases, losing one's most sympathetic listener. Now each of them had found a truly interested confidant.

Patsy and Gordon often discussed whether the U.S. was actually entitled to demand sociological changes in emerging countries asking for its support. Had our government always backed the morally right factions, or had it too often favored those more economically favorable to our "interests"? Did our "interests" change with administrations and their political and financial supporters? What was the morally correct litmus test of that all-encompassing and ubiquitous phrase "in the best interests of the United States"? How much time should emerging nations be given to catch up with modern democratic thinking and human rights programs? Can a tribal chieftain become a Thomas Jefferson overnight?

Patsy had been spending some sleepless nights herself. Here it was, late fall of 1989. The bills she had dreamed of proposing were going to take at least another year to prepare, and in that year there would be elections. Quite content with her role in the Senate at present, she had been stunned when a member of the State Committee mentioned that the "inner circle," those nonelected but indispensable party strategists, were actually considering her as a candidate for Congress. This was ridiculous, considering what a newcomer she was, and she had said so. The only answer had been a shrug of the shoulders and a grin. Ordinarily she would have laughed it off and put it out of her mind, but nowadays her mind did have a way of swinging around to Washington. Not to what went on there, particularly, but to a certain person living there.

Now, her big old house seemed to know it would be full again and took to its holiday cleaning and polishing kindly. The maples in the yard hung on to at least some of their brilliant leaves, and the euonymus flamed by the front walk. Pots of chrysanthemums were warm welcoming signs on the porch and ears of Indian corn hung on the front door, pecked at occasionally by birds who should know better.

All was ready. Patsy felt as nervous as the night her very first date had come to pick her up for a movie. Then the question had been, would her father disgrace her by saying something dumb? He had of course, all fathers do. Now, just a few generations later, would her children or grandchildren be guilty of the same faux pas?

On Wednesday she drove to the airport, and the plane was mercifully on time. There he was, handsome, tweedy and so nice, hopefully scanning faces in the crowd. He saw her and they moved toward each other. Putting down his carryon bag he opened his arms. Patsy walked into them, and reveled in how good it felt.

The whole weekend was perfection. The traditional Deering-Portland high school football game was a cliffhanger, the weather was superb, and many old friends of Meg and Charlie seemed to appear at all hours with their children. A highlight was attending Portland's Christmas kickoff in the Old Port shops and oohing and aahing as the hundreds of lights suddenly blazed from the huge tree set up in Monument Square. Little Fanny and Billy thought Christmas must be tomorrow. Four weeks would be eternity.

Gordon took it all in stride and, like a chameleon, fitted right in as if he'd always been there. Patsy lost count of the number of winks, thumbs-up signs, and leers she received from supposedly well-brought up family members, though for the most part everyone behaved well. The only one who really kept his cool was Hank. He and Gordon took to each other immediately, and acted like reasonable adults.

A long, windy walk on Scarborough Beach Sunday morning, with gulls swooping and surf strong enough to crash with a roar, took care of those unwanted extra calories. All relished what might be their last visit to the shore till Spring, and this was a fitting finale.

That night the airport teemed with students bearing backpacks full of mother-washed laundry and untouched textbooks. Grandparents kissed sleepy babies one more time, and lovers clung to each other as if one was off to the wars, not just another work week. Gordon, foreseeing all this from long experience, refused to let Patsy join him to wait for takeoff. She parked by the curb.

"I'm really considered quite a big boy now and can handle this mob scene myself." He turned, grinning, to face her, and his eyes grew serious.

"Patsy, I hope this weekend was as important for you as it was for me. You have a wonderful family, and your home is truly just that. First place I've relaxed in months, even years. Bless you. We have a lot of thinking to do, but just remember this."

She hardly dared breathe.

He softly said, "You are in my heart and head every day." He paused, then whispered, "and every night."

Leaning over he kissed her, really kissed her for the first time, kissed her again, retrieved his bags from the back seat, and was inside the terminal before she could recover.

She hadn't realized how very lonely her lips had been, or how every other inch of her had long ached for a gentle touch. Fifty-plus widows need TLC just as much as a tiny new baby does, she thought, but are more discriminating in the provider. Thank goodness she had Christmas to think about as well as her work. That plane was taking a big part of her with it.

Pragmatist that she was, Patsy had deliberately sought this new life, accepting that the old one was gone for good. Now she welcomed each opportunity to grow. Bill had been a realist himself, and she knew he would never begrudge her any happiness. She felt his trust and generosity and was grateful for them.

A few weeks later Patsy received a call from the Chairman of the Republican Committee.

"Any chance of you getting up here to Augusta tomorrow? We're having a special meeting of the Committee's Executive Board, and the governor has asked to be there. OK, two o'clock, at the Blaine House?"

She was not a member of the Executive Board. The Blaine House? His Excellency? What was going on?

The governor's mansion was situated on the corner of State and Capitol streets, directly across from the lofty State House. It had been home to the man historians considered Maine's most outstanding politician, James G. Blaine. Since 1920 it had also served as official home to nineteen Maine first families and lodging to many visiting U.S. presidents.

Approaching the beautiful old house next day, Patsy Hudson wondered to which door she should go, the informal side entrance or the impressive front door. She had attended a few large receptions here in the past years but had been just one more face in an immense crowd, practically unnoticed.

Pulling into the drive she found her question answered as the chairman himself emerged from the side door, which was festooned with Christmas greens. He escorted her into a house sparkling with red and green decorations and smelling of Maine's Christmas perfume, balsam.

In the gracious sunporch the District One members of the state committee were gathered, as well as the executive group. They were soon joined by the governor, who took over the meeting.

"Thank you all for coming at a busy time. Senator Hudson, thank you especially, as you are still in the dark about what this meeting will cover." He crossed his long legs and leaned back in his chair.

"As you undoubtedly know, neither I nor the State Committee, for the sake of party solidarity, can have any public say in who should run for what office or whom we may support until after primaries. This meeting is therefore totally off the record. Any leak would be devastating to us all.

"By this time next year the elections will be past history. Maine will have chosen a governor and a U.S. senator, as well as two congressional representatives and a full legislature. We are always hopeful that Republicans win all openings.

"The congressional seat for the First District is wide open, as you all undoubtedly know. The Democratic incumbent is not seeking reelection, and so far no one from that party has announced intentions to run, in spite of many rumors. Not so in our party. We have, from Waldo County, a very fine though very conservative candidate. We also have a candidate from York County who is pledged to environmental issues, period. Both are newcomers to the political scene, but will be well financed by like-minded supporters.

"If you look back on the recent history of Maine Republican candidates, you will see that in federal elections the ideologically moderate R's have generally won. The true Conservatives are becoming stronger and stronger within the party but are not yet acceptable to Independents, without whose vote we get nowhere. And of course they're anathema to Democrats.

"Both of these declared Republican candidates are fine people, but limited in interest and therefore appeal. We need someone who can win.

"Senator Hudson, your record in the House and Senate has shown you to be a moderate, an independent thinker rather than a knee-jerk party person, and a person with strong fiscal principles who is also sympathetic to human needs. You are a whale of a campaigner. Can you see what I'm driving at?"

Patsy sat transfixed. She could not believe what she was hearing in spite of those earlier rumors, and this was coming from the governor himself! She didn't know whether to address him under these circumstances as "Your Excellency" or "You Idiot," so she just started out with nothing. He was young enough to be her son anyway.

"If you are asking me to run for the Congress of the United States of America after not even three years' experience, with no real financial backing, and certainly no PACS wooing me, I am totally flabbergasted. I've made a small name for myself with just one little bill, I am working on a few more but nothing earth-shaking. My constituents are just beginning to call on me for services. I don't even have the name recognition of Mrs. Bush's dog. You must have more reasons."

The Governor laughed, stretched his six-foot frame in his chair, and answered.

" OK. You have a great personality, meet people easily, and have a sense of humor, which is mandatory. Your bill on juvenile crime can be the chief issue of your campaign. It was good enough to get you to the Washington conference, wasn't it? Both your landslide victory last November and your Senate victory in February, again in Democratic territory and over the Democrat's ideal candidate, Don Vassalo, are like money in the bank for you. That last campaign was unforgettable. As far as we know you have made no enemies, particularly in the special interest groups. Voting with the other party on several occasions, particularly on Portland bills, has given you a reputation for independence and for putting your constituents' needs ahead of knee-jerk party discipline. If you have a lurid past we have yet to hear of it.

"There will be a primary. No word of our support can come out till that is over. I guarantee that you will be funded, both for the primary and for the general election, above and beyond what you can and must raise yourself. And it goes without saying, you will have to work harder than you ever have in your life. We will augment any staff of advisors you have, give you lists of volunteers, and so forth, but we can't hand it to you on a silver platter, as the legislative races need our help too."

If Patsy were the fainting kind she'd have been having fullscale vapors by this time, but this group had unerringly come to the right person. Here was the challenge of a lifetime. And if she won, it meant Washington for two years at least! Go for it!

Later that night, ready for bed, she was amazed at how appallingly independent her actions had become. It had never even occurred to her to ask for time to talk it over with her children. That was scary in itself. Now she was on her way; the announcement would be made in the spring.

In the next few months she would have to keep her name before the public during the session, working extra hard and in headlining ways for the right bills. She could afford to make no mistakes. There would have to be almost immediate steps to build up a campaign staff, find a manager and headquarters, and plan both a primary and a general election campaign that would set new standards for excellence and appeal. She had a lot to learn; her adrenaline better behave itself.

She looked at her watch, ignored what it told her, rolled over in bed and, grasping the phone, punched in a number. A sleepy voice answered.

"Gordon, can you keep a secret?'

"That's my job."

"Try this one."

* * * * *

Little Sebago Lake, Maine

The wintry skies of 1990 were things of the past, but the really soft, warm blue of spring had not yet taken their place. As Don stood in his office window he couldn't decide which was more depressing, March in the city or March in the country. Dirty snowbanks were the same either place.

He was restless. Last month the family had gone to Orlando, spent a sun-and-fun-filled vacation week enjoying the rides and marveling at the imagination on display, the cleanliness and efficiency of the parks. But now that was over and he needed something new to anticipate. The goal-oriented pattern of his life was lacking an immediate carrot. So, though it was only noontime, he put on his overcoat and boots, told his secretary he would be gone until the next morning, and sought his car.

Heading out of Portland on Rte 26, he drove through Gray and eventually took a left, the road to the family camp on Little Sebago Lake. A spring inspection visit before mud-time was almost a valid enough excuse to go AWOL, and the rustic cabin on the lakefront never ceased to restore him.

He had spent happy and irresponsible childhood summers here, surrounded by grandparents, aunts, uncles, food and laughter. And, of course, innumerable cousins. If he ever wore anything more than bathing trunks there he couldn't remember what it might have been, or what he might have eaten other than hot dogs, corn, and watermelon. Though sometimes even now he could bring back the caramel odor of burnt marshmallows, always dessert.

About a mile in on this road, at a fork, there was a small convenience store. Today, for some reason, quite a few trucks and cars were parked in front, and a group of men was engaged in excited talk. Finding a spot for his own vehicle, Don went into the store to get an Italian sandwich and a Hershey bar to eat at the camp.

He saw no familiar faces, so while waiting for his sandwich to be put together he asked what all the agitation was about.

"Kid lost in the woods." Olive oil was drizzled on the contents of the long roll. "Mother thought he was at school, but got a call that he wasn't on the bus. Little feller, six, I think. Some other kid said he'd been talking about finding the Easter Bunny. How about that? You from around here?"

"Summer person, cottage on the lake, near the far end. I'll keep my eyes open for him, have sons of my own about that age." He picked up a can of Coke, paid for all, and went out.

Turning to a man who seemed to be allocating search areas he said, "I'm going down the shore road till just about the end. Is that area covered?"

"Not yet it isn't. Pretty far for him to get. Do what you can. Dogs are being brought in, and a helicopter. We want Scotty out of them woods before dark."

His car was now on a dirt road, bumping over potholes and slithering a bit in mud that would be much deeper in a week or so. Don's eyes missed nothing on either side. There was still a little snow that might show footprints. Occasionally he stopped and sat quietly, listening for cries of help.

Then he saw, lying on the ground, one small blue mitten. He got out of the car, calling "Scotty, Scotty, yell if you can hear me." No answer. He got back into the car and moved along, soon coming to a barely defined logging road off to the right. He took it without even considering how he'd get out if it proved a dead end. Stopping, calling, listening, and then thinking he heard an answer. Glad that he had thought of wearing his boots, he ran from the car in what he hoped was the direction of the sound. "Scotty, I'm coming." He had to go some distance, but the voice seemed to be nearer. That kid must have lungs of iron to keep up the cries.

There! In an ancient pine tree, at least fifteen feet off the ground, a little guy was crouched on a not too sturdy branch. Dead lower branches seemed to have been recently broken and were lying at the foot of the tree.

Plunging ahead, anxious to comfort the child and wipe away the tears, Don didn't look where he was going. As he floundered through a pile of loggers' slash, one foot sank down into that pick-up-sticks mess. His forward thrust couldn't be stopped, and down he went. His right leg snapped.

Fighting the faintness and nausea of agonizing pain, he slowly lifted his head. The kid's tree was only about ten feet away. Don's accident had at least made the little guy forget to cry; he sniffled, wiped his nose on the remaining mitten, and managed a weak smile.

Trying to sound natural and confident, Don called out to the boy. "Hey, Scotty, cheer up! We're going to get you out of there, and whaddya know? I've got lunch for both of us!" Actually, lunchtime was well past. The shadows were getting longer, and they'd be lucky if they could call it supper.

If he could manage a stable grip with his hands on the slash branches around him, then push with the good leg and pull the other out of the hole, he might be able to wriggle on his belly over to Scotty's aerie. The first tries were agony; the branches just snapped or shifted without giving support. Finally he began to make progress, and reached the foot of Scotty's old tree. What he saw in the mud shook him.

Newly broken branches surrounded the tree, and in the soft earth on which they lay were bear tracks. Not terribly big ones, but big enough to impress him.

"Howdy-do, young man, pleased to meet you. My name is Don, and I know you're Scotty. I understand that you're looking for the Easter Bunny. Seen any traces?" Keeping his voice and words chatty might give them both confidence.

The little head shook. "But I did see a bear." Proudly.

"No way! You mean to say a great big bear just appeared, said hello, and went off to look for a better supper?"

"Yup. He came over to me and I didn't move at all. Then he sniffed me. Then I sniffed him and boy, he stunk. He stunk sumpin awful. I said 'peeyew' real loud and he went away."

"Good boy. I'll remember to do that myself next time I'm sniffed. Did he come back?"

"Yup, but I'd thought getting up in this tree was a cool idea in case he did. He tried, too, but the branches broke. I yelled some more and he went off. But now I don't dare jump down."

Don agreed that his judgment had been faultless.

"How good a catch are you? I think it's time for lunch."

"I'm on a T-ball team and play catch with my brother. Try me."

With difficulty Don dug into one of the big pockets of his coat. Unwrapping the sandwich, he broke it in half, then rewrapped one section. From the remaining section he tore off a large part for Scotty and kept a little for himself. He carefully lofted Scotty's share, which was caught by a pro. Don bit into his portion and they munched companionably, though no closer to a solution or even to each other.

The injured leg was really pounding. His stomach was reacting to the stress, and occasional waves of faintness would sweep over him.

"Hey, y'know what?" Scotty piped.

Why did kids always try to grab your attention with that meaningless query? His own did it, too.

"No, I don't know what. What?"

"It's snowing."

Thanks, buddy. He hadn't noticed. Oh Jesus, that's all we need.

Time to fish or cut bait. On the plus side was a good little kid who could catch a sandwich and yell "peeyew" to bears. On the down side was the fact the kid was way the hell up in a tree, Don was badly injured, and night was falling along with the heavy, wet snowflakes. It was cold.

"Hey, Scotty. If I built a real bed of those soft branches, and then lay on them ready to catch you, would you jump?"

The little head shook, expressing a clearly negative reaction.

"Ever been to a circus? You have? In Portland? That's just where I live. OK. Pretend you're one of those acrobats on the high wire. Just close your eyes and jump when I yell 'ready'. I'll bet you can fly."

"No way. There's no net."

"Yeah, but you have something they don't have. You have me! I catch my flying kids all the time, never dropped one yet."

Whether it was because he was tired of being in the tree, or hungry, or cold, something gave that little six- year-old confidence and he launched himself into space. He knocked all the wind out of his rescuer temporarily, but he was down!

With a bit of gymnastics, together they got him inside Don's coat, and they clung to each other. It felt just great. Grinning, eyes warm with happiness, they bonded, with mutual need and trust.

"Now we've got to think. First, the bad news. I have one broken leg and you're not quite big enough to carry me. So we'll have to find something to use for a crutch. We have no flashlight, we have no matches as I gave up smoking years ago. But, d'ya know what? There's good news."

"What?"

"In my other pocket, way down at the bottom of it, lying there just waiting for your hand to find it, is ... guess what?" Two can certainly have fun with the "guess what" game.

"The other half of the sandwich?"

"Nope, I'm saving that for an emergency, in case we run into one." He hoped the kid didn't ask why this wasn't already an emergency. It was beginning to fill his own definition of one quite adequately.

"What is at the very bottom of my pocket is dessert, my absolutely one hundred percent favorite dessert. See if you can find it."

After wiggles, and grunts, and some very sharp pains in Don's leg, a triumphant Scotty produced the Hershey bar. It wasn't one of the skinny ones, but thick, in squares. The kind you suck and let melt on your tongue. Serious dining began.

"And there's even more good news. We're going to be just like Boy Scouts, or soldiers, or cowboys, take your pick. We're going to camp out tonight. I like you too much to send you looking for my car in the dark, and I need you right here to say peeyew to that bear if he comes back. We're going to try to make some kind of shelter out of these dead branches, and snuggle up close to stay warm, and tell each other good stories till we go to sleep.

"A lot of men were out looking for you this afternoon, your Mom is probably pestering all of them to look harder and longer, and now my wife and kids are saying 'where's Dad?' So the woods will be full of nice people by the time the sun gets up. Let's get comfy. Help me pull some of this slash over us to make a little tent. And then we're going to think about that Easter Bunny. Do you know a song about Peter Cottontail?"

"Yeah, he came down the rabbit trail, hippity-hoppity, Easter's on the way."

"Ya got it, chum. And who is your favorite bear?"

"Pooh, of course." All bears aren't stinky.

"For that you get a goodnight kiss." How he wished he was at home kissing his own little guys and tucking them in.

It snowed all night and well into the morning. March storms are generally wet and heavy, and this was no exception. Breakfast was the other half of the sandwich. Don was awfully proud to be a member of the nationality for which that sandwich was named. The mixture of salami, cheese, onion, green pepper, tomato, olives, and pickle, all doused in olive oil, electrified every taste bud he had. He'd always been told that the Italian sandwich was invented in Portland, a whole well-balanced meal to put in the lunchboxes of working men. Call it a sub or a hero other places, in Maine it was definitely an Italian. Right now he strongly believed that it was actually the secret of Caesar's successes in all three parts of Gaul.

By noon, still unrescued, they decided to move on. Scotty was proving to be just the lad for such an adventure. Together they finally found a branch of the right shape, size, and condition to act as a crutch. Don had to make sure his good leg wasn't sound asleep; then, gritting his teeth, he rose from his nest, waited for his head to clear, and took his first step. With Scotty cheering him on and more or less clearing a path, he very, very slowly retraced his route of the afternoon before.

Covered with snow, his car had enough gas to encourage the heater to thaw them out. They could be entertained by the radio, and at intervals could blow the horn to attract rescuers. Lunch was the remains of the Hershey bar.

They had the fun of hearing on the radio news what a stir their disappearances had caused. Scotty cried a little when he heard his Mom's voice begging people to keep on searching. Don almost cried himself when he heard Marilyn's voice saying she was sure the two were together, that Don was certainly the man who had stopped at the little store, bought lunch, and gone on to his camp, except he never got there. The two lost sheep must be somewhere between.

About four o'clock, when the sun was lowering again, Scotty nudged Don. "I hear something. Shall I blow the horn?" No answer. Don had passed out from pain and exhaustion.

Scotty reached over and blew the horn the way Don had taught him, the SOS of three longs and three shorts. After a while he heard a roaring, and could see in the rear vision mirror a snowmobile coming up behind them. They'd been found.

* * * * *

Portland

Three days later Patrick O'Flynn tiptoed into Don's hospital room, emanating a pseudo-reverence.

"How are you doing, Congressman?"

Don stared at his old friend and mentor, puzzled. Patrick settled into the chair provided for visitors.

"I couldn't have done it any better for you if I'd planned it myself. Name recognition, boy, name recognition. You've followed all those plans we laid out a few years back, and done well. You certainly got your name around Cumberland County in that state senate race, though I'll always think that was a screwy campaign.

"But now you've got something perfect to capitalize on and you want to strike while the iron is hot, to coin a phrase. The whole state was holding its breath while you were lost in the woods with that kid. You're a household word, the darling of the evening news, a bloody hero. But not for long. Some damn fool will get lost in the fog, or on Katahdin, or ice-fishing too late in the season. Someone else will rescue them, and you'll sink down to the bottom of the list."

Don broke into this euphoria.

"Pat, I'm in a very delicate condition. This leg will lay me up for at least six week. What the hell are you blathering about?" Depressed, he really believed what he said.

"Donny, you are not stupid. The Democratic state convention will be in three weeks. The state committee is solid behind you though, as you know, there'll be primary competition. We'll take care of that. At the Convention you struggle up onto the stage on crutches, pale and pitiful. You wipe your brow, give whatever political spiel you feel like, and then just a hint of how your experience strengthened your values and your dedication to youth, blah, blah, blah. You're a natural. We all know the governor's going to be reelected, Senator Bill Cohen will also be reelected, and we've been praying for one really good Democratic candidate for Congress. You're it, and you're ready."

A few days later Patsy Hudson was occupying the same chair beside Don's bed. After a bit of sympathy and some friendly banter, she said she wanted him to be one of the first to know a secret she'd been keeping for several months. She truly believed hot political news would be therapeutic. His defenseless condition gave him the courage to ask her if she was pregnant, but she gave him a token slap anyway.

"No, no, no, you boob. Now listen. I'm in the race to be nominated as the GOP candidate for Congress, from the First District. The campaign is all organized on paper and known to just a few, still a secret."

Looking at her unbelievingly, he let out a whoop of delight. The pallid sick man came to life.

"Thank God I'm not in here for abdominal surgery, as this laugh would have pulled out all the stitches. Because I've got news for you, too. Lying here with nothing to do but daydream, I've been considering running for the same job, though the word 'run' is hardly appropriate right now. A few of my friends are behind the idea. You and I have a lot to talk about, as your announcement has just made up my mind. Thanks."

In the following hours and days, they examined the situation. This race, if both won their primaries, would be very different from the one they'd earlier run against each other. They would be able to do much as they chose in the primary campaigns, with a little deference to their individual leadership groups and advice from their personally chosen kitchen cabinets.

The general election would be a different kettle of fish entirely. That would be big-time, and not only their separate State Committees but their National Committees would be calling many of the shots. Big bucks would be involved, special interests and PACs would have to be considered and dealt with, and they would both lose the independence they had enjoyed earlier. Each party would pour not only money but personnel into Maine to aid all races in this election. Each candidate, in order to earn these perks and to keep supporters and staff happy, would have to accept becoming a commodity to be marketed by experts, the Madison Avenue types bought by the party. They would not only no longer be in charge but, in many ways, would be pawns.

Each major candidate would have an omnipresent aide to keep lists of every person met for use in future personalized mailings, and to serve as chauffeur so that not even a minor accident or ticket could damage the candidate's image. These aides would serve as the "bad guy"' when it was time to break away from a coffee or meeting in order to keep to the schedule for the day, and would be the liaison between the candidate and campaign headquarters. Checking on whether the candidates' socks matched, if a slip showed, or if it was time for a "pit stop" was part of the job, as was the challenge of keeping the candidate optimistic, upbeat, and remembering to smile, smile, smile.

Schedulers would be in charge of the commodity's program, supervised by the campaign director, the big hired gun. Setting up each week's interviews, speeches, rallies, and debates, detailed but also flexible and utilizing every moment, was truly a mammoth task. No factory gate could be overlooked, no business leader slighted. Directions to each site must be flawless; time was one resource that must never be wasted. Sleep would become a memory.

Other staff members would be in charge of news releases, publicity, signage, even speech writing on occasion. An accountant was needed to keep accurate records of donations and expenses as required by election laws.

Energetic volunteers and political junkies in every community would have to be found to make endless phone calls, stuff endless envelopes, and give endless wine and cheese parties. Local party organizations might have to be tactfully demoted, as the pros often found them enthusiastic, but more social than effective. For campaigns of this importance vigorous and dedicated workers would spell the difference.

Every community's voting list would have to be checked for accuracy. Absentee voters' ballots had to be obtained for the handicapped and travelers. No voter could be ignored, and each must be made to feel that his or her vote was especially important. "Get out the vote" was Challenge #1. Personalize, personalize, personalize.

For the top-of-the-ticket candidates fund-raising dinners, cocktail parties, and rallies, usually planned by Washington, had to be organized and integrated into the minor candidates' calendars. If the acceptances to these didn't seem to guarantee the necessary enthusiastic crowd, warm bodies must be invited to fill the hall. This list of supporters who would like to get in free must be up to date and based on how many votes they could deliver. Photo-ops of supporters shaking hands with the drafted Washington headliners at the high-priced affairs were mandatory.

Position papers on what were perceived to be the main issues had to be written, generally by bright political science graduate students, good at research and with a gift of salesmanship, to be mailed to voters asking particulars. Good pictures of the candidate, his or her family, spouse, and children, and even a dog, borrowed or legit, must be available and ubiquitous.

Familiar with all this, both Patsy and Don promised each other to still follow the Phoenix philosophy as much as possible, though realistically. They both owed a certain fame to it, having created a legend for themselves that would be hard to replicate. Now, with the ridiculous coincidence of this, a possible second face-off, they both felt it would be disastrous to revert to questionable political patterns. The Phoenix plan had a superb freshness and appeal that they certainly should not abandon. After all, Phoenix had worked. Would peer pressure, party pressure, and good old-fashioned ambition sway their decision making? Would they have the backbone, each wanting the prize so much, to play the game of democracy in its purest form?

Though their campaigns would not be as lavish as those for senator or governor, Maine was a state important to both parties. This was a big-league ball-game, and both were realistic in accepting that challenge. Their training days were over; they would both enter the lists well-armed.

Both the Republican and Democratic state conventions in April had been well attended, with national leaders invited by each party. A U.S. Senate seat, the governorship, and two seats in Congress were all seriously targeted by each party as possible wins. James Baker, Pete DuPont, and Elizabeth Dole had told the Republicans what they had come to hear—that with hard work it could be a winning year. Dick Gephart, John Kerry, and Maine's own Senator George Mitchell had made the Democrats more eager to win than ever. None had found a new way to sound the same old war cry, but at least their jokes were new, and their resumes impeccable.

As potential candidates both Patsy and Don had been given chances to meet with their party's notables for a bit of quality time and the inevitable photo. These events were considered first steps in being called up to the majors.

At the First District conventions both had solidified their positions with good speeches and rallies. Don appealed shamelessly to the multinational labor groups with Irish-Italian-Franco music. Patsy had featured teenage talent, reminding voters of her bill. Neither had many doubts about winning the nomination in the June primaries. Patsy and Don were both successful. Up went the curtain as the Maine stage was now set for the election of 1990.

The scramble for candidacy for the state legislature was unusually spirited, with more and better qualified candidates from each party than in the recent past. Was Phoenix at work? Was politics becoming an acceptable interest again? The campaign methods would tell the story, but the Phoenix Board was excited.

There have always been three criteria for a successful candidate: money, name recognition, and a message, sincere but based largely on what the electorate wants to hear. Since the advent of TV another element had been added: charisma. With which candidate are you most comfortable?

Which shows leadership qualities? Which looks most like Robert Redford, or Meryl Streep? With which do you identify most strongly as to lifestyle, spouse, dog, or speechwriter? Whom do you believe, and why?

Swamped with advice by experts on all these requirements, Patsy and Don had gotten into the rhythm of their challenge. They were instructed to prepare good, convincing answers to questions about their positions on veterans' rights, gun control, conservation, abortion, and other issues. Washington, as foreseen, began to call the shots, send suggestions along with money. But, as in their earlier race, they both refused help that depended on negative ads. After all, they pointed out, voters had liked that stand before.

In addition to the philosophical decisions to be articulated, more practical matters had to be implemented. Both candidates chose to have their campaign offices in Portland. Don's headquarters were downtown in a recently vacated store on Congress Street. Patsy was lent a building in a suburban shopping center, not quite as accessible to voters but far more convenient for workers, with no parking problems. Patsy's manager, experienced Ben Livingston, explained his campaign plan to the staff and keyvolunteers.

"I plan to study the current voting records of every ward in the whole district, then color-code, on a map, every town as to Republican strength, Democrat strength, and Independents. Then we'll look over past records to see how many swing voters are in those groups. With the influx of new families moving into all parts of our district, the figures from even two years ago are no longer accurate. Correct ones are vital to winning.

"We'll start visiting in the heavily Republican areas, possibly picking up workers and contributions, but also because we may never get the opportunity to get back there. Then we'll hit the neighborhoods and communities rich in Independents and swing voters. Traditionally Democratic areas will come last, but by then voters are the most interested and we may pick up some surprise support." His workers were impressed. And challenged.

In addition to the volunteers who had helped win the primaries, a larger army of workers was to be enlisted and trained by early September. Middle-aged housewives were a great pool in which to fish for volunteers, though often their hours depended on their children's programs, health, or vacations. Male aides and workers might be a mixed bag, ranging from recent college grads to ideologues, quixotic, mercurial, yet sometimes brilliant. Retirees, often veterans of many earlier campaigns, were loyal, quiet, and glad to have something to do. They caused few ripples and got the work done while enjoying the little dramas swirling among the younger group.

A good campaign manager could, with luck and talent, weld these disparate people into an unbeatable team, like an extended family. It was the manager's job to create a mystique for the candidate, wrapping him or her in transparent armor that deflected negative news, but at the same time gave off an almost holy glow to be seen by the faithful.

First, with just skeleton staffs, personal mailing lists were brought up to date and more created, begged, borrowed, or stolen. Fund-raising letters went out.

Next came the organizing of the hinterland, with personally selected city and town committees in each county. Both Patsy and Don were "middle of the roaders," too liberal for some of these oldsters, too conservative for those whose philosophy demanded immediate changes.

Their earliest public campaign appearance was on Memorial Day. Patsy chose to march in the Portland parade and later in a smaller one that actually wound through the cemetery where Bill was buried. She was glad to have him share this beginning. Don—on crutches—also took part in the Portland parade and then in one to the historic Eastern Cemetery on Munjoy Hill, the bastion of his family.

Meanwhile their schedulers studied all the lists they could find of summer events in the district that appealed mostly to the local inhabitants. Others were more tourist oriented and therefore unproductive, unless good TV coverage was promised. There were festivals of all kinds, strawberry, potato blossom, lobster, chicken, blueberry, and the final pumpkin. There were county fairs, art shows, lobster boat races, and windjammer days. All-day swings through distinct areas were planned for the summer months, making sure to take in a Rotary lunch, a walk down Main Street with a popular local party resident, and some Kiwanis and Lions connection. Calls on local newspaper editors, TV, and radio stations were a must. Courtesy calls had to be made on all local party leaders, past and present, as well as many CEOs, and even religious leaders, with pleas for their active support. If a campaign could claim to have visited every city and town at least once by Labor Day, if only to lay the groundwork for the real push ahead, that team would be satisfied.

In addition to all she had learned from her legislative years, Patsy now made a point of studying Maine conditions and issues in greater detail.

Jerry Warner had generously agreed to lend her much of his research material, with the understanding that he would also make it available to Don if asked. Because of its objectivity, it was a gold mine.

Don and his family planned to take one week off at the lake. Southeast Asia seemed to be behaving itself, so Gordon was planning to come to Maine, for a vacation and to help Patsy, in mid-September. So much for relaxation for either candidate.

Patsy visited Washington in June for a Republican candidate training session after the primaries. She learned a bit more of what Gordon's lifestyle was, and liked it. He usually attended only those social functions he would truly enjoy or those definitely part of his job. The peace and quiet of his home meant a lot to him. They had spent evenings there enjoying the garden, the sunsets, and dinners produced and left by his housekeeper, rather than at the Kennedy Center or Embassy Row receptions.

During this visit she once again saw his sister Alice, first met at the beach on Rhodes. While Gordon was busy bartending before dinner one evening, Alice whispered to Patsy, "We are so glad you have come into Gordon's life. He has been so lonely, but also gun-shy."

"Gun-shy?" asked Patsy, not understanding.

"Yes. He probably told you he was a widower, which is true. But his wife died after she had left him, an event that tore him apart. We were afraid he'd never be able to trust a woman again. Thank you for being here for him."

It had never occurred to her that this poised, amusing, and seemingly self-sufficient man might need anything or anybody, much less Patsy Hudson. Thank you, Alice.

* * * * *

Across the nation, mailboxes would soon be stuffed daily with fund-raising letters, campaign literature, position papers, and notices of events and rallies. Even home entertainment was already mildly affected. The ubiquitous antacid TV commercials were replaced with thirty-second appeals by candidates, often bringing on greater digestive distress. One national candidate even planned a TV commercial of total silence for thirty seconds, with the simple printed message, "This respite is brought to you by ______________. Remember that name."

Voters knew that all this was going to take September and October to peak and finally dissipate, finally giving way to Christmas shopping ads. All would probably be kept spicy by charges and countercharges, hours of analysis by "talking heads," and polling reports ad infinitum. Very few voters would believe even half of what they heard. When cynically asked why such manipulated elections even took place, one wag replied, "To find out which polling group came closest to the final figures."

While for years voters had piously stated that negative campaigning turned them off, this campaign would be a test of that myth, and the greatest test of Phoenix. Americans love exciting competition that is tough and blood-stirring if not actually bloodletting. Good manners are nice to live with but can often be appallingly dull.

Patsy and Don had accepted the stupendous challenge of making their race just as newsworthy and provocative as those not limited by idealistic Phoenix rules. With both senatorial and gubernatorial races in the state, those of the congressional districts so far were not often on the front page. This was frustrating, challenging each team to do some creative campaigning.

One night in early April, just before the convention, Patsy attended a vaudeville revival show in Gardiner. She was intrigued by the real appreciation shown to time-honored jokes, one-liners, and tales dealing with the everyday lives of the audience. Corny but great. As a result, during the summer Patsy collected stories rich in Maine humor or that could be made applicable to a Maine campaign. These might be remembered by voters more than serious topics, though carrying the same message. "A spoonful of sugar makes the medicine go down" was a song Patsy found herself humming quite often. It might work. She and Gordon talked nightly, and he finally admitted that he could hardly wait, not for the sound of her voice, but for the joke of the day.

Her opponent was not idle either, also seeking new ways to get and hold attention. Though no great soloist, Don had a pleasant tenor voice and had been practicing Italian, Irish and French-Canadian songs, sea chanteys, and a few old favorites, with guitar accompaniment. Fooling around with the lyrics, he put some of his political arguments to familiar music. Subliminal politics, or maybe just an honest attempt to make the race interesting without dirt. He had done his homework over the years, building a good resume as a citizen, with impressive connections. Now he was facing the test he had dreamed of for so long, and he was ready.

By Labor Day both Patsy and Don were satisfied with their fortifications, attack plans, and troops. Their offices had become war rooms, with maps tacked to the walls and multicolored pins coding the possible voting pattern of a district. Phone banks were manned by volunteers encouraging city and town teams, polling voters, and already asking who would need rides to the polls or absentee ballots. Campaigns on every level swung into full action, their bases built, their weapons ready, and their war chests filling up. Let the games begin!

Chapter 12: Summer 1990

Boston

Immediately after that historic May 1988 board meeting, before word had gotten out to competitors and investors, Roger, with Phyllis' approval, had called a press conference to announce the withdrawal from the world market of the company's questionable fertilizer , and why. Phyllis had finally told him the whole miserable story of the baby, her subsequent treatment of Webb, and finally, of the fund in Webb's honor dedicated to the renewal of mutual trust, honesty, and civility in business, government, and private lives. Challenging the board as she had was her endorsement of that ideal, her "one small candle," a more personal gift than all her checks. And an atonement.

Needless to say, none of that personal material was given to the press, but the Phoenix Fund had received good coverage. The articles were not limited to trade papers, and the *Wall Street Journal* made a big splash with the story. The eyes of the industry had been immediately concentrated on the stock market reaction. A step such as this would probably spell the end of a very successful company. But after a few vacillating days the stock had soared, surprisingly boosted by the competition. Sensitive to the somewhat less than popular regard in which they were held because of scandals in the past, leaders of the industry had jumped on the bandwagon of safe long-term conservation, and the public purse responded. The Phoenix philosophy had scored again, and in very practical terms.

In the course of the following year safer formulas had been developed and Phyllis had the satisfaction of personally coming up with one of the first on the market. Her confidence had soared like the stock, and Rog found his protective attitude toward her becoming one of admiration instead. Visits to her "shrink" became less and less frequent. Best of all, she was developing a small circle of real friends.

Rog invited Phyllis to spend some time with him and his family on the ranch in August. He wanted to have her see from whence he came and, selfishly perhaps, he wanted his parents' opinion of this lady. Transplanting an orchid into a sagebrush lifestyle was a tall order, and he needed wise opinions. The "orchid" agreed to the plan, though nervously.

First, however, in May 1990, she attended a class reunion at Wellesley, the first time for her, and found she really enjoyed herself. Everyone was surprisingly friendly, and far more interesting than she had remembered. She was sorry she hadn't come before. More importantly, taking this trip alone was, in her mind, her graduation into the world of normal living.

On the last day, with her bags packed, she found she had time to visit the gallery where Carol McLean worked. It was situated in the attractive Wellesley shopping area, surrounded by fine specialty shops. The very handsome young woman at the desk told her that Carol was on vacation, but cordially urged her to look around.

The gallery was made up of several airy, well-lighted rooms, very cool and pleasant after the glare of the streets. Much of the work was conventional, safe and pleasant, but some was quite abstract, a good mix. Two rooms held a one-man show of landscapes and a few portraits. As Phyllis studied the landscapes she realized that they were all images of a rather small area, perhaps a farm. Like Monet, the artist had presented each subject in many lights and at different times of day and year. A favorite motif was a majestic blue spruce, overlooking fields leading down to a lake, with mountains beyond.

Each painting was dated, and Phyllis was fascinated with the changes in style and vibrancy that had taken place in the last few years. Earlier paintings were almost sentimental, or wistful, in comparison to the later much stronger ones. Their sunlight warmed the viewers' skin, and shadows were inviting, not ominous. She wished she could know what had happened in the artist's life to cause this development, similar perhaps to what had happened in her own life. If she herself was creative, how would the changes of the past months be reflected? Interesting.

Knowing she had to have one of these paintings, she spent some time making her selection. There was one of a couple sitting under the tree, looking out over the lake, happy in their setting and with one another, the way she was beginning to feel with Rog. As a non-artist, she was always fascinated by a painter's ability to express personal feelings by use of color, composition, and light. Before deciding, she moved into the adjoining gallery, which contained portraits by the same artist.

She had to catch herself from falling. Webb Lewis seemed to be staring out at her from one painting after another, bearded, changed, but still himself. Of course this was impossible, but there he was, framed and looking right at her.

When her heart stopped pounding and her breathing was more normal, she studied the paintings carefully. Only one was Webb as she had last seen him, shaven, wearing a business suit, tired and almost grim. Others were of an equally tired but also injured man, bearded and a bit frightening, in a faded flannel shirt. The latest were of a happy, vibrant Webb, still scarred physically and still with the red beard and hair, but whole emotionally, a Webb she hadn't seen for many years. In several he was portrayed with a lovely girl, whom she soon recognized as the gallery receptionist. One of these was titled *Cousins*. One with a striking older man, both in profile, was simply *Father and Son*. All were signed "Susan Warner." The date on the earliest was 1987.

She finally returned to the desk and asked if the receptionist could tell her anything about the subjects of the portraits. Brightly and proudly she was told, "Most are of my cousin, Jerry Warner. You may recognize me in some, too, and there is one with his father, Stan Warner. His mother is the artist. We're all from Maine, and the setting is the Warner farm."

Phyllis shook her head in confusion, thanked the girl, and returned to choose a landscape, though certainly not the one in which the couple were sitting so happily together. She made arrangements for shipping, wrote her check, and left.

That night, on the plane, her mind raced. The paintings were in Carol's gallery. Carol, Joel, and people named Stan, Susan, and Jerry Warner were all on Joel's Phoenix board. Obviously too many relationships for a coincidence. But why, how? The impossible had taken place!

Her primary feeling now was of anger, brought on by a sense of incredible betrayal. Webb, Joel, and Carol were obviously in this drama together, keeping so much from her for so long. How much did that lovely "cousin" know? How could Joel, the soul of honesty, be active in raising memorial money for someone so alive? The "widow" was hurt, furious, and puzzled, but also left with a strong affinity to this Susan Warner.

Her plane was still on the runway, preparing to take off. She looked out the window and realized it was raining. The drops on the glass quivered as they hit, then slid down, to be replaced by others. At first they simply gave her something to look at, an escape from her own thoughts. A metaphor or simile grew unbidden in her consciousness. Was she like that pane of glass, buffeted by this storm, but strong enough to keep the rain at bay? The drops hit, then fell away. In time the sun would come out, the window would have been cleansed, the view and future clearer.

Slowly she relaxed. The doubts about Webb's death were over, and she realized she was free, emotionally. He was alive and she was relieved for him about that. He was engaged in a project for which she had great respect, and he was evidently making a fine new life. The recent portraits were of a happy man. Did that girl know the truth about her "cousin"? Phyllis couldn't bring herself to believe that anyone so charmingly straightforward could have been deliberately lying.

By her own financial support of Phoenix, Phyllis had made the only amends she could for her years of wretched behavior. Whatever the means and reason for faking his death, he had forced her to first seek help and then gain independence. Two miserable people were now better off than before; one of them was finally able to think of individuals other than herself with genuine interest.

Some day she might get the whole story from Joel. Until that time, she decided, Webb's secret was safe with her. She owed him that at least. Comfortable with that decision, as the plane knifed westward through the night, she slept.

Later, as they went through the landing routine, Phyllis' heart beat faster as she knew Rog would be there to meet her. If his arms were open she would go into them, with no reservations.

A few days later Phyllis wrote a note, a very carefully worded one:

Dear Carol and Joel,

How sorry I was to miss Carol at her gallery this past week. I should have written ahead.. It is charming and you must do very well. As you may know, I bought one of Susan Warner's paintings, and it has just arrived. Superb!

You will be interested to know that I am filing for divorce from Webb, to take care of any loose ends. My lawyer advised it as in time I might wish to remarry.

I have been impressed with the good publicity Phoenix has received and hope it continues to thrive.

Best to all,

Phyllis Lewis

She reread it, slipped it into an envelope, and addressed it to them at the gallery.

Opening the mail was one of Heather's jobs. When the note arrived she read it, considered it of little interest except to hear that the painting had arrived in good shape. She filed it under "Lewis, Webb, deceased." So that was the widow she had heard about. She didn't seem as bad as depicted, though kind of nervous. Occasionally in the past she had wondered what Webb Lewis had been like. Would she have liked him?

* * * * *

North Dakota

A Maine car sped along a North Dakota highway on an August afternoon. Mountains in the distance were deep purple, the plain flat, and the driver pointed out to his wife and children, for at least the tenth time since lunch that "this is the real West." OK, Dad, OK. Back packs, bedding rolls, coolers, and a tent filled the back of the station wagon. One more nice American family en route to high adventure vacationing in the national parks and sure to consume more meals at McDonald's than the parents had counted on.

Approaching the outskirts of a small town the car slowed down. The driver's head turned from side to side and then he seemed to relax, spotting a small restaurant down the main street.

"I'm going to drop you guys off here for a snack and see if I can find a service station. There's a funny little noise I don't like." His wife hadn't heard a thing but knew better than to argue, though they'd just passed a service station. Maybe he needed a break.

When his family had trooped into the eatery, the man turned the car around, drove back about two blocks, and turned down the only side street in town. On one side was a brick schoolhouse with "Roosevelt High 1910" carved over the arched portal. On the other side a large Victorian mansion sported the sign "City Offices" and beneath that, discreetly,

"Police Hdqtrs." Nothing had changed. The traveler parked in front and got out.

He mounted the steps and entered through an ornate beveled glass door. To the right was the assessor's office, to the left the city clerk's. The police office was still downstairs, in the basement; down he went.

A bored and rather aged deputy sheriff sat behind a desk, leaning back in the swivel chair. He still wore, as he had before, a Red Sox baseball cap. Were his feet still in tired canvas lace-up sneakers? "What can I do for you, son?" he asked, unsmiling, but not intimidating.

The younger man shifted from one foot to another, and cleared his throat.

"A few years ago a friend of mine had the, er, opportunity to be the guest of this town office overnight, for a small offense. You wouldn't believe how impressed he was with the way he was treated, the hospitality he was shown, and the caliber of the dinner he was served. As I was passing through I remembered his tales and thought I'd like to see this municipal Ritz for myself and thank you again on his behalf."

What awful malarkey that speech was, but it was the best he could do, even after hours of planning what to say. He had never been a good liar.

"That's real nice to hear. Have a look around. Not much to see, don't even have real cells, just the motel yonder and a kinda sitting room here. I'll show you."

Damn, damn, he wanted to get in that sitting room alone. The Deputy was on his sneakered feet and heading toward the door when mercifully the phone on the desk rang. The visitor was motioned to go ahead; the deputy regained his chair and was soon involved in a discussion regarding this coming evening's bowling matches. Bowling was big locally, very big.

The visitor, moving swiftly, entered the room, looked around, and quickly found what he sought. A log book containing names, addresses, and offenses of every miscreant held here since the town was incorporated, lay there on a table for anyone to study. It had entertained him and his companion all those years ago as they waited for judicial—and, worse yet, parental—axes to fall.

He knew exactly what date he needed, August 16, 1977. It had happened on his mother's birthday; he had begged his friend to make the one family call they were to be allowed by law rather than calling his own on that particular evening. His mother deserved that much respect. But the friend's family line had been busy, so it was his mother who had answered the call he finally had to place. He remembered every word.

"Hi Mom, Happy Birthday. Just wanted to let you know I was thinking of you. Where am I? Oh, in a nice little town in the Dakotas. Hard to believe, isn't it? Yuh, we're having a great time. I'll write you all about it."

The sheriff, or whatever the guy called himself, hadn't acted patient. Chatting had nothing to do with the legal process.

"Mom, I'd like to have a word with Dad too. OK?" He recalled now that the few minutes it took for his father to come to the phone had been the longest so far in his life.

"Dad? Hi there. Oh yeah, we're having a ball. One little thing though, and don't shout at me 'cause it might upset Ma on her birthday. Dad, um, I'm in jail, and I need money and advice. Dad, Dad, please cut out the yelling. Look, we got stopped 'cause one headlight was out. No big deal. But we're young, we're from the big bad East, we have long hair, guitars, and torn jeans, so they searched the van. Dad, we had just a bit of pot on board. It was going to be a present to the guys we're going to visit. Dad, calm down, OK, we have occasionally sampled it, the dried stuff. What else was there? Oh, we had some plants, too. Some guys had bet us we couldn't keep 'em alive all across the U.S. of A. Yes we're dumb, Dad. Yes, Dad, really d-u-m-b. But we're not in irons, and they only shoot drug offenders on Thursdays here and it's Monday today. Sorry, I know it's not funny. What'll it cost? Lemme ask."

He'd turned to the officer who shrugged and indicated that about $200 would take care of the matter, plus court costs and keep. The kids really didn't have that much pot with them, and obviously weren't dealers. Just a case of illegal possession and lousy judgment.

That had been the summer of his junior year at college, and this incident had been the highlight of the trip. Good for laughs at the frat house, but not anything his kids ever needed to know.

Now, in hardly any time, he found the page, their names, addresses and crime. Looking over his shoulder, he saw the deputy making himself more comfortable as he talked. With hands that were no longer trembling as much he carefully ripped that page from the book, pocketed his treasure, and returned to the office.

Out of courtesy to his guest, the deputy wound up his conversation. "Not much to look at, but if that's what you wanted I'm glad I could oblige. Hope your friend has stayed out of trouble since then."

Rejoining his family, he assured them the car was fine. On the wall near the door of the restaurant was a postcard display, and he bought one, of a busy-looking gopher.

That evening an envelope containing the purloined police record and the post card was mailed off to Donato Vassalo Esq., candidate for Congress. On the card was a note reading, "No telling who might have found this during your campaign. Can't be too careful these days. Cheers, old buddy. You're clean, Best to all. Norm." It might give Don a laugh, and it was a bit of business that had been on Norm's mind ever since Don had announced his candidacy. Good man, good friend.

* * * * *

Montana

Their Western vacation was more successful than either Rog or Phyllis had dreamed possible, though begun with some very real misgivings. Phyllis had thought of it not just as something to enjoy but also as another test, and one she most desperately wanted to pass. Set in a part of the country completely strange to her, both physically and culturally, this in itself had been a challenge. Common interests with the elder Millikens would undoubtedly be scarce.

Shy fondness for her own father had made meeting Roger's dad fairly easy, though he certainly didn't play second fiddle in his home as hers did. His gentle kidding, occasional flirting, and a never-ending store of amusing tales made her actually seek him out, rather than avoid him. Comfortable with himself and his life, he presented few complicated attitudes, much less the parental neuroses she was familiar with. His eyes were as clear as the Western skies.

Her only image of a mother was her own, and she was prepared, if necessary, to cope with someone similar. But after a few days of receiving genuine warmth and interest, Phyllis truly loved Rog's mother. Her self-esteem bloomed like the colorful flowers "mothered" by the same lady.

This was a family made up of all the traditional Norman Rockwell requisites, Phyllis thought, yet completely foreign to her. With so much materially, had she actually been a deprived child? She knew that answer but had progressed to a point in her thinking at which the present finally mattered more than the past, and she would build on it.

Roger delighted in watching these relationships grow and in hearing relaxed laughter as they all worked and played together. The "orchid" was doing just fine.

Riding out by truck or horseback every day, either to help with ranch work or to just explore, gave both of them a healthy sense of their small importance in this huge prairie surrounded by towering peaks. This sense was familiar to Rog, but necessary to him for personal renewal; it was new to Phyllis. Both experienced a healing diminution of what they'd believed were onerous problems.

One night they all went into town to a dance, a real foot-stomping, fiddle and accordion shindig. Phyllis had left her severe barrette on the bureau and let her hair flow soft and free. Rog had said nothing, but from then on treated her with none of the formality she had had to accept. The little clasp was gone for good and western breezes had a fling.

Just before supper on their last night Rog's dad had taken him out to the corral on some pretext or other, then handed him a small box.

"You're a big boy now, son, and I wouldn't dream of saddle-breaking you into another marriage before you're ready, but you're not a kid any more either. Your Ma and I would like to see you settled when the time is right."

In his mid-forties, Rog knew his parents were more than a mite concerned about his future, and he chuckled to himself. This kind of personal talk was not his father's style. He guessed he was about to get a clumsily worded assessment of Phyllis, probably composed by his mother. Not so.

"Open the box, damn it. What's in it belonged to my mother and she thought the world of you as a little tyke. She'd want you to have it, and so do your mother and I."

Then he had turned and walked deliberately back to the ranch house. Mission accomplished.

In the box, wrapped in faded silk, was a ring, solid gold, and obviously made by semiskilled hands from a nugget. In the center was the tiniest diamond Rog had ever seen, though surely treasured for many years. His parents had spoken.

After the supper dishes were washed, the kitchen floor swept, and the dogs' water dishes filled, he and Phyllis drifted out onto the porch that stretched the length of the house. Hanging from the porch ceiling by chains, a creaky old canvas hammock moved gently back and forth in the soft evening air. Phyllis and Roger, relaxed on its faded pillows, quietly watched the golden glow of another day disappear behind vast purple mountains. Jack slept near the steps, twitching occasionally as he dreamed of chasing more rabbits than he'd known existed.

Letting one foot drag along the porch floor to slow down the hammock's movement, Rog turned to look more directly at Phyllis. Then he leaned forward, hands clasped, eyes focused on his native hills.

"Phyllis, I've got a problem."

She stirred and sleepily asked if she could help.

"I think you could, at that. You know that I'm pretty much on the cutting edge of our business, right up-to-date and maybe a bit ahead. But maybe you also know by now that I'm a conservative, old-fashioned guy, brought up by parents who believe in certain traditions. Well, I've been taught that when a man wants to marry a girl he should ask her father for permission to propose. My problem is that the father in question is somewhere in Europe, and I want to ask that girl right now this minute. Got any suggestions?"

Phyllis hadn't found the West as wild as she thought it might be, but her heart was certainly acting wildly now. Then a delicious, sweet happiness swept over her and, looking at him with dancing eyes, she said gently, "Ask Jack."

At the sound of his name the dog raised his head and thumped his tail with enthusiasm.

"Thank you, Jack." Rog turned to the woman beside him. "I'm all prepared, because my little old grandmother Milliken, who came West in the wagons, left this for you." He opened the box.

They had decided to be married very soon, quietly and simply. Mrs. Jarrett had complained, of course, but was reminded that she'd already stage-managed one wedding for her daughter. Now was that daughter's turn. The Millikens all came, as did the entire staff from the office, the bride's housekeeper, her psychiatrist, Dr. Burton, and her lawyer, Mr. Atwater, with their wives.

Waiting in the rear of the little chapel for the wedding music, Phyllis' father whispered, "You're better than any son I might have had, and you prove it every day. How I wish I'd told you sooner. Best wishes, dear child. I love you. " He had squeezed her hand, winked, and they stepped forward. With her head high, sure of herself at last, Phyllis Lewis approached the altar, the Rev. Morris, Roger, and her future.

A few days later friends and those relatives not present received large and elegant envelopes, the sort generally used for invitations. On the front of the enclosure was a photo-portrait of an exceptionally ugly though well-groomed dog. He was dressed for an occasion in a custom-tailored cutaway, complete with ascot tie and white carnation. Over one eye was what seemed to be a black satin patch. Opening this folder, the recipients found the following:

> "Jack Hathaway (of the Shirt Hathaways) is pleased to announce the marriage of his mistress, Phyllis Garrett Lewis, to Roger G. Milliken on August the fourteenth, nineteen hundred and ninety."

Phyllis, proud of this lighthearted break from stuffiness, was tempted to send one to "Jerry Warner," but didn't want him to worry about her knowledge of his deception. Upon receiving the announcement, Joel and Carol were amused and delighted at first. Then conservative Joel was caught up, appalled.

"She's a bigamist. Oh my God, what do we do now?"

Carol reminded him of Phyllis's note, telling them she was filing for divorce. After some discussion they decided to tell Jerry of both events later, when the campaign stress was over and the time seemed right. Why take the chance of upsetting him when so much was on his mind? Carol sent a nice landscape signed "S. Warner" as a wedding gift.

Chapter 13: Fall 1990

Cobscook Bay, Maine

Fog had moved into the little town on Cobscook Bay. The street lights were blurs and the neon signs on the few stores glowed in indistinct hues. As Hank Longbow walked down the road into town slap-slapping a basketball ahead of him, he saw the lights of the little bar go out. He hadn't realized that it was so late; closing time was eleven.

He had spent most of the evening with the family of a young Indian boy, a senior in high school, an exceptional senior. Wally's grades were well above average, 3.8 average and very good SAT scores. He had varsity letters in soccer, basketball, and baseball, and was active in student government. The only elements lacking were the aspiration and faith of the parents and the self-confidence of the boy. No member of his family had ever attended college. To succeed, as a member of a minority, in the world outside a little town in a small, isolated state, seemed most unlikely.

Hank's challenge that evening had been to persuade all of them, including Wally, that he should apply to the United States Military Academy. One of the few examples Hank could use to convince them was himself, yet what had he really accomplished other than earning degrees? Certainly not earning money. He didn't live or work in Washington, New York, or even Portland. He still lived in this tiny town in Washington County, Maine, devoting his time to helping his people move out and beyond. Some argument.

After talking himself out he'd invited Wally to shoot a few baskets on the grammar school playground, to rid themselves of tension and bring things back to their normal relationship. Then they'd said goodnight and

Hank had headed home.

As he approached what might be called the center of town, really just a little crossroads, he noticed a group of men spilling out of the darkened bar, a bit unsteadily and very noisily. They were strangers, and unhappy strangers at that. Their drinking plans had been interrupted and none were in the mood to submit to this interference in a strange hick town.

Hearing the slap of the basketball, they peered into the fog to find the source of the sound. Hank realized that to stop now would be to admit they mattered. He proceeded, but slowly.

One of the five snapped forward, like a snake. Intercepting the ball, he continued to bounce it himself. He passed to a companion and the ball went the rounds, leaving Hank to stand and wait till he could retrieve it. He thought he saw an opportunity, moved in, and knew immediately he'd made a mistake, a bad mistake.

What light there was shone down on the little group and one of the strangers yelled, "Hell, we've got us an Injun. A f ——— redskin." Another blurted out, in rough, hiccupping voice, "And look at that necklace. Bet he's gay. Boys, this evenin' ain't lost yet, if we've captured an honest-to-Gawd f ——— injun queer. Who likes Injuns?" They moved in on Hank, closer and closer.

He stood still, erect, with dignity, sensing that if he tried to run it could prove dangerous, but they were too far gone for such niceties of thinking. One gave a vicious yell and struck out at him, catching him on a shoulder. Another landed a blow in his middle, and one in his groin. They were all on him like a pack of wolves.

Joe Perkins, the bartender, heard the noise from his upstairs bedroom and looked out the window, appalled by what he saw. He recognized Hank, a good friend, and was outraged, but knew there was nothing he could accomplish by joining the melee. All he could do was call the sheriff's department, and trust to luck one of its cars was near enough to get there in time. Help better come soon.

In good condition, and trained, Hank put up a good fight, but was hopelessly outnumbered. Hit around the head, below the waist, wherever the mindless ruffians chose, within a few minutes he was down on the cold, fog-wet pavement. Knowing the evening habits of his neighbors, he accepted the fact that only a lucky chance would bring someone driving by at this hour. Charlie would have been asleep for hours, having to be up five A.M.

A laugh came from the obvious leader, a porcine slob of impressive dimensions. "Hey, guys, let's get even with Injuns. We got us one. Let's scalp him."

Hank was on the brink of passing out from pain and exhaustion. He opened his eyes to see a knife blade catch the light as it descended in an unsteady hand. He felt the prick and the cut as the point entered his forehead just by the hairline. He was almost grateful for another kick to the head that knocked him cold.

Minutes later Joe Perkins saw headlights zooming in very fast through the fog, but no blue lights, no sirens. Who the hell was coming from that direction anyway? Screeching to a stop under the lights, a disreputable old pickup disgorged half a dozen enraged Passamaquoddy men armed, not with tomahawks, but with tire-irons, jacks, and empty beer bottles. Their scanner had picked up Joe's call for help.

It was all over in minutes. Just as a sheriff's cruiser came snarling in to the spot, the young Indians had tied up the last of the ruffians and had them stacked like cordwood, waiting for the law. Several squatted by the motionless body of Hank Longbow. "I've got a pulse," cried one. The deputy reached for his car phone and called for an ambulance, pronto.

Joe thought to call Charlie, who got there in minutes and was shattered by what he saw. Face bruised and mauled, eyelids swelling, blood trickling from split lips, Hank was not a pretty sight. The knife had cut about one-quarter of the way around Hank's hairline. There was no doubt of intent. They all knew that these details were evidence of obvious injuries only; much more might be found by examination and X-ray.

Charlie took the pulse himself, was reassured, and grateful to Joe who appeared with towels and cold, clean water. The deputy, with more first-aid training than the rest, checked on other vital signs and gave a positive report.

White-garbed and efficient, an ambulance crew soon gently bundled Hank onto a stretcher, invited Charlie to ride along, and headed for the hospital in Calais.

Joe rose to the occasion. "I don't care if this is after hours, I don't care if half my guests are cops and the other half Indians, probably under age. The bar's open and it's on me. C'mon inside." The lights went on again.

* * * * *

Portland

Dolly Winslow, Patsy's aide and constant companion, stopped the car and looked at the sleeping candidate beside her. They had been on the intense campaign trail for three weeks and were both exhausted, but the pressure was mounting and would not abate till Election Day. Like the glorious fall foliage, the race grew ever more intense.

Politics, to Dolly, was the ultimate extension of PR. It involved merchandising, a keen sense of why and how people react to what, and a real flair for drama. Manipulation by choice of words, an understanding of what produced which knee-jerk responses, all while exhibiting a semblance of innocence, had intrigued her. Psych courses in school had helped, but she now knew that real success in this field boiled down to creativity and the lure of power. Like a sponge Dolly had soaked up proven practices, and had keen eyes and ears for sensing the moods of gatherings. Her reports were masterful and generally quite funny, a joy to read.

Now, sitting in the dark car in front of Patsy's home, she hated to wake her. An important dinner meeting in Waterville, addressing many of Kennebec County's leading health providers, had been just the last appointment of a full day. Tomorrow they were scheduled to breakfast in Sanford with an industrial group, attend a coffee in Alfred, and swing over to the coast for lunch with the Ogunquit Rotary. The most important event, however, was meeting one Gordon Abercorn at the Portland airport in the late afternoon. Her curiosity about this man would finally be satisfied. That name had a way of popping up in Patsy's chitchat while they drove from meeting to meeting. Dolly stretched, stifled a yawn, and poked Patsy. It took several such pokes to rouse her. Turning on lights, feeling the welcome warmth and the always satisfying rush of affection she had for her home succeeded in waking Patsy fully. Ignoring the blinking light on her answering machine, she went into the kitchen and made a cup of cocoa.

Everything was going so well. She had developed real self-confidence in speaking, her silly jokes were well received, and her honest statement that she would make no promises she couldn't keep had made a good impression everywhere. Party issues, the Phoenix philosophy, and her personal approach to the job were her main themes. Every letter, every phone call, every meeting was based on her courteous respect for that individual and his or her opinions.

Patsy lit into partisanship and gridlock, stubbornness and even bigotry. She stressed the need for familiarity with issues and informed thinking prior to voting. She reminded listeners of the old Big Box, by which Mainers could vote the straight party ticket by just checking one square on the ballot. A no-brainer.

"Upstate there are towns pretty solidly Republican over the years, actually centuries. At the time of a recent election one town clerk found a ballot voted straight Democratic! Flabbergasted, he put it to one side, not really knowing how to handle such an aberration. Then, unbelievably, another Democratic ballot showed up. Greatly relieved the clerk announced, 'Damn fool voted twice, so we'll have to throw both out.'"

As she brushed her hair and prepared for bed, choosing a well broken-in old flannel nightie, she chuckled. So far they had had only two debates, and they were both loaded for bear. Don had appeared first with his guitar, ready to entertain. Little did he know she could play too. As his rhetoric waxed strong on his personal capabilities, she had picked up his instrument, strummed awhile, and then, interrupting, broken into song, "Anything you can do I can do better, I can do anything better than you." She was no Ethel Merman, but made her point.

Both candidates were well spoken of as individuals; the real difference was in party positions. Less government interference versus more government help. Pro-life and pro-choice, gay rights, and prayer in school were issues they hardly touched on, both feeling those were personal decisions, not political punching bags. Maine's economy, educational programs, and environmental concerns were the most popular subjects.

The press had a field day comparing their race to the "politics as usual" race in the Second District, so their unique contest was getting publicity because of its element of surprise. Few other candidates had the confidence yet to break old patterns, though generally, campaigns seemed markedly cleaner.

Finishing her cocoa, Patsy pulled back the bedspread, arranged her pillows, and was about to wearily climb into bed when she remembered the blinking light on the answering machine. Taking her mug with her she pattered barefoot back down to the kitchen. There were two messages. One was from Gordon telling her he had gotten off a day early for his visit and was even now at his hotel in Portland. Hooray! But too late to call him.

The second was from Charlie, an incoherent, sobbing Charlie. She listened, horrified, to his story, then called him back at the number he gave. The Calais hospital, on the Canadian border. Crying herself by this time, she heard him out. Her first instinct was to dress and start up there immediately, but he made her promise to wait till morning. The doctors felt sure that Hank would live, though with a long recovery period.

The lateness of the hour did not matter now. She called Gordon.

"I'll be there as soon as I can throw some things together. Leave the door open for me and try to relax."

Still shaky, Patsy lit a fire in the living room grate and lay down on the big old sofa in front of it. Bill had often urged her to get a more modern couch if she wanted one, but this old one, large and deep, was a loved member of the family. It was big enough for the whole family to enjoy an occasional snuggle, and one could really stretch out on it for a nap or a good read. It had even been a splendid trampoline for the children years ago,

Not caring that she was in the old flannel nightie, or that her face was tear-stained and swollen, she curled up in misery, waiting. The warmth of the fire and her exhaustion crept over her, and Gordon found her asleep in the darkened room with just the flickering firelight defining the location of chairs and tables.

For a moment he stood beside the sofa, touched by her grief and wondering how he could best help. It was heartbreaking to see this spunky, independent woman so devastated. A log fell in the fireplace, crackling, and that slight noise brought her back from sleep. She weakly smiled her welcome and gratitude to him, and opened her arms. If ever in her life she needed to be held, it was now.

Gordon saw that there was ample room for both on the generous old sofa, and slipped down beside her, cradling her close to him. With her head on his shoulder, tears came again. She spoke in gasps, in outrage.

"How could they, how could humans act like such animals? We read terrible stories in the paper of crimes like this, but they don't seem real or maybe we refuse to be believe they are real. And they never, never happen to people we know and love."

Gordon smoothed the messed-up hair from her forehead and kissed her gently where it had been.

"Do you want to talk about it?" Getting the tale out of her system might be the best therapy. He had learned little but the bare details on the phone.

Slowly, with hesitations, she recounted what Charlie had told her. All he knew, or could tell her, was based on the reports given by the tavern owner, the police, and those wonderfully avenging young tribesmen from the reservation.

What bothered her most was thinking about what Hank had felt, from the very start, the unexpectedness of the attack, its violence, his helplessness, and finally, the terror and pain. Would he ever speak of it, or was it too private, too appalling? How does the human spirit recover? How does one with his dignity, pride, and talents live with such memories, such debasement?

"What can be done to prevent such things happening again?" she wailed. "To my Charlie? To other fine men who are 'different'? These creatures who attacked Hank are under lock and key, but for how long? And how many more ignorant bigots are out there to replace them?"

As she went on Gordon held her gently. She turned toward him a bit and relaxed against him, shifting occasionally for both comfort and closeness. Finally, talked out and exhausted, she just lay there, spent. His mind was racing. He loved this woman, truly loved her for her spirit, her humor, her companionship. He trusted her, something he thought he'd never be able to do again. He'd known for some time that he needed her to complete his life. What did she want of him, need of him this night? Not wanting to take advantage of her and possibly jeopardize their future, he nevertheless sensed that she was searching for loving comfort and support, maybe in the simplest way he could provide. Love was so often the best medicine.

Slowly, with his free hand, he began to stroke her back, moving down to her hips and then up again, toward her breasts. Gently he cupped the nearest; she gave a contented little sigh and moved even closer to him. His hand moved to her chin and, lifting it, he kissed her softly. Mouths opening, they slowly sought each other and then explored with eagerness. His hand found the hem of the old flannel nightie and slipped up inside it, up her thighs, over her smooth buttocks, and finally around to places neglected for so long.

Content for a time, they lay quietly, letting natural rhythms guide them. She pressed harder, closer. Her hand found his zipper and gently released that which was waiting behind it, hard and ready. Their bodies were so close she could hardly tell where hers stopped and his began, as if they were one. Joining was so right for both of them, and so inevitable.

Much later, the ship's clock in the hall rang four bells, six o'clock; a faint light from the windows told Patsy that another day had arrived. Lying on her stomach, at first she was confused, then stretched and one hand miraculously found a warm and bigger hand to slip into. It gently closed over hers.

This moment, this act, of waking and knowing she was no longer alone, was perhaps as beautiful as the sharing of love completely last night. It was in daylight, it was real, love had happened. She felt whole again for the first time in three years, and belonging. She knew all was settled. Both were needed and needing by the other.

Then her mind raced back to the horror in Calais, to her responsibilities to Charlie, and even to her campaign. Good God, Dolly would be picking her up in half an hour!

Awkwardly climbing over the still-sleeping Gordon made her giggle, and she knew she was on the way to recovery. Reaching the kitchen phone she rang Dolly's number and caught her between showering and walking out her door.

"Hi, it's me. Today is scrubbed, maybe the next few days. I'm on my way to Calais; my son has been involved in a terrible tragedy. I'm a mother first and a candidate second." She was glad that at some point she had told Dolly about Charlie's relationship with Hank.

"This is not for publication, but Hank was horribly beaten up by some red-neck homophobes last night, and almost scalped. Yes, scalped. He will live, but he's still critical. Charlie's a mess, of course, and his mom isn't much better.

"Call Ben, find subs, if possible, for today's appearances and tomorrow's, at least. Ben can cover them himself; tell him I said so. Oh, some good news. Gordon Abercorn arrived last night and will drive me up there. That little nugget is off the record, of course. Ben will know how to handle the press, but right now the less said to anyone the better. I'll be in touch."

Gordon had woken during this conversation and was picking his rumpled clothes off the floor. They met at the kitchen door for a hearty good-morning kiss, then headed upstairs for quick showers.

Patsy packed quickly, called Meg to let her know she was on her way, and made a semblance of serving breakfast. It was hard because she wanted to stop and hug or kiss Gordon every time she passed him en route to the stove, sink, or fridge. How could anyone be so miserable and so happy at the same time? She had an anchor again.

It turned out to be a glorious day, foliage more and more fantastic as they headed northeast, and they had so much to talk about: Hank, Charlie, themselves, campaign, even foreign policy, Maine's Southeast Asian trade, and Gordon's expertise and understanding of same.

All the while a little termite was gnawing hard in Patsy's mind. For the first time in her life she was thoroughly outraged and at the point of wanting to dedicate herself to righting an appalling wrong. Her juvenile delinquent bill, worthy as it was, had also definitely been intended to further her political position. That aspect had no place at all in what she was feeling now.

Hate crimes, whether racist, religious, antifeminist, antigay, or antiabortion, had the elements of real evil. This attack on Hank symbolized all of them. Now they had become, to her, anathema, a vile disease living in all levels and in all parts of the country. Herewas a subject calling for far more commitment than a mere campaign. Could it be waged most effectively in the Congress of the United States or locally, family by family, town by town, state by state?

Her children had led charmed lives, had never been threatened or lacked for security. Or so she had thought. As they matured she had loosened their leashes and finally let them run free while she pursued her own interests and, now, her career. Since last night she had discovered that she was a crusader not for just her kids, but for all those children and adults unfairly picked on, bullied, attacked.

"Do you know that Native Americans, whom we used to call savages, are often more tolerant of homosexuality than whites? Gay men are almost never shunned, and in some tribes are even venerated because of being different. They are called 'bedarche.' Quite different from our discriminating against an 'inferior' minority."

Rattling on to Gordon as they swept northward, she was amazed at the lack of self-interest in her arguments. No need to prove anything, just a real hunger to put what talents she might have to the best use. Why fight so hard to get to Congress where she'd have to spend hours thinking about such things as most-favored-nation trade agreements, farm subsidies, and defense department budgets? Why not just change course and concentrate on this one horrible problem?

They called Charlie from Ellsworth and were overjoyed to hear that Hank was conscious, and the prognosis was good. They agreed to meet in Calais for lunch, then go to the hospital together. Patsy wanted to ascertain Charlie's condition before tackling Hank's.

Going through the everyday normal activity of ordering and eating a satisfying meal of clams, rolls, and pie put them all in better spirits. Charlie had pulled himself together, gone home and showered and shaved, and his appearance relieved his mother considerably. Patsy kept her problems to herself and was thoroughly supportive. Gordon, with skill, assumed a not-quite-father role, ready to be called on if and when needed.

The hospital visit allayed Patsy's fear further as Hank had been stitched up, bandaged neatly, and looked actually ruddy in contrast to the white of his hospital johnny and sheets. He expressed no bitterness and Patsy found herself very grateful to Charlie for having introduced such a man into their family circle. She found she had truly loved him for quite a while.

His parents came in during the visit. Patsy was glad to meet them and gave his distraught mother a most understanding hug, which was returned. Charlie suggested that they'd be back again later and they drove to his cottage, picking up takeout food for dinner.

After one more day there Gordon and Patsy realized they were no longer required, and left, but not before picking Charlie's brains on the subject of hate crimes and his mother's future. Hank was obviously improving daily.

Not knowing when they would be up north again they decided to stop in on Meg and Peter to talk over all these subjects, so from Ellsworth they went inland to Brewer. The children, as children always do, brought all down to normal reality. Meg's legal background gave Patsy material to ponder; then she let slip that her office had been picketed for her support of an abortion clinic.

"Oh, no, not you too," moaned Patsy, holding her daughter close.

Though assured that the demonstration had been quite peaceful, she could not forget it. By the time they finally saw the Portland skyline, Patsy's mind was made up. On arriving at her home she called the state Republican chairman and submitted her resignation as candidate for Congress.

She made it clear that her decision was not based on trying to protect her son's reputation or even her own. Nothing as selfish or self-serving as that. Nor was it because of threats to her daughter. It was based quite simply on her desire to devote one hundred percent of her time and energy to eradicating this festering national sore of narrow-minded hate wherever it showed up. She had learned that the dedication of a handful was as powerful as a mob, and was swapping a career for a cause.

The chairman was flabbergasted. He tried not to show his anger, but wondered what the party should do next. After consulting with the committee's attorney, he relayed the procedure back to Patsy. A committee, elected at each First District convention to handle just this sort of thing, would be responsible for nominating a new candidate. Did she have any suggestions as to her replacement? For once she knew enough to keep her mouth shut.

This hadn't been exactly the vacation Gordon had planned, but they finally stole a few days to unwind, to day-sail in a borrowed boat, to beach-comb, and to love each other. When she left him at the airport they laughed at their lack of plans, but had faith that all would work for the best, and soon.

The party and news organizations had generously given Patsy these few days to put her thoughts in order. Now interviews were arranged so that she could personally explain to the voters the reasons for her decision. With Charlie's permission she laid all their cards right on the table, hoping that fair-minded people would recognize that she was expressing the depth of her commitment. No phony excuses or reasons. This thing was too important for anything but total honesty.

Her former staff gave her a simple but warm farewell party. Little did they realize that it was a true farewell to a woman whose whole life so far had been lived to prove herself. She had now carved out a far more important and selfless mission.

* * * * *

Augusta

Republican State Headquarters were located on the second floor of one of Augusta's fine old mansions on State Street. It consisted of just three rooms, a kitchenette, and a lavatory. These premises were presided over by Ginny Waterford, secretary for so long that few could remember who preceded her. Surrounded by filing cabinets, bookcases, and office supplies, she seldom moved out of her nest. It was furnished with a swivel chair, a typing table, computer, and a desk covered with GOP memorabilia. The fat Rolodex beside her phone contained names and numbers that Democrats would die for, but it wouldn't matter if they pulled a Watergate and swiped it, because every one of those numbers was indelibly printed in Ginny's mind. Chairmen could come and chairmen could go. They all learned very soon who actually ran the party, who had even occasionally held up mass mailings of which she did not approve, and who could time after time fill ballrooms with diners at $50 to $100 a head when campaign or operating funds were needed.

This day she greeted the chairman of the First District Committee and told her that the other members were waiting in the conference room.

The group was already tossing names around, voices getting higher and higher with irritation at Patsy Hudson's decision. This particular committee generally had little to do. Membership and chairmanship were pretty much honorary jobs, recognizing loyalty or financial support. Putting her Republican tote bag down at the head of the table, the chairman took her seat and asked for quiet. Her leadership qualities had not been tested before this.

"Let's not mince words, but let's not be critical about Sen. Hudson's decision. Any of us in her place might have done just the same thing." A good firm start.

There was muttering and some shaking of heads.

"We have less than six weeks—exactly thirty-eight days, counting Sundays—to find and then sell to the voters another candidate, another one who can win. You were all asked to bring in a list of five names, no more, of people you think might fill the bill."

She rose, went over to an easel holding a pad of newsprint, and picked up a marker.

"Each of you, in turn, read off your list. As we go along there will surely be duplication, so I will put a checkmark beside those repeated names every time they're mentioned.

"As this list is made, study it carefully, with the following things in mind: name recognition, political connections and clout, availability on such short notice, reputation for successes, and finally, personality. The ability to raise money is secondary. It will take a lot to market this candidate, but I've heard from Washington that the RNC is willing to foot a lot of bills. This situation is colorful publicity for them. Let's go. You first, Sam."

She kept things moving, cutting short any opinions at this point. When the list was complete seven names were followed by at least three checkmarks.

"Do you want to start by going over these suggestions, or would you rather review the names that were suggested by just one or two of you, but probably with good reason?"

A member from the Brunswick area raised his hand.

"I like the second suggestion. With all due respect to the other seven, every one of them, every single one has already served in Congress, as governor, in the state Senate, or as chairman of the State Committee. All are respected, capable, even brilliant, but old hat. They are exactly the people the Democrats hope we will come up with, creating no excitement whatsoever. If we're as smart as we all like to think we are, now is the time to pull a good healthy young rabbit out of the hat."

Those around the table enjoyed that last simile, laughed a bit, but then settled into silence. The chairman, amused herself, waited for someone to speak, to take the ball and run with it rather than putting the decision back on her shoulders. Finally, looking somewhat hesitant, a young man, new to the group, asked to be heard.

"I'm very aware that I lack the experience of most of you, but maybe that is in itself a good thing. Maybe I represent the younger voters, Republican or otherwise, who would welcome a new personality. Not meaning to be disrespectful, I agree that those seven, though distinguished, are retreads, and by choosing one of them we would be showing that our bench strength and imagination are very limited."

A middle-aged woman from the Gold Coast of York County signaled her wish to be heard.

"My bailiwick is becoming more and more sophisticated, interested in new ideas, new solutions. We have a great many immigrants from the megalopolis who are tired of politics as usual and would be intrigued with courageous innovation. What does GOP stand for? The Grand OLD Party. Maybe we should think instead in terms of being the Grand OPPORTUNITY Party and prove it by our choice. Can we improve our sometimes fuddy-duddy image by breaking new ground? I'll bet there's new leadership out there."

"Thank you all. Let's get going on those not on the so-called retread list."

The chairman flipped over to a fresh sheet of newsprint and wrote down the qualifications she had earlier stated as necessary. "As each name is discussed we will put it beside the essential quality or qualities that we think that person has."

The first few names to be weighed were actually "favorite son or daughter" suggestions, people who were hardly known in the state or district. Several more were CEOs of large businesses who might find a move to Washington for two years out of the question at this time. Others had records of such strong positions on the abortion question, pro-life or pro-choice, or were such champions of other volatile issues that their nomination would automatically cost many votes and possibly split the party. Some, though respected in their particular field, had little political experience. They would need an intensive orientation (a polite word for education) not only to campaign convincingly but, if a winner, to do a respectable job in Washington. A few were perennial candidates who had never quite made it to success.

Of fifteen names, only one appeared beside every single one of the qualities, and not just once, but several times. There was only one problem about this candidate. No one knew whether he was a Republican or Democrat.

Ginny was called in and given instructions. Within minutes she was back and stated with authority, "Jerry Warner, resident of Augusta, is a Republican."

Around the table everybody relaxed. In the following discussion about Jerry much came out that made him a natural. His knowledge of the state and its needs, his understanding of government and particularly that of Maine, his contacts with politicians, educators, business men and women and civic leaders, were impressive. They all gave him credit for inspiring the Phoenix movement, which was the highest recommendation of all. It was felt that he would be a natural successor to Patsy in freshness, integrity, and message.

One person mildly raised questions about Jerry's background, education and former employment, but was practically shouted down.

"Good God, he's superbly educated here and in Europe, has an MBA from somewhere, has worked in large internationally known companies. He's a born State of Mainer and his dad is probably the most loyal Republican I've ever met. Forget it."

The chairman asked Ginny to locate Jerry, if possible, by phone. The rest agreed it was essential to meet with him as soon as possible, even tonight. They felt it might take some doing to talk him into the slot because of his commitment to Phoenix; he might, quite reasonably, ask for time to decide.

"Got him," called Ginny, and the chairman took the phone.

"This is awfully short notice, Mr. Warner, but a group of us from the Republican First District Committee would be honored if you could join us for dinner tonight?" She smiled at her group and soon made the OK sign with thumb and forefinger.

"Really, that's great. How about the Senator Motel, at six-thirty. I'll try to get a private dining-room. You're a good sport, not even asking what this is all about, but believe me, you're in safe hands. See you later, Mr. Warner. OK, see you later, Jerry."

* * * * *

"Well, well, well, aren't we some gussied up. Going somewhere, fella?"

Mark had caught Jerry standing in front of the kitchen mirror, adjusting his tie, straightening the coat of his one and only suit, and checking on the neatness of his hair.

"What gives?"

With a shrug, Jerry turned to face him and very seriously said "I haven't the faintest idea. All I know is that I've been invited, or ordered, to have dinner with the GOP First District chairman and friends tonight at the Senator. I'm the one who should say 'what gives.' "

A whoop of delighted laughter from Mark didn't help matters. Sobering up, the journalist said, "You've heard about Patsy Hudson, haven't you? That's probably the answer."

"No, not a thing. Is she OK? Not hurt or anything, I hope? And what does Patsy have to do with me, anyway?"

"A few nights ago her son's Passamaquoddy boyfriend, up near Eastport, damn near got scalped by some outta-state hooligans. Beat up really badly. He was rescued by a bunch of young braves who picked up the call for police on their scanner. A magnificent brouhaha followed, a real switch on the time-honored theme of the U.S. Cavalry arriving just in time to save settlers from the Indians. Times change.

"Patsy rushed right up there, was really shook up, and now she's furious, just wild. She's decided to give up not only her campaign but her whole political career to really go after hate crimes of all kinds, any way she can."

"Wow, that's a terrible story. Still, what's this got to do with me, oh learned one?"

"The GOP obviously needs a candidate pronto, and I have an idea that they think they've found one. Jerry Warner."

Mark gave him a playful punch on the shoulder, then added, seriously, "I think they've found just the man. Bright, well-known by name, well connected, with no baggage and lots of good, reasonable ideas." He just couldn't resist, "and oh so handsome in his city-slicker outfit."

Jerry began to see that what Mark said made sense, that this was the explanation for the dinner invitation. He was astounded by what Patsy had done, and was realist enough to know that naming a new candidate ASAP was crucial. That he was considered a candidate, perfect or not, was certainly a moot point. Actively nonpartisan for so many months, it surprised him to even be considered a Republican, though how could he be registered anything else and sleep under Stan Warner's roof in safety?

Before leaving the cottage Mark had spelled out for him in more detail the probable reasons why he had been picked, if this was actually what had happened. Theoretically, they perhaps made sense, but it was all beyond his imagining. He wondered, as many men had wondered before him under similar circumstances, "Oh Lord, why me?"

Driving in to Augusta, he had time to assess the pros and cons of the situation in case Mark was correct. On the plus side was a magnificent rostrum from which to actively promote Phoenix, locally during what was left of this campaign and on the national level if he won. Adhering very publicly and sincerely to its principles, he could proselytize endlessly. Heady stuff.

In itself, having a political career held no charms for him, had never entered his head. The possibility of power, personal or partisan, was foreign to his thinking. He was, however, fairly comfortable with most of the Republican platform. Patsy had laid good solid groundwork for him through her campaign platform and tactics, and it would be easy to simply continue on that path.

On the minus side was the very real and frightening possibility of being recognized as Webb Lewis. There would be inevitable and intense public exposure during the campaign, not to mention national exposure if by any chance he won. Lucky so far, he knew that recognition would undo all he and so many others had worked for in the past years. Had he been an ostrich because he cared so much? This threat had been there all along.

The thought of leaving Maine, the Warners, and Heather was heartrending. Up till now Jerry had had no idea of how much they meant to him personally; he'd been too busy living his happiness to stand back and appraise it. At several points he was tempted to just turn the car around and head for home. But that would be a black mark on Phoenix, having a mannerless boor for a leader. The least he could do was to listen to what these people had to say. That had always been his modus vivendi, listening and weighing. Pulling into the Senator parking lot, he left the truck and walked with straight back, firm steps, and a quaking stomach into his future.

Lying in bed later, listening to the familiar and soporific lap of lakewater against Mark's dock and the gentle sighing of a mild breeze through the pines, he could hardly believe what had transpired during the evening. Mark had been right on the button about why he had been invited. The group had made no bones about it at all, quickly explaining the spot they were in, their methods for choosing a candidate and, without much subtlety, trying to talk him into acceptance. He agreed that time was of the essence, but that this was something he would have to talk over with the Phoenix board, by which he was employed. Agreed. A reasonable request.

After another round of drinks the questions of his positions on certain issues were examined, and they were found to be pretty much in accord with those of his interrogators. No personal questions, of any nature, were asked. With dinner, there was discussion of his role in relation to the party and to the opposing party. The chairman had given a disappointingly trite talk on tactics.

"We need someone willing to fight the other party every inch of the way. We hope you will not only fight your opponent and his supporters, but that you will also fight for those principles and issues Maine Republicans stand for."

This little speech was given almost by rote, so sure was the lady of his agreement. Where the hell had she been all these months? Jerry pushed his dessert plate away from him, placed his hands firmly on the table, and began to speak, carefully but with total conviction.

"This may be where we part company. With due apologies to our chairman, during every campaign that I can remember, I have heard the word 'fight' ad nauseam. I personally believe that promises by candidates to fight the other side only fuel more partisan hatred and an increased lack of respect for, or loyalty to, one side or the other. War clubs are always raised, swords are always drawn.

"As I've explained, Phoenix is my chief concern. It is based on collaboration, which means listening to the other side with genuine respect, jointly examining a problem and, with patience, arriving at solutions agreeable to all. Thank God, signs of that philosophy are showing up every day in many Maine races, particularly in the race we're discussing. I know, because it's my job to know.

"If I accept the candidacy, this approach is what I shall talk about. Not very good at telling jokes or singing songs, I'd concentrate on stretching out our hands to those across the aisle, hopefully finding theirs reaching for ours. There's too much that needs doing, too many concerned people waiting with diminishing patience, to waste time in continuing to play cowboys and Indians. You can't shake hands with a clenched fist. I am not, and never have been, a fighter; I am a builder and mediator. Believe me, and I say this with real humility, over the years these tactics have actually accomplished quite a bit, here and abroad."

His listeners were shocked, not because they were necessarily pugnacious, but simply because this newcomer was denying almost in toto the traditional way things were done. This man was almost taking the fun out of campaigns.

Jerry had continued.

"Don't misunderstand me. I have no qualms about fighting evil conditions such as violence, waste, and corruption. But I truly believe that a respectful approach to the opposition is the answer to breaking the power of special interests, to overcoming the cynicism of voters, and to correcting the appalling paucity of really distinguished candidates. In the last two elections the Phoenix approach has proven not only popular, but effective. Just study the figures."

He had paused and looked around the table, smiling, but with firmness.

"Probably the best way to leave things is for me to agree to check with my board about my- being a candidate and, more importantly, for you people to think over what I have just said. I will understand if you decide I am not your man, and will now state that I have been honored, tremendously, by your choice.

"Campaigning in any other way would be impossible for me, believing, as I do, that good listeners are more effective than noisy fighters. And," he laughed, "building alliances and mutual respect actually takes much less time, energy, and even money than attempts to destroy. I'd probably be able to campaign a lot more effectively than someone weighed down with heavy verbal artillery."

The group had broken up shortly, still friendly but obviously a bit uneasy, though he was promised they would be in touch.

As he lay there he decided that though they might withdraw their nomination of one Jerry Warner, he sure as hell had given them something to think about. And that was the most important thing. He had known all along that Altitude Adjustment had to be built slowly, brick by brick, and one more brick had been put in place tonight. Why hadn't it been put in place earlier? Where the hell had these people been for the last year or so? Obviously too many supposedly politically savvy individuals thought Phoenix was just a vagrant idea, nothing with roots. He'd learned something tonight too. His recent farming education was coming in very handy; Phoenix certainly needed strong fertilizer, weeding, and constant cultivation. With no regrets as to the evening, he finally slept.

Next day, polled by phone, the Phoenix board gave him their excited go-ahead, with hearty congratulations on his stand regarding campaign style and promises of support if and when needed. The Warners and Mcleans both volunteered their loyal backing if he were recognized, no matter what it would do to their own credibility. What friends!

A call from the First District chairman came around noon, warm, sincere and surprisingly positive. Even over the phone she radiated pleasure.

"That was quite a lesson you taught us last night and it took some digesting, just like" and she spoke as an obviously experienced mother, "presenting a new vegetable to a picky two-year-old. We could spit you out and go back to peas and carrots, or give you a try and do some growing up. The job is yours if you still want it. Losing is the worst thing that can happen, and that may be inevitable anyway. Winning, by the Phoenix techniques, might be the saving of the party."

"Hooray," chuckled Jerry to himself, "she's hooked!"

Plans were made for an immediate press conference. Patsy would be asked to give not only a further explanation of her resignation, but her strong endorsement of Jerry. When she was informed of the Committee's choice her first reaction was delight. Jerry would be a great candidate and congressman. He was bright, honest, attractive, and obviously dedicated to good government. A fresh face was just what was needed. Then a little bell began to ring in her head. To her there was an element of mystery to him, and she was going to get to the bottom of it before she went out on a limb for him. She had a few clues and knew where to start.

Driving immediately to Bangor, she went to the microfilm files of the *Bangor Daily News* and sought stories dated early 1987. And there it was, the answer to the riddle. The plane crash, located reasonably near the Warner farm. Webb Lewis, Harvard, Harvard Business School, and former Namakant camper, had died on that plane. There was unfortunately no picture. But she knew that Jerry Warner, the little-known son of reclusive parents, had coincidentally returned from Europe at just about the same time as that blizzard, carrying dreadful scars from a recent bad accident.

Though very active in Phoenix, Jerry had managed to dodge publicity till now. She had heard him tell little Billy that he had been Piglet once. Had he been a camper, also coincidentally, with Joel "Pooh" McLean? At first she was almost sickened by what she had discovered. Mr. Clean, the epitome of honesty, was not what he seemed. Why the masquerade? Were the reasons justifiable, and by what values? Did Jerry's identity make a real difference in the political race? What did his actions tell about him, as a person? How much weight should partisanship play in her decision?

Patsy thought hard. Her own political future was no longer of importance, but she still wanted to back the right candidate. She liked and respected Don Vassalo; she could essentially hand him the seat. What had she learned in the past few years? What counts?

* * * * *

The State House lawn, always a good site for interviews, was covered the next day with both autumn leaves and Republican faithful, contacted by Ginny. The State Committee was well represented, from Fort Kent to Kittery. Much of Patsy's campaign organization was present to underline her expected endorsement and to add to an excited crowd scene. Other party leaders had been carefully picked to be present, showing a genuine though calculated range of support.

Camera crews from the networks were in place, mikes had been tested and, at the stroke of noon the First District chairman and the party chairman stepped forward, on either side of Jerry. The party chairman spoke first, saying simply that this was a memorable and exciting occasion, a first in Maine history. The First District chairman, stunning in an orange linen suit that matched many of the carpeting autumn leaves, took her place at the mike. This occasion was a first for her in the television spotlight and in statewide news, and she hoped to do her part with humor and grace.

"Fellow citizens of the First District, Republicans, Democrats, and Independents, we have great news. Faced with the task, very late in the game, of finding another real star to take Senator Hudson's place, I am honored to tell you we have found such a candidate.

"Miracles do happen, or magic takes place, whichever way you wish to think of it. Someone said jokingly, as our committee was discussing possible candidates, 'Gee, if we only had a magician who could pull just the right rabbit out of his hat.' Well, let me introduce our rabbit, a wonderful great big rabbit like Elwin P. Dowd's Harvey, our next Congressman from Maine's First District, Jerry Warner."

Seasoned public relations people gasped with horror at this appallingly cutesy gaffe. Heather almost gagged. Would Jerry go through the campaign, or even life, as "Harvey"? What kind of a candidate is a charming rabbit? That woman should have her head examined. The crowd was laughing at her, not with her, but she didn't have a clue. "What a test for this Warner guy," reasoned members of the fourth estate. How would he handle this hot potato with grace? Reporters held their breaths for what he would say. It would be a measure of the man.

Jerry stepped to the mike, waved, grinned, looking relaxed and happy. His tweed sport coat and chino trousers were the perfect compromise between his usual jeans and his suit.

"Good afternoon, and thanks for coming. First, to straighten things out, how many of you know what noises a rabbit makes? Can any of you mimic a rabbit's conversation?" He waited.

"Nobody? Not a one? And you're absolutely right, because a rabbit is generally mute. Ladies and gentlemen, Jerry Warner is far from mute. What the magician has pulled from his hat is actually a little tiger kitten, soft, cuddly, but also capable of spitting, snarling and taking on the wrongs we're all concerned about. And because it's a magic kitten it will be full-sized and ready to start by the time I'm through with these remarks. 'Tiger' Warner will be on his way."

Patsy Hudson, unbidden, moved over to stand beside him.

"It is with great pleasure and gratitude that I heartily endorse Jerry Warner. All of you are probably aware of the violence that has touched my family, and of my decision to concentrate on a crusade against hate crimes. Thank you for your understanding, sympathy, and," she paused and looked right at Jerry, "particularly for the respect and trust you have shown my very personal decision.

"Just as I myself started out on a new life four years ago, today Jerry Warner is following the same path, starting a new life by also going into politics. Already, through Phoenix, he has made the profession more honorable, and so" she turned to him, "I wish you all the very best, Tiger, Rabbit," she laughed, seemingly casual, "even Piglet or whoever you turn out to be. Your name isn't important;, your deeds are what count, and we already owe your decisions and judgment our deepest respect because of what you have accomplished."

Jerry felt a great warmth and strength sweep over him. Patsy had somehow learned his secret and had pledged much more support than the crowd realized. His secret was safe at least with her, and that promised support might be needed. He regained the mike, giving her his warmest thanks with his eyes.

"Thank you, Senator Hudson, for your very kind words and support at this important time in your career. It will be up to the voters to decide what metaphor is most appropriate." A warning bell had been rung, but the verdict had been mercifully delayed.

"I may be going into politics but I am not a politician, never have been and probably never will be, in the usual sense of the word. I'm a mediator. I work with people instead of against them. And I make all of you a solemn promise: you will never hear me use the word 'fight' in relation to the opposition, individually or as a group. Never. You will hear me use that word only in reference to the wrongs of waste, corruption, and particularly, Senator Hudson, hate crimes. I like to think we will fight those wrongs together, all of us, shoulder to shoulder, Republican, Democrat, and anyone else who wants to help."

Addressing the viewing audience more than those supporters around him, he continued.

"If you've heard of me before it has probably been in relation to the Phoenix Association, a nonpartisan organization that is dedicated to helping us all restore to our daily lives mutual respect and the integrity that results in accountability and sincere collaboration.

"The character of your legislature has already changed markedly because of Phoenix, and you may have noticed diminished gridlock, more voters going to the polls, and greater interest among young voters. Campaign ethics have improved, campaign spending is less open to suspicion, and the term politician is coming back as worthy of respect, not the butt of cheap jokes.

"My campaign will be much like that of Senator Hudson's, except I don't know many good jokes and would probably louse up all the punchlines. I'm looking forward to debating Don Vassalo on many issues, partisan issues, though we might favor you with a duet at the close. When he and I are not competing for a seat in Congress we will continue to devote a lot of our time to working together on the next Phoenix subject: Education.

"These very few campaign weeks we have left can be fun, a learning experience for us all. Don and I will give you good solid philosophical reasons to vote for one or the other of us, more significant than how we comb our hair or our choice in ties. It will be a campaign of values and plans for the future, not personalities.

"And now I will take some sage advice. A good beginning and good ending make a good speech if they come close together.

"Just one more word to those of you already working with me. Yogi Berra, when his team had suffered too many losses, tried to console his mates. 'All we gotta do is win ten of the next five games.' We can do it, together, all ten of 'em."

* * * * *

On the Campaign Trail

Mild September ceded to a brisk, sometimes rainy October. After a short, frantic period of regrouping, the Republican campaign for the First District congressional seat surged forward, fired by the challenge of introducing a new candidate at the last minute. With the inspiration of so many supporters, Jerry worked harder than he knew was possible, covering the district from Kittery to Belfast, and inland, town by town, even village by village. He and Don had debated twice and had thoroughly enjoyed it, each explaining their differences clearly and without rancor.

One of their best evenings had been devoted to questions concerning the elderly. Don had produced his grandmother, and Jerry put Stan center stage. The head-on collision of a genuine old-time labor-oriented matriarch and Stan's chauvinistic, laissez-faire capitalism seemed made to order for a lively encounter.

Susan had been worried about the meeting, as Stan was so wrapped up in the campaign that even she had no idea to what lengths he might go. When, on stage, he was introduced to Grandma, steely blue eyes met and held anthracite-black ones. Then a courtliness emanated from him and he bowed low and respectfully. She almost smiled. Both pairs of eyes softened.

When it was their turn to speak, Stan had entertained the audience with time-honored jokes about prune juice, absentmindedness, and self-starting rocking chairs.

Grandma countered with, "I will admit that some days I spend a lot of time thinking about the hereafter. I go somewhere to get something and then wonder what I'm here after." She added, after the laughter "Most people have no respect for old age unless it's bottled."

She had said her lines faultlessly and was not prepared for Stan's next move. He reached under the table at which they were all seated and produced a package.

"I was going to give you this at the end of the evening, but now seems an appropriate time. It is a bottle of blackberry cordial, made by me on our farm, and just the right age for people like us." She tried hard not to show her pleasure.

He stood and looked out over the clapping crowd.

"These two elderly personages were deliberately brought here tonight to show up the differences in the philosophies of the two candidates, but I think we actually have a great deal in common. We are both rugged individualists who wish to control our own lives and those of our families. The signorina was brought to Maine from Italy as a baby by parents who were anxious for a better life, one of independence. I came here as an adult to leave behind a business style that was beginning to dictate how I should live. Her parents made the courageous trip not looking for entitlements but for opportunities to succeed by their own labors. I did the same, in a less dramatic way. She and I can recall well when life was simpler, and probably more fun, even without so-called modern conveniences."

He turned to her and continued. "Do you remember following the ice-man's wagon and picking up, to suck, the slivers chipped off the blocks he cut to fill each home's need? Circuses under tents, coasting down snow-covered city streets, taking the trolleys to the beaches and parks, gas-lit streets, even walking to school."

Her head nodded happily, reliving those days.

"I think our boys are both hoping to bring back the values of those years, but with different approaches. Yes, ma'am, we have a lot in common." He bowed again and sat down.

The "enemy" was completely disarmed. She leaned over and patted his hand,

"We have two good children, and they both have the good sense to still come to us for advice. Come share this wine with me some time."

Susan was embarrassed to think she had ever doubted her gentleman and amazed to realize that his every word had been sincere.

Some communities, however, were confused by the friendly atmosphere of the race, missing the biennial excitement of political bloodletting. One traditional Republican, using an old simile, had referred to Don as a man with as many faces as the town clock. Jerry had lost no time in answering "Maybe, but all those faces are giving us the same time. Sounds honest to me."

Both men were well-informed, both were personable, and neither seemed touched by anything suspicious or tales of skullduggery. More and more voters began to be conscious that this was a contest of philosophies, not a staged battle of personalities, propriety, or sex appeal. The Phoenix standards were not only lived by, but praised by both.

Finally the last weekend was reached. Nothing or almost nothing was left to be said, and the one remaining task was the classic GOTV, Get out the Vote. Last rallies were aimed at just that, to build bonfires of enthusiasm under the activists who in turn would rout out the uncommitted. On Friday night the two candidates, in their third and last debate, had underlined the importance of activating large numbers of voters by singing the duet Jerry had promised earlier. As the debate ended they stood together, arms over the other's shoulder and belted out a familiar tune, pointing to people in the crowd as they sang,

> We each want *his* vote, we each want *her* vote,
> From inland forests to each coastal fish boat
> From New Hampshire borders to our verdant farmlands.
> You'll give this seat to him or me.

The crowd was clapping in time to the song, stamping feet and cheering.

> Each vote is crucial, we ask that you shall
> Urge friends and neighbors to respect our labors,
> And vote on Tuesday, make a real big newsday,
> Proving that Maine can lead the way.

People stood and kept the rhythm going, clapping and stamping. The two men had to repeat the whole song again, to cheers.

Polls showed that they were still running neck and neck, as Patsy and Don had done. Had it even been a personality race, or automatically partisan? Maybe issues were important at last. Tuesday would tell the tale.

No surprises were expected, no new elements were left to throw into the pot. Just three days to go and then polls would open all over the country. Though not a presidential year, the many big senatorial and gubernatorial races would reflect the mood of the nation after two years of President Bush. The economy wasn't bad, foreign situations were seemingly in hand, and no one major issue or even scandal was generating excitement.

With a last major foreign policy speech ahead of him, Jerry was still concerned about how the Phoenix philosophy might be applied realistically to U.S. dealings with its global neighbors. If the United States felt it could legitimately demand higher civil rights standards in countries receiving its financial aid, did that not also mean that the fundamentalist Christian Right could legitimately insist on legislating social and moral changes in the U.S.? Where does tolerance stop and bigotry begin? When does giving rights to some rob others of theirs? If all men are created equal and entitled to life, liberty, and the pursuit of happiness, who has the right to define the meanings of those entitlements for other cultures or religious doctrines? Has any group or nation the right to consider itself impeccable? No matter how noble the purpose, where is the line drawn between missionary zeal and moral blackmail or violence? Tolerance, respect, and open communication were required in all areas, not self-satisfied arrogance.

Setting examples of behavior and attitudes rather than dictating them was the Phoenix answer, just as applicable to nations as to businesses or even families. Would Phoenix's popularity among idealists hoping for attitudinal changes actually have any effect when it came to marking ballots? Would those thousands of colorful little birds carrying messages of honesty, courage, and civility influence any but the children, unable to vote? In spite of all the positive reports, would the result be decided by lethargy or self-interest?

With these questions uppermost in his mind, Jerry, late for a lunch appointment, almost pushed his way past a group of teenagers lollygagging down the sloping tunnel leading to the State House cafeteria. They caught his attention as they all wore familiar Boys' Club jackets and were probably on a tour.

Dog-tired, shoulders sagging, just as they had for the years before the disaster, he couldn't relax now. He'd promised to do his best for moderate Republican ideology on issues, and he was also pushing Phoenix as hard as he could in a bipartisan way, to any who would listen. He was almost at the end of the tunnel when a young voice rang out, echoing off the walls.

"Mr. Lewis? Hey, Mr. Lewis!"

Heart pounding, he found he couldn't swallow. After all these months of planning, working, and building a new life, had it come to this, a sorry end in an underground trap? He felt like a woodchuck hopelessly hemmed in by Jack Russell terriers. Who had recognized him?

He could pretend not to have heard, or that the name "Mr. Lewis" meant nothing. It was so tempting to just keep moving, so tempting. But two other thoughts battled for his attention.

The phrase "you can run but you cannot hide" swam into his mind and he knew that what he had long dreaded had finally happened and would undoubtedly happen again. Living in constant anxiety was demeaning, as a guilt was definitely involved, though buried deep. The second thought was much more important. He could take this kid aside, and he was pretty sure it was Tommy, explain what effect public knowledge of his true identity would have on the election and on both his future and that of Phoenix. Could he, or should he, demand the kid's loyalty to save his own skin or the campaign? What would Tommy learn from that? In past years they had talked so much about playing fair, integrity, trustworthiness. All of Tommy's adult life was ahead of him, to be influenced by what he himself, the boy's adult role model, decided now within seconds. Just seconds. A speech he'd made in a high-school play swept into his head, coming from that hidden memory bank that is inexplicable.

"Mine honor is *my* life, both grow in one. Take honor from me and my life is done." Those lines from *Richard II* made complete sense at last. Good old Shakespeare. Jerry Warner's life as it stood now was done in any case, a no-win situation, but honor could be rescued.

Stopping, he slowly turned as a bigger and more attractive Tommy than he remembered came loping down the incline. Jerry held out to his hand, but seeing the joy in the boy's eyes, opened his arms and embraced him.

"Gee, it's really you! I recognized you from the back, the way you walked, you know. If I'd seen you face-to-face I wouldn't have known you. You're alive!"

It was done. Surprisingly, a tremendous weight seemed to be lifted from those drooping shoulders. One bridge was crossed; would he find the strength to cross the next?

* * * * *

Portland

Election excitement warmed the crisp Maine air; the electorate had been awoken and was stirring. On Saturday night the old Exposition Building on Portland's Park Avenue was filling up rapidly. Portland voters and many others from all over the First District had come to hear Jerry Warner speak on foreign policy at this last big event before Tuesday's election. The speech would be broadcast on both television and radio.

A low stage had been erected at the far end of the hall; the bleachers, folded up except for basketball games, were in place to accommodate people who could not find chairs. Every inch of wall space was decorated with bunting and posters; a small but enthusiastic band was helping to build excitement.

Vassalo's forces were meeting that same evening in the huge auditorium of City Hall. Both men were breaking a cardinal rule of campaigning by their choice of venue. Conventional wisdom warned that candidates always pick sites smaller than the crowd they hope will attend. Empty seats spell apathy, standing-room-only screams success. This campaign had created such interest that they had both decided to gamble.

At the Expo a roar went up. People got to their feet and turned their heads to watch Jerry Warner jog down the aisle, smiling, nodding, and exhibiting stamina they could only marvel at. The chairwoman of the Cumberland County Republican Committee, tall and impressive, met him as he gained the stage, and they stood together waving to the happy crowd.

She spoke. "Good evening. What an extraordinary display of interest this is. I'm not going to waste a minute going into details as I introduce Jerry Warner. We know him, we like him, we want to hear this particularly important speech. So I just say 'Welcome' not only to Republicans, but to the many Democrats and Independents I see among you. Our next congressman from the First District of the great State of Maine, Jerry Warner."'

Again and again Jerry asked for silence, and finally the crowd quieted. TV cameramen turned on their bright lights and Jerry adjusted the mike.

"Thank you, thank you so much for your warm reception." More clapping and cheers.

"This is my last address to a large live audience such as yourselves. Tomorrow and Monday are set aside for last-minute visits to towns needing perhaps a little more encouragement, and for at least one good nap before Tuesday." Sympathetic laughter.

He reached into his pocket and drew out the pages of his speech. People settled down, ready to listen. He did not place the speech on the lectern, but held it at arm's length and slowly and deliberately tore it in pieces, letting the shreds flutter to the floor.

There was an audible gasp and faces became puzzled.

The candidate began to speak.

"For the past three years I have studied the assets and needs of our state and district. I have also worked very hard and with real devotion for the Phoenix plan, which, as you know, is dedicated to a renewal of integrity, respect, and civility in all relationships, not just politics. The Phoenix Association chose politics as the first area in which to try to change attitudes, as politics affect us all. I think you know what a heartwarming success we have had. It can be seen in the new attitudes of our legislature, the caliber of our candidates, our campaign techniques, and in Maine rapidly becoming a model for other states."

The clapping rose to the rafters, and many of the crowd stood. This was a program of which they could be justly proud, Maine-produced, Maine-delivered, and as fresh and invigorating as Maine air.

"I believe wholeheartedly in everything we have stood for, everything. Because of that belief I must admit to you that for over three years I personally, though championing integrity and honesty, have been a living lie."

He paused to let that truth sink in, watching as the eager expressions turn to concern and then shock. The silence was profound.

"You may remember that in February 1987 a plane, flying from Zurich and about to land in Bangor, was caught in a snowstorm and crashed. Found a day later, it had burned almost totally, obviously leaving no survivors. Wrong.

"I survived that crash, how and why I shall never know. I now introduce you to my real self, Webb Lewis, a midwestern businessman who first came to Maine many years ago as a camper.

"Joel McLean, chairman of Phoenix, is my oldest and closest friend, as devoted to Maine as I am. Stan and Susan Warner rescued me after that blizzard and took me in. Only the Warners and the McLeans have been aware of the truth of my identity, and they also care so much about this program that they have accepted the possibility of my being discovered and what that would do to their own reputations. My everlasting thanks to all four of you. No one else on our staff had any idea."

He waved a hand toward where the four were seated. Looking at the crowd, he found a white-faced Heather sitting near the front with Tommy, and gave her a little nod. Patsy, seated nearby with Gordon, now relived the meeting she'd witnessed at the Bunyan statue so long ago, and appreciated it all at last.

Jerry continued with his story.

"Crawling over the snow, searching for some living beings and appalled at what I found in the wreckage, I began to believe that perhaps I'd been blessed with a second chance. In recent years my life, both personally and in business, had become far from satisfactory. No answers that I could live with happily seemed to exist. Was this all that I had been created for or could I find another role I was meant to fill?

"In a state of shock, I did some serious and possibly flawed thinking. Now, I reasoned hopefully, I might seek a cause or principle so exciting and so worthwhile that it would not only challenge me to make a real difference in some way but would also justify this miracle of my survival, I might even discover a cause for which I would gladly give my life. You may feel I have overdramatized my situation, but please imagine yourselves in the same position."

Telling them briefly of the fire, his rescue and adoption by the Warners, and the beginning of the search for a goal, he was careful not to glorify or romanticize his role. He led them through the formation of Phoenix, the Namakant experiment, and the recent months of other challenging programs and guidance, stressing Maine's continued role as the pilot project.

"I have been privileged, in recent years, by luck and by Phoenix, to repay a bit of what Maine meant to me as a boy. It is an even more wonderful state than I realized, with great promise, great natural talent, and quite capable of leading the country in a return to honor, respect, and civility, the attributes that made this country great."

The joy he had felt in his work was obvious, but he also wove through his tale the constant thread of fear that his true identity might be discovered. The purity of Phoenix might not just be threatened by that, but possibly destroyed. He stressed his decision to keep a low profile so that what he cared so much about would not be jeopardized, but recent events had forced his hand. When, in an emergency situation, he was approached to run for Congress in Senator Hudson's place, he had been faced with the hardest decision of all. He believed in most of the Republican platform and knew that his name recognition as a leader of Phoenix gave him a great advantage. Above all, a seat in Congress would be a perfect position from which to further the Phoenix philosophy. Should he take the chance of being recognized as he appeared on platforms, on TV, on posters, possibly hurting the party, the program and destroying himself? Did he want to spend his life always looking over his shoulder, afraid? With the permission of the McLeans and Warners he had taken that chance, made that commitment, and had campaigned hard and openly. The cause was worth it.

"Actually I have done nothing illegal, nor have my partners. Any pleas for financial support of Phoenix were worded in honor or in memory of individuals. We checked all that out with counsel."

Then, quietly, he told them that, just this afternoon, an episode had put the whole situation in true perspective, and to a test. Tommy.

"As a former role model for that young man, how could I destroy his faith? I could have denied my identity, but he truly knew who I was. Asking him to lie for me and live my lie with me would have been reprehensible.

"I mentioned some moments ago I had hoped for a quest or goal for which I would give my life." His voice quivered a little, and he lifted his chin.

"The real Jerry Warner was a very special and loved child who died in a boating tragedy when he was just eight. His parents most generously gave his name, his persona, to a total stranger, someone they trusted to treat it with respect."

His eyes sought the Warners, with whom he had talked earlier. He was encouraged by their brave smiles and a thumbs-up sign from Stan.,

"Tonight Jerry Warner dies again. It is obviously too late to withdraw from the race as the ballots have been distributed and some absentee ballots have already come in. The name Jerry Warner will still be there on Tuesday, as will the name Don Vassalo. As you probably know, pollsters have us running neck and neck."

He took several steps away from the mike, shifted his position and, taking a deep breath, returned to open up a new subject for discussion.

"Ladies and gentlemen, Don Vassalo is a fine, fine man, a strong supporter of Phoenix, and just as devoted to the principles of his party as I am to mine. He would represent Maine well in Washington and, to make sure, you Republicans can become a very lively, loyal opposition if and when necessary. Our campaigns have driven home, clearly, the differences in our positions.

"I have one last request. Do not give up your support and dedication to Phoenix because of my duplicity. Make it even stronger. It is my total belief in what it stands for that gave me the strength to level with you tonight."

A heavy silence hung over the audience. He gave them an opportunity to hear, digest, and evaluate what he'd said.

"As someone 'from away,' I can't thank you all enough for the friendship and support you've shown me, and for all you and others have taught me. Now, before I get maudlin, I'm going to say goodnight."

The stunned crowd was silent for just seconds, then responded to his speech with overwhelming applause. Many stood, and some were in tears. A slight commotion in the back of the big hall caused heads to turn. Donato Vassalo came running down the aisle, followed by the reporters and cameramen from his own rally. He ran lightly up the platform steps, grabbed Jerry's hands, hugged him, and headed for the mike. The crowd quieted instantly. The drama was not yet over.

Don grinned, seemed to be relaxed, and started to speak.

"I've got a pretty good rally of my own going on across town, but I couldn't resist crashing this one." A few friendly chuckles relaxed the listeners too. He continued.

"Jerry came to see me this afternoon and told me what he felt he had to do, actually wanted to do. He may be 'from away' but I think he's a helluva fine Mainer in every respect."

The crowd came to life again and roared its approval.

"At the risk of your thinking this is a case of monkey see, monkey do, please bear with me for a few minutes.

"Since my teenage years I've dreamed of being a politician of some stature, representing my family's city and possibly their state. Since those years I have followed a blueprint for such a career, drawn by experts. I have enjoyed every minute of the tasks and contacts that the blueprint required.

"Patsy Hudson beat me fair and square for the state senate seat, and I've had the pleasure, until lately, of running against that fine lady again. When Jerry stepped in and took her place I was delighted, as I knew he too was a fine and worthy adversary who would play as fair as she had. We've had a darn good time too." He glanced over at Jerry who signaled agreement.

"Since he came to see me this afternoon and dropped his bombshell I've had an awful lot of thinking to do myself. You see, I've been living a lie too, not as colorful as his but a lot longer."

Again, the gasp of the crowd was as audible as a cheer would have been. This speech, like Jerry's, was being broadcast and telecast live, locally. Friends were phoning friends to tune in. Some networks were even picking it up.

"Men in glass houses have to be darn careful not to throw anything much harder than marshmallows or feathers. How many of us are perfect, how many do not carry some little secret we pray never surfaces, some damn-fool thing we've never dared tell our mothers?

"Since my junior year at college I've had that kind of a secret." He drew from his pocket a rumpled piece of paper with jagged edges.

"This summer my loyal fellow criminal rescued this piece of evidence from what passes as a jail in a tiny North Dakota town. It is evidence that he and I, as college juniors, were booked and convicted of transporting marijuana. Some was dried and some was also growing splendidly in flowerpots stored in the back of the pickup truck in which we were touring the country. We'd accepted the stuff from buddies, with bets that we couldn't get it intact to a classmate on the West Coast.

"We lost the bet because the local constabulary out in the Dakotas stopped us for having one burned-out headlight. Imagine that, one lousy light bulb. Our out-of-state plates, filthy jeans, and pitiful attempts at beards made us prime suspects. We thought we were cool, really cool. That deputy didn't.

"After being booked we were held in the basement of the little town hall, fed a great meal, and then put up in what passed as a jail, the local motel. My dad wired us enough money to pay our fines and we were on our way after a morning court appearance. My mother, believe it or not, phoned the judge and sheriff, thanking them for scaring us most to death.

"But, I have a criminal record, and I have lied about that on every application and interview since. No big deal, no magnificent adventure like Jerry's, but just as dishonest.

"This isn't easy to confess. I don't know what it will do to my standing in the Maine Bar Association, or more importantly to my wonderful wife or the two little boys who look up to their dad. And then there are my parents and, God help me, my grandmother! This record does not deny me political office as it wasn't a felony, but it surely destroys my Boy Scout image.

"I'm confessing because I could never live with myself if I didn't; I've lived with it long enough, not bothered by the crime as much as by the lying. Actually, I'm grateful for finally having to get it off my chest.

"Jerry and I are not only proving we're human and fallible but together we're hopefully setting an example of real candor and honesty to all those candidates who follow. We are jointly asking you to vote on Tuesday; don't let our confessions keep you home. Vote on the issues rather than on the personalities, if you can stomach our failings. Issues and ideas are what elections are all about. Let's set a record for turnout and voter intelligence, and have something good come from this drama."

Turning, he embraced Jerry again. They both waved away the reporters swarming up on the stage and, heads high and with smiles, departed swiftly from the building by a side exit, leaving bedlam in their wake.

Moving faster than the transfixed members of the press, Jerry waved good-bye to Don and sprinted to his campaign van in one corner of the parking lot, hoping Dolly would be inside and ready to move. Instead he found Heather at the wheel. Slamming his door shut so no dome light would alert those soon to follow, he collapsed into the bucket seat, drained.

Her voice, soft and controlled, washed over him and helped fight down a panicky compulsion for instant flight. It was over, almost. Relax.

"Jerry, Webb, whoever you are, I am so very, very proud to be your friend. What a story, what decisions you've had to make and what self-discipline you've shown. You are a very special person., even more special than I'd realized." Her voice was like warm honey, soothing and sweet, her words supportive.

There was a long silence. He no longer had the energy to take any initiative or any sense of what might be required of him.

"Don was pretty special too. Did you have any idea that he was going to do that?" No answer. Was he asleep?

"But," and her voice became warmer though now almost a whisper, "I have realized that this admission gets rid of that cousin nonsense I've been fighting for so long."

Those were the words that finally sank slowly into his tired mind, taking a bit of time to enter his consciousness and arrange themselves clearly. Patterns of thought were rearranged.

She continued, her voice stronger, more intense. "Now life is so good, life is wonderful, and politics be damned." She moved closer, found his hands and held them hard.

In spite of all that had battered him today, the inevitable results of his confession, involving so many people, he miraculously found himself switching gears. Somehow he pulled himself from the miserable paralysis held been feeling and responded to what she had said. He was at last able to concentrate on what really mattered to him the most and had for so long, this girl beside him.

"Cousin business? Cousin business?" His voice was dry, almost cracking. "You may find this hard to believe but that particular problem never once occurred to me as of course I knew it didn't exist. Oh lordy, oh my Heather, how stupid I've been. What you've been put through."

Then, after a few seconds, he slumped again and added, "Don't, forget, my love, there's still Phyllis."

The silence in the van was profound. Heather reached for the ignition key, ready to move on, totally defeated. She suddenly straightened up, turned and faced him, her voice shaking.

"Phyllis, is that your wife's name? I never knew. Phyllis, Phyllis Lewis. Oh, Jerry, listen to me." She clutched his hands again, and continued, trying to control her excitement.

"An attractive lady with that name came into Carol's gallery, in May, while I was filling in. Remember when I did that? She bought one of Susan's paintings, but was also very, very interested in the portraits of you. I told her, of course, that you were the son of the artist and my cousin. Was she, do you suppose, your Phyllis?"

Jerry's head came up, slowly.

"Phyllis was in Wellesley? She saw those portraits? Then she's known ever since May, known the whole story except for the how and why. And she never let on." His voice held wonder, and warmth.

Heather continued. "She wrote a note later, to Joel and Carol, saying the painting had arrived OK. But there was more. Didn't Joel or Carol tell you?"

"Tell me what? They haven't mentioned her for months."

"Her lawyer had taken care of a divorce, as a sort of a housekeeping detail in case she ever decided to remarry. Oh Jerry, poor dead Webb Lewis was of course a total stranger to me, and his wife's love life was of no interest at all, or I'd have told you all this myself."

Heather felt herself relaxing, finally, realizing the wall between them was down.

"What's more, Jerry, she recently sent the McLeans a wedding announcement, a funny, happy one."

All this took time to sink into his tired head, but soon all of him responded, with warmth, joy and, at long last, freedom. The "No Trespassing" signs were gone.

The bewildered crowd was finally leaving the Expo and flooding into the dark parking lot. Headlights were turned on, car doors were slammed and engines started. Exhausts made smoke signals in the cold night air. In every car the events of the evening were discussed, with heat and bewilderment. One vehicle remained in the lot, off in a corner, dark and quiet. For those inside, their most pressing problems solved. The years of waiting were over.

* * * * *

No public relations expert could have dreamed up a better script to bring candidates before the voters. A nation bored to death with months of even more banal campaigns than usual suddenly had not just one but two real human dramas. And the stage was in Maine, of all places. Beginning with *Meet the Press* at 9:00 AM, then *This Week*, and so on through Sunday, the pundits, gurus, and even men on the street shared their opinions of this Maine performance and its leading actors. Heroes? Scamps? Reformers? On the eve of a deadlocked Congressional campaign two outstanding rivals, devoted to good government and active in promoting old-fashioned honesty, had each voluntarily admitted behavior just short of criminal. How could the media ask for more than that? No one had ratted on them; the opposing camps had not dug up these tales earlier and saved them for a surprise. Pollsters were told, time and again, "Those guys in Maine made us feel needed; we can't let 'em down." These two guys both seemed to have something called consciences and were leveling with the electorate spontaneously! Not even their campaign managers had been forewarned of the confessions. Incredible!

Historians dug back in the American political past for similar tales and came up empty-handed. There had been plenty of skullduggery in those "good old days" but little that was so perplexingly noble. Here was drama that didn't count on murder, corruption, or even sex. Certainly their early promises to respect differences and to put aside paralyzing partisanship in favor of constructive compromise were not only unique, but were promises obviously made to be kept.

By noon the "As Maine Goes" campaign philosophy and the Phoenix program were as familiar to the national listening public as the fact that one eats turkey on Thanksgiving. Pollsters frantically jettisoned all plans for the next days and worked into the wee hours on new questions, new statistics. Unexpected results in many states were credited to the Phoenix program, radiating from, of all places, a summer playground and winter icebox. Other states, torn apart by the usual bitter elections and vicious tactics, began to quietly study this event. All eyes and ears were on the small and distant state of Maine, a state, incidentally, that was handling it all with characteristic understatement, calm, and temperance. "No hurricane, just a bit of a gale."

Not to be found were the two candidates, protected by families, friends, and the loyalty of their backers. Even the press eventually ceased the manhunt and settled down with the rest of the country to watch the Sunday football on the tube.

Donny and family went as usual to Munjoy Hill relatives for Sunday dinner. The decibel level of conversation and comment had hit new highs until the grandmother, the matriarch, took control. On Don's arrival she had marched him into a bedroom, for privacy, and given him the piece of her mind he would have received if she had been privy to the incident when it happened so long ago. She owed herself this splendid explosion, and he too would have felt cheated without it.

As that smoke cleared, like the sky over Vesuvius following the Great Eruption, her voice became softer, her eyes less flinty, and he began to be congratulated on his present courage and honesty. That speech was followed by a hug to her massive bosom. Then she opened the door and they joined an apprehensive, watchful, and unusually silent clan.

Don winked at his boys as Grandma spread her arms wide and boomed "What are we waiting for? Where's antipasto, the lasagna, the wine?" Children stared at their parents, took a cue from their smiles, and all was once again a normal deafening Vassalo Sunday.

Stan and Susan had stayed overnight in a Portland hotel where they were joined by a relaxed and radiant Jerry and Heather about noon. One look at their faces told Susan that the problems she had sensed between the two were more than resolved. She hoped that at some time she would learn what it had all been about, but at this point she simply decided that God works in mysterious ways. Almost three long years of frustration and misunderstanding were obviously past history.

Earlier Jerry had given Phyllis Milliken a call of gratitude and congratulations. It had been a warm, happy talk, each wishing the other well and laying the groundwork for a reunion in the near future. Old hurts were banished, old problems obviously buried. He and Heather stopped at Amato's deli and acquired classic Italian sandwiches, apples, and beer. Because of the unusually mild weather, all were soon headed for Two Lights State Park, where they found an isolated picnic table overlooking massive gray rocks and the steel-blue, restless, cold Atlantic Ocean. Nothing suggesting smoke-filled rooms or noisy rallies was in this setting. Crashing surf and the cries of sea gulls were the only music, and much appreciated. Seagulls don't vote. Unlike the Latin Vassalo gathering, these laconic Anglo-Saxons said nothing about much of anything, though Susan marveled that Stan for once didn't feel called upon to sum it all up. They were all just happy, close, and respectful of one another.

Both Don and Jerry were contacted Sunday evening concerning a joint satellite appearance on Monday's *Today Show,* and both agreed to participate. It would be Phoenix's first appearance on that show and a chance to continue selling their ideas to the country, showing that even rivals can be friends, respected and trusted friends. After that Jerry spent the rest of Monday closeted with his team, going over Getting Out the Vote plans, details for transportation to the polls, and the usual absentee ballot work. He also made an important trip to City Hall.

Heather picked up Nana at the airport, a Nana demanding the whole, entire, and unexpurgated story immediately.

Don canvassed a few key neighborhoods, received official assurances that he would not be disbarred, and attended an afternoon soccer game of second-graders to watch Don Jr. exemplify "lost motion" with enthusiasm and expertise..

Hasty local polling showed little change in the standing of the two candidates. They were still neck and neck. National network polls all showed strong numbers supporting the courage and candor of each, and sympathetic acceptance of what they had revealed.

Tuesday dawned bright and clear, and both men took stands outside busy voting places. Legally, they could not campaign there, but they could shake hands and look pleasant. Jerry had thought of sharing a chartered plane with Don to visit Waldo, Kennebec, and Lincoln counties, but decided that would probably be overkill.

Senator Cohen's victory party was scheduled at Portland's Holiday Inn, and he had graciously invited Jerry and other Republicans to share that venue for their own celebrations. The place was jammed early, noisy and excited. TV cameras from the major networks with their cables snaking across the floor gave a sense of the importance of the occasion.

While the faithful gathered in the large function room to exchange war stories of the day's events, Jerry's campaign staff, like Cohen's, occupied a suite upstairs, in touch with spotters by phone to get earliest figures as they came in. Computers and statisticians were in place to analyze returns as they were reported.

Nana, like the Warners, had voted absentee in the past week, and was thoroughly enjoying the excitement of the windup. The McLeans had driven up after voting in Massachusetts. Joel had really been looking forward to seeing many of his Namakant workshop friends and was soon mingling happily downstairs, endlessly repeating his hopes that "As Maine Goes" would become not only fact but a national model. Would results in turnouts nationwide reflect the influence of Phoenix?

Three days of "big city living" were proving more than enough for Stan and Susan, but they were determined to see the process through. No one wanted dinner; they were all too excited to eat, or too tired.

Don and his team were celebrating with other Democrats at the Ramada Inn, also with a suite of their own. There would be little real excitement there either till after the polls closed at eight, though there was mild interest in occasional exit poll reports, no matter how low a percentage of precincts they reflected.

By ten o'clock Cohen was adjudged the winner. Not much later the governor, in Bangor, received a concession call from his opponent. Most local legislative races were, as usual, the last to be reported, considered of minor interest except for aggregate totals that would determine control of the two Maine houses. The Second District Congressional race went to the Democrat at about eleven, in good time for a brief speech by the winner on the late evening news.

The First District race continued to be much too close to call and some glitches in counting ballots were also holding up the decision. A driver headed for Boothbay Harbor swerved to avoid a deer, hit a utility pole, and the area was plunged into darkness. Neither the deer nor the driver were casualties, just the electronic vote counting system. An ancient voting machine in Augusta belched smoke and gave up the ghost. Those ballots not yet counted had to be done by hand. And in York County a flat tire on the vehicle transporting absentee ballots to their destination caused considerable delay.

Mark Lowell had written two winners' stories, one for each candidate, so he would be ready to file something when the news came. In rereading them he realized they were more about Phoenix than the men. He hoped he would be writing Phoenix stories for a long, long time.

Both Don and Jerry made cameo appearances on the eleven clock news, exuding confidence, good nature, and stamina. They were actually so tired they probably could not have accurately given their dates of birth or mothers' maiden names.

By midnight the crowds were thinning at both locations. The Maine vote was estimated to be over 75 percent.

At one o'clock their race was the only one of interest to Maine voters that was still undecided, and each candidate told supporters to go home and learn the results in the morning. At 2:30 Jerry announced that while Nixon had stayed up till 3:30 in his race against Kennedy, he did not feel this was a test of his own manhood and he was going upstairs once more and getting into his pajamas. Don followed suit a few minutes later from the Ramada. In a phone call to Jerry they decided that one of them would probably get a congratulatory call from officials before breakfast and they would keep in touch.

At 4:10 the phone rang in one man's motel room.

"Hi," groggily. "And a good morning to you. Oh, we won, did we? Thanks for telling me. What was the vote? Wow! Hardly a mandate. Do you think they'll ask for a recount? Yes, I have his number, I'll give him a call right away, though I'm sure the poor devil would rather sleep. See you later, and many thanks." So that was that.

Keeping his promise, the winner then rolled over in his rumpled bed, turned on the bedside light, and punched in the numbers. A phone rang several times in a room across town before it was answered.

"Good morning. It's me, and I guess I won, but only by a hair, at least that's what I'm told. Thanks for a damn good campaign, for support in tough times, and for the example you set for future candidates. Yeah," with a chuckle, "we sure made history, maybe even good history. Thank you, thank you very much for such generous words. If you want a recount, let me know."

He paused, then added, "Though in my opinion neither of us won; the real winner is Phoenix."

There was a long silence, neither man wanting to hang up. An important relationship was entering a new phase, not terminating. Finally one spoke.

"Life is going to be different now, isn't it? Like today, no schedule, no speeches, no coffee parties. Probably just one press conference. What are you doing for the rest of today?"

There was another silence, broken eventually by a warm peal of laughter.

" What am I going to do today? I'm going to get married."

* * * * *

Two nights later Stan and Susan lay in their own big bed, still wide awake, too energized by politics, the wedding, and traveling to get to sleep. Suddenly Stan began to shake with laughter and his laugh turned into a whoop.

"Woman, you'll never guess. I can't keep it to myself any longer. After all these years this old curmudgeon of a husband of yours voted for a Democrat! Yes I did, and I'm still living to tell the tale. That nice Robinson guy, our neighbor, running for county commissioner, got my gold-plated, priceless, sacred vote because he deserved it. The Republican running against him was a certifiable ass. His lights may have been on, but nobody was home."

Susan reached over and patted him, smiling quietly to herself in the dark.

Old Rousseau had been woken by this outburst but soon settled again on his rug at the foot of the bed. Grandma Moses dropped gracefully from the sofa in one corner of the kitchen and padded into the bedroom. Susan felt the soft, warm body land on her back and then settle down between herself and Stan. She heard the contented purring.

She wanted to purr herself, about so much. Nothing had ended and so much lay ahead, so very much.

Afterword

For the reader's interest: In the last decade Maine has taken leadership nationally in reforms of campaign spending and campaign ethics, and has held her place regularly as one of the top states in voter turnout. Also, for those who wish to read further, the book used as a model at Camp Namakant is *Collaborative Leadership*, by David Crislip and Charles Larson, published by Jossey/Bass Publishers

About the Author

Nancy Payne, a graduate of Radcliffe College, still takes course from her four chldren and ten grandchildren as well as from more recognized institutions. She has woven many of her experiences, as well as her concern with attitudes of this young century, into a thought-provoking but delightful book. Her love of Maine, with all its beauties, warts, bumps, and promise, is a strong theme throughout, thought she admittedly was born "away."

Widowed, she served in Maine Legislature and for a period was Republican National Committeewoman for the state. She has served over the years on the boards of the Portland YWCA, the Area Agency for Aging, and the Osher Lifetime Learning Institute.

Her first book, *Widowing: A Guide to Another Life*, was successful in helping many through the early years of aloneness. Living in Falmouth, Maine, she paints pots, gardens, and writes, all with enthusiasm, whimsy, and enough success to keep her going.

Order Form

Please send ____________________ copies of Phoenix/Maine to:
Name (please print) ____

Address ____

____
City State Zip

Telephone: ____

Price per copy: $12.50 ____________

Maine Sales Tax @ 5% (if purchased in Maine): $.62 ____________

Shipping and handling (per copy): $3.25 ____________

TOTAL ____________

SEND CHECKS TO:
Rathaldron Publications
P.O. Box 66792
Falmouth, Maine 04105

or order through your local bookstore.

For further information: (207) 781-3868